ALMOST
PARTNERS

Liminal Books is an imprint of Between the Lines Publishing. The Liminal Books name and logo are trademarks of Between the Lines Publishing.

Copyright © 2023 by TammyJo Eckhart

Cover design by Cherie Fox

Between the Lines Publishing
1769 Lexington Ave N, Ste 286
Roseville MN 55113
btwnthelines.com

First Published: November 2023

ISBN: Paperback 978-1-958901-68-7

ISBN: Ebook 978-1-958901-69-4

ALMOST
PARTNERS

TammyJo Eckhart

Chapter One

"Do what?" shouted Joanna, standing up and glaring into the screen. "You're crazy if you think I'd do that!"

"It's already been done," stated Mi, her face looking calmly back at Joanna, as if she'd been prepared for this reaction.

"What do you mean?" Joanna asked as she stared, her voice lowering just a fraction. Around her, Hilda, her house computer system, adjusted the ambience of the alcove, turning the walls a light sea foam and adding a soft yellow tone to the lighting to counter the stress it could detect in her tone of voice, heart rate, and muscle tension. Although many would be hesitant to upset a McMillin, Joanna knew that her GNA director didn't stand on formalities. Hilda was programmed to make sure that the Scion of one of the Great Families of Gaia was in optimal physical condition at all times. Joanna noted further color and lighting changes as Mi's next words caused her even more stress.

"We've picked him out and paid for him. All you have to do is go look him over – at Dells Escort Agency, over in Neuvo. The agency has assured me that everything will be ready to leave when you are. If you need a time extension, we've preapproved that. The goal is for you to get the best story possible, so don't rush though this. We have two backups who will meet you there as well, someone from MOI with drug knowledge and an Intragalactic Authority agent."

The IGA spanned the galaxy and relied upon planetary news agencies and agents to help maintain the peace by uncovering multi-system threats as well as spreading the word about the benefits of peaceful coexistence. Their allowing Joanna to document and even assist in this particular investigation spoke to the GNA's reliability and stability within the interstellar neighborhood.

Joanna sat down in disgust. "This is not chill!" She pushed an auburn curl behind one ear and rubbed her temples. "I can't believe you'd do this without consulting me!"

"I thought you wanted to catch Judy's murderers. This is a guaranteed way to do that, plus it will get galaxywide play, not just on Gaia. Good for you, good for the Gaian News Alliance."

It was true that she wanted her betrothed's murderers to pay, but this just felt wrong on every level. Joanna knew that Mi wouldn't have called if she hadn't cleared this with the McMillin family first. There had to be another way to get out of this assignment. Joanna narrowed her eyes for a moment, then growled through clenched jaw, "And Mothers' Original Intent? You rarely counter their goals, Mi."

"Our goals and MOI's are the same in this case," the other woman replied evenly. "When can you go look at him today?"

"We're talking about a human being, not an object!"

"I'm aware of that, you're aware of that, but you'd better remember that we live in this world, and changing it means working from within." Joanna opened her mouth with a huff of indignation that finally got her director's calm to crack. "Don't give me that look, McMillin," she said, using her family name as a dagger. "This is the way the world is, the way your family helped recreate it. You know that Joanna, better than most of our members."

"How dare you use my name against me, Mi! You know if I could disown it, I would. I use it," she said, waving her arm around to include the condo that was part of her family's holdings, something she'd pass on to her own daughter one day, if she had one, "to further our cause, to fight for justice, for balance. I thought we, MOI, even GNA, fought for that. Or have we given up and taken the easy way instead of the right way?"

"No." Mi sighed, pushing back her short black hair as she reclaimed her calm, then continued, "We have analyzed your situation and believe this will provide you with a new perspective on stories."

"Stories?" Joanna rose to her feet once more, and the lights and colors around her adjusted again. "Wait a minute. You said for this one story, not more. If you're thinking of buying …?"

"Only if you find the arrangement workable," the woman interrupted.

"Oh, then just forget it, Mi, because it's not going to be workable at all."

Mi folded her arms over her chest and tilted her head to one side in silence for a few moments. "Don't make me call you a hypocrite, Joanna, please," she sighed.

"Excuse me?" Joanna gasped as she leaned down. "I haven't owned – oh, excuse me, 'held' is the current euphemism, right? – a boy in years."

"The Chain," Mi said simply, and this made her operative's face drain pale.

Both women were quiet for a few moments, and the lights turned up slightly, while the colors on the walls took on a more yellow hue. After a few seconds Joanna pulled her arms closer around her before straightening up and looking directly back into the screen. "When?"

"Always. When you joined us, we did a very thorough background check, everything, and we keep monitoring; you know that." Mi emphasized with a pointed look.

Joanna chewed on her bottom lip for a moment then looked at her desktop. "That isn't the same thing," she insisted softly.

"How is it different, exactly?"

"First off, Betty says that her boys all enjoy it – they're wired that way; she finds them because their mothers are horrified by what their boys do, and she gives them a place to feel … normal." It sounded weak now that she said it out loud.

"Dells prides itself on discovering boys with talents and abilities and enhancing those. This one we rented is an imagist, and a very good one, both with stat and vid production. He also enjoys the work."

"How do you know that?"

"I spoke with him briefly and saw his profile, which I've sent you under his name, which is Scott, by the way."

"Of course, he wouldn't lie …"

"Would Betty's boys lie?"

Joanna coughed, shook her head, and tried to look more confident than she felt. "Not to me; they can't lie to me about that."

Mi simply arched one eyebrow at that naïve thought but let it pass. "When you meet Scott, you can ask him yourself. Ask him anything you want, in fact, during the hour you have to check him out."

Rolling her eyes, Joanna shook her head again. "I'll cradle the idea that he has some skill with imaging, but I need someone of Judy's caliber."

"Scott's skills are just as high, but he may be hyperthymesic or at least eidetic; that's rare regardless of gender," Mi emphasized. "True, he won't have worked with you as closely, but over time I'm certain the two of you will flow."

"There's that multiple stories thing again," Joanna said. Her annoyance was more for show than true anger now, so the walls and lighting adjusted back toward their normal blue-green tones. "I've been doing fine on regional stories; I've even picked up a bit of imaging skill myself." She was rambling now, spouting off the pathetic successes she'd had with interviews and commentaries on her previous work.

"McMillin!" The sharpness of the word made the redhead drop down into her chair as Mi's knife turned into a club. "It's been a year! Mother up! Time to stop mourning and get back to work!"

"It's too soon," Joanna whispered, her strained words and wounded eyes unable to express all the pain she still nurtured daily since the death of her future wife. "I can't do it without her." The walls turned toward the pink region of the spectrum, while the lighting took on a sharper yellow tone to try to cheer her up, because Hilda never gave up.

"Joanna, she is dead. You are living, and the living have responsibilities. Judy would want you to keep living, wouldn't she?" Mi leaned forward in her own seat and focused her full attention on her agent. "And you want revenge even more than the rest of us for her death."

"Yes," Joanna resigned with a growl as her head snapped up. Hilda paused in adjusting the atmosphere, because the readings were mixed now, then settled into a silvery white theme that highlighted the black desk and chair. Joanna slowly lowered her head onto her hands. "Chill. You win. I'll try him."

"Good. Are you free at thirteen hundred this afternoon?"

"Yeah, yeah, I'm between stories, and there's no family thing for a few moons."

"I know. It's one of the reasons we negotiated with IGA for this opportunity to tag along on their final preparations."

Joanna interrupted quickly at this further information. "They think they have her now? Are they really arresting her?"

"Those details will be revealed later," Mi said, repeating the oft-used phrase Joanna suspected that she had to tell every one of her investigators, whether they ended up on the evening news or testifying in court. "I'll confirm the viewing at Dells Escort Agency. I suggest you take someone with you. Perhaps Kathey Jenson?"

"I don't know if I'm ready to talk to her yet," Joanna said, looking up at the monitor, her face pale, but the ambience of the alcove stayed the same.

"She can understand your grief better than anyone else."

"I know, but ..."

"She's helped you before; she's the one who introduced you to Judy, as I recall. I'll call her if you want," Mi offered with a slight smile of concern. "She does know I'm your director at GNA, after all, and the Jenson family benefits from exclusive stories through us from time to time."

"I suppose it couldn't hurt," Joanna agreed as she sat back in her chair again. After a few moments of silence, she sighed. "Thanks."

"Of course." The woman on the monitor was silent for a brief second, smiling before she continued. "Let her help you the way she helped Judy. You need to re-immerse yourself in the world we struggle daily to change. You have great potential power, but you've been ignoring it. If you witness and report on an IGA success of this magnitude, your mother will be impressed, and she might listen to your suggestions; she might give you the information you really want. You know that." The monitor went blank as the caller hung up.

Joanna remained silent as a tear rolled down her check. Angrily she wiped it away and struck her fist on the desktop. "This is so cocked up!"

After a few deep breathes and a cycle through lighting and colors, she was calm enough to call the most important person in her life. "Contact Raven."

"I'm sorry, Scion, xe is set as working. Would you like to leave a message?" Hilda asked.

"Yes." After a pause, Joanna began speaking. "Raven, I got a sudden assignment from GNA that I can't turn down. It has to do with Judy's murder, so I know you'll understand. I will try to call you as often as I can. Love you." Another pause, then Joanna instructed, "Send the message." With determination she rose to get ready for the viewing.

Scott slowly lowered the barbell to his chest, then thrust it up. A shadow fell over him as his spotter steadied his lift. "How much do you weigh, Scott?"

The sandy-haired man set the barbell up in the rack, then sat up. "That's a personal question, Todd." He grabbed a towel and wiped the sweat from his face. "Why are you asking?"

The larger, darker man grinned at their body trainer to get permission before sitting down next to him, placing his hand on his shoulder. "You're about ten mills shorter than me?"

"That's about right, I guess."

"You're in real good shape?"

Scott suddenly grinned. "Your clients looking for a little white sugar?"

"No. My clients are very satisfied with this chocolate chunk, thank you very much," Todd replied with a smile. "Are yours?"

"None have complained that I know of."

"Then why are you down here almost every day?"

The blond rose jerkily. "Got to keep in shape," he muttered, but his friend stood up and refused to remove his hand.

"That's what the schedules are for, calculated specifically for our body types and clientele. So why do more than what's necessary?"

"I want to please my clients."

"Is that the real reason? I think you're just trying to work out your frustrations over Jones."

Scott eyed his friend coldly before turning toward the showers. "I have a new customer coming at thirteen hundred, and this is a long assignment. I need to be at my best."

"Which is why you should talk to me. Even right now you are just vibrating with tension that has nothing to do with a new client," Todd whispered as he pursued him across the gym. Their body trainer gave them a glance, but her attention was required elsewhere as a new acquisition did a pose wrong. "Aren't I your best friend? Your lover? Don't I live the same life you do? I'll understand."

The blond whirled around angrily. "How often does Jones take you?"

Todd stopped short and fell silent for a moment before answering, "Only once a year to evaluate training, and I know ..."

"Once?" Angrily Scott hit his own chest. "Once a week for ten years! You can't possibly understand what I go through, because you aren't living the same life I do!"

Todd reached out and roughly stopped his friend. "And how the hell is this supposed to help? Your clients, none of them stay around for long, and it isn't because of your body," he hissed as he pulled his lover closer. "You reek of desperation, and women don't like that. You gotta talk about it so you can let it go."

"Just leave me alone." Scott pulled free and raced into the showers, doors slamming behind him.

To passers-by, the deluxe red Vega IV was an unusual sight, but not half as unusual as the driver who emerged. She was dressed in dark pants with a dark jacket whose hood was pulled up but didn't quite cover her long auburn curls. She was working too hard at being inconspicuous, given the vehicle she'd arrived in, and this only drew more attention. On a normal day, Joanna would simply have walked where she wanted, answered any questions tossed at her with a slight smile, and even agreed to sign a few autographs. Today was far from normal for her.

Joanna walked up the steps to where her friend Kathey was waiting. "Your smiling at them is only encouraging them," Joanna growled when she reached the top step.

Kathey laughed and waved at the small crowd. "They know Jenson Motives' work; they know you; why be so mean to our adoring fans? You know, any other Scion would be enjoying this with me."

"You should call one," Joanna grumbled.

"You know I could call several."

"Balls," she replied, stopping, and looking around. With a grunt she pushed the hood off her head and let her curls fall out, revealing that she had her hair pulled back in her "let's get to work" style. Then Kathey started to laugh softly. "What's so funny now?" asked Joanna.

Kathey steered her toward the building, taking her arm as she did so. "The fact that you're coming here is very amusing, because clearly, you're not here by choice. I imagine you don't need this sort of place very often. Judy told me that you had mothers and aunts creaming just to get you to talk to their boys."

"This is strictly business," Joanna replied, ignoring the all-too-true comment about the constant stream of requests to meet potential sires, husbands, and fathers. She and Judy had planned to do that, of course, but not until they were ready to settle down and think about kids after Joanna assumed a more active role in the McMillin empire. Getting married had even been secondary to their work with the IGA and GNA, going anywhere the flights connected to find the next big secret that might rebalance Gaia itself.

"Of course," Kathey mocked, schooling her face to seriousness.

"It's the truth. This is only for business."

"I know that; I talked with your GNA director, after all. I just wonder what kind of business you might do between business."

"I don't kiss and tell," Joanna replied half-heartedly as she opened the front door for the other.

Kathey walked with familiarity to the reception desk and was greeted by name, though she didn't have an appointment. Joanna gave her name, and the receptionist's ears perked up at the sound of one of the founding matriarchs' surnames as she stood up and smiled widely. Unfortunately, this also resulted in "special treatment," so they had to wait for a host to greet them formally. "I'm Sandy; I'll be your host today. Please follow me."

As the group proceeded down the hall, Joanna looked at her fiancé's sister with uncertainty. "You've been here before, haven't you?'

With a coy smile, Kathey replied, "I doubt I know him," in a whisper, then added out loud, "What's his name, Sandy?"

"Scott. I'm sure you'll find him pleasing, Scion McMillin." The title made Joanna tense up, so her companion merely took her hand again.

"All the items here are quite pleasing," Kathey added. Joanna glared at her. "No, I don't know him; I do generally remember most of their names."

"Here we are, our viewing room." Their host led them into a room with a mirror-covered ceiling but otherwise rather nondescript decor against the mostly white walls and floor that were much like every home and building. A large semicircular couch sat to one side, leaving ample room in front of a dressing screen. "Please be seated; it will be just a minute more. May I have one of our boys fetch you some hot cocoa or snacks?"

Both women shook their heads, and Joanna waited until their host disappeared behind the screen. "You come here quite often, don't you?"

"Once a week. I'd have brought you here as I did Judy, but now that you've come on your own, there's no need."

"Judy came here?"

"She did once to check it out; she thought you two might want to get a husband after the wedding. Better than going with what your mother suggests, right?"

"Speaking of which, why do you come here when you and Ann have Owen at home?"

"He's here." Kathey stopped the questions with a nod toward a dressing screen that Joanna hadn't noticed before. She did note her guide's hungry smile, which reflected the viewing room's change of hue; the walls were red now, and the lighting was still white, but lowered.

Joanna stood to greet the man she was renting but stopped at the sight of his naked male body. "Not what I'm here for," she muttered before walking out of the room.

"Scion McMillin! Stay here," the host instructed the man before following after the client. "Scion McMillin!"

Scott watched the host leave with a worried frown. As a feminine hand touched his wrist, he straightened to attention. He held his breath as the hand moved up his arm and across his shoulder blades to rest on his other shoulder. Out of the corner of his eye, he recognized the other woman who'd been in the room when he came out; she did not act as though she recognized him. He was certain that he hadn't served her. He had an excellent memory, much to the horror of many clients and the joy of exceedingly few. His breath came quickly as her other hand journeyed down his chest to his thigh.

"Nothing wrong with you as far as I can see. You look a bit familiar, but I don't think …" the woman started to turn his face to her but was interrupted by the returning host.

"Excuse me, Ms. Jenson, but Scion McMillin would like to meet with Scott alone now."

Kathey nodded and walked to the door. "You're right," she commented with a glance back toward the escort, "she'll be very pleased."

After the other client left, Scott spoke up. "Have I done something wrong, Madame Sandy?"

"It's hard to explain." As she turned around to face him, he knelt on the floor, which was now softly blue.

"I will beg her forgiveness. Please give me another chance?"

"Scott, it's nothing that you did. You look fine; you presented correctly." She reassured him by running her hand through his hair. "It's her first time renting from an escort agency. Perhaps she's a virgin, I imagine the Greats do keep a tight control over that sort of thing, though, at her age," she added in a whisper. "Just do whatever she wants, make her comfortable. Understand?"

"Yes, Madame."

"I'll send her in."

As she exited, Scott hurried to his feet, looking around worriedly. The woman, Mi, had told him that she was sending over a reporter. This woman was a Scion, the heir to one of the Great Families; this was way beyond his fantasies. The closest he'd come to such an important client in the past had been the head of a prestigious import/export service for farmers; he'd managed to hang on to her for almost half a dozen rentals before she just never requested him again. As the business computer system adjusted the room's atmosphere with red and gold hues, Scott became so engaged in checking out his hair, face, and physique in a nearby mirror , that he didn't hear the door reopen. He froze in place when the sounds of a throat being cleared startled him.

Scott turned around as gracefully as he could. "Scion," he greeted her, using what he hoped was the appropriate title, even though he wondered if it were correct for a woman of her status, given his own position in society. He was thinking too much again, so he fell back on training. He bowed deeply and took a step toward her as she held up one hand's palm toward him to keep him back. "How may this boy serve, Scion?" he asked softly as he stopped.

"Do you have clothes you could put on, please?"

Scott blinked but nodded a moment later. "Yes, Scion. Right away, excuse me." He bowed again, then hurried behind the dressing screen.

Joanna sat down on the couch. As she waited, she played anxiously with her gold pinkie ring, which had been a gift from her fiancé. She frowned at the cushions and glared around the room until the colors started to fade into a softer tone with some aqua highlights. How dare they try to turn her on when she was here strictly for business?

"Scion?"

Joanna sighed with relief when she saw that he was now dressed in white shorts and a loose white shirt, nothing too tight, nothing too revealing, probably just what he wore around the building. She allowed herself a smile. "Hello."

"Hello. Is this more to your liking?" he asked softly as he stepped closer but didn't raise his eyes to hers.

"Yes. Thanks for changing. I'm sorry if I upset you earlier … Scott? That's your name, right?" Joanna asked quickly as the man kneeled in front of her.

"Yes, Scion." The blond bent his head in submission. "It is I who begs forgiveness for offending you, Scion."

"Please stop calling me that," Miss Joanna replied with a tired sigh, then frowned when he jerked back just a bit. "I'm not here in an official capacity," she offered.

Scott slid closer on his knees. "Anything you want, Miss, I will do. It is my duty to please you."

Miss Joanna twisted a strand of her auburn hair as she looked down on him nervously. "Would you sit next to me?'

"Next to you, Miss? On the couch?" His tone suggested that he was surprised by the request.

"Yes. It would make it easier for me to talk with you." She held out her hand with a tight smile. "Please?"

His hand started to reach for hers, but with a blush he simply slid up next to her. "This pleases you?" he asked as his eyes met hers for a brief second. With another blush he lowered them. "Forgive me, Miss? Please?"

"No." Gently she lifted his chin with one of her fingers so that his eyes could meet hers, but he avoided her gaze with his own eyes. "Let me look at you."

"As you desire."

"I can't really see you unless you look at me."

He glanced up, and then a slight shudder went through him as his gaze relaxed.

Miss Joanna studied him carefully, and he knew what she would see. His light tan showed off his sandy hair, which was short except for the bondage braid in back and the bangs that hung over his left eye. His bright aqua eyes were protected by delicate long lashes and were studying her cautiously. The silver tag on his right ear and the medium silver chain around his neck, which marked him as corporate property, caught her eye as the light glinted off them.

"You have amazing eyes," she said, releasing his chin and standing up, "but eyes aren't enough." Taking a deep breath, she turned to face him as he continued to gaze up at her, swallowing once but saying nothing, and moving not at all as the blues of the room deepened. "Scott, I'll just say this plainly."

Respectfully he straightened his back and lowered his gaze on her hands.

"I didn't ask for you, and I really don't want you to go anywhere with me." His gaze fell to her feet. "But unfortunately, circumstances demand that I take someone with me on this trip."

"I'm sorry that I displease you, Miss." He tried to fall on his knees in front of her but was stopped by her hands as she pushed him back onto the couch, then joined him.

"It's not you, really." She touched his hand. "How old are you?"

"Twenty-four, Miss." Scott trembled slightly under her unexpected touch. He had less than a year to find a private holder, or who knew where he might end up when retirement from Dells fell upon him.

"You're three years younger than me. Do you know how old that makes me?"

"Twenty-seven, Miss," he replied without hesitation.

Miss Joanna smiled. "Fast with numbers, but are you good on your feet and not just on your knees?" She frowned slightly, then laughed at his confused stillness. "Did anyone tell you why I rented you or where I'm taking you?"

Scott paused before answering, glancing cautiously at her as he spoke. "Not specifically, Miss, only that you are a reporter, and you need an imagist. And that it would be a one-month lease with an option to renew."

"I don't have a lot more details to share now. I'm told you know vid and stat processes. Is that correct?"

Scott's gaze came up at the information, and he met her eyes again. "Yes, yes, my mother was an imagist; she taught me everything she knew, and Dells has continued my education. I did a good deal of the vids on Dells' site as well as the prints."

"Do you have a portfolio I can look at?" she asked but then made him frown a bit when she added, "The news agency I work for actually arranged this; I haven't seen your work yet, but I need to before I can agree to this."

"Yes, Miss," he responded. Turning his eyes to a touchpad on a nearby table, he said, "If you use that yellow button, Madame Sandy will come back, and you can ask for my portfolio. I don't even have to be present while you look," he whispered.

"Of course, you have to be present. I need to know that you really understand the tech. I want to hear why you used angles, lighting – you know, that imaging stuff," she replied as she reached over and tapped the yellow button.

He grinned and met her eyes

Madame Sandy accessed the portfolio on the computer in the viewing room and then left them to look through it. There were stat and vid images, short and long form, narrative and solo, mostly of other men but also some of the agency and outdoor scenes. Many of them were sexual, but Miss Joanna just skimmed over those to focus on the advertising while she asked him questions about how he might capture images without someone noticing, what formats he would use in different environments, and the few specific questions about the tech.

After listening to his answers, Miss Joanna sat back and considered him for a few seconds. "One more thing you need to know, Scott. I'm leaving Gaia for this story, and it could take a month or more for me to get what I need. I'm going to be working with people from different worlds where things aren't like this," she emphasized with a wave of her hand back and forth between them. "No one will expect us to be anything we aren't, but I also need you to be able to adjust so you don't get in the way of the story but can actually help me. Sound like something you're up to?" she challenged him.

"I shall try to faithfully perform all you ask," he replied as she smiled gently, then added, "I learn quickly, Miss. It's my duty to please you at all times."

She took his chin momentarily and forced his eyes to meet hers once more. "I hope you can learn quickly. Flexible may be woman's middle name, but I believe boys can be flexible, too. This is a very important story for me." Miss Joanna rose to leave. Scott stood, and accompanied her to the entryway, the slight difference in their height making him hope she's see them as fairly matched. She smiled at him and held out her hand as she would to a woman. "It's been nice talking to you. I'll see you tomorrow?"

"I look forward to your use, Miss," he whispered as his fingers lightly touched hers and his lips brushed the top of her hand. "I hope I have pleased you, Miss."

Miss Joanna's face flushed, and she muttered, "It's been a pleasure, Scott. See you tomorrow morning." Joanna left quickly, grabbing Miss Kathey by the arm as she hurried out of the escort agency.

"Scion McMillin!" the host ran after them. "Is something wrong?" Scott just stood and watched as the women went down the hallway.

"No, everything is fine. I'll be here for him in the morning as per contract. He must have all his preparations done for off-world travel by six sharp. Sorry. Busy busy, in a hurry."

"Scott! What happened?" Madame Sandy demanded as she shoved him back into the room. "Scott, what did you do wrong?"

He turned quickly around with eyes lowered, his heart pounding in his chest at the tone of voice and the question. "Wrong, Madame?"

"Scion McMillin just left in a flurry. What happened in here? I'll watch the vid," she reminded him as the room reflected more cooling blues.

"I think she had a lot of prep to do, Madame. Very important story, she said, and that I'd need to be ready early tomorrow. She said it had been a pleasure," he added nervously.

The host released a held breath, so Scott relaxed just a bit. "She must have prep to do then, as will you, but for now go back to your quarters," Madame Sandy ordered. "I'll go see what prep needs doing and come get you. Get rested; this is an early morning assignment."

"Yes, Madame." Scott rose, bowed, and hurried out of the room and down the hall to the quarters he shared with five of Dells' other boys.

"I don't believe it," Joanna muttered as she sipped her cocoa. "I was there, but I don't believe it."

"Don't believe what?" Kathey asked, sipping her own beverage.

"I don't believe I went to an escort service," Joanna hissed back, her eyes darting around the café where they had stopped per Kathey's suggestion after leaving the agency. This place was also one that her fiancé's sister was familiar with, so Joanna was feeling unnerved.

"It's fun. Perhaps it would make you a good Christmas gift?"

"He said 'I look forward to your use.' Can you believe that?"

"I'm sure you'll have fun."

"But the way he came out. I didn't ..." Joanna shook her head in disapproval.

Kathey chuckled as she set her tea down. "I didn't see anything wrong. Everything looked like it was in working condition, and so beautifully proportioned."

"Kathey, that was not why I was there!"

"Joanna!" the other mimicked her outraged tone. "You act as though you'd never seen a naked man before or even used one before. I know that's not true. Your family certainly had a dormboy for you back in university, and that wasn't so long ago, plus you are older than sixteen; I'm sure you had your first ride to celebrate – we all do. Judy and I went there once to see if there were any potential husband material there, as I said. She told me you were a bit bent; you don't get that way without some good rides."

"I just wasn't expecting him that way," Joanna broke in, interrupting the uncomfortable string of sentences coming out of the other woman's mouth.

"Then what did you expect?" Kathey frowned at the younger woman's naiveté. "It was a viewing, you know."

"I expected to see some of his imaging! His vids, his stats, that sort of thing. This is a business deal, you know."

"Only business?"

"Only business."

With a doubtful sigh, Kathey pushed her chocolate cream pie across to Joanna. "You'd better eat mine, too. You're going to need it on this story."

"You don't know anything about this story, other than I need an imagist."

"Nor do I need to."

"So why would I need more pie?"

"Energy. I have the feeling that you're going to need it."

"Why, or don't I want to know?"

"Oh, I don't think this assignment is going to go exactly as you planned. I get the feeling that his idea of business isn't your idea of business."

"You have a very boyish mind, Kathey." Joanna stared into her cup with a frown. "It had better go as planned. This could be very important for both you and me."

"Why?" Kathey pushed, but Joanna only shrugged. "This has something to do with Judy's death, doesn't it? Of course, you can't tell me?" Kathey nodded with an annoyed but silently accepting frown; Joanna knew this was exactly how Judy had dealt with things over the past two years, once the two of them had started working more covert stories. Jensen Media didn't benefit directly from Joanna and Judy's investigations, but GNA did offer other types of pieces to the Jensen coterie of publications and shows.

Kathey pushed her cup away and leaned across the table with a grin. "I have just one more question. Are you going to take him?"

Joanna frowned angrily, "This is a business trip. Nothing more, Kathey!"

"Then I have one last comment: You're stupid."

Joanna folded her arms across her chest and tried to stare the older woman into silence.

"Did you see him when he walked out?" Kathey continued as she ignored the redhead's glare.

"More of him than I wanted to."

"If you don't use him, just think of what you'll be missing." Kathey leaned up on her elbows, resting her chin on her hands, and looked dreamily over Joanna's head. "I bet he's a great ride, and I'm sure he can saddle well, too. All of Dells' boys are thoroughly trained, but they aren't just little sex toys either."

Joanna just sat still for a few seconds, pushing the fantasy these words created aside but returning to an earlier dismissed subject. "So, you don't go there for the sex, then, even though you have Owen and Ann?"

Instead of getting defensive Kathey just chuckled and took her dessert back by using a spoon to scoop up a bite as she shook her head. "Jenson is a minor family. As de facto head of our business while my grandmother takes care of politics, and my mother currently enjoys her temporary retirement, I could have three guardianships, but I only have one. Ann gets a little …

needy." Using that term clearly made the other woman uncomfortable, so Joanna didn't push. Judy had said that her sister's life had been a bit complicated, so Joanna just listened and took another sip of her cocoa. "When I took on Owen as a husband and father, his grandmother made me promise to clear any new contracts with her. To be blunt, Owen's simply too tired all the time for sex, with taking care of Nell and the house, both of us, and prepping for another baby." Joanna noted that her companion moved her wedding ring around a bit as she said that.

"You're pregnant? Ann?"

"Not yet," Kathey said with a chuckle. "We're waiting for Nell to finish her first year in school before I have another. Ann isn't interested."

It wasn't uncommon for younger daughters to lack a desire to have children these days, given that they couldn't inherit family status and, if they were married, any children followed the greater of the parents' family lines. If it were a marriage of equal status, then Joanna knew of at least two couples where each wife had a child but only the eldest inherited everything. That had been the reason why Judy hadn't been interested in having children and sometimes joked about how she might as well have been a fifth-gender, unable to have children. But this was a sidetrack from the original point of figuring out why Kathey went to Dells or any place like it at all. "So, you have an amazing wife at home and a father to take care of everything; why Dells?"

Kathey smiled. "I'm a bit like you in that I like sex with men just a touch more than women." Judy had repeatedly pointed out that being bent like her older sister was chill in their discussions about The Chain or getting a husband as a wedding present. Judy had even delved into how many male contracts they could hold (five for a Great Family, plus two for her status as second daughter in a minor family) once they were wed. Judy had even told Joanna they'd all be for her, even though Joanna had insisted she didn't need any. That was a lie, as her continued membership at The Chain proved.

"Plus, I like variety in my men, at least," Kathey quickly amended. "Ann likes males from time to time but doesn't want to expand our holdings right now. It isn't worth the fight, you know?"

Joanna did indeed know. She had agreed to let Judy conspire with her grandmother, not her mother, about a contract as a wedding present, but that had ended with her fiancé's death. It didn't get rid of her sexual desires. Getting involved with another female felt like a betrayal of Judy. Boys were another matter. Without another word, Joanna paid the bill and left.

Kathey just called out "goodbye" and didn't push. Yes, Judy's older sister was the type to insist you open your private life to her, but she also knew when to back down. The café was not that far from Kathey's office; come to think of it, Dell's wasn't far from her office either. That explained her knowledge of the place. Sharing the car in her current state of mind felt too risky to Joanna now. Better to just leave than risk saying something to isolate her from Judy's family. They were all she had left other than vids, stats, and her memories, and she wasn't quite ready to give that up.

Plus, she had an appointment to keep and some worries to be quelled.

Scott entered his quarters with a puzzled expression as he found the other five men who shared this dorm room – Cal, Elias, Keaka, Polo, and Todd – just watching him silently. Gently he lowered himself onto his cot.

His five roommates all rose. Todd stepped forward, speaking for all of them. "How'd it go?"

"It was the weirdest viewing I've ever done. I'm still not sure what happened."

"Well, tell us about it." The other men sat down on Scott's bed. "Come on," Todd urged as he punched his lover lightly on the shoulder, "tell us what she did."

Scott sighed and ran his hands through his bangs before starting. "First of all, when I walked in, she just got up and left. Madame Sandy convinced her to come back, alone. Then she asked me to put on some clothes."

"Weird," commented Cal, a younger boy who was specializing in garden and lawn care. "Weren't you afraid of what she might do to you? I mean, that sounds like the reaction of an unstable woman." Keaka, the resident musician, who had only been in active service for three years, made a face and gave Cal a little push to show his opinion on the matter, resulting in the normal blues of their room deepening, along with a lowering of the lights.

"A little, at first. But what she did next blew me away." He sat up and leaned toward them, pausing dramatically before continuing. "She sat down and had me sit next to her, on the couch."

"On the couch? Next to her?" Todd repeated unbelievingly.

"Yeah. Then she touched me, on the chin, and made me look at her, right in the eyes." All five men exchanged stunned glances. "Then she placed her hand on top of mine and talked to me almost like I was a woman. I never had a client treat me like that."

"Did she take you right there?" Elias asked as he leaned forward. Big surprise that the roughboy of their suite would ask that question.

"That's what I thought she would do, right?" Scott didn't notice the large figure that loomed in their doorway. "She didn't. I can't figure it out."

"Why not? You're hardly worth taking." The deep feminine voice brought all six men to their feet. Emma Jones, Dells' chief disciplinarian, walked in to stand in front of Scott. Immediately, all the boys fell to their knees. "Everyone else out. Now! Scott!"

At the sound of his name, he brought his head down to xyr feet; xe might never be able to be a mother, but xe was still a woman in every other way that mattered, plus xe held great authority in Dells. His body trembled as he heard his roommates leaving quickly. "Do you know how long she's rented you?"

"A month, Ma'am."

"A month, with an option for longer." Scott's smile of relief vanished quickly as he was hauled up to a kneeling position by his bondage braid. "That's a long time to be without my favorite toy. I am very displeased."

He cringed as xe released him and turned to leave. Automatically he grasped xyr ankle and began the ritual of forgiveness. He started kissing xyr left foot, then the right. "Take me and make me please you."

"I don't know," xe teased cruelly; "you're hardly worth my time."

He continued kissing xyr knees, thighs, lower stomach, and finally xyr belt buckle. Breathing heavily, he pleaded with xem, "Beat me, bruise me, take me, use me."

With a cruel laugh, Jones led him by the braid, down the hall to xyr discipline suite.

Joanna leaned back against her apartment door as she closed it; the roughboy she'd picked up turned around to face her, his hands resting behind his back, which opened his simple shirt up to reveal his naked firm chest and flat stomach over low-riding, tight pants. It was a submissive pose, but his look was brash, face toward her, eyes on her. Jack was her favorite, the one she saw the most often; even though she suspected Jack wasn't his real name, he seemed the sincerest of all of the ones she'd hired through Betty, the woman who owned The Chain. He'd become her regular at the club since Judy's murder.

Goddess, she was a hypocrite! She didn't *see* him; she rented him, and tonight she'd use him until she dropped him off on her way to pick up the other one.

Her face must have betrayed something because Jack was suddenly right in front of her. "You can always take that out on me, you know," he said in his gravelly voice. His voice was perfect for his features, rugged but not too bulky, pale skin that marked up easily but took some effort to maintain a bruise. She'd never seen him with a mark from a previous ... client was the honest word, wasn't it? Right now, he was looking into her eyes with his almost matching hazel ones, daring her with his directness to do what she wanted to him, but he wasn't touching her; his hands were still behind his back.

"Do you want me to hit you?" she said softly as she kept her hands at her sides.

He blinked, then half smiled. "Let's get into it."

"Do you want me to hit you?"

He frowned now and moved just a touch away from her before he chuckled and leaned his head toward her with a grin. "That's what I'm here for."

"I'm being serious, Jack," Joanna ground out as she stepped away from him. "I need you to answer as you. Not what you think I want to hear, but what the truth is for you, as you, not as a role you're playing."

"I am, Miss," he replied as he straightened up. "The truth is that you called, Betty told me to get ready, you picked me up, and now I'm here for you to do whatever you want with me, which usually involves a fair amount of fun hitting."

"Is it fun for you?"

He let his hands fall to his sides at this and pushed his weight slightly onto one hip, thrusting his groin out just a bit. "I think my dick always proves that."

"Now you're being vulgar," Joanna stated as she crossed her arms over her chest but otherwise copied his stance.

"You're being off." He even raised his voice slightly, then sucked in his breath at the same time as did she. Being smug was one thing, and pushing just enough was a dance, but he was never disrespectful. He dropped his gaze and looked at her feet planted on the floor while his hands found their place behind his back again. "Forgive me, Miss? Please?"

Joanna grimaced at the words she had heard not more than two hours ago from another boy she had agreed to rent, to use, to do whatever she wanted to do. Hypocrite. There had to be a way to salvage this, because she wasn't taking him back until the arranged time tomorrow morning. He might get rented out if she brought him back early, possibly punished. Those thoughts stirred jealousy and fear in her until she made a decision about what to do next.

"I need to show you something," she told him as she approached him, disgusted that he flinched back just far enough that she had to reach a bit further to put her hand on his arm.

Joanna led the roughboy into the family room, and they stood silently in front of her sixteenth birthday portrait. She smiled, remembering how angry her mother had been at the thought of letting her brother pose with her. "That's my twin, Joseph. We grew up together until I went to college. When I came back after my first year, he was gone."

She caught Jack glancing at her when she said that, but then his eyes were back on the image. "I don't know who has his contract, private or public, business or guardian, but it hurts me to think that somewhere out there he's expected to just take whatever is happening to him with a smile and maybe some ballsy phrases."

Jack frowned at that and looked down at the floor as Joanna mused, "I like to hope that he's doing something he likes, something he's good at, that he isn't just some saddle to climb on or a toy to break or some grunt to load up. I want to be a sister he could be proud of …"

"You are," Jack whispered but fell silent as she continued.

"I need to know that I am. I need to know that you would choose me if you could choose."

Joanna held still while Jack looked up at the ceiling, took a deep, slow breath, and then turned to face her again. "Miss, since we're sharing all this stuff, may I tell you what my mother told me?"

"Please."

"She said I was a sick fuck that no one would want for a husband, certainly not a father. I didn't," he paused and took another breath, "keep myself from the girls in my neighborhood or the daughters of my mother's friends; I just let them do whatever. I liked it rough even then. I liked knowing it wasn't proper."

"You still feel this isn't proper, then?"

He glanced away and shook his head as he let his arms fall to his sides again, his palms rubbing his jeans slowly as he continued. "No, Mistress taught me that this is proper; this is the way some folks are, boys and women, too." He looked directly at her now. "But you asked if I wanted to be hit. I don't want to be hit by just anyone at any time. I have fun when it's with specific women and when I'm not with one of them … you are correct, I can fake it."

"I understand," Joanna started to reply but then found her eyes following him down as he knelt at her feet, his eyes still locked onto hers.

"I have never faked it with you. Never. I can't grasp any boy faking it with you. You asked this question; it felt off, but it really is how you are. You care, you take the time, you check in, you slow down … you care."

It seemed he wanted to continue, so Joanna just grinned and tucked one lock of hair back behind an ear as her face flushed.

"Fun? I always have fun with you … well, not so much with this entire question thing right now, but otherwise," he ended with a shrug.

"Are you done talking?" she laughed back at him.

His eyes flashed as he gave her his signature smug grin. "Make me," he said, then gasped as he licked his lips after her palm connected with his face.

Joanna stepped closer and caressed the cheek she'd just slapped. "You're right, we do have fun."

As she was about to replace his smugness with cries of pleasure, Hilda interrupted. "Raven calling for you, Scion."

Joanna rolled her eyes at the interruption, and the man at her feet smiled. "Put xem on the screen," she ordered as they both got up to sit on the bed.

After the screen was lowered from the ceiling, both smiled at the woman who appeared on it, calling out together, "Raven!"

The darker woman with short nearly black hair grinned back at them. "I'm glad you were able to keep your normal schedule, Ma'am." Raven was a member of an elite force of the Neuvo Authority that dealt exclusively with Great and Minor families, but the honorific was also a term of affection from xem. Her own family was Minor ranking, though her decision to become fifth-gender had taken xem out of any inheritance or responsibility for them.

Just as Jack had just said, rough sex, just being rough, could be enjoyed by people across the genders. It had taken Joanna a while to accept the term from her lover until they'd gone over consent and desires with Judy sitting in and helping them clarify what they were saying. The memory of her fiancé made Joanna close her eyes for a moment.

"I think about her most every day, too, Ma'am," Raven offered. Jack leaned his head over and placed it on Joanna's shoulder. "That's a good boy, taking care of our boss," Raven teased.

"Anytime she wants," he echoed back. The two of them had bonded over two years ago when Joanna had introduced them. While not strictly necessary, it was important to her that all her lovers were chill with each other regardless of their legal status. Joanna leaned over and kissed his face, then blew a kiss at the screen.

"I wish I could be there, Ma'am, but I'm actually still with the client. I wanted to check in and see if there was anything I could do for you before you leave on your assignment."

Joanna sighed, pressed her lips together, and then blurted out, "I went into Neuvo today, met up with Kathey, went to Dells Escort Agency."

"What?" both of her lovers demanded in near unison.

After she explained for a couple of minutes with reassurances all around, Joanna let out a long breath. These two accepted her as she was. That was something she should build on. A house with a firm foundation was life's goal, after all.

"I can arrange to have a team member meet you at Dells, Ma'am; no need to do it alone," Raven offered.

Joanna frowned but was beaten to reply by the roughboy, who was now up on his knees next to her. "Miss Raven, I just got the boss in the mood, and now she's radiating stress again. See?" He motioned to the light and color changes that had been happening for the past few minutes.

"Sorry, Ma'am. You let me know if you need anything. I'll try to clear my schedule for your calls, whenever you can send them through. You," Raven added, fixing her golden-brown eyes on Jack, "take good care of her tonight."

Jack just grinned and lay back, making both women laugh for several seconds.

Scott fought his desire to bolt as Jones left him alone naked in xyr red and black punishment room; the computer never changed things here, so he always felt aroused and horrified at the same time. He remembered each encounter with the various devices around the room. His breath quickened as he tried not to think of what xe had waiting for him now. As he stepped back, he was flung upside down, suspended from the floor, legs parted by a metal bar that tightly clasped his ankles. His back protested, but he bit back any verbal response, since he couldn't be sure what xe wanted from him.

"I see you found my new toy." Jones returned to stand in front of him. Xe was dressed in a loose black top and skirt with knee-high boots, playing with all the sexy triggers that he'd been programmed with by Dells, society, just being male. For a moment he told himself that xe had to do all of this because of what xe lacked, but it offered him little comfort as soon as xe began to touch him.

He braced his hands on the floor as xyr gloved hands started sliding over his legs and squeezed his buttocks.

"Whose toy are you tonight?"

"Yours," he whispered, all smug thoughts tossed from his mind by fear. In here, in xyr room, xe could do anything to him, and no one would believe it wasn't appropriate.

"Whose toy are you forever?"

"Yours," he gasped at the pain as one dry finger drove in between his ass cheeks. As Jones added another finger, Scott clenched his fingers in the carpet. A drop of cold sweat fell from his forehead as a third finger was added. A cry escaped through his clenched teeth. Immediately the pressure was released. His breath slowed as he tried to relax, only to be stopped short as xyr bare hands explored his buttocks further.

"Did that hurt?" xe asked acidly.

"My pain," he automatically replied, "is for your pleasure." The rote replies freed him from thinking and from fully being here while xe used his body; it was the way he had survived for a decade.

Jones moved xyr hands to his inner thighs and down to squeeze his testicles. "I hate thinking of that Great bitch taking you for two months. You're going to have to make up for that time." Xe loosened xyr grip on him. "You're in for a long night, cock."

"My duty is to please." A second later, he felt xyr hand replaced by the whip's handle. Suddenly Jones pulled the lash around his organ. Scott clenched his teeth as he tried to keep the pain under control. Xe lashed his testicles once, smiling as they started to grow and throb against his will.

"Would you like me to beat you more?" Jones asked as xe hit his cheeks.

"If it pleases you."

"Do you want me to beat you?" Xe parted his cheeks and placed the tip of the whip handle just between them.

"If it pleases you," he whispered.

"I didn't ask that! Do you want me to beat you?" xe demanded, shoving the dry handle in hard.

His scream was swallowed by the padded walls as his body arched with the pain. "Yes! Beat me!" he lied, trying to play into xyr mood.

"Did you just give me an order?" xe asked as xe twisted the handle once.

"Please forgive me, Madame? Please beat me, please."

"Beg me," xe ordered, pushing the handle in more.

Tears now squeezed from his closed eyes. "Please, please pity your slave. Please beat me, bruise me, take me, use me."

After several minutes a knock on the door drew Scott's attention away from the silent counting he did to control his body. Dells, and Jones, did an excellent job of training their boys to respond in any way a client might want, but deep-down Scott had never enjoyed such rough use. He was left hanging, swinging slightly, as Jones cursed and stalked off to find out who was interrupting them.

Scott blinked when Madame Sandy came into his view. She tilted her head and frowned at him. "He knows how important this client is; he wouldn't have misbehaved, especially not to any degree that necessitates this," she said, and now both women entered his line of sight.

"He was bragging to his suite buddies about his client – dogs, every one of them," Jones said, but stopped when Madame Sandy just moved around xem. "Hey, you don't know how to do that!"

Scott felt his ankles released, and his arms helped cushion the fall, which wasn't that far, onto what was actually a mat for safety, where he lay crumpled, breathing slowly, as the two women argued. At Madame Sandy's word he pushed himself up to his feet and went to get his clothing from a chair in the other room. He couldn't help hearing them continue to argue as he hissed and pulled them on. It didn't matter what they said, really, but he could piece together that his next stop was the clinic, then wardrobe, then equipment before a night's sleep, and then breakfast and pickup early in the morning.

He fell into step behind Madame Sandy and just kept quiet as she continued to voice her opinions of Jones, ones he frankly agreed with, though the vitriol against her gender seemed a bit harsh even now as he walked trying to ignore the pain in and on his body.

The clinic stop was another round of angry discussions about the problem with Jones. "If it's such a problem, dismiss xem," Scott thought, but shoved that forbidden idea deep down as he continued to listen. Then they talked about xyr having something on the Dells family and how that meant xe could pretty much do what xe wanted, something xe repeatedly told every boy in the place. It was all over his head, so he just tuned it out after a while. Healing took only a few minutes, and he felt tight afterwards, but he just stretched out as best he could during the walk to the wardrobe room.

As usual, his clothing had been chosen either by the client or based on her requirements. He helped pack a suitcase with the nicest suit he'd ever seen, a couple of casual but modest outfits with multiple layers, and even pajamas, not one single sexy item in the entire selection. His look must have been obvious, because Madame Sandy reiterated that this was a professional imagist gig, not just a ride and then home job. "However, if Scion McMillin wants to use you in any way, you will provide her with the best service, correct?"

"Yes, Madame," Scott hurriedly agreed, but he couldn't keep a grin off his face. To be valued for what he could do, what he could think, what he could create, and not just his body and the rote expressions he might recite, was a rare thing. Maybe he could find a way to keep this client. He'd have to think about it some, and he knew almost nothing about her other than her Great Family status. "Madame," he ventured as they walked next to the equipment, "would it be possible for me to see a vid or two about the McMillin family or my client? I want to provide the best service."

"You have to get rest, too, but if you think you can handle it." He nodded seriously at the concern. "I'll find something and put it into your account, then."

"Thank you, Madame," Scott replied with a deep bow as they went through the door to the equipment room.

The tech he was being sent with was just basic, but the manager told him that the client would also provide her own. This was just backup to show that they could be prepared for anything she needed in the future. He smiled at that thought, glad he wasn't the only one hoping this could become something more than a one-month rental … with option to renew, he reminded himself.

Eckhart

That night he lay in bed and considered the information from the vids he had watched in the reading room right outside their dorm. He knew it all; he wouldn't forget anything he'd seen and heard – some sort of gift, his mother had called it. Now he knew whom he had to impress, and it seemed so daunting. A direct descendant of two of the Great Mothers, someone destined to lead her family into the next millennium of natural order and harmony. No reason for her to ever look to a rental again for anything, unless of course he had amazing skills and a helpful attitude.

Now he just had to prove how useful he could be.

Chapter Two

Joanna woke up at the alarm and smiled at her bed companion as he lay silently, looking back at her with a growing grin on his face. His face was looking a touch mottled this morning, but that was something The Chain would take care of once she returned him. "Good morning," he said, his voice husky, as he reached out and simply stroked the side of her arm.

"Indeed," she replied as she rolled over so that she could straddle him again. "Did you sleep well?" she asked as she guided his hands to rest on her hips but otherwise didn't move further down his body, though she could feel the heat from his still-eager cock just inches away.

"Yes, Ma'am, I did. Do we have time …" Jack began, then frowned with a sigh as she shook her head, "… for breakfast, then?" he amended.

"We do have time for that if you can stand eating separately. I shower first," she added as she swung over him and out of bed.

"I'm not good in the kitchen," he replied as she undid the chain that had connected his left ankle to the bed frame.

"Hilda," she said, looking up at the ceiling, "let Jack order whatever he wants for breakfast and help him make it. He'll need easy instructions. I'll be done and out in fifteen minutes or so." With that she kissed him and then sauntered off to the en-suite bathroom.

Approximately an hour later she was kissing him again through her open car window as she dropped him off at The Chain. "I've paid Betty to keep my weekly appointment for the next two months, but I'm not sure how long this will take me."

Jack blinked and crouched down by the car door. "You didn't need to pay for time you aren't using, Miss."

"I want to make sure you don't get another regular that takes up my spot."

"It is true that I'm difficult to do without," he teased and was rewarded with a slap. "Thank you for the memories."

"Dick," she chuckled back as she waved him off and took the road into Neuvo.

"Scott?" The blond looked up to find his best friend among the boys from his room crouching down in front of him as he slipped his gray leather shoes on. He was dressed well, yet casually, to begin the trip.

It was exciting. He'd lived in Neuvo his entire life, first with his mother, then here at Dells, once she had signed his guardianship over to her employer. He knew it wasn't the normal way that boys came to the agency, but it was all he knew. Most of them were like Todd, simply turned over when they didn't neatly fit into their mothers' idea of appropriate behavior that had something to do with sex. At least, that was what Scott had pieced together because few of them discussed the details after their initial training at Dells.

"I'm sorry I woke you up," Scott offered with a glance upward. Normally they just wore slip-on shoes for something like this, but he'd been given nicer shoes that required a bit more care to put on and take off. Foolishly he hadn't practiced last night once he had started looking into his new client's background.

"You didn't; I asked my clock to get me up shortly after you – told it I wanted to do some balance work this morning."

"You'll have to now, or you'll get written up."

"Oh, well," Todd grinned. "You've never been rented for so long. I've never been rented for so long. I wanted to see you off."

Scott paused, then finished his shoes. "How am I doing on time?" he asked, standing up anxiously.

"You have a few minutes yet." Todd stood up at the same time and then sighed as Scott turned to the full-length mirror. "Did you sleep all right last night?"

"Why wouldn't I?"

"You didn't get back until after midnight. That's a long time to be out when you have such an early pick up the next morning."

"I've been out later with clients. I'll be gone a lot longer this time."

"Jones isn't a client." Both men tensed. Not using an honorific for the disciplinarian was risky, it was small defiance they shared, one Scott nurtured in his mind whenever he could.

Scott sighed. He so did not want to get into this right now when he had an opportunity like this in front of him. "I wasn't with Jones the entire evening. I was getting packed for a client, then I was reading up on her."

Todd's stance relaxed. "Oh, that's good. I mean, other than you being gone for a month or more, you didn't tell us much else."

Scott stepped back and decided he looked the best he could. Dark gray trousers, leather shoes, button-down light blue shirt tucked in under a dark gray vest. His braid wasn't showing any loose hair, and his bangs were lying at an angle just hovering over his right eye, while the lashes on both eyes were darkened just slightly and the hint of color for his cheeks and eyes seemed almost natural, highlighting his features, not hiding them, or drawing too much attention to them. Makeup was a skill that every boy did well to learn, and Dells had refresher courses on the latest trends from time to time.

"You look good," Todd told him firmly as he picked up the dark gray coat and held it out for him. "I might help you look better if I knew who you were strutting up for."

Scott turned with an eye roll and stepped a bit closer. "She's a Scion of a very important family, Great Mothers important. I can't screw this up."

"No, no you can't, so ..." Todd picked up Scott's hands and examined them one finger at a time, then walked entirely around his friend twice, touching him there, adjusting a fold here. "I'd ride you," the other man declared with a nod.

"Thanks," Scott replied with a chuckle. The two leaned in and briefly brushed their lips against each other for a second, then moved back just as the door beeped.

They both stepped forward when Madame Sandy came in, and she frowned at the darker man. "Why are you up, boy?"

"I wanted more time working on balance, Madame. I have a two-day client picking me up, and if I'm not in balance it's difficult to help her."

That was entirely possible, since Todd was routinely booked for two- and three-day sessions with women whose high-stress jobs benefited from his holistic body care specialization. Whether he'd been trained because of his naturally chill personality, or the job had necessitated his developing such an attitude was unclear, since he had always been the calm one since the day Scott had met him.

"Good, good, way to think ahead," Madame Sandy replied with a smile before turning to Scott with the same smile. "I was very pleased to see that you spent a good deal of time on the reading last night. I hope it pays off because this could be a huge boost for us. That will be undone if you're late."

Scott nodded and glanced back at Todd before following her out the door. His luggage would be waiting at the entrance for him, giving his client a chance to look through it and discard or change out anything she didn't like.

"Scion McMillin, is there anything else I can get you?"

Joanna shook her head again at the eager employee who was bothering her again. "Amanda, yes?" she asked, and the woman beamed at her. "We do have deadlines to meet; I hope it won't be much longer."

"If you're bored, we can go through his bags," the disciplinarian, Jones, interrupted.

Joanna managed a weak smile for the larger woman and shook her head. Just how many people worked for this place? It was taking a good deal of self-control not to bolt from the building as Joanna stood waiting in the outer lobby of Dells; the escort agency was too public, which made her uncomfortable, unlike The Chain, which was an exclusive private club she'd worked months to get invited to. Perhaps she should have accepted Raven's offer to assign an escort, but it was just one stop; she could handle this on her own.

Her refusal had clearly earned her the larger woman's ire. Frankly she wasn't used to people not fawning over her slightly, or at most ignoring her, so the annoyance was only fueling her own. Then Joanna realized that the face and name were familiar from her college days, where they had been on opposite sides of several campus debates. Women like Jones tended to treat boys very badly, and it wasn't surprising xe'd end up in this job. It could only be something like this or perhaps the military, after all, once a girl chose fifth-gender status.

"Where did you say you were going, Scion McMillin?" Jones inquired harshly, refusing to simply ignore her.

Joanna returned the favor by not reacting to the tone of her title. "I didn't say, but I'm going to Bragg to do a vacation article." Joanna turned away to look at the reception desk, hoping the man would soon be coming.

"Jones, some respect," Amanda hissed.

"Isn't that a little out of your field?" Jones snorted. "It doesn't have anything to do with the poor abused boys of our world. Or are you expanding now to fight the plight of the male animal on a galactic scale?"

"Guess you haven't been following my work very well, then," Joanna replied over her shoulder. It was true that many of her stories looked at the lives of men in some way, but at least on the surface they primarily dealt with economic policies and trade issues. Not her favorite subjects, but MOI required that she hide her agenda while she worked for GNA, with the promise that later she could focus on more social issues once she'd proved herself as a solid reporter and not merely a Scion playing until her family needed her. Joanna turned back to Amanda before Jones could speak again. "Will he be much longer?"

"He shouldn't be, but you know men," the host answered, looking toward the hall. "Ah, here he comes now."

Scott entered with the host from yesterday and then stopped three feet from Joanna. He looked good; no, he looked great, if she were honest, but Joanna just forced herself to frown and step toward him quickly – but not quickly enough to get to him before Jones. The other staff member stepped back, looking worried, Joanna noted, before studying what was happening in front of her.

As Jones neared, he stood at rigid attention. "How does he look? See the way the vest draws the eye to the important parts of a man," xe commented, moving xyr hand over the front of his trousers.

Joanna gave a short nod, to hide the fact that she wanted to slip those hands away. She didn't know this boy from any other dick; how could she feel protective or possessive of him? "Very nice, I'm sure."

"Come look for yourself," Jones suggested strongly.

After encouraging looks from the three employees, Joanna approached the man. His aqua eyes lowered as she approached, and a smile rose slightly to his lips. Joanna walked slowly around him; arms crossed. His bangs had been brushed back over just one eye to show more of his face; the rest of his hair looked recently washed and braided. The clothes emphasized things she didn't want to deal with at all on this trip, but then, what could she expect from a place like this? "Yes, he looks very nice."

"Here," Jones said suddenly, grabbing Joanna's hand and placing it on his chest, "feel how firm he is." Jones tried to force the younger woman's hand downward as xe watched her eyes and face carefully. "Feel him everywhere."

"You're being mannish," Sandy stated as she stepped forward but stopped when Joanna held up her other hand.

With a disgusted look, Joanna pulled her hand away. "No, thank you. We really have to go," she added firmly, moving toward the door.

"Wait a minute," Sandy interrupted and ran behind the front desk. "You need his leash." She returned and handed Joanna a silver chain with a dark gray leather handle.

"The leash is the law in Neuvo," Jones added.

"Yes, I know." Joanna frowned. This Jones clearly remembered her as well and was trying to stomp in every room of Joanna's mind to get a stronger reaction from her. Knowing that allowed her to curtail some of her immediate responses.

"One more thing. We have a little ritual," Sandy added.

"Is it really necessary?" Joanna sighed but kept her eyes on the disciplinarian.

"Yes," Jones affirmed, standing right behind the male.

The look of fear that clouded Scott's eyes decided the matter for Joanna. "Fine. Tell me what to do."

"Give him your hand," Sandy instructed. Joanna reached out and gently touched his outstretched palm. "Now tell him that you are his guardian and clip the leash onto his collar. It will make a voice and DNA match to his collar when you do that."

Joanna tried to shake his hand as she spoke in a monotone, "I'm your guardian." She fumbled a bit with her other hand as she snapped it onto the front ring of his collar. It had been a long time since she'd done such a thing; she never used them with the men she got through The Chain, and she did not like the minor thrill that leaped through her as it clicked. It sounded too permanent, too intimate, and that was not what she wanted him for.

Scott knelt, placing her hand on his head, then replied, "I am your obedient servant. Your grateful servant," he added in a whisper.

Joanna looked down at him with a worried frown. "It's time for us to leave." The escort hurried to get his bags and followed her to the door. "I'll bring him back as soon as possible."

"Just call if you need him longer, Scion McMillin," Sandy reminded her.

"Or if he gives you any problems," Jones said, hurrying to the door, "I'll take care of it when he gets back." Xe grabbed the man by his collar. "Did you hear that?"

Joanna noticed the fright that filled the boy's voice as he managed a weak reply that sounded more like a trained phrase than any true promise. She turned back to the disciplinarian with a smile. "I don't think he'll be any problem." Taking him also by the collar, she forced the other woman to release him. "In fact, I think he'll be quite a pleasure," she stated before pulling him close enough to give him a firm kiss on the lips. With a gentle pull on his collar, she got him out the door. With a final calculated smile at the three women watching, she led her escort out to her car.

Joanna watched the escort out of the corner of her eye as she drove down the road toward the highway that would take them to the lunar shuttle port. Her hands beat the steering wheel along with the music from her crystal of golden oldies, "A Millennium of Women's Songs," though it was a bit misnamed, given that the anniversary was a few years off, but it seemed everyone was cashing in. The attention to her family would only grow more extreme, too, as the anniversary ticked closer. She wasn't looking forward to it for many reasons. No. No thinking about what might happen; time to change the subject. "I take it that you like my car," she stated, referring to the way he had stared at it when they had first left Dells.

"Yes, Miss."

Joanna waited for him to continue, but he neither looked at her nor added to his simple reply. She gripped the steering wheel more tightly and searched for something else to say. "You can drive, can't you?"

"Oh, no, Miss."

"Why not?"

"It's against the law."

"No, it isn't. I've seen men drive before; I've been in cars driven by men. Limos are often driven by men, if you port in or fly in for a visit to another city. I've even seen a few mass trans piloted by men." She paused and waited for a reply, which did not come. "So, it can't be against the law for you to drive, can it?"

"I'm sorry, Miss. That is what I've been taught." He glanced at her meekly, "I'm probably wrong, Miss."

"Someone told you that? Why would they say it was illegal for you to drive?"

"I was taught that driving was not my job and therefore illegal, Miss," he reiterated in a softer tone.

Joanna frowned as her attempts to press a conversation failed. This was one of the reasons she could empathize with a boy's condition and still find him annoying; they just seemed to be every damned stereotype she'd been taught, with rare exceptions. One would think that an imagist …

Finally in exasperation she gave him an order. "I like a little conversation when I'm driving, especially once we jack into the highway. Please try to hold up your end of the conversation."

"Yes, Miss. I'm sorry I've displeased you." He looked at her now and offered a small smile. "I'm a little nervous, but I shall do better, I promise."

"That makes two of us, Scott," Joanna assured him as she allowed the car to jack into the automatic system for the next stretch of the drive. Now she could turn more of her attention to her companion with just a cautious eye on the highway from time to time. She was far more used to roads than highways, and while the uniform highway system had been in use for centuries, it still made her nervous. Accidents were rare, but when they happened, they could be devastating. "What exactly did your supervisor at Dells tell you about me?"

"Not much, Miss. I was told that this was your first time and to be attentive to your needs."

"My first time for what?"

"Renting from Dells," he hedged.

"Yeah, well, it really wasn't my idea to go to Dells. My director at GNA arranged this whole thing." Her voice was practically dripping with anger, but the escort didn't seem to notice, so she continued with a sharper edge to her voice. "She said it would give me a new perspective on things, so I decided to try."

"I will try to please you, Miss."

"So, you've said again and again." Jonna recalled the café conversation with Kathey. "What exactly did they tell you I wanted from you?"

"Every client is different, Miss. They couldn't give me exact details about my use." Scott looked at his client imploringly. "I know a lot of techniques. If I don't know what you like, I'll learn, Miss. I'm a fast learner, I've been told."

There were a few seconds of pause as she turned his words over in her mind. "I get the feeling that we're not talking about the same thing. You do recall that I've rented your imagist skills, right?"

"Yes, Miss," he said, but his voice held a hint of something new.

"I know this probably isn't your ideal situation," she began and was surprised to see him look directly at her. "What?"

Scott grinned and looked at his hand, then back up at her. "Actually, it is ideal, Miss. Really, it is," he insisted at her unimpressed frown. "I rarely get to use my imaging skills outside of the agency. I really like being behind the camera, figuring out how best to do a shot or frame a segment with the goal in mind. I did some research on you last night, and while I've never done news work, I know I can learn fast and give you what you need."

Joanna's mouth had fallen open just a touch as he had continued speaking. It was so obvious from the way his face and eyes lit up, the upbeat tone of his voice, and even his hands moving with emphasis that he was telling her the truth. There was more to him than she thought. Then he shut his mouth and looked down at his hands again with a mumbled, "I spoke out of turn, Miss. Forgive me, Miss? Please?"

"Scott," she replied, and he glanced up at her with tears already lining his eyes. "No, don't cry, you didn't speak out of turn. I'm just surprised you talked for so long. But," she hastened to add when he flinched, "it is clear to me that you might really know what you're doing."

His mouth twitched as though he wanted to reply, but he just glanced away.

Way to go, now she'd offended him, and she hadn't intended to do it. "I'll tell you more about my goals once we're on the trip. I only have basic background stuff myself right now," she offered, and that earned another glance from him.

Scott nodded, then licked his lips before offering something in return, since it was clear she was being forgiving when she didn't need to be. "Your imagist on the stories I saw last night was really good. There might be better ways to deal with total darkness if you like."

Her reaction was to sit back a bit further and look out on the highway, where other cars were all moving along with precision in both directions. "That could be useful. I know that Judy said it was a challenge when we did dark shoots."

"She's right. Is she on another story now, Miss?"

"She's dead," Joanna bluntly stated. "That's really the only reason I rented you."

There was silence for a few moments between them. "My condolences, Miss," he offered in a shaky voice.

"Thank you," she replied as she blew out a breath she didn't know she'd been holding. Great, he was back to studying his hands again, her glance confirmed.

She let them sit in silence for a few minutes before bringing up another subject. "Emma Jones works at Dells." His body stiffened at the statement. "I knew xem," Joanna said. "Well, I knew of xem; I had the misfortune of crossing xyr path several times in college, is more accurate. It's a small world to find xem waiting for me this morning. Xe said that you like a firm hand." His body stiffened even more. "Is that true?"

"If it pleases you, Miss."

"Which means xe was lying."

That got him to look up at her sharply, his aqua eyes wide, his mouth mumbling, "I would never accuse a woman of lying, Miss."

"I know. I can tell you want to be a good boy," Joanna added as she glanced away but kept an eye on him.

"Yes, I will be a good boy, Miss." Scott was now turning toward her, and his body was radiating fear and nervousness on an entirely new level. It would have been hot if she had been looking for that reaction, but right now it was simply confirming her thoughts about the disciplinarian. "If Madame Jones says that I like a firm hand, xe must be right," he submitted with a grimaced smile.

"Bullcock," Joanna said, and that made his eyes widen further. "That … woman … has been a self-serving barren since before I knew xem!" Neither of them flinched when she used the derogatory term, suggesting either that he was well trained not to react to the use of vulgarities or that he held a similar opinion about Jones. Most fifth-genders she'd known never acted like Jones and xyr college crowd had. Every memory of those debates and school investigations just pushed Joanna to be more enraged.

"The things xe and xyr sisters tried to get passed at school would make your hair fall out." He touched his hair reflectively and seemed to sink into himself a bit. "If xe says that you need a firm hand, what you probably actually need is a bit of encouragement. Not that I can hold the door for you the entire time. I need you to step up here. Work with me, help me document everything that's going on, because I need to be focused on my part of it. I can't be telling you what to do every single moment."

"Of course, Miss, I understand," he replied to her pointed look. "Sort of," he added, then bit his lower lip.

"No, no. Conversation, remember?"

Scott nodded once and continued, "Behind the camera I will make sure you get the best images that I can manage. I've never been with a virgin before, though ..."

"A what?" Joanna felt a giggle burst through her lips as she interrupted.

His eyes widened again; he swallowed, then repeated what he had been saying. "A virgin with males," he clarified. "I've never been with an inexperienced client, so I would appreciate guidance, lots of feedback, in that regard, please ..." Each word was slower coming out of him as her laughter increased. "They told me ..." he whispered as he felt his face burn in embarrassment.

Joanna was grateful her Vega wasn't on manual right now because they would have crashed. "Good Goddess, are you jerking me around?" His miserable look confirmed he wasn't, so she jostled his knee with one hand as she laughed. "This is hysterical. Why the hell would they think that?"

Scott took a breath before he replied. "You left the viewing room in a hurry when I came out and told me to put on clothes."

"Oh, for the love of Gaia, really? That equals I'm a virgin? I didn't hire you for sex, Scott; I don't know how often I need to repeat that, but I hired you to be my imagist for this story."

She put her hands on the steering wheel for a second while they both just sat there silently. "I'm not a virgin with males or women," she stated, and he slid down his seat just a bit, lowering his head. "Understand that my not jumping on for a ride has nothing to do with your job or your body, can you cradle that?"

"Yes, Miss, as you say," he offered automatically as he looked at her but didn't sit back up. "I'm here to please you in any way you want. I'll try not to assume to know what that is until you tell me."

Joanna's hands clenched in frustration. Kathey was right; he might be saying he wouldn't assume, but clearly he did. Once they went over the background for this assignment he'd understand, so for now she changed the subject. "If I turn on some music, could you sing along with me?"

That got him to sit up and grin at her. "I can open my mouth and growl out some words, but I wouldn't call it singing, Miss."

She chuckled at his sudden humor. "It's good to know that your artistic skills aren't all-encompassing. What else can you do?"

Scott sat up in his seat, tilting his head to one side for a moment before he replied. "I can read and do basic computer work, to do the imaging and research."

"Like you said you did on me last night?"

"Yes, Miss. I try to learn a bit about clients so I'm better prepared. Is that a skill? I can think ahead?"

"That's a very good skill," she confirmed. Most believed that men simply couldn't plan ahead, but she'd seen that wasn't true in her own life with whatever father was in her mother's house. Lily Marla McMillin had gone through husbands and fathers fairly quickly after her twins' sire had died, and while that was often heartbreaking to the kids, it had also given Joanna many examples of male ability that frankly didn't match the stereotypes. It really hadn't been so hard for her to understand that the popular ideas of what men were rarely matched reality. In college she saw many types of dorm boys, even if she'd only kept hers for a year. Once she had access to family histories, she could see that men played roles in world events, and not always negative or unimportant ones.

Scott smiled again at the compliment, and she found that meant a lot to her, so she added, "It's also helpful for the work I need from you, though you also have to be flexible, because we never know what might happen during an interview or filming."

"Yes, of course, Miss. That sometimes happened at Dells, or with my mother. Weather would change, or the lighting wouldn't work, or a subject had difficulties," he added. His smile suddenly faded as he announced, "Oh, Goddess, I've been calling you Miss!"

His face was much paler now, so she put a hand on his knee again. "I prefer it over hearing Scion repeatedly," she offered him. On one level, she knew it was an attempt to bond with her by using that title rather than a more neutral Ma'am. As the ceremony back at Dells had emphasized, right now, for all legal and social purposes, she was his guardian, his mistress, just as he was her servant, her slave. She closed her eyes for a second over those words. "Just using Miss is chill for now, Scott."

"Yes, Miss, thank you," he sighed back.

"What else can you do?" she pushed after more silence.

"I have basic cooking skills – at the level of using a wave or a toaster – and the same for cleaning. I could easily learn, though; Dells offers domestic classes. I have an excellent memory. Dells tested me and everything to document that. I think my data says it's hyperthymesia with almost eidetic qualities. I hope it doesn't make me seem vain to say that, Miss?"

Joanna shook her head and smiled at him to encourage him to keep talking.

"Um, what else? I can dance," he finished with a shrug as though he was embarrassed somehow by his list of skills and talents.

"Dance but not sing, huh? What kind of dancing?" she asked, sliding her eyes to look at him, though she had a suspicion about the answer.

"I don't know how often you get into Neuvo, Miss, but when we're still young we dance at the Haven, a club that Dells owns." She was nodding her head, so he continued, "Then we continue to do gigs there a few times a month, depending on the need and our schedule. I'm usually there three nights or so each month."

"That's a themed escort club, right?"

"Yes, Miss. You can't rent the boys out, but if you rent a room or a boy there you can spend the night. More like a hotel?"

"I haven't been there, but I've heard of it. I live in Cape Elizabeth, so I don't need to go into the metro that often. It used to be on an island – or islands, actually; did you know that?" she again changed the subject.

"Neuvo? Yes, I think I heard that somewhere, Miss. One of the side effects of male foolishness, right? The oceans rose and took away land, so cities had to move or die? I'm pretty sure that's what I learned."

"That's what I was taught," Joanna confirmed, though she left out the fact that the old world wasn't ruled only by men when the big natural crisis developed, and the world started slipping into chaos that eventually provoked mothers worldwide to rise up. Those were minor details, as many of her teachers and others would repeatedly say to her, and she doubted he could even participate in any type of debate. She wasn't here to free his mind, but to use it, after all. That was definitely being a hypocrite, but before she could speak again, he surprised her by continuing.

"One of the boys I know has a client who is a scientist who does dives in the old city. He's seen some of the stuff she's brought up. Sounds creepy to me," Scott confessed with a lopsided grin.

"I think I saw a docu on that recently. I'm sure there are going to be a ton of those docus and research with the millennium approaching. I have a friend who is an archivist, so I might be looking into that at some point."

"Exciting time to be alive," Scott tossed out a comment that sounded a bit fake.

"Yeah, I guess so," Joanna chuckled. "However, we are about to do something more exciting, I assure you," she told him as they approached the highway exit toward the shuttle port. She jacked out the car and manually drove down the off-ramp.

In just a few miles she exclaimed, "There it is!" She pointed out the shuttle port, shiny and tall with domed buildings around it, just ahead of them and to the right. "Have you ever been off-world, Scott?"

"No, Miss." He looked up at the sling that shot the shuttle off into space toward the moon through the window.

"Don't worry. Transport to the moon base is safe, and I'll keep an eye on you. I think you'll enjoy it."

"Yes, Miss," he replied with a tense smile.

"After that we'll take another ship to the Gate, and then of course there's the hyperspace leg of the trip, then onto another ship taking us to the base we're headed toward. So at least five or six steps before we meet up with the rest of the team."

"Rest of the team?"

"Yup, this is going to be a big story. We're going to document the IGA taking out a criminal who is threatening the entire galaxy."

"Wow," Scott simply said as he looked at her, then back at the shuttle port.

"Wow indeed," Joanna chuckled as she turned into the parking garage to store her car.

Chapter Three

Joanna stood and just looked at the frustrating scene before her. Scott was kneeling while security agents went over his ID again and discussed something that made them both chuckle. You couldn't always tell a fifth-gender by looks, but their job and their attitude suggested that, if they weren't barrens, they were at least second or third daughters, angry at the world for their birth order. There had been a second daughter every now and again in the McMillin family, but not often, and normally they helped run the family businesses. While other Great Families were highly specialized, the McMillin family continually expanded its interests, so there was plenty for even distant cousins to help with. Usually, second daughters didn't have children, though it wasn't unheard of either. It wasn't fair, but it wasn't unfair either; it was just the best way to preserve family interests, particularly among the Great lines. If Joanna had a younger sister, she would have seriously thought about handing over her birthrights just to get away from the cocked public attention she struggled with.

There had been another band of gossip parlor reporters waiting at the shuttle port when they'd arrived. She'd paused to vaguely answer a few questions about the man right behind her, then hurried inside where only ticket holders were allowed. She wasn't like them; she did real investigations and news stories, but it was important to play nice with them for her family's sake. Joanna had foolishly thought they'd get through security quickly because of her name. Even her gun, a privilege or duty of the Great Families depending on how you liked to view it, hadn't slowed her down in the past. It had never taken Judy and her more than a minute or two, but now, with the focus on Scott, it was approaching a good ten minutes. With a sigh she stepped forward, drawing the attention of the two guards. "Excuse me," she ground out with a fake smile, but it was a statement, not a question.

"Oh, yeah, yeah, we're almost done," one of the guards told her as she motioned for Scott to stand up.

"You should take your clothes off," the other guard ordered, and at that Joanna took the few remaining steps to get between the escort and security.

"No, he shouldn't. He's been through the scanner, his ID checks out, and the company I've rented him from has signed all the waivers; there is really nothing else you need to check," she said exasperatedly, going through the entire list of required security checks.

The two guards looked at each other, then shrugged. "Don't blame us if he's hiding something in his body to damage the shuttle. Remember Nottingham," the senior guard said, tossing out the old example of the failed male-led city from nearly seven hundred years ago. Set a community up to fail by suddenly changing the authority structures, and of course you create corruption, terrorism, and violence that can then be used to justify any damn thing you want centuries later.

Joanna touched the fingers of one hand to her temple and rubbed it briefly. "I have confidence that the scanner worked well enough," she offered with another sigh.

Another guard came out of a nearby room, and Joanna almost cursed as this one approached her directly with a concerned look. "Is there a problem?" she asked politely, looking between passengers and her own women. Her nametag and uniform indicated that she was director of security.

Time to use her rank again. "I'm Joanna Lily McMillin, Scion. I'm trying to check into my shuttle with my imagist, but apparently there's a problem, which seems unlikely, given my people's attention in planning this trip." She said it all with a firm condescending smile, even offering her hand to be shaken to show she knew this guard would be able to sort things through.

"Is there a problem with his ID?" this new guard asked her underlings, who just shook their heads and closed Scott's luggage up before handing them to him. The head of security turned back to Joanna with a smile. "Sorry for the delay, Scion; please have a safe trip."

"Thank you so much, Director Simmons," Joanna replied with a friendlier smile. "Come on, boy, we've a shuttle to catch," she called out as she turned and started walking, leading him by the leash. She couldn't help but continue smiling as she heard the director mutter about how stupid the other guards had been. Sometimes it was good to be a Scion.

They shouldn't have much of a wait before boarding at this point, so something good did come out of the delay. Seats were assigned, so it didn't matter when they arrived, as long as everyone was seated for slinging at the right time. There were certain times of day when launching from this point on Gaia's surface resulted in a maximally energy-efficient path to the moon; these efficiency-maximizing times of day changed as the moon revolved and over the course of the year. Weather didn't matter, only timing, and that was something that was relatively easy to predict. There were Slings at several other points on Gaia as well, but this one was the closest to Neuvo, as well as her home.

"Don't be nervous," Joanna told Scott as he stood next to her, seemingly as close as possible, their bags in his hands, his shoulders trembling just a bit. "We'll be sitting down soon enough."

"Yes, Miss," he replied softly but leaned in even closer to her.

This was going to be a long trip, Joanna decided right then and there.

Scott followed his client through the terminals to their boarding gate, staying as close to her as he could. Once there, he took a few deep breaths and tried to relax, but it was difficult. He had known that this rental was going to be different, but already it was feeling overwhelming.

He'd been out of Dells numerous times every week, but usually he was just urged into a car and driven to the client's house, hotel, or party and turned over to her. Rarely did the women who'd rented him pick him up themselves, because they were too busy running the world to do that, he guessed. When he was with them, they were very focused on using him as fully as possible for the time contracted, generally a couple of hours, before another company car came to pick him up. He didn't know what Scion McMillin had been talking about when she'd mentioned men driving; he'd only seen women doing that.

Dells vehicles had darkened windows to hide the boys during transport, and they often had folders of information reminding the boys of a client's needs or requests, so they weren't tempted to sneak peeks out the window or talk to each other. Would he have gotten any information before she clipped the leash on him, if he hadn't requested it last night? That leash was just hanging loose right now; she'd never bothered to pick it up once they were past the security checkpoint. Not having that connection had spurred him to stay closer to her, yet a moment ago she'd seemed annoyed by this fact.

Miss Joanna was tricky to navigate; he just couldn't cradle what she wanted from him yet.

There was what she'd said – conversation, thinking ahead, acting with the knowledge he had, no sex – but then there was what she did; sometimes she was looking at him appreciatively, or with an annoyed frown, sometimes within seconds of each other. Women were like that, thinking all the time in ways that were beyond any man's understanding. That complexity made them ideal as mothers and natural managers of the world, but Scott was just a boy with simple desires and needs.

"Buck up," he whispered, and she turned toward him, stroking his arm, and telling him to take another deep breath. Great, he'd said that out loud.

He took the time to look around him as covertly as possible. He wasn't surprised by the lack of other men. It was unusual for men to travel off-world, and even the staff he saw here and there were all women, though there were probably a few older men somewhere in the background doing the dirtiest jobs. This sort of future might not be too bad if he turned 25 before he found a private guardian, but the rumor mill around Dells was that they sent all their used boys to hard labor jobs where life expectancy was just a few short years. It might be only a few short years here, too, since he really didn't know what men at the shuttleport did, if they did anything at all.

Then he saw him: another man trailing behind another woman, and he was looking fancy in a colorful suit, carrying a bag over one shoulder across his torso, holding a computer in his hands as he followed her … without a leash, and without a collar, in fact, marking em as a mas, not male. Scott closed his eyes for a second. Why would anyone want to be a man? It made no sense to him. A fem, on the other hand, a boy who had identified as a woman when ze was growing up, made a lot of sense; it gave you access to some autonomy, though the price was steep if you valued your cock. Did a mas have surgery? Scott just turned away from the thoughts, blocking them out. He was too old to wish for any such change and getting older by the moment.

He had a job to do and a future to think about, so he asked his client a question about the Sling and got a bright smile in return before she started talking about gravity and orbits and other such things. Scott nodded a lot, made interested sounds, and asked a few other questions until the line started to move for boarding.

There was only one class for the shuttle, because regardless of tech advances, going off-world was expensive; it was expensive in every part of the galaxy, so people only did it for important reasons or if they had a ton of wealth. This was only her fifth time off planet, Joanna calculated as she settled into the seat and let the attendant help her buckle in. When she turned to watch Scott getting fastened into the harness, she was surprised by how pale he was.

She reached out and touched his knee, and he glanced at her with a visible swallow. "You aren't claustrophobic, are you? They should have told me that, 'cause most of our journey will be locked down for our safety." He blinked at her as though he didn't understand the word, so she clarified, "You aren't afraid of small places or being confined?"

Scott released a breath as the attendant finished the last strap. "No, Miss, just surprised." His hand twitched, so she turned hers over on his knee, and he placed his palm in hers with a smile.

Joanna smiled back, then shook her head and pulled her hand away to fish out the information she had preloaded on a player just for this leg of the trip. "The journey to the lunar station is a couple of hours, so why don't you just relax and listen to this? Save any questions you might have until I ask you for them," she instructed as she motioned for him to put the earbuds in.

Scott nodded silently and put the devices into his ears. Joanna put her own earbuds in and turned up some music. She could feel his eyes on her, though whenever she opened her own, his gaze was just slipping away. He'd better be listening to what she'd recorded. The slinging made her tighten her grip on the arm rests, but she noted how tense his entire body got. Women handled pain so much better than men, just as they handled being off-world better.

Once they were under way to the lunar station using the momentum the Sling had given them, Joanna opened her eyes again and gave Scott another squeeze on the knee. After the information about the Sling, she'd recorded some basic information about the Vancazies and the Transway or Gate on the crystal she'd given him, as well as information about where they were going, and after that there was some of the music that was currently popular.

Scott's body looked more relaxed. The time she'd spent recording that during the drive from The Chain to Dells had been worth it. Joanna turned to the porthole and watched the sky change colors until it became the blackness of space highlighted by pinpoints of light. Slowly the stars seemed to flow together as her mind recalled the two most important people in her life. Two faces seemed to float in the blackness, waiting for her to choose. Closing her eyes, she pictured the perky blonde's face growing and coming to life. The scene faded into a memory from her last assignment.

"I believe we are having problems," Judy stated as the two of them hid behind a door.

"No kidding!" Joanna wiped the sweat from her brow with an annoyed glance at her partner.

"Just slightly more than normal," the perky imagist smiled back assuredly.

"We're being shot ..." Judy's hand stopped the redhead short. Both young women held their breath as the footsteps grew louder. As the armed guard stopped right across from them, Judy raised her gun quietly. Before she could shoot, the woman hurried by.

Joanna released her breath, then whispered, "We have to get this story out. It's got to be more than simply drug transactions and slave trafficking if they want us dead. Lots of worlds allow both, so it isn't as if those are especially dangerous or high profit." She glanced in the direction they needed to go. "If we'd only had more time in that lab."

"We came too close to getting caught. Let's just make sure that what we have gets further investigation." Judy glanced around the wall down both corridors. "We'll make a break for the slip-pad. The ship should be waiting." Joanna nodded. "On three: One... Two... Three."

Joanna led the way quickly down the left corridor toward the storage room where they'd left their slip-pad and other equipment. As they turned a corner, Judy stumbled. "Can you get up?"

"Just keep going," the blonde instructed, putting the video crystals from her pocket into her partner's hands. "I'll hold them off for a second or two so you can make contact, Scion," she teased, but that only made Joanna frown and pause. "Just move!"

As soon as Joanna was in the door, she hurried to the board and contacted the ship. "FlashNews to Press Beta."

"Contact, FlashNews. We have only one of you locked in," responded the female voice from the IGA ship that had brought them there.

Joanna was about to step off the pad when Judy barreled around the corner and into the room, nearly knocking them both off balance. "I had to kill her," Judy smiled weakly as Joanna looked at her.

"Slip us now!" Joanna ordered the ship.

The slip took nanoseconds, but both women tumbled out onto the floor of the IGA ship awaiting them. The technician called med as soon as she spotted the blonde woman's pained look.

Joanna tried to help her partner to stand but instead felt hot slickness under her hands. "You had to kill her because she shot you?" she whispered as the horror hit her.

"I'll be fine," Judy replied with a cough of blood.

Medics took the blonde from Joanna's numb arms. One of the medics touched her, but she simply shrugged her off. "Scion, you might be hurt."

"I haven't been hurt! Let me through," she ordered as she pushed her way past the woman to her mate's side. "Judy, I'm right here with you. Everything is going to be fine."

"Did the equipment make it back in one piece?" the blonde grasped her hand tightly.

"Yes, it's safe. You just have to do what the medics say now," Joanna offered. Any injury to the body risked amplification upon slipping, simply because the process wore on the body, which itself was far more complicated than any machine.

"Have you started writing the story?"

"No, we just got back. But don't you worry about it. We'll write it together after you get better."

"Joanna," and Judy's gray-blue eyes locked onto her hazel ones, "I've been shot."

"No kidding." Joanna swallowed her tears. "But you're going to be fine. Medics will fix you right up."

"No; they can't," Judy suddenly said, coughing up another mouthful of blood. The medics paused before the surgery room. "You'll have to write it for both of us. I'm sorry I won't get to meet Joseph, Joanna. And I'm sorry I won't get to be your wife."

Joanna stood helplessly back as the medics took Judy into the waiting surgeon. Slowly she paced in front of the doors, muttering to herself, "You're going to be all right. You're going to pull through this."

After several hours Joanna had calmed enough to sit down. Suddenly the steady thump of the heart monitor in the other room became a continuous buzz. "No!" Joanna burst through the doors to the surgery. "What's wrong?" she demanded of the medics surrounding her best friend.

"Get her out of here!" ordered one, covered in bright red blood. Two medics started to push the redhead from the room.

"No! Judy!" Joanna fought both medics wildly as they forced her to leave her lover. "I have to be with her!"

"You can't help in there," one of the medics told her. "Let us handle it from here."

"Then what am I supposed to do? Just sit out here?"

The other medic held her by the shoulders, looking at her soberly. "If Gaians have religion, pray for her."

Joanna stood momentarily before lifting her hands upward right where she was standing. "Please, Goddess, Divinity. Don't let Judy die. I need her; we all need her so badly." Her voice broke as she started to weep and beg, "How can I live without her? Please, don't let her die."

After minutes of pleading, she slowly rose to seat herself on one of the nearby chairs. As Joanna waited, she was unaware of other crew members coming to wait for news of the hurt investigator. After what seemed a lifetime, the chief surgeon emerged. "Scion Joanna?" The young woman looked up hopefully. "I'm sorry. We did everything we could. The shot itself was from an old-fashioned weapon, difficult in the best of circumstances to heal, but given the slip … I'm sorry."

"No!"

"No!" Joanna jumped at the shock from the memories.

"Miss?" the escort next to her asked, looking toward her. She glanced down and found his hand on top of hers, then back at him, as her memories faded into the now.

"Is there something I can do, Miss?"

"No, I was just remembering something," Joanna said slowly as she looked back down at his hand on top of hers, then with a wiggle got him to remove it.

"Sorry, Miss," Scott replied with as much of a dip of his head as the harness allowed.

A quick glance at the clock on the wall in front of them gave her reassurance. "You didn't do anything wrong. You'll know exactly when I think you've done something wrong," she added with a lopsided smile that only made him get a bit paler. He looked so lovely right now, so fragile. Why did he, of everyone on Gaia, have to be the one MOI had picked to help her? "We should be reaching the moon in just a little while," she forced out to get her mind centered on the goal.

Scott watched with mouth slightly agape as he silently followed his client out of the shuttle and into the lunar station. True to the information provided right before they'd landed, his body did feel lighter here, but the artificial gravity used in some locations made everything seem normal. "Don't run, don't jump, take purposeful steps," was what the shuttle voice instructed them all.

Another round of check-ins followed, but this time they were far faster than the ones back on Gaia. In fact, there was a woman holding a placard with "McMillin" written on it waiting for them, and she took them to what the signage said was the finest lunar hotel. Rarely had he stayed in a hotel, since clients either took him back to their homes or just rented a bedroom at Dells.

He had to submit to his IDs being scanned, which wasn't a problem, except for his client. A lot of things seemed to annoy her, probably because they slowed her down. He was what he was; he couldn't blame anyone for wanting to be careful. Not that he was violent or too moody, but, well, it came with being male, after all, and the world needed a mother's concern to thrive, even if that world was the moon.

The moon? He was on the moon! His gaping turned to a grin as he followed his client up to their room just a floor above. He noticed domed buildings, which his client's recording said were to hold in the artificial atmosphere. There had been the huge dome the shuttle had touched down next to, then a tube connecting the shuttle had pulled out, letting them move into the next dome. Yet inside the dome itself were smaller domes over clusters of buildings, or, in the case of this "finest lunar hotel," over a single building. Every now and again there were domes on Gaia, but usually the building itself was that shape, or it operated as some sort of greenhouse or agricultural or garden center. He recalled visiting such places on mother's assignments before settling at Dells.

Scott let his eyes focus on his client's back as he followed her with their bags. She said she'd been remembering something back there on the shuttle. At the time he'd thought she was taking a nap, something he would not allow himself to do once rented unless ordered to sleep. After the music, the recording continued about her mission, so he'd paid close attention. But she'd never said what the memory was about, though her reactions upon waking up suggested it was a nightmare.

Scott just held onto the bags silently as his client walked around their hotel suite with a small pen-like device. He stayed put as she went into the bathroom and held it along every wall, every fixture, and even every control panel and powerport. With a satisfied look she replaced the instrument in a pocket and sat down in one of the two nice chairs in the room, signaling him to do likewise.

He moved to her and knelt in front of her, but she only sighed before launching into a speech. "Question: What was I doing? Answer: Scanning the room for spy devices. I do that wherever I go, especially when the subject of the conversation must be private." Miss McMillin eyed him carefully before holding out her hand. "Player, please. Thank you. Now, do you have any questions about what was on that crystal?"

Scott frowned nervously at the floor. "I have a lot of questions."

"Do you understand any of it?"

"Not really. Except it sounds dangerous." He glanced up and was encouraged to continue by her nod. "You aren't just a Scion with a part-time reporter gig, are you?"

Miss McMillin shook her head with a sudden chuckle. "You're a very clever boy. I'm a reporter, an investigative reporter, which you knew from your research on me, but I don't just look into Gaian issues or the typical stories you might see on the news. Sometimes I just report on things that our media outlet wants – I have a contract to do a certain number of those each year – but I've also investigated matters I'm more invested in, and even some that public authorities want documented."

She leaned forward and lifted his head up by his chin. "What sort of story do you think we hired you to help me with?"

"Public authorities?" His client nodded solemnly. "I've never done anything like this, Miss. The things I've filmed were for a client's pleasure or to promote Dells boys. My job is to please you first and foremost, Miss, so I'll try my best."

Miss Joanna ignored his attempt at sexual innuendo. He felt a flush of shame; she had said she hadn't rented him for that. He just didn't want to believe it. "We have two or possibly three days here on the moon to get to know each other. Then we'll take a ship to a Gate and use the Transway to go to a planet called Bragg. Once there we'll connect with IGA. I've been working with them on this particular case for almost two years now – Gaian years, that is," she added. "We'll talk more about what exactly is going on there when we meet the rest of the team.

"Team?" Scott asked, then looked down, making Joanna frown with a loud release of breath.

"Look at me." When he did, she continued. "You have to get over your problem of monitoring what you say to me in private. I have to know when you don't understand something or have a concern. We are off-world now and only getting further from home. If we can't rely on each other, we are going to fail, and that could be dangerous."

"Your crystal mentioned a drug ring and a shooting," Scott offered immediately, letting his worry come out in his voice and on his face, since she claimed that was what she wanted. He spent so much time hiding his emotions and thoughts that it felt fake to let them out, but the client was always right.

"Not all drugs, foods and other things are legal, on Gaia as well as elsewhere, and some people decide they'd rather harm others than follow the rules."

"Men," Scott stated with a shake of his head. Rebels and loose cocks made them all look bad; that story apparently held off-world as well as on, but her next words made him frown.

"Sometimes, but in this case it's a woman. A very nasty one by the name of Maggie Rebecca Richards, born on Gaia but exiled." His eyes widened at that thought, but Miss McMillin continued, "I'll tell you more about her later. If you want to please me, helping me uncover enough evidence to get her locked up for life would please me more than anything else."

Maggie Rebecca Richards … Scott searched his mind for anything he had ever heard about her. No, nothing, but before he could ask another question Miss Joanna stood up, so he automatically rose as well.

"Not much of a reason to unpack for just a couple of days, but let's go over the menus just in case MOI didn't get your order right."

She'd dropped the acronym without thinking. She caught herself too late and stared at the boy, who just stared back at her. Mi would have mentioned only GNA when she arranged everything at Dells. If they'd told Scott anything, he would have heard only GNA. After several seconds, he swallowed and replied softly, "My order, Miss?"

Joanna had to tidy up the mistake as quickly as possible, so she just smiled, picked up the remote, and encoded herself on it so she could speak to the room computer for the rest of their stay. "I am Joanna Lily McMillin, room 207. Encode my voice now."

"Welcome, Scion McMillin, to the Hyacinth Hotel at Lunar 4. My name is Jane, how many I help you?"

"I know the Hyacinths," Joanna told the boy softly as she smiled at him, and he simply regarded her seriously. "Jane, is it possible to add my boy here to the control system?"

"I'm afraid not. Males are not allowed to encode at the Hyacinth."

Now Scott was giving her a surprised look but didn't say anything. It was worth a shot; she'd seen father use their home computer system, when she was growing up, and Hilda let the boys she brought back to her apartment ask questions, if not direct her program. Males simply couldn't do that, given the differences in the basic brain chips they were implanted with at age five, but also simply because it was considered the highest form of treason, punishable around the globe with the death penalty. Such treasonable offenses were few, and rarely was anyone caught breaking these laws, but Joanna could remember at least one public execution in her lifetime. As much autonomy as she might want to give men, she herself wouldn't take that risk.

"I understand, Jane. Could we see the menu for our stay? I believe we have six meals with the option for an extra one to four."

"That is correct, Scion."

Before the computer could continue, Joanna interrupted. "Would you not call me that all the time?"

There was a very brief pause, and then, "Of course, Ms. McMillin. Here is your meal schedule with highlighted options where substitutions may be made."

A large display popped up in front of them, and Joanna motioned for Scott to look as well. Her meals were on the left, his on the right; highlighted in yellow were meals with options, starting with tomorrow's luncheon. Joanna pointed to the first optional grouping. "Oh, look, we can still get a picnic to eat out in one of this station's hortidomes. Sound interesting?"

Scott blinked just once, then nodded with a smile, "Sounds very interesting, Miss."

Joanna swiped the option to the main board and looked on. That same evening, she could choose between three desserts, but she noticed that Scott didn't have desserts listed for any meals. She considered the options and made her selections with a small sigh. Hyacinth was known for its cuisine, and she knew from past stays here that it was as fine as any place in the base could muster, given the limitations inherent on the moon, where plants served two functions – maximum food or maximum oxygen, preferably both.

"Jane. What is the schedule for our ship out; is it on schedule, or do you think we'll be staying on?"

There was a pause, then the system replied, "Predicted storms around Saturn and Jupiter may delay the arrival of the long shuttle. Please feel free to choose your extra meals; we can always delete them should you not need them."

Joanna continued making selections, asking for Scott's input. His answers seemed more like reflections of her thinking out loud more than actual opinions, but she still tried. Even Joseph had increasing difficulty making decisions over the years they grew up together, and his condition, as she liked to think of it, only worsened with puberty and the training their mother arranged. If it were a condition of both nature and nurture it could be changed a bit, so it pleased her to believe this was the case with any man or boy she met.

Then he surprised them both by asking a very good question. "Why does day two of the breakfast meal still have two options?"

Joanna smiled and rubbed his shoulder with a hand as he blushed and ducked his head down. "No, that's what I need, your asking questions when you don't understand. See, if the ship's on time, we'll get a larger breakfast than if it's late. But if it's late, we'll also have lunch. The food on the next ship isn't as good, just focused on what we'll need for the Transway sleep."

He moved his feet a bit and frowned down at them. "Will the next ship feel like the base, that gravity thing," he whispered.

"Yes, the gravity is lower on the next ship, it simply can't support the mechanics needed to fake that force. If you weighed yourself here without the adjustments, you'd weigh a good deal less."

That made him perk up with a smile that she shook her head at. Many men tended to be too thin for her personal preferences. She finished their selections and thanked Jane for her help before turning back to Scott.

"We have hours to kill before dinner, which will be delivered here, so let's see what entertainment we have." At his nod she asked Jane to display the various venues and events around Station 4 during their stay. It didn't even occur to her that she was planning almost date-like activities as she fell back into ideas of what she and Judy had enjoyed in the past. There was a lunar hydration demonstration they'd always meant to go see, and the music pavilion had a new show, not to mention the mixed strip club they had managed to get to the last two visits. "Oh, look, the image gallery has a new exhibit; you always like that," she said with a smile that immediately faltered as she turned and saw Scott. She wasn't here with Judy. That was the previous visit to the Lunar Base.

"It all sounds great, Miss," he told her with a huge grin.

Joanna paused, swallowed, and nodded. Mi had said to take the time to get to know him – doing things with him outside the hotel was better than staying here, where he might expect other things. His smile was fading now as his aqua eyes started to lower with the tension. "Yeah, I think it will help us learn how to get along better," she offered as she wiped the corner of one eye with the back of her hand. Mother up, right?

Her comment only made him blink and move uncomfortably as he waved his hands slightly and muttered, "I am here to please you; I would not defy you."

Joanna rolled her eyes and grabbed one of his waving hands. "Hey! Chill! You're a good boy; I cradle that. You don't need to keep saying it."

"Yes, Miss," he agreed as his other hand went behind his back, which stiffened up as his head bowed lower.

Thank Goddess the hour was almost up, Joanna discovered as she looked at the corner of Jane's display. She spent the last few minutes reading the description of the demonstration they'd attend later that afternoon.

Scott listened and watched politely during the lecture about how water was captured, transported, transformed, and injected into the cycle on the moon. He'd never thought about it before, but apparently the moon was basically just a big rock, and it had taken a good deal of planning and continued hard work for it to become habitable. Earth had never been good at the level of cooperation needed for this project until it became Gaia and unified under the natural rule of mothers. "Was that too boring for you?" his client asked him as they stepped outside afterwards.

"No, Miss McMillin, it was just a bit much. I never really heard of a comet before," he added, remembering her rules from the car, and hoping this would get her talking. She seemed pleasantly surprised, and then she repeated some of the information he'd just heard in the lecture with a bit more about comets and Gaia or the sun when he asked another question.

He could remember things he heard or saw immediately, but he'd discovered over the year that understanding those memories took effort. Since this was one of his key attractive points, he never told his clients or the staff at Dells how much effort it really took to truly cradle something, as opposed to just recalling it. If it was meant to be easy, then any boy could do it, but most of the others he knew simply didn't care to venture outside their skill sets or to really go beyond acting like they cared about their clients' interests. Most clients didn't care either, which is why his desire to know more could put them off. Luckily Miss Joanna seemed to like his questions, but he was still wary.

Miss Joanna? Scott smiled as he realized that he was starting to think of her in more personal terms than Scion or her family name, not that he could afford to let her first name slip until she said he could. Even that HCS in the hotel room hadn't been that familiar, and it was feminine.

Afterwards he was disappointed when his client took his arm at one point as they walked along one of the canals, then suddenly released him like it burned her. There was something going on, and he bet it had to do with her former imagist – who had also been her fiancé – and this job. The crystal's information had made that strong suggestion when he'd listened to it a second time during the initial trip. Scott tried, but he couldn't think of a polite way to ask questions about that, at least none that wouldn't shut down any conversation.

He found himself blushing several times when shopkeepers and even visitors recognized his client and then turned their attention however briefly toward him. He'd have that to look forward to for, well, forever, if he managed to show her how much help he could be. He'd get used to it, he told himself as he walked beside her carrying whatever bags they acquired. Normally Scott would walk to the side of and a few steps behind a client out in public – not that he'd done it much, but he knew the protocols – but for her he made a conscious choice to be as close to her as reasonable to keep the leash loose. Her fidgeting made it clear that she was not used to leading a man around, and the one time someone's excitement at seeing her had slowed him down causing the leash to go taut, had resulted in such a glare that he'd started making sure he was only half a pace behind and a pace to her right.

The upside of that mishap was that she could now see him more easily, and after a few hours she was even conversing with him again, not just talking at him. Occasionally he offered real opinions, not just mimicking back her own, such as the fact that "clothing or food was always useful and didn't take up space just to be pretty" as she shopped for gifts for her family and friends. With each sentence out of his mouth her smile seemed more genuine. With each brighter smile he felt more comfortable being closer and speaking. He kept his voice low and respectful and tried to be helpful, such as when he'd asked, "Miss, do you think that woman over my left shoulder has been following us?" when they'd paused before exiting a jewelry shop where the items were made from minerals from various planets in their solar family. Miss Joanna was friendly but firm, polite but in control, and undeniably lovely to look at, to the point that he needed a firm bite on the cheek to limp his overeager cock.

By the time they got back to the hotel room it was only a few minutes before dinner would be delivered, and he barely had time to start unpacking her purchases. She'd mentioned never having time before to get gifts during the layover on the moon, so she was taking advantage of it.

Women did that a lot: planned for things, prepared; it was probably the one big reason that Scott was glad to be a man, he reminded himself as he watched her frown over her phone before Jane let her know that the food delivery was right outside. Once more it was brought by a woman, and the escort found himself shaking his head as he organized the purchases by the names of the people she'd mentioned when buying them.

"Think I bought enough to please everyone?" Miss Joanna asked, but her voice was light, so he just looked up with a smile. Then he followed her gaze to the five piles. "Wait. You …" She looked at him, then continued with a chuckle, "you organized these by who I'm giving them to. Grandmother, Liz, Kathey, Raven, and you."

"Me?"

"Who else would I get this for?" Miss Joanna said, picking up the aqua colored microblend shirt with mid-length sleeves that said "Lunar 4 997 MR" on the back and had the station's logo on the front in a discreet place on the left lapel. She held it up to him and tilted her head to the side like she had in the store. "You could remember who got what for everything else but didn't know this was for you?"

"No, Miss McMillin, you didn't say a name when you bought it; I …" He trailed off and just ducked his head. "I've never had a client give me a gift before." That wasn't entirely true. When he was with them, they had a responsibility to feed him, give him water and shelter, and if he were to need medical care, call the agency's clinic and arrange for his transport. Only one had ever given him something to take back to Dells before.

Miss Joanna shrugged. "The contract didn't say I couldn't get you something extra, just that I had to provide the basics, as if I wouldn't do that," she added with a huff. She shook the clothing at him until he took it into his own hands. "Wear it as you like; it's yours now."

"Thank you, Miss, thank you," he repeated as he held it against his chest.

She wrinkled her nose at him and then shrugged again. "I have a similar one from 995 when we first came here … seemed like the thing to mark your first off-world trip."

Scott nodded with a grin, letting his fingers feel the fabric as she blushed slightly. She'd said it first, and he'd heard it: she was open to the idea of bringing him back, of renting him again, then maybe … he was interrupted as she urged him to come over and have dinner with her.

The rest of the evening they went over images she had of the team as well as the only shot she had of Richards. Joanna was impressed by his memory but noticed he needed a bit of time to pick up many details beyond just matching names to photos. Luckily, he asked questions and listened to her read the official dossiers, which allowed her to also learn a bit more about the people she'd be working with or watching during this gig. She hoped it was more than just waiting around, but then again, doing more had killed Judy, so perhaps waiting might not be a bad thing this time around.

It took some urging, but Scott enjoyed half of her dessert, a fruit-filled tart. There was just something about lunar food that didn't taste quite the same, but he seemed thrilled by it, nonetheless.

When they were both yawning, she decided they'd had enough and locked up the crystal. She frowned at the only bed in the suite but just brushed that off for the immediate moment with another yawn as she stood up and he rose from where he'd been kneeling all night. How did men do that? Didn't it hurt their knees or their hips? Her twin had once told her with a shrug that you just got used to it because there wasn't anything else he could do. After he'd started at the training center at age 10, she couldn't get him to sit on a chair except in her room, and then only when their mother was out of the house.

Joanna picked up her overnight bag and headed for the restroom. Suddenly she paused and turned back to the escort. "You brought pajamas, didn't you?"

"Yes, Miss. As you requested."

"Good." Her sigh of relief turned to another yawn. "Get ready out here; I'll be back in a few minutes, then you can use the facilities to do anything else you need to."

Joanna looked at her reflection in the mirror as she held onto the edge of the sink. "Are you being stupid, woman?" she asked out loud. "Getting him a souvenir, feeding him dessert, worrying about his knees," she pointed out half-heartedly.

She cleaned her teeth and face, pulled on her pajamas – a pair of loose bottoms with pockets, a tank top, and a loose short-sleeved top – and combed her fingers through her curls for a few seconds. "Balls! What am I doing?" she snarled at her reflection again. She waved at herself and stopped primping like she had a date in the other room. Not that she'd wear this if Raven were spending the night … she needed to call her girlfriend soon before the other woman took her silence for lack of interest. The three of them got along beautifully, Raven taking on the rougher roles that Joanna needed from time to time so she could give Judy all of her gentleness, but Raven was a free spirit; she wasn't interested in joining a marriage.

"Jane?"

"Yes, Ms. McMillin?"

"I want to place a call Gaiaside."

"There is a surcharge for that."

"I understand, and I accept."

"Do you wish visual?"

"No, just audio, please."

In a few moments there was the ringing, and then Raven's husky voice on the other end. "Miss Joanna? I thought you were off-world?"

"I am, but I was thinking about you, and I wanted you to know."

There was a very brief pause, then, "I'm glad, Ma'am, because I worry when you leave. How long this time?"

"Month, possibly two, but I'll call you if it's more. I," Joanna swallowed, then added, "I got you a gift from the lunar station I'm at."

"Finally," the other woman chuckled.

"Brat."

"You love it."

"I do."

There was another pause. "Are you going to be able to find a partner while you're gone? I worry about your needs, Ma'am."

Joanna swallowed and looked at the closed door, thinking about the boy on the other side, but shook her head. "I'll be fine, geesh, I think I can go a month without the rough and tumble."

Another pause followed before Raven replied, "Sure, sure, but call me on the way back, and I'll make sure I'm free for a few days."

That made Joanna smile, because that was what she loved about Raven, about Jack, their eagerness to be with her, to take all those rough edges she had, all those dark places inside, and smile at her like they adored her the next morning. That boy out in the other room might have training, but no way could he give her that. A month wasn't that long, not really, so she just told her girlfriend that she loved xem again and closed the call.

Scott quickly changed into the pajama pants that he rarely needed to pack, though these were kept in the dorms along with basic clothes for between-client times. He could count on one hand how many times he'd taken them to meet a client, and on zero hands how often he'd actually worn them. It felt wrong to be wearing them right now, but the client's wishes came first.

He checked his reflection for bruises as he passed the mirror on the way to the big bed in the room. Jones had been hard on him the previous night, but the medics in the clinic were skilled, so the bruises were minor, probably only visible because he knew where to look. With a smile, he turned the blanket and top sheet down for her.

"Thank you," Miss Joanna's voice suddenly said behind him, making him turn, "but you didn't have to do that."

"Just trying to please you, Miss."

Miss Joanna paused as she walked by him, one hand almost trailing down one of the bruises before she sat down on the bed. Scott knelt when she just looked at him, hoping it was the correct thing to do. "That's very important to you, isn't it? Pleasing me?"

"Of course, Miss. That's my job," he said as he reached for her feet and placed one quick kiss on each before she pulled them away with another blush.

Miss Joanna looked at the ceiling, then back at him. "If I wanted to hit you, to tie you up more than the nighttime bond, to, well, be rough, you'd be fine with that?"

Scott almost tilted his head in confusion but stopped himself and forced a smile to his face. "Of course, Miss. If hurting me pleases you, I'm happy to suffer."

At first, he thought her flinch was a sign that he'd said the wrong thing, but she just sighed and patted the bed. "We have one bed here, so we're going to be sharing, but," and now she looked directly at him and held up a palm toward him, "we are sleeping. No sex of any type."

Not tonight, he filled in silently and hopefully, as he nodded and agreed, "Just sleeping."

He hurried off to the bathroom to clean up and put on his pajama shirt, then came back to find her standing by the bed looking upward, her hands raised. She was praying; he hadn't seen a client do that before, at least not during a rental; he assumed they all did it in private if at all. Men rarely did it, though older ones gossiped about ancient stories of loving sky mothers who might care if you were lucky. He'd never prayed until he'd become Jones' favorite target. Not that it helped, but it also didn't hurt. He watched silently and still as his client finished and relaxed her entire body, letting one big breath out.

A client who was religious … that could be good or bad, so he just walked the few feet to the bed once she was done and getting into bed.

Once under the covers he lay on his back, legs slightly spread and arms slightly above his head in what he hoped was an appealing as well as comfortable pose. He'd spent many nights chained or tied in a client's bed, but not in Jones's room, so it was a relaxing position to sleep in. He turned his head to find her lying on her side watching him, but she kept her arms close to her.

After a few seconds she tossed out, "Good night," and then rolled to her other side.

Scott looked up at the ceiling and said his own prayer that Goddess might help him figure out his flaws so that he could do better at pleasing her the next day and all the days that followed, or this was going to be a very long month. For a moment he thought about pulling a Todd, reaching out and caressing a shoulder with one hand, commenting on her stress. No, that wasn't him. Unless he was behind a shot, trying to hold the best image, he needed to let her direct.

He looked at her again and then back to the ceiling, biting one cheek hard to curb his erection. No wonder his prayers went unanswered most of the time. He wasn't much more than a piece of cock, he berated himself. It took a good hour for him to finally relax enough to get to sleep.

Chapter Four

Scott's eyes fluttered for a few seconds. Something was different this morning. His memory was good, but it fell victim to early morning grogginess like everyone else's. He did an assessment of his body to find pajamas – no, not much unusual there, but the bed felt different, and his right arm was up by his head while his left … his eyes opened as he turned his head to the left. His hand was holding hers, the client's, the McMillin Scion – no, she didn't like that title, just Miss McMillin. Scott considered his pajamas and then the fact that he could see the sleeve and neckline of her pajamas, plus he would remember if she'd taken him last night.

Definitely no sex last night – in fact, she'd told him that wasn't part of his job on this trip. He was hoping that declaration wouldn't hold for the entire month of this rental. She'd also rolled to face away from him last night, so why was she lying on her side now, facing him, her hand resting on his chest, his hand on top of hers?

As though she could hear his thoughts, her eyes opened and stared back into his, then glanced down to see their hands touching. She released a breath and pulled away as she sat up. "I'm glad this helped you sleep better," she mumbled as she stretched.

Scott blinked and sat up as well, mimicking her stretching with his own and a nod of his head. That's right. He'd had nightmares again, the constant plague of his sleeping life, possibly a reason he had no steady clients. He pushed those negative thoughts aside and bowed his head as he said, "Thank you, Miss McMillin. I'm sorry if I disturbed you last night."

She just shrugged. "Must be a bit scary to sleep in such a new place."

"I wouldn't know," he whispered, but this she caught and gave him a look that urged him to continue. He'd already spoken out of place so often with her, at her request, that he stated, "I've never slept in a client's bed before. If I stay the entire night, I'm generally on the floor." That was partly true; even on the floor they could hear his nightmare-fueled thrashing and screaming and generally woke him up with a nudge of their foot, or, rarely, a kick to the side.

Joanna snorted and rubbed her eyes with the back of her hand, "Of course, the floor, and I didn't think of that."

Scott grimaced at the realization that he may have given her the idea, so he hurriedly added, "I'm very grateful that you allowed me to sleep on the bed, Miss. I'm fully awake for anything you want today."

She looked at him and sighed. "I'm not kicking you out on the floor, but I am taking the first shower. Get the door when breakfast comes."

"Yes, Miss McMillin," he replied as he stood up and gave her retreating figure a bow. He considered the bed for a moment. Did hotels want him to make the bed or not? Did his client? He thought back and easily recalled that in all the information she'd entered into the HCS yesterday she had told the hotel to clean but not bring new towels or sheets, so should he make the bed? He decided to do that, so it looked neat and showed he was able to take care of domestic things.

His hair was doing that thing it did in the mornings, his braid loose, the bangs angled off wrong. He was trying to use his hands to adjust the bangs when he jumped at the sound of the alarm going off. "Miss Jane, can you turn that off? We're awake," he pointed out, but of course his voice got no response from the HCS.

In a few moments he heard a few vulgar words from the bathroom after the water stopped, and then the alarm shut down. It was odd that the computer didn't realize they were awake, but then he hadn't noticed any color or lighting changes either. Maybe computers just weren't that sophisticated here. Scott shrugged and went back to trying to fix his bangs.

"Jane!" Miss McMillin's voice made Scott step back from the mirror as she came out wrapped only in a towel, not glancing at him, her hair still wet, a rather annoyed look on her face. "I need you to monitor us more closely so that if we get up before the alarm you don't sound it. Can you do that?"

"Of course, Ms. McMillin."

"Good, I mean, I appreciate not mothering so much, but still, that was annoying," she said, shaking her head, then stopped and looked directly at Scott, who lowered his gaze to the floor immediately. "A few more minutes, then it's yours," she threw out as she headed back to the bathroom.

Scott just nodded and kept his eyes on the floor until he heard the door shut. She was pretty, even when wet and angry, not that he wanted to ever make her angry, but he found himself smiling at the information, nonetheless.

The breakfast cart arrived just moments later at the scheduled time, so he took the two trays and set them on the table, thanking the woman for her delivery. He'd figured out yesterday that women on the Lunar Base primarily worked, while men of both genders were rare. It was still a bit unnerving to have one deliver something for him like this, so he just reminded himself that it was really for his client. With that in mind he didn't look under the lids and simply went to grab briefs and hygiene products to use in the shower when he heard the water in the bathroom turn off again.

"Miss?" he began as they passed on his way into the bathroom. "If you lay out what I should wear, I'd be grateful."

She frowned at him, and he almost apologized before she nodded and agreed to do so. Normally clients dictated what he wore, his mother had had guidelines, and Dells had sets of clothing for different activities. Perhaps it was one of those things she wanted him to learn her preferences about and follow, but so far, other than what he'd packed, dictated by Dells, he wasn't sure.

Scott hurried with his shower but took a bit of extra time afterwards re-braiding his hair and applying some subtle makeup. Normally he used heavier colors on his face, but Miss Joanna seemed like she would prefer the subtle, and yesterday she hadn't commented negatively, so he tried these tones again. When he thought he looked as good as he could, he pulled on his briefs and stepped out into the main suite.

He didn't have to go far to find a set of clothing laid out for him on a chair nearest the bathroom just on the other side of the wall separating the private and public areas of the suite. Ah, she didn't want to see him until he was fully dressed up. That was disappointing on one hand, but on the other it confirmed her comments about not needing his body so much as his mind this trip. Scott clicked his tongue a few times as he pulled on the pants, shirt, socks, and shoes. His hand hovered over the jacket, and he decided to push his luck and just draped it over an arm for now.

He came out into the main suite and found his client watching what appeared to be the news. Not that he watched much news – boring, really – but he'd seen it from time to time, and of course his research on her the previous night had included watching segments of newscasts. What was interesting was that she was watching two channels at once as well as scanning a print article when he stopped just a foot from the table. She didn't notice him, so he cleared his throat, earning a look from her and a smile.

"Have to keep up while I can. Once we get on the next ship, communication back home will be limited until we're on the other side."

She didn't comment on his clothing or appearance, so Scott just nodded silently and took a seat at her suggestion. She asked the computer to go on privacy mode and then pulled up the photos from last night.

"Do you think you have these people straight?" Joanna asked Scott a bit later after they went through all the photos again.

"Yes, Miss."

Joanna nodded. "Your memory is going to be a huge asset for me, for this story," she corrected herself quickly.

"Thank you, Miss McMillin."

They were quiet for a few minutes, and she saw him open and then close his mouth once. "Do I really need to repeat my order about speaking up and asking questions?" Joanna growled as she stabbed a piece of fruit with a utensil before stuffing it into her mouth.

"No, Miss, sorry, I …" He blushed and set his own utensils down before taking a deep breath and looking at her. "I don't have many regular clients, so if I please you, my imaging skills please you," he amended at her frown, "I could be available for future stories."

Joanna paused and swallowed before sitting up straighter. She'd told him to speak up, but not even Jack, as bold as he could be, ever suggested that she hire him again, only that he'd enjoyed the evening with her. Why did this annoy her? Wasn't it what she wanted to hear? She thought for a moment and then smiled. "We haven't even officially started yet, so I have no idea if your skills are real or all just talk, do I?"

His eyes narrowed just a touch, and his lips pressed together for a mere second before he bowed his head. "Quite true, Miss."

Great, now she felt bad for what she'd said, so she added, "We'll see how the month goes. Let's just try to see how well we get along over the next few days before I need your imaging talents. Chill?"

"Chill," he echoed back, but Joanna could tell by the way he now picked at his food that he was disappointed. Too bad, because this hadn't been her idea to begin with, and she would not be pressured into anything that would interfere with seeing the woman behind Judy's death put out of circulation for the rest of her life.

The rest of the day was quiet, spent sightseeing around the base's publicly accessible domes. Joanna dealt with a call from Mi and then one from her mother, both of which she kept as short as possible. She didn't mention the boy to her mother at all and told Mi only that he hadn't been too much of a problem so far, a comment she knew he had obviously overheard, given his formality for the next hour after that, until she reminded him that he wasn't being much of a companion by acting that way.

"Sorry, Miss," he muttered as he bowed from the waist down. His apology, again, was both embarrassing and a turn-on. That would not do; she wasn't with him for that, only for business – her business, not his. To kill that feeling with a distracting pleasure of another sort she steered them to the nearest dessert parlor that also served light meals. It was an added expense to eat outside of the schedule she'd set at the hotel, which MOI was paying for, but it wasn't as if she lacked for credits, and one look at her ID almost always got her a discount if not complimentary service or products. What shop wouldn't want to say one of the Great Families had visited and was a satisfied customer? Plus, she'd purposely left this afternoon open for just this situation.

Businesses here didn't change ownership much, but they changed styles frequently to make the base seem lively. Aside from the mining and scientific operations on the moon, tourism was the lifeblood of everyone who lived and worked here. Coming as a repeat tourist and a reporter had opened Joanna's eyes to the realities here. Some of those realities were not nice. That brought Judy up again in her mind, so she turned her attention to the boy at her table.

He sure didn't eat much, and that worried Joanna a bit, but his stomach never made noise, so perhaps he was just used to eating less food, or less rich food. She suspected that Dells boys were kept on a very controlled diet. Dells seemed like a place that kept its boys on a regime. Even her mother and whatever father was around had strictly limited what Joseph could and couldn't eat and when, while Joanna had been allowed a much wider range and amount. Men, after all, were supposed to be angular, thin, and straight, while women had curves and mass, to take up space in the world they ran.

By the time they were out at a scheduled dinner he had returned to the level of relaxed companion that he'd managed to be by last night. Joanna told herself to be careful because he was clearly a very sensitive man and men's egos were fragile. Just what she needed, a precious little glass figurine to worry about on this story. She pushed that thought from her mind as he voiced an opinion about his food when it arrived, saying that he thought it looked lovely, something he hadn't said about the other meals they'd had so far. It was true. To make up for the fact that it was the same dozen or so ingredients in different combinations no matter where you ate it in the station, the restaurant had used a decorated plate, laid out the food differently, and added just a touch of spice.

After a few minutes of trying the food, she asked what he thought of the day they'd had, and he replied. They fell into an easy conversation about their day over the rest of the meal, until he brought up his own question, pleasantly surprising her. He was bouncing back from the morning faster than she'd feared he would.

"How did I get into reporting?" Joanna repeated his question as they waited for their dessert. "Well, as with many women, I'll spend my twenties in one career then transition into another when I become a mother. In my family there's a tradition of having a post-college career that touches upon one of the family's business holdings. We own Newsnet, the metacorp behind several news outlets, and I always loved spending time at the various studios, so I decided to try that. But I'm not much for hanging around a studio, so investigation seemed like a good excuse to get out. Of course, once I'm 30 I'll be pressured do more on the management side so I can think about having a daughter." If only her mother and grandmother would wait until she was 30.

"So," he continued, looking up for a second, then back at her, "that's another two or three years of doing all of this?"

"Yeah, yeah, since I don't have a partner anymore ..." He didn't reply but just looked down, so she twisted the topic a bit. "You mentioned your mother was an imagist? That's how you got into it?"

"Yes, Miss McMillin, Mother did freelance but also worked with Dells regularly."

"Is Dells that big?"

"The largest escort agency on Gaia, with locations planet-wide," he said, sounding as if he were repeating a factoid from a brochure. "Mother worked at the Susanville office for most of my life. She turned her attention solely to the Neuvo house when I was twelve because they were starting a new layout for their books," he stated, referencing the collection of promotional materials for each man owned by the company.

Joanna frowned and thought back to their conversation in her car. "You were acquired by Dells when you were fifteen?" At his nod she added, "That seems a bit young. I mean, dorm boys and husbands aren't parted from their mothers until they're eighteen to twenty; fathers have to be mid to late twenties at the earliest."

He paused, then shrugged. "Mother had an opportunity to travel a bit, so she made sure I was taken care of."

Before Joseph had been sold off, Joanna would have believed that turning a boy over to another woman was a good thing for him and the family but given that her mother refused to tell her who the guardian was so she could see her twin, she now doubted it. With each new revelation she had about men's lives she doubted Gaia's laws and customs more and more. Scott sounded resigned to his life, but not bitter; one way to find out. "Have you seen her often in these past ten years?"

"Nine," he replied sharply, looking directly at her. "I'm only 24, Miss," he added more softly.

That was the second time he'd made a point of his age, as though it was important for some reason. "Oh, right, 24, sorry," she offered, and he just nodded once and put his fork down with a release of a sigh. "So, you see her often? At least on your birthday?"

"No, Miss, not since the contract was signed." He told this fact more to his plate than her, and his voice sounded a bit strained. Joanna was about to ask another question when Scott stood up abruptly and then stepped over just enough to kneel at her feet, bowing his head nearly down to the floor.

Joanna could hear the low buzz of conversation around them at the restaurant go silent for a moment before picking up again. She frowned and then realized he was apologizing for his correcting her chronology. "Get up!" she hissed with a tap of her foot, years of male management training in school kicking in before she knew it. "I was wrong, you pointed that out, I don't have a problem with that," she whispered when he just looked up at her.

"I shouldn't have raised my voice, Miss McMillin," Scott insisted, but he sat back up and then stood to return to his seat, pausing for her nod before he sat.

"Don't be a puppet." She tossed out the insult with a frown and stabbed her food, using it to motion to his own plate. "You have a sister? Brothers?"

Scott's eyes widened just a touch, then he shook his head as he took up his utensils again. "Not that I know of, Miss." This time his voice did sound sad.

"I'm sorry," Joanna offered with a half-smile. To lack a sister ... Joseph had told her repeatedly that he was so glad he had a sister and so lucky that it was her. The fathers they'd had growing up had pointed out just how lucky the little boy was and doted on her to the point that it often angered her to see her twin ignored. The truth was, without a daughter a family died out, no matter how powerful they were. The first pregnancy was fully covered by worldgov healthcare, another one might be covered if the first had resulted in a male or fem or mas leaning child. Most women didn't want to invest the credits or the wear on their bodies to try again. The McMillin line had been threatened a few times but had always managed to create a daughter, even if the mother was a bit older than usual, including her own grandmother, who had been 41 when her mother was born. This probably explained her mother's attempts to set her up after Judy's death.

Joanna pushed out another question to stop that thought. "You want to do some Gaia viewing before we head back? I think we can catch the final glimpse of it before we turn too far."

"Yes, please," he replied with a grin.

"You know, if this goes well, and we accomplish what I want, I'll get you some ice cream once we're back Gaiaside. How's that sound?"

He nodded but didn't look enthusiastic.

"You don't like ice cream?"

"I've never had it, Miss McMillin."

Joanna felt her mouth fall open. "How about this then? You start calling me Joanna instead of using my family name over and over again, and then success or not on this story, I'll get you some ice cream. I promise."

He blushed and she immediately feared she made an error when he replied, "Yes, Miss Joanna, thank you for letting me call you this."

Scott made sure everything he wouldn't need in the morning was packed up once he finished in the bathroom. Their ship to the Transway was on time, so they'd have time for a very quick breakfast, and then they'd need to head out.

He paused at the edge of the wall to watch his client double-check her luggage. So far, she really wasn't letting him do very much, and he doubted she'd use him tonight either, given how early she'd set the alarm. He wasn't sure what he'd done to get her to touch him last night and really wished he knew so he could repeat it. Maybe he could subtly ask if he was careful.

"Miss Joanna, I'm all packed for tomorrow morning, sweater set out to wear," he added as he stepped to the end of the bed; he'd folded down the covers while she'd been in the bathroom.

"Thank you, Jane. Goodnight," Miss Joanna said to the computer, dismissing the system before turning toward Scott. "Good, it gets a bit chilly on the ship. Once we're in trans it won't matter, but we'll have a few days to get to the gate." She sat on the bed and patted a space next to him, so he smiled and perched on the edge, not assuming she wanted to do more than just talk, though he was good to go at her word. "You have any questions about the next ship?"

"I think you explained it well, Miss. Small room, communal meals, lighter gravity than here, but not bad, transfer to the main ship at Eris for the slide."

"Apparently I explained it very well," Miss Joanna chuckled as she slapped his knee and let her hand linger for too brief a moment. "Let's get to sleep so we can get up early."

Scott stood up, went to the other side of the bed, and crawled in. He raised his arms and hands, then lowered them. "Miss?" She looked at him as she settled down, facing him this time, so he pressed on, "If you wish, I'm happy to be a pillow again."

She frowned and sat up, making him sit as well. "Well, I, I didn't do that for me, really. You were upset; I was trying to calm you; it apparently worked. You don't remember that?"

"I remember the nightmare, not when you took my hand."

"I did that because you kept saying, 'Please don't,' and 'I'll be good, my pain is for your pleasure,' and other such rot." She rolled her eyes when she said the last one.

"Oh, I'm so sorry. I should sleep on the floor, not bother you ..."

"Do you have nightmares often?"

Scott swallowed. The truth was that he did; that was a fact that Todd and the others in their room had reported to him often. They were worse after an appointment with Jones, but still, he had them more often than not. She'd told him that she wanted him to talk, to be honest with what he said, and to speak his mind, and she did already know about it firsthand. "I've been told so, Miss. I don't generally remember their details."

Miss Joanna rubbed a hand over her face and just shook her head for a few seconds before waving him to move closer and lie back down. "I can't have my sleep disturbed, so I'm going to pillow you, but just for your sake," she added as she moved closer on her side, moving her actual pillow on top of his arm and under shoulder. She clipped the arm nearest her to the top of the bed as was required by the hotel's rules. She draped a foot over his calf and put an arm over his stomach, which allowed his free hand to rest next to it, then pulled that closer and placed her hand on top.

Women tended to be just a bit shorter but also a bit wider than men; overall, women were slightly larger than men. Scott adjusted his position to make his angular body as comfortable to her as possible and then smiled when she sighed and just patted his hand on his stomach. "Have to get used to it, anyway," she muttered, but he didn't reply; he just went to sleep with a huge grin and no ill dreams.

Joanna woke up with the alarm and called for the lights, stopping both the alarm and any attempt either of them would have to go back to sleep. The rest of the trip would be boring with long stretches of sleep, so no point grumbling about it now.

She lay there and considered the boy lying right next to her. They hadn't moved apart, as she'd expected; if anything, they were closer than they'd been at the start of the night, with her one leg now fully over his. The hand on his stomach inched toward her when she released it. No, that wouldn't do at all! Joanna sat up, and he opened his eyes to follow her movement.

"Good morning, Miss McMillin," he said sleepily.

"Didn't I tell you to call me Joanna?"

"Sorry, Miss Joanna," he said, but he was grinning now.

She should have stuck with the formalities, but it was too late now, plus it sounded like someone addressing her mother, and that she could well do without. Plus, she hadn't lied last night when she'd mentioned that they'd have to be sleeping together more on this trip. Both the ship to Eris and the one through the Transway were small, and anyone sharing a berth had to share sleeping space as well. That hadn't been a problem with Judy, but with him … "You're a bit sharp to sleep next to," she said, aiming a barb at him as she unclipped his cuff and then got out of bed.

"Sorry, Miss," he muttered as he, too, got out of bed.

"Need to eat more," she added as she headed to the bathroom. After a moment she came back with his clothes that had been laid out there. "Change here. We're in a hurry this morning. Jane, when will breakfast arrive?"

"In three minutes, Miss McMillin."

"Three minutes," she repeated, handing him his clothes.

He just nodded, so she retreated to the bathroom. Dressing warmly was required for the next stage of their journey. Gravity was lower, temperature was lower, all to be more efficient for such trips. In one of her college classes she'd read different masculine works about the future, generally not set as far as the present, but almost all of them had unrealistic ideas of how luxurious the world would be, especially space travel. Oh, they'd gotten some things correct, such as travel using a sort of Transway system, the innate connection between computers and society, better energy, longer lives, but most had thought that the planet and the solar system would be bent to their will, not that humans would have to live in harmony with Gaia and by extension the galaxy. Routinely they imagined great wars, which had simply become unnecessary once everyone realized that they needed both resources and each other equally.

Joanna frowned at her reflection and winced when she finally gave in to the fact that she was aroused this morning. She could take care of it herself in three minutes, less than that now, but that wasn't as much fun. The boy was right outside, but she was not going there. She took out her phone and considered it, then just sent a note to Raven's message folder, telling xem they were taking off and that she'd call as soon as they were back on the moon. Another note to Mi and her grandmother giving an update on her status, and she was done. Finally, she lingered over a photo of her twin and recalled the holidays when she'd discovered he was never coming home. That dried her up fast.

Scott was setting out breakfast on the table when she came out. He was dressed in what she'd picked out and smiled at her when she approached. "Looks like a lot of food, Miss."

Joanna nodded at the mounds of breads, fish, fruits, and even cheeses laid out. This was an expensive meal but given the food situation for the next two stages of their trip, it was a reasonable expense, or so Judy had convinced her. She'd just been ordering and doing what she'd normally do with her mate, she realized, and that made her sigh, drawing a glance from the boy as he stepped back from the table. He wouldn't sit until she did, so she took a seat and nodded for him to do so. It was tiring being with a man.

During this meal he asked a lot of questions about the ship to Eris, and she was able to fill him in a bit more on the mundane matters she'd just let slip previously. He took the arrangements all very well, even trying to hide his pleasure at learning they'd be sleeping together in a much smaller bed. It was only with the explanation of the pods for the Transway that he frowned.

"We'll be unconscious for that part of the trip?" His voice was strained.

"Ah, yeah, a very deep sleep to protect us during the folds and flows. You didn't know this?"

He shook his head and brought a shaking forkful of egg to his mouth.

"I guess you wouldn't. How many people on-world really know about this, huh? It's just something I've always known about, even before I used it. Family has off-world business, so it's just one of those things I've learned."

"It's safe?" His tone was hovering between question and statement, so Joanna shrugged as casually as she could.

"There's always a risk; life has risks no matter how prepared a mother is," she replied, offering a saying that was supposed to be reassuring, but he only swallowed and nodded as he played with the rest of his eggs.

"Jane. When was the last Transway injury reported for our stop?"

"The last Transway injury was in 892, over a century ago, before the usage of the pods became standardized and human engineers were added to the local gate maintenance crews."

"See? Very safe and set up for our people to use."

Scott nodded and took another bite but didn't ask any more questions.

Chapter Five

Scott looked around the smaller room on the ship and noted that the bed was indeed smaller, but still not as tiny as Miss Joanna had suggested over breakfast just an hour or so ago. There was a netting over it that they were supposed to draw down once they were settled for the night to help with the lower gravity. There was no table here and no separate HCS, though there was an entertainment unit in front of the bed. His client was doing that thing with her little device again, so he just wandered around to check it all out. The clips they had been given and told to put under their shoes helped walking with the lower gravity, but he could still feel a slight floating sensation as he moved on the metal floor. There was no carpet or padding anywhere that he'd seen; his knees might be a bit sore after this trip, but maybe the lower gravity would counter that too.

He found a locker to store their luggage off to one side, which he opened and started loading the bags into, with the imaging equipment on the bottom, since he doubted he'd need it until they reached their final stop. A small bathroom area with a shower, toilet, and sink was the only other space, and it was separated by nothing more than a half wall; it smelled like chemicals, too.

Not the Hyacinth by a long shot, but still, it might have more room per person than his dorm back at Dells. Not as warm, though, he realized as he pulled his sweater down over his hands as far as it would go. They'd only lifted off a few minutes ago. Before they were released to their rooms, everyone had sat strapped down on safety benches, not nearly as comfortable as the shuttle.

The mas and eir mistress were there, and ey was the only other masculine presence as far as Scott could tell. He'd tried to return the other's smile but had only managed a weak one that seemed to disappoint, given how quickly the other had turned away. Was he going to have to talk to em at some point? What was the proper way to do that?

"Bathroom that bad?"

Scott looked up at Miss Joanna's teasing question and found she'd moved right into his space. He was getting too comfortable around her, and too quickly. It turned off clients if you didn't remember your place, or if you were too formal. But she wasn't like his other clients. It was all so confusing, and he couldn't afford to cock it up this time around. "Chemical smell," he told her with a roll of his eyes in that direction.

Maybe they'd just stay here in the room for the entire trip, so he'd just never have to deal with the mas.

Joanna looked around the mess hall and spotted the woman with the other boy she'd seen back at the shuttle and then on the takeoff benches earlier. Sokolova – that was her family name, she recalled, after several moments of observing her and cudgeling her memory. The Great Families were a small group that met every couple of years to discuss world policies outside of the Gaia Council, or worldgov as it was commonly known, but still, they numbered 283 individual families, each with at least two or three important members at any given time. It had been years since Joanna had attended a Great Council, though her grandmother insisted she read the reports. That was either Natasha or Dariya Sokolova over there, most likely Natasha, since that woman appeared to be perhaps a decade older than Joanna at most, and the Scion of their family was a child.

Standing behind her was a slender young man in a large bulky sweater and a pair of gold eyeframes. Must be her boy, Joanna decided as she touched Scott's arm to urge him forward. She paused when he didn't budge for a second and looked at him to find his eyes wide and staring straight at Sokolova. Goddess, Joanna hoped she wasn't a regular client of his, because that was the last thing she wanted to deal with right now. "You know Lady Sokolova?"

He blinked and looked at her before lowering his gaze. "No, Miss McMillin," he said, falling back on a formal address that made her sigh, "I … I'm surprised to see her … companion."

Joanna glanced around and thought for a second. Was there something special about the boy other than the obviously too large sweater and flashy eyewear? No, now that she looked around, she noticed it, too. The only men in this room were Scott and this yet unnamed boy. In fact, now that she thought about it, she hadn't seen very many men at all on this trip. Not that it really mattered to her one way or another. What decent mother would sign her son over to someone just to have him taken off-world? Everyone knew that was dangerous. What kind of mother would do that? Oh, now that was something she should tell Mi to look into; why hadn't she thought about it before? Her own mother might do that with Joseph. "Thanks," she said to Scott, causing him to just blink several times again. "We're going to go see if we can have lunch with them, since you boys are so rare on the ship."

A soft noise came from him, but this time he just followed her over.

"Lady Sokolova?" Joanna asked in her best reporter voice and noticed the other woman's shoulders tense up for a second.

"Really, can't I get away from you people –" the other woman started to say as she turned, then stopped as a smile grew upon recognition. "Ah, the McMillin daughter who is trying out the world of reporting. Your mother and grandmother say so much about you at every meeting," the other woman said as she opened her arms.

Both women hugged as their companions stood back and eyed each other. "What brings you here? Oh, reporting, yes?" Natasha teased as she took Joanna by the arm and led her to a table.

"Indeed," Joanna confirmed. "Business, I assume, for you as well?"

Natasha shrugged, "Always, but at least I have Ivan with me to keep me entertained as well as take care of the little things. Ivan, this is Scion Joanna McMillin."

The slender man bowed with a hand on his heart but didn't speak. When introduced, Joanna noted that Scott mimicked the gesture well. "Do you mind if we join you for lunch?"

"Of course, of course, I didn't know that you were on this flight, or I would have contacted you sooner. Perhaps we could have met up at the lunar station as well. But Ivan can show – Scott, was it? – how to get the food for us all," Natasha added, with a nod at her companion.

"Scott, just follow Ivan's lead," she ordered and then frowned when Scott's eyes widened a moment before he bowed silently. He was acting as he had when he'd first met Joanna – would he always be this awkward whenever he met anyone from a Great Family? Another reason why he would never work out beyond this one story, because even if she didn't attend the formal meetings, she still interacted with others from the Great Families multiple times each year.

Abiba Hala Michieka was head of StarNews in Nazambia and Lena Anna Drexel headed VoiceNews in Aufania. Joanna sold stories to each of those companies as part of an ongoing contract via GNA, though her main audience was still in Korawinia, her home continent. If he couldn't handle this, perhaps they knew of an imagist looking for a partner. If Mi, GNA, or MOI wouldn't help out, she'd go around them.

Her attention was snapped back to Natasha at her next comment. "They will gossip, of course, but what can we expect when we are about do so ourselves?"

"True," Joanna agreed, then listened to a very proud report about Natasha's young daughter Dinar.

Scott followed Ivan without a word, listening to that just slightly too high voice that confirmed his ideas about eir gender, doing his best to hide his shock at being near a mas for the first time in his entire life. He wasn't doing a very good job, he realized, when he answered, "Yes, Miss" to a question from Ivan.

The other stopped and looked at the floor, then the ceiling, before rolling eir shoulders and head. "Damn," ey whispered, taking Scott by the arm, and moving them both out of the way of the women getting in line to get food. "Don't call me that, please." Ivan's voice had a begging edge to it, and that made Scott swallow. "My voice, right?"

Scott shook his head before whispering back, "no collar," and motioned to the silver around his neck. He didn't mention Ivan's height or build, because really there were at least two boys back at Dells smaller than ey. Voice, too, wasn't a sure sign, just a possible identifier.

Ivan frowned and then pushed back the sleeve on eir right arm to reveal a wide band of golden metal engraved with English and some other language. "We use these where I'm from for boys like me." Ivan's eyes flickered back toward their guardians, and ey sighed. "Can you at least work with me to get lunch? I won't bother you after that, since I'm a problem," ey tossed out with a snort.

Goddess, he was cocking this up, because he wasn't sure of the formalities he should be following right now. Scott squeezed his eyes shut for a second and took a deep breath, working hard to shove down his reaction to the other. "I'm sorry, I shouldn't be so rude."

"No, you shouldn't be," Ivan stated, putting eir hands behind eir back and tilting back on eir heels once. "I'm owned just like you. I'm treated just like you, maybe worse, but you probably don't want to hear that ..."

"Actually," Scott interrupted, "I'd like to learn more. I just never met ... someone like you before."

"A mas," Ivan offered the term, and Scott nodded. "That isn't offensive; it's a legal term. I've heard much worse – from my own mother, in fact," Ivan confessed. "Let's go get the food, please."

"Yes, Ivan," Scott agreed and didn't really notice how his tone still used eir name as a title.

"Would you like to spend some time with Ivan during the trip?" his client asked once they returned to their room after lunch. "They aren't staying for the entire trip, but they also aren't leaving for another forty hours, so Natasha, Lady Sokolova, suggested it. Seems that Ivan doesn't have much of an opportunity to interact with other boys."

Scott didn't say anything, though once they were in the small room there was no way he could avoid her. She continued to talk about what she'd learned about Ivan from Lady Sokolova and that it might be good for them to spend time together. It was clear that she didn't really understand what ey was, and after several minutes Scott simply blurted out, "Ivan isn't a boy. Ey's a mas."

His client just paused, frowned, said "Oh," then shrugged and frowned at him. "How is that not a boy?"

Scott opened his mouth and then closed it when he realized that he didn't really know how exactly Ivan was different from him now, only how ey'd been different before. "I, um," he sighed and sank to his knees. "I'm happy to spend more time with Ivan, Miss Joanna. As you wish."

She crouched down in front of him and frowned. "Why is Ivan's legal gender a problem for you? I don't get it. I'm not going to make you spend time with em, but normally if one family asks a favor from another …"

"I'm just rude, Miss," Scott offered immediately, and while that stopped her talking, she remained where she was on the floor staring at him. "I've never met one before; I called em Miss, and that offended em."

"As well it should. Ey realized what ey was and made a decision that changed everything for em. Legally, ey's not that much different from you. Ey had more years of formal education; I think they have slightly more database access, but ey's owned …"

Scott looked up at her use of that word, surprised for a moment. Normally only boys used that word unless a woman was making a point. Like Jones.

"… contracted, must be under guardianship to a woman, just like you. Look, Scott …" He kept his gaze on hers at that to show that he was going to fix this situation however she required, "you're going to meet a lot of new types of people on this trip. If you can't handle that, you're no good to me."

He reached out and touched her ankle as she started to stand up. "Forgive me, Miss? Please? I've been bad; I deserve punishment. I accept it. I beg for your correction."

She crouched back down and ran a hand over her face with a sigh. "This isn't about punishment, Scott. It's about what I hired you for; well, an extension of it. To do your job well you have to be able to get along with everyone we encounter. If you can't do that," she ended with a shake of her head.

"I'll be more flexible, I'll figure out how I should treat others faster, I promise. Please give me another chance, Miss Joanna," he pleaded, adding her name in the hopes of pleasing her, since he had cocked it up far worse than he could have guessed just an hour ago in the mess hall.

"Fine; it isn't like I can claim some social or moral high ground, huh?" she added with a roll of her eyes but didn't explain. "I'll set up a time for you and Ivan to hang out. Please do accept em," she emphasized that pronoun, "being a boy like you? Granted, eir guardianship," and her tone suggested she didn't like that word, "is private, but maybe someday you may be in that same position. Ey might be able to teach you something, too."

Scott blinked at her knees when she stood up. That was true. Regardless of how ey'd started, Ivan had a position that Scott deeply desired, not because of some birth identity but right now in the hands of the law, in the arms of society. Ivan had discovered ey was a boy, given up the privilege that pretending to be a woman would have assured. Scott had made it work. Scott rose at her word and listened to her arranging the meeting for after dinner that evening.

Joanna took the time when Scott was with Ivan to go over the information that Mi had sent with her. These were details that the man didn't need to know, even though at some level she realized she would have shared them with Judy. The boy simply didn't have the necessary background to offer constructive ideas or feedback.

Maggie Richards was the eldest daughter of two in an average Aufanian family on the Seine River. Her family had once been major pharmaceutical researchers for four different Great Families over the centuries, though her grandmother had done something – the documents were unclear on exactly what – that had offended the Great Council and got them banned from doing business.

Joanna ran a hand over her mouth as she thought about what that offense could have been. By and large the Great Families oversaw investments in smaller families rather than directly dealing with manufacturing, distribution, or creation in any form, unless it was time for a Scion to prove her abilities by starting up a new venue. That was the McMillin way, though not every Great Family had the same traditions. It would take a terrible sin to get one of the families associated with a Great Family banned, yet there was no report on it. Grandmother might be able to help her access those records once she was on-world again; she should have been doing that research for the past months, not mourning uselessly.

UGA, the United Gaian Authority, and IGA records, though, were very thorough in every other way, so she kept reviewing. Maggie's mother had sent her to explore xenopharmacology, which wasn't all that new, but a challenge for the average family without the connections of the Great Families. Maggie was described as charming, though a bit condescending toward men, again not a big surprise, and had made important business contacts among several peoples. Then five years ago she started showing up on the donor lists for political events in the third quadrant, where Gaia was located, though her influence didn't reach home. Joanna noted that seven years before that, Maggie's mother Rebecca had died suddenly from unknown causes. Maggie herself couldn't go home without having to deal with the UGA regarding that case – something else Joanna knew she should have dug further into.

Mi had been right; she had lost a lot of ground after Judy's death. Joanna took a sip from the water she'd brought back from the bland small lunch and continued reviewing. IGA noticed Maggie's political connections coincided with changes in the legal definition of slave and a higher rate of enslavement on each planet she had those political ties with. Most worlds weren't dependent on slavery, though the line between "slavery" per se and other forms of inequality was often blurry, but this uptick in the raw percentages of planetary populations considered slaves by the IGA was noticeable – a five percent increase in just five years. Activist pressures resulted in the investigation that had come to the attention of the UGA and MOI, and thus FlashNews had been created as a cover to "report" on it merely for the curiosity of the public. Joanna and Judy had been the prime investigators because they were relatively new and unknown.

Now IGA had traced Maggie to the resort planet Bragg, where she was due to make a new business deal with the owner, Evan E'Lige, who had readily cooperated with IGA when they had come to him with information, some of which FlashNews had gathered. E'Lige's resort was the largest in the galaxy, and apparently Maggie had been remodeling the underground network beneath it in a way that E'Lige found "distressing," which was saying quite a bit for Karkans, who tended to be very laid-back people. Now she was back – no, they were back – no, FlashNews was back, to document the final stages of the investigation and Maggie's arrest.

Joanna had never met a Karkan before, though she found it quite interesting that they could live off sunlight to some extent … how would Scott react to not just seeing men in positions of authority but ones so very different from those he lived with, worked with, and learned about? He was trying to get along with Ivan, so he wasn't as rigid as men were supposed to be, which was just another sign to Joanna that sex or gender status didn't really determine personality, at least not always.

She looked at the time on the display in the room and realized it was time to meet Natasha and the boys as she shut down the documents, for their Mixed session before dinner. This time she hoped they might be victorious.

Scott looked at his client and nodded his head as he wiped a bit of sweat from his brow. He'd done some active things with previous clients, but none like Mixed. The first time had just been Miss Joanna and Lady Sokolova to show him what to do, though Ivan played every time they traveled, as ey'd explained before that first game.

As Ivan talked about the game, ey talked about eir life, gaining more and more respect in Scott's eyes with each conversation. Ivan had done so much more than Scott thought possible for any man. In fact, ey told Scott about males and mases ey met regularly at events on- and off-world. If ey could be a galaxy-trotting boy who helped eir mistress with all her concerns, then there was hope for someone like Scott.

Ey'd also suffered a lot, which shocked the imagist. Scott had been afraid of the future when his mother had signed his guardianship over to Dells, but that first year or so he'd gotten a message from her a couple of times. Poor Ivan had had the gender reassignment one day at the age of fifteen and literally that same day had ended up at a training facility, never again to hear from anyone from eir birth family. Scott narrowed his eyes at the smaller man and then smiled when he realized he really did think they were both just men. Now he understood what Ivan had given up to be eir more authentic self, as the expression went, as well as how much they had in common.

Even more so if he helped Miss Joanna win this tied game of Mixed. It was a game specifically designed to be played in a small, low-gravity space, such as a spacecraft. There were ten targets around the court, and you scored a point by getting the little ball into one of them, but the trick was that a player had to score with a different body part each point. You could use your legs, feet, arms, hands, head, butt, hip, chest – anything, if you didn't repeat within the same game. You also couldn't score on the same target twice in a row – the last target used was always inactive. Of course, depending on how low the gravity was, you wore weights on your limbs, or your ankles and wrists. The goal was to score the most points in 30 minutes, which was obviously easier to do with a teammate if you could coordinate. Over the course of three games, he and Miss Joanna had gotten better, thus the 9-9 score instead of the 3-20 and 7-12 of previous matches.

When women played, either singles or doubles, they tended to be more strategic and precise, but when he and Ivan had played last night for a small curious crowd they'd tried to score whenever they could – sometimes a target wouldn't even register a score because they'd hit it too hard. It was a game of fine muscle control, not merely power. With mixed doubles, it was easiest to combine raw power with precise targeting, with the men capturing the ball but the women doing most of the scoring.

Miss Joanna rolled her eyes back toward one of the targets when they looked at each other, and he nodded but directed his gaze to the left, trying to mislead. It was their turn with the ball, and when it dropped from the ceiling Scott turned left but angled his foot to kick it straight back, stumbling backwards as he did so, allowing him to see Miss Joanna use her butt to push the sphere into the target just as the buzzer sounded. The crowd around them clapped loudly as Ivan fell to his knees with a groan and Lady Natasha simply clapped slowly.

"Finally!" Miss Joanna stated as she thrust a fist into the air and gave him a grin. Scott steadied himself and gave her a little bow that seemed to please the crowd, who added a few hoots and whistles to their applause. She came over and clapped a hand on his shoulder, making him blush, as Lady Natasha offered a hand to Ivan, who accepted it with an apology, as well as taking the light cuff she gave his head with a shy glance toward the floor.

"That's a good memory to send them off with," Miss Joanna told him as she used her hand on his shoulder to pull him a bit closer as they left the field for the next match on the schedule. "Of course, it will be just you and I after this for our matches."

"The next stop is where she disembarks?" He made it sound like a question, though he remembered clearly.

"Yes, and she's taking Ivan with her – sorry, I know that you seem to have gotten closer," she told him with a wider smile. "I'm glad, because I was getting worried about you dealing with more new experiences once we reach Eris."

"I shouldn't have been so rude, but thank you for pushing me, Miss. Sometimes a boy just needs a little push."

"I've heard that before. I should have known," she replied, but didn't explain what she really meant as she let him start removing the weights from her limbs before turning to his own.

The next morning everyone on the ship had to sit on the safety benches again for the landing on Europa. Most of the passengers were debarking here with only a handful continuing with Joanna to Eris. She whispered to Scott that he should say goodbye to Ivan while she did the same with Natasha, who pulled her into a big hug.

"You give any thought to my idea about a follow-up mining operations story?" Natasha asked.

"Yes, I'll spin that by my agent and see if any of the newscorps I'm contracted with might be interested. However, I also think you're right that I need to get back into the circle again, reconnect with my peers," Joanna offered with some sincerity. It wasn't her first choice for socializing, but it could be fertile ground for her goals; someone might know where Joseph was or have other story ideas she could use for MOI after Richards was in IGA custody. A good reporter must always plan several stories ahead.

Natasha nodded and moved back yet kept her hands on Joanna's arms. "I'd like Ivan to spend more time with other boys. Since your Scott has gotten along well ..."

"He isn't mine," Joanna interrupted, loudly enough that the two men glanced at them but didn't seem to know what exactly was being said from their curious looks.

Natasha leaned in to suggest, "Perhaps he should be. I can see how well you work together. That is difficult with a man, especially with a male," she added with a nod and wink before stepping back and calling for Ivan.

Joanna ran her tongue over her bottom lip and looked down at the floor of the ship until she felt the boy in question standing close to her again. "Did you say goodbye to Ivan?"

"Yes, Miss; thank you for allowing that."

Joanna snorted and turned to restrain herself on the safety bench before she did something stupid like try to have a conversation with him during the descent. She was saved when he asked if he could watch out the open hatch until it was time to go; allowing him to do so made it less likely she'd say something. After a few minutes she found her eyes trained on him as he looked out the window and then again as he grimaced during takeoff.

Her eyes kept finding him throughout the rest of the trip. Most of the time there was a good reason; for example, his improvement in Mixed required her to study his body language more. She wanted to keep an eye on him just in case any of the others on the ship made a move on him in the mess hall when he picked up the meagre rations.

At other times she struggled to come up with an excuse for keeping a close eye on him. Even though he never got a pop quiz on their assignment wrong, she made sure he looked at everything each day – it helped her stay on top of it too. Their room was quite small, so it was unavoidable that she'd catch him undressing or dressing. The bed really did require that they share space, and that was hard to do unless she looked at him.

Each time he looked back at her it was in a more acceptable manner than the last. At first, he'd blushed and quickly looked away. Later he glanced away after a few moments, even though he was still flushed by her attention. Now he was smiling at her and asking an unnecessary question or offering a comment, watching her closely but not with fear anymore. His nightmares even stopped that seventh night they shared a bed.

When they transferred to the transship, she was very grateful to see the pods they'd be frozen in. She needed a break before she started thinking that Natasha and Mi's idea about using a rented imagist had been a good one. Unfortunately, the transpods didn't stop one from dreaming, and when they arrived and he came out shivering with wide, terrified eyes, she found herself smiling and aroused.

"How was your trip, Miss Joanna?" he ground out through chattering teeth after the Vancazie crew settled them into the recovery area with rising temperatures and lots of food and water. He was a bit pale and clearly miserable, but he knelt in front of her, wrapping his robe around him, rather than sitting next to her. "You're probably used to it, huh?" he added when she just sat silently.

Joanna blinked and shook herself. "Sorry, effects still," she mumbled and tore her eyes from him for a second. "You'll recover faster if you sit up here," she told him with a jerk of her head to the left that made her head throb for a second. She knew better than to move that fast until the effects of the freeze wore off.

The Vancazie and Gaian medics all said that it was the safest way for humans to travel through the Transway, though conveniently this always meant that humans could never control their own travels around the galaxy. Judy had questioned whether it was really a scam, since according to the Vancazies most of the peoples of the galaxy were unable to safely travel unfrozen through the slip. She hadn't been impressed when Joanna had pointed out that their hosts had invented the method of accessing hyperspace, built the system of gates, and had been happy to work with various planets to find ways to allow others to travel through it. The Vancazies could have ruled the galaxy by keeping the gate technology to themselves, or just by operating as the only interstellar traders, but instead they'd adjusted the tech and shared their gate stations with the populations of most systems. They'd even helped some of the non-conformist and more radical factions of humans settle on five colonies after the War of the Great Mothers.

Oddly for her naturally trusting and easygoing mate, Judy had just snorted at those facts. She hadn't been impressed by the Transway and had repeatedly emphasized that there was work to do at home. Scott, too, seemed unimpressed by his experience as he frowned when another traveler was escorted into the room.

"You didn't have a good trip," Joanna merely stated once he was settled next to her on the warming seats.

He paused, then nodded as he looked at the floor before lifting his legs and tucking them under himself as she had. "I think I was dreaming, Miss, not all of it very nice. I'm very glad to see you here," he added with a weak grin as he looked up at her from underneath his wet hair, which had been loosened from his braid before he'd been placed in the pod next to hers.

"Eat, drink, warm," one of the Vancazie crew said as they placed a basket of edibles on a table that rose from the floor in front of them.

"Thank you," Joanna told them with a grateful smile. Everything tasted and felt so intense after a slip of this distance.

"I kept seeing that," Scott whispered next to her.

She looked at him as he watched the crew member glide away to offer a basket to another traveling duo, two women who had introduced themselves as vacationers with a fascination for the exotic back on the ship from the moon to Europa and then again on the trip from there to Eris. Truth was that Joanna had jumped at the chance to talk to more women as a way to distract her from him, but now he was clearly not adjusting well to this leg of the journey. "What did you keep seeing?"

"Those eyes," Scott whispered as he turned his own wide ones back to hers. "I knew they had four of them, but seeing it …" His voice just trailed off as he shook his head.

Joanna found her lips trembling, and soon she was laughing, which started a wave of laughter around the room as each of the other six passengers joined in. Scott's shoulders hunched over, and he looked down until she bumped him with a shoulder as gently as she could.

"I'm sorry, Miss; that was rude. I know better than that; why can't I control my big mouth?" he hissed softly.

"No, no, we've all thought it," she told him, and as though overhearing, the Vancazie crew member across the room paused to make an exaggerated face, pointing to four eyes with four hands and looking around the room, earning more laughter in the process. "See, they are fully aware of how they look to us. I'm sure they laugh at us as well."

"Really?"

"Really. Like I've said before, Judy, they are a very good people."

Scott jerked back from her, and this made Joanna stop. She'd said it out loud this time. She was so worried about him cocking things up that she'd let herself do it.

"Go ahead and eat, eat a lot; you need it, Scott," she told him firmly. They had only hours before they were picked up by IGA, so she just ignored the error as best she could, and it was clear from body language and voice tone that he was trying to just act as if it hadn't happened. He was not her partner and could never replace Judy.

Chapter Six

Scott found it a touch more difficult to handle their luggage this time than it had been before the Transway – the information his client gave him said that muscles could be affected by low gravity as well as the cryo state, but it hardly seemed like it had been enough time. As if he'd know how much time it would take. He almost chuckled at everything he'd already experienced. Wait until his roommates heard about that, among the other weird things he had to recount. Their minds would be blown; he himself was struggling to cradle everything as he was experiencing it.

Right now, as they stepped from the transship to the station at someplace called Lemui, he was struggling with more than luggage, since he could only understand his client's side of a conversation with a woman with horns coming out of the front of her head. The Dells boys would not believe that for one second, even though she looked fairly Gaian otherwise, with a brownish skin tone not as dark as Todd's and a build similar to Jones's. Were they a fifth-gender? He wasn't sure and didn't want to assume. Miss Joanna called her Chief Traffaz Blim and introduced her as their liaison at IGA for this story.

"Not the most comfortable sleeping, that's for sure," Miss Joanna said, and the two women laughed with a glance at him. Great, he was being spoken about as if he weren't there, which was normal, really, but he couldn't understand half of it this time. Not a safe position to be in, so he moved as close as he could to make sure he caught at least his client's words.

Scott was surprised when she touched his arm and spoke directly to him a few moments later. "You can't understand her, can you?" He shook his head but looked at the floor as he felt a heat creep over his neck and face. The horned woman, perhaps a fifth-gender, said something, and Miss Joanna replied, "You're correct; he can't understand, but I worry about messing with his chip." Chief Blim, Scott repeated the name to help his memory override the feelings of confusion he was currently experiencing.

His chip? MTS chips were placed into the brains of every boy who reached age five. The Male Tracking System was designed to protect both the boy and society should his mother or another guardian not do her duty. It also allowed for some integration with various networks for very limited access to the BCS at Dells or his mother's HCS. He didn't like the sound of anything being done to it, given where it was located, right above primitive basic functions in his brain. Attempts to change the chip could result in death, a familiar story repeated among men whenever they were talking about something they shouldn't be. He was debating saying something when another woman's voice he could understand interrupted.

"I can do that easy, and no one will be the wiser."

"Renee, you beat me here," Miss Joanna called out, so Scott looked up to find a smiling woman about twenty years her senior approaching for a welcoming hug. That was the specialist they were meeting, Renee Brownlow, doctor not just medic, he reminded himself based on the information his client had given him near the beginning of this rental.

"I was closer, studying a disease on one of our colonies, when I got the notice for this." She stepped to the side, and Scott lowered his head as he felt her gaze wash over him. "Ah, they did get you a boy, then? I have to say I was shocked by the suggestion."

"I know," said his client, glancing at him, "I mean, he has imaging skills, but this is more than that."

"No, no, I was shocked they'd ask you, given some of the stories you've done before."

As the two women talked, Scott recalled a few of the pieces he'd found when he'd done research on his client. She did seem oddly concerned with how boys were treated, especially given that her family was one of the reasons the natural rule of mothers had been restored. He was jerked from his train of thought as Doctor Brownlow touched his head and tilted it down so she could find his chip scar.

"It would be easy to do – that's why we leave a scar at all, so we can upgrade the things," Doctor Brownlow said as she let him go and gave his butt a gentle pat. He made himself stand still, but it had been the most sexual contact he'd had since his client had picked him up. It had been so long that he almost flirted with the other woman.

He turned his attention to Miss Joanna when she made a displeased sound, then replied, "We aren't part of that. I just rented him; actually, MOI rented him for me," she added, and he couldn't help but bite his lower lip to keep from saying anything stupid. What was this MOI she mentioned again? Doctor Brownlow knew about it, apparently so did Chief Blim. Scott tried to push the word to the back of his mind and pay attention to what was important right now.

"Did they give you the access code for it?"

"The access code for it?"

"They probably did, so you could set him up on your home computer, or the car, or whatever you wanted. I mean, he is using some of your equipment, right? How would he do that without access?"

His client sighed and rubbed her forehead with a hand as she nodded, "True, true, yes, they did give me that, but ..."

"This is just making him more useful to you, plus you'll actually be adding to his value, so you could get a discount in the future ..."

"Oh, brilliant, you got the 'let's gang up on Joanna' memo."

Scott was tempted to ask about this memo but instead just followed Miss Joanna, Doctor Brownlow, and Chief Blim into another room. At the door another person with pale green skin and the whitest blond hair he'd ever seen, took the luggage and set it in a corner. At first, Scott assumed it was another man because of his angular built and submission attention to their luggage. He was wearing light grey pants and shoes and a tunic that covered him from mid-calf to neck. On the right breast of the tunic was a universal medic symbol.

Could men be medical assistants off-world? The chief agent introduced the green person, and the two Gaian women shook the green hand. The four of them seemed to discuss Scott's chip and something to do with translation. Scott frowned, torn between worry about them messing with his chip and being left out of half of what was being said at any given time.

Doctor Brownlow had a bag with her that he hadn't noticed before, a shiny case that also had a medic symbol on it, along with the symbol for computer systems used back on Gaia. Maybe she was an expert in the chip, but his client's next statements surprised him. "Does he know how the Gaian male brain works? I'm not doubting your expertise," she said directly to the green person, "but I've learned the hard way that the dominant species are different enough for seemingly minor medical mistakes to turn deadly."

The green person was the one who would be in his head? Scott backed up until he bumped into someone and turned to find Chief Blim right behind him with a smile. Her hands – did they have four fingers? – gently helped him stand still as he couldn't help but stare at those four fingers before his gaze rose to the horns on her head.

"See, this is upsetting him," he heard his client say, and then the gentle touch on his ass made him turn again to face Doctor Brownlow, who also placed a hand on his arm.

"He's upset because he can't understand everything that's being said. Right, Scott?"

Chief Blim patted his other arm and his other ass cheek. Scott jerked away from both women. "I'm sorry, I'm sorry," he found himself babbling and scurrying to his client to hide behind her.

Miss Joanna took a deep breath and reached back to touch his arm, but he grasped at her hand with his. After a look at him she nodded and squeezed his hand, letting him keep hold of her. "Scott? We've been talking around you, and that's not right; that's not what I'm … it just isn't right. Sit down, please." When he looked at the only chair in the room and whimpered, she turned to face him more firmly, pulling the hand he held toward her and exchanging grips with her other hand but not losing contact with him. "The medic won't touch you unless you say that is chill with you. Just sit, and we'll talk."

Scott nodded and took a seat at her order but continued to hold her hand. "You have the access code, so you have the right to make a change, Miss," he forced out, but he didn't really feel the words.

Miss Joanna just looked at him, then back at Doctor Brownlow, Chief Blim, and the medic. "A bit of privacy would be helpful," she told them, and that got them to leave. She turned her attention back to him, considering him silently for so long that he started to apologize until she cut that short. "Stop with the apologies. They annoy me, especially when we're discussing serious matters. This is serious."

Scott just closed his mouth and looked over her shoulder for a second before bringing his eyes back to meet hers. Hers were quite beautiful, with that hazel tone that seemed to change color with her mood, a trick that Todd had told him about years ago that complemented their training to notice signs of tiredness, anger, and, of course, arousal in a client's face and gaze. She looked tired and a bit angry, though her pupils were wider than they should have been, unless she was turned on right now too. Angry sex wasn't the best sex, but it was something he could work with, so he wet his lips with his tongue just once to signal he was available if that was what she was feeling.

Once more he'd read it wrong, and she stood up straighter and paced for a few seconds. "Look, here's the deal. In our own solar system, which is primarily inhabited by Gaians, everyone speaks common, a mixture of various languages once used on-world. The Vancazies have a translator they use which is why you could understand them, because their ability to reproduce common isn't great, and we can't make the sounds of their language too well either. But outside of our system we all use a universal translator program; it's probably not really universal, but it works around the galaxy with the five major peoples, so everyone who travels gets this installed. The Vancazies introduced the technology, and we've adapted it to our needs. Most women these days just get the translator as a matter of course, because we are getting more and more information from the rest of the galaxy. Plus, it has allowed the revival of the old languages on Gaian for scholars and others who care for some reason."

She was speaking in a rush of words, so he just sat and listened, watching her pace as she continued to talk. "On the one hand, it would be useful to me and to you," she emphasized by looking directly at him as she paused, "to have the translator. Legally speaking I think we'd be safe, given that it could be argued that it's an improvement, plus they did give me the access code, but I don't know Dells; I don't know what they'd do to you when they found out." She stopped again and looked at him with a serious expression. "Do you think they'd be offended if … IF you agreed to do this?"

Scott frowned and then shook his head. "There was a boy, a few years back, who got a chip improvement from a regular client; I don't remember Dells being offended or upset, but that client bought his contract when he turned 25 … I'll be 25 in ten months," he added softly.

That comment seemed to annoy her, because this time she rubbed her hands over her entire face with a low growl. "See, there's that, too. Granted, we have gotten along fairly well during the trip, but we just got here, and we're getting ready to start this story. I don't know how well you're going to do as my … an imagist for this sort of situation until we've finished. If we put in a translator, do they – do you see that as my saying that I'm going to buy you?"

Yes please, he thought, but just pressed his mouth together for a second before answering as she looked expectantly at him. "I can't really speak for Dells, Miss, but I don't expect anything from you other than the opportunity to serve you during this period." His voice sounded flat and full of lies to his ears, but she just tilted her head to the side with a loud sigh.

"Beyond all of that is the simple fact that it's your brain and your chip, Scott. I won't let anyone touch that while you're with me unless you say you want the translator program." She stepped up to him and put both hands on his as they gripped the chair arms. "You take as much time as you need and ask whatever questions you have. I can get Renee and Medic E'Leun back in here to answer your questions."

Scott flipped his hands over and held hers again; this time she smiled at him and just seemed to relax a bit at his touch for one of the few times since he started this rental. "Miss Joanna, would it help you to not have to explain what is going on to me? Would it help this story if I could be better informed of what my subjects are saying?"

"Obviously, yes."

"Do you trust Medic E'Leun and Doctor Brownlow with this upgrade?"

"I haven't worked with Medic E'Leun before, but I do know Renee professionally, and if she and IGA and MOI trust him … yes, I do. I know they have the skills and good intentions, even if they're a bit pushy."

Scott nodded and licked his lips again. The green person was him; he filed that information away and moved ahead. "Then I have just one question, really, if a boy may be so bold."

"It's your brain, Scott; ask whatever you need to."

"Would you stay in the room with me and hold my hand during the procedure, Miss Joanna?"

She closed her eyes and took a deep breath, saying upon releasing it, "I can do that. But you do have to let go of my hands to get them back in here for the upgrade."

Scott released his fingers as slowly as he could and still be obedient and then grinned as she went to the door to call everyone back in. He was a bad boy, lying to her about expectations, but he had to prove himself good enough to stay with her, and if that meant fiddling with his head, they could fiddle all they wanted.

The recovery time was almost zero, though it did take the boy a day or so for his brain to adjust to the odd little lag that happened with the translator. He was talking smoothly, though much faster than Joanna had expected, and she was pleased enough to cuddle into him that first night on the ship toward Bragg without the excuse of curbing his nightmares so she could sleep. Put on ten pounds or so and he might be comfortable to sleep with, though that was just a stupid thought, really, not a plan, she repeated silently the next day when she studied him before the alarm woke him up.

IGA let them set up cameras around the room for the first official meeting and even insisted that Joanna sit in the same room and ask questions while Scott monitored their recordings in the next room. He demonstrated his ability to manage four screens and calibrate the sound on a test run, so she agreed and sat down with Chief Blim and her five IGA agents, casino owner Evan E'Lige, his assistant Jinn O'Rray, and Renee. Planning sessions might be boring, but she hoped that by having the different angles they could edit it into something at least vaguely interesting, perhaps interspersed with the carrying out of the various stages. With that in mind, she'd asked Scott to take some close-ups and turn the cameras when he thought they might make a more interesting shot, getting a huge grin from him at the suggestion. She turned now to one of the cameras and gave him a nod with her own professional smile.

Chief Blim stepped to the front of the room, and the low chatter died down within moments. "We'll arrive at Bragg in one universal day, even though Mr. E'Lige and his assistant are leaving on a faster ship right after this meeting. Once there A'Tarick, Markeni, Noulayia, O'Heironul, and A'Jaliou will report to Mr. O'Rray." Each agent stood for a brief moment as they were introduced, and Joanna was pleased to see that the cameras were focused on each and zooming in to make the connections.

"After they have two days to settle into their new jobs," she continued, and this generated a few chuckles, "Scion McMillin, Doctor Brownlow, and Mr. … Scott will go to the resort under their cover." The chief stumbled a bit on Scott's lack of any surname.

"What?" Joanna nearly coughed out the word at this news. "Our cover?"

"You did want to document what was happening, correct?" the chief replied, though she looked to Renee for a response.

"We haven't had time to really pull our cover together yet," Renee replied, then looked at Joanna. "We have days to sort it out."

Joanna felt her mouth go agape for a moment before she closed it with a frown. Going undercover had resulted in Judy's death, and she wasn't pleased to be expected to do that again this time, especially without consulting her. MOI and IGA were just a bit too motherly at times, planning out events without even the decency of discussion.

"Are you going to be able to work out a cover, then, or do we need to keep you on the ship, simply monitoring the situation with me?" Chief Blim directed that barb to Joanna.

"I'm sure once we talk through it, we'll be fine," Joanna agreed with a tight smile.

"Excellent. Maggie Richards will arrive two days after that to meet with Mr. E'Lige. Between him and our Gaian investigators, we hope to get Richards to reveal more of her plan, but regardless, as soon as her labs are operational and have their first experiments underway, we take them down. Officers will have standard undercover weapons; investigators … we can make that part of our talk. Any questions?"

Joanna just watched for a few minutes, noting any gaps in the information given, then raised her own hand. "Won't the regular staff and guests notice five new employees in such public positions?"

"Mr. E'Lige, would you care to take that?" Chief Blim nodded at the casino owner.

He stood, his skin almost a mint green, his hair light blond and his eyes a deep brown. He nodded at everyone until he met Joanna's eyes. He paused and then clutched his chest for a second, making his assistant turn to stare at her, and then nod and turn away.

"Mr. E'Lige?" Joanna pushed, using the title easily, since she'd been silently practicing off and on during their trip.

"Forgive me, but your hair, they said," he glanced at both the chief and Renee, then back at Joanna, "but I didn't really expect so much red. It is very, very rare among my people and considered a sign of great fortune." "We'll have to see if that's true once we're in your casino," Joanna humored him, then quickly steered the topic back. "Would you explain how these new staffers are going to fit in smoothly at your resort? I'm a bit concerned about Richards' knowing who I am," she went on, adjusting to using the surname for now, though it felt off when not discussing the matriarch of a family, "but if your staff and guests talk about a suddenly high rate of turnover among senior staff, Richards might notice and pay closer attention, regardless of my cover story."

E'Lige was nodding and holding his hands in front of him as he leaned toward her, even taking one step before his assistant put a hand on his arm. "Ah, we have a high turnover rate already, and I have been advertising for senior staff now for some time since Richards insisted on making these changes to our business arrangement. I often bring in groups of new staff at once. I do not think it will cause much trouble, as long as the officers can do the job."

Each officer tossed out a line or two that they thought showed how they might interact with underlings or guests, but it was A'Jaliou's "I'm here to make your stay more fun," coupled with a toss of her head and a wink, that made everyone chuckle.

"There is some time to work on it," E'Lige offered, and his serious tone and look only made the room laugh more for a few seconds until the chief held up her hands.

The casino owner looked at Joanna again. "I think I can help with your cover; I will send you a proposal as soon as possible."

"Oh," Joanna didn't know what to say for a moment as she realized that everyone's eyes were on her at this moment. Men, Gaian men, weren't this forward with anything that wasn't sexual, and even then, most could keep it under control until there was privacy or until given permission. Of course, this probably wasn't sexual; they weren't the same species, after all, so why was this even entering her mind? "Renee and I, and Scott," she added quickly, "will look at your suggestions. It is your casino, after all, and we simply want to see the IGA in action protecting us all from criminal activities."

"Yes, yes, this is what we all want," E'Lige agreed with a wide smile, showing his very large, flat teeth for a moment. The rest of the room turned back to the chief as the officers raised a few more questions about their roles and IGA's measures to protect civilians, so Joanna continued to make notes.

At the end of the meeting, she found E'Lige watching her but was grateful that his assistant took him in hand and led him away. "I wonder what his proposal is going to be," Renee's voice chuckled next to her, so Joanna turned with a frown.

"I wonder what your proposal is going to be, because I wasn't consulted about any undercover anything."

"Think of us as a family," Renee started as she hooked her arm through Joanna's and led her into a small meeting room.

"We'll need to set up cameras where the various conversations are going on," Joanna insisted, refusing to sit down.

"This is your story, so do what needs to be done."

Joanna almost rolled her eyes but forced herself to smile instead and then went to the monitoring room to get her imagist – her rented imagist, she reminded herself on the way. He wasn't there, but she could see him on one of the screens taking down the cameras in the main room. She hit the voice button on the camera nearest to him that he wasn't undoing. "Scott? When you get done, we need to place cameras in the rooms where planning is going on."

He looked around for her first few words, then turned to the correct camera and nodded his head, saying, "Yes, Miss Joanna. Do you know what rooms those are?"

"We're in the room to the left; the officers went into the right room, and I'm going to grab an extra cam and try to catch the resort owner before he leaves. After you set them up, move the monitors into the left room. You, Renee, and I need to talk."

"Yes, Miss Joanna. I will hurry."

She didn't even bother to acknowledge his reply and picked up one of the other cameras to use as a handheld. Judy had had a half dozen cameras, and Scott had brought another three with him that gave them ample coverage, especially if they could tie into the security at the resort. Of course, working with IGA meant letting them receive transmissions as well, but they reciprocated, too, giving even more coverage. This was going to need a lot of editing, though it would go faster with another set of eyes. *I guess that means I'll be extending the rental*, she thought.

Joanna found E'Lige and his assistant in the Chief's office, and all three turned to look at her when she knocked on the wall before entering. E'Lige stood up, so she glanced at him, then held up the camera. "I was granted access, and I know we already have two cameras in here, but would you mind if I set this up at the docking port? I thought the departure of the beleaguered casino owner might be a good addition."

There was a slightly longer pause, and Joanna silently cursed herself for using a complicated word, but after an extra second or two E'Lige nodded. "Yes, yes, whatever you think will be best I am happy to do."

"I don't think you need to go that far. I'll have to rely on your expertise about your facilities once we're down there." He was definitely looking at her hair, and that made her touch it reflexively. "You are really fascinated by my hair, huh?"

"I apologize," E'Lige said with a slight bow. "Only our females have red hair at all, and then very, very rarely. Normally they become the high priests for our people."

Joanna thought quickly, then smiled. "Maybe we can do an interview once I'm on Bragg to talk about Karka and its colonies, your customs, and environs. I think a little cultural education would be a good thing to add to this documentary."

"Gaians do not travel much," O'Rray piped up, earning a glare from his boss.

"The majority don't, but a few travel quite far. Like Agent Markeni," Joanna added with a look to the Chief, who spoke up.

"One of my best – been with our unit for five years now. Why don't you set that up, then, and I'll do the rounds to check in with everyone before Mr. E'Lige leaves?" the chief insisted.

Joanna knew a matriarch's voice when she heard one and reacted instinctively to go do her task. It only took minutes, so she was able to get back to Renee before Scott was finished and could join them.

Joanna sat back and folded her arms over her stomach. "So," she began after a few silent seconds, "was there a big MOI/IGA cookout I wasn't invited to where you all decided to put me back into a situation that could be dangerous?" The hair on the back of her neck rose as she remembered a similar situation only a few months before.

"I don't think we should leave yet." Judy took the backpack from her partner.

Joanna's mouth fell open at this suggestion. "I don't believe you, Judy. We just heard them say they know we're sneaking around here!"

"They said they strongly suspected that someone -- *someone*," the blonde emphasized, "was snooping around this base. They don't know it's us. As far as they know, we're just newlyweds on a honeymoon trekking around the galaxy for a few months."

"I'd like to keep it that way, thank you." The redhead grabbed the backpack from the other woman and stuffed more data crystals and other equipment into it.

Judy sat down on the chair right in front of her partner. "Just a little more time and we'll have all the evidence we need to close this place down."

"We have enough evidence to fill the courts for months, plus we aren't agents; we're just reporters," Joanna pointed out quickly.

"But the more evidence, the better for the authorities, and the more information, the better our story." Judy leaned close to her future wife. "Don't you want to get them? Joseph could have been sold through a place like this. You've seen the records here; they sell to some of the toughest mining stations, brothels, and ports in the galaxy. Only the Sorzlex system would be worse, and they don't deal with alien slaves."

Joanna stood up straight, her eyes flashing. "That's one of the reasons I want them fully and legally investigated. Then we can get to the official records – heck, perhaps we'd be invited to the big arrest and trial; that would be the first time in over half a century that Gaians will have a firsthand look at how IGA operates."

"A little more evidence, courtesy of us, will help assure that." Judy stood up so their eyes met. "Just one more hour. What harm could come from just one more hour of nosing around that lab again?"

"Sorry," Renee's voice interrupted her thoughts. "You didn't hear a word I said. What are you thinking about so hard?"

"Memories about the last time I decided to go beyond just being a reporter. It didn't turn out well."

Renee sat back and nodded slowly. "Your fiancé … I'm sorry, I heard – hell, read about it; it was everywhere in the system."

It had been big news on Gaia and around the system, perhaps reaching to the outside colonies as well, though most didn't keep close ties – or ties at all – to the motherworld. That might be an interesting story for the future: how are the colonies faring? It was an idea to bring up to Mi the next time they talked. For now, the sympathy was a bit too much, so Joanna just shrugged. "Thank you, but that was some time ago, and I have to think about you, me, and him, right here and now."

"One advantage we have that I believe you didn't is that the IGA is heavily involved. The agents will outnumber us at the resort, shadowing Maggie and us as much as they can. They may even have agents we don't know about already on the ground."

"How many will she have?"

"Maggie? Well, E'Lige said she is coming, and she might have an assistant, though none of the reports I read about her says that she travels with anyone."

"Someone is setting up the underground for her. That could be dozens."

"I don't think construction workers are a big worry ..."

"If I had crews setting up something that was going to get me a lot of power, not to mention money, I'd make sure they were armed, and armed well."

Renee lifted her chin and shook her head slightly. "It's a bit scary that you can think that way, but I guess not surprising for a McMillin."

Joanna huffed and relaxed her arms a bit. "We did aim the first bombs, after all. Kind of in my line to think of the bang solution."

Neither woman had time to say more before Scott was standing in the door with the monitor cases on a trolley the ship was letting him use. They both just smiled and helped him set up the equipment before getting down to business.

Scott was studying his hands so he wouldn't say something to reveal how excited this little plan they were formulating made him feel. Miss Richards liked wounded boys, but she didn't like to harm them herself. Their being Gaian would get her attention, but if Doctor Browlow was going to take that extra step so he could get close and get more evidence, that would take effort from them all.

Yes, the plan was scary, but the mere idea of Doctor Brownlow, he bit his tongue and corrected his internal way of thinking of her. The mere idea of Miss

Renee slapping him was making him hard. He wasn't a roughboy, but then it didn't take much to get a boy aroused, especially if he'd been ignored sexually for more than ten days. It wasn't like he had a client every day, but even when he didn't, Jones called him in for a session, and as xe'd pointed out, he'd been designed to get off on the smallest of things, as well as the meanest.

Chief Blim had joined them at one point, followed by one of the shipmates, rolling in a selection of food to let them know that they'd missed the evening meal. She joined them, not eating but adding her opinions to their plans. Right now, they were discussing Miss Richards' interest in ill-used boys and how that might play into their hands.

"I'm not hitting him just so he can attract her attention," his client insisted.

Scott was torn. On the one hand he couldn't say that he really enjoyed the rougher stuff, but his dick still usually reacted, and it really seemed like a good plan. He hadn't said much, unsure how Miss Renee might react to his input, but now he spoke up. "I'm chill with bruising, even a broken bone, if you think it will help."

"What?" Miss Joanna turned to him with a horrified look that surprised him.

She had told him that she liked it rough; but the frown she was now showing him, and the tone of her voice was telling him the opposite. Damn it, he was cocking this up. He should kneel; he should say the formal words, but he recalled the times she'd pulled him up or snapped at him for doing that since this assignment started, so he just sat still and looked at her with his own confused look.

"Joanna," the specialist started, but his client turned on the woman who was going to pretend to be her lover.

"There is no way you can tell me that broken bones are a part of this deal or that even thinking that is chill!"

"No, it isn't," Miss Renee said as she turned to look directly at him, but her voice was calm. From the corner of his eye, he could see the IGA Chief watching in silence, her head tilted slightly forward as though she was very curious, but he hadn't yet figured out her body language to be certain of that reading. The specialist continued to look at him but directed her next word elsewhere, "Please calm down, Joanna; this is not what I was expecting from you, given your reputation, boy or not."

Scott glanced at his client as she took a deep breath and let it out, giving him a moment to think before he spoke up again, "I don't want any broken bones, Miss Joanna. I didn't mean to suggest that. I just ..."

"Just what?" the specialist urged him, putting one hand on his arm as he fidgeted with his hands sitting on the table. He couldn't remember moving them up there, and it wasn't very presentable to be acting that way, so he, too, took a deep breath and stilled his hands.

"I've had worse treatment." He let his eyes scan the three briefly before settling back on his client. "Miss Joanna, if you want to use me to lure Miss Richards in, you will have to have evidence she can see. A cast would be visible ..."

"We can put a cast on you without really breaking a bone," Miss Joanna ground out through tight lips. "I get that Dells isn't a nice place; but I'm not like everyone else back home." She tossed the specialist a look that the other returned before turning back to Scott. "I'm not Dells, you're a good boy, and I don't believe in damaging someone, anyone, unless there is no other choice."

"Our reports say that she frequents very harsh brothels," Chief Blim suddenly added. "Not that she herself engages in those activities, but she only buys time with the 'damaged,' to use your word."

"Father sucker," Miss Joanna whispered as she sat back and looked up at the ceiling for a second. "I can't." She looked down at him and then at each of the other women. "It goes against everything I believe in. Judy would never forgive me if I went against my morals like that."

"I think with Medic E'Leun's help we could do a controlled sprain that wouldn't do serious damage but could require a wrap of one hand and wrist; visible, but not very limiting. I could play the baddie, and you could be the softie, as we discussed," Miss Renee pointed out.

"This is beyond wrong," Miss Joanna said as she folded her arms over her chest and shook her head.

"Would you let your male decide?" Chief Blim asked, then let her gaze fall on Scott.

Miss Joanna took a deep breath as the medic touched her arm and leaned in toward her. Scott could hear the soft words, though he wasn't sure what exactly "isn't that part of what we're working toward?" meant.

His client nodded and muttered her agreement, though only the medic looked at him as she did so. Scott took another deep breath, then held out his left arm with a single firm nod.

When they reached Great Bragg Resort days later, Joanna adjusted the scarf over her head, then squeezed Scott's right arm as they waited for the express doors to open. This was one of a dozen individual hotels that made up the resort, along with numerous shops, parks, waterways, and other facilities. The trip down a long-tracked tram was unusual, but not unpleasant compared to the Sling, and it had allowed them to work out a few more details. "Are you ready for this?" she asked the boy at her side as the tram lights signaled they had arrived.

"Yes, Miss Joanna."

Joanna gave his arm one last squeeze before picking up two of her bags. Scott gathered the remaining luggage as best his wrapped wrist and hand allowed and followed her out as the tram doors slid open.

"Welcome to Bragg!" the intercoms blared out over the crowd of visitors. "Welcome to the luckiest place in the Federated Galaxy. Newly arriving guests, please register at the nearest desk. Have a wonderful vacation, and may the spirits guide your bets!"

"There's check in." Joanna led them to the familiar smiling Karkan man at a nearby receptionist counter.

"Welcome to Bragg!" the undercover officer greeted them in Gaian.

"Thank you. I'm McMillan, Joanna. I have a reservation for a suite."

"I'll check the register; just one moment." His pale green fingers flew over the keypad, then he nodded. "There you are … for three people?"

"This," Joanna said, motioning to Scott, "this is our potential husband. My wife, Doctor Renee Brownlow, should have checked in a while ago."

The receptionist frowned a bit as he touched a few more pads, then nodded. "Yes. You're in room 289. I'll have to check his ID number, though," he added, this time allowing his voice to hint at his displeasure with the task. Karkans did not use slaves on their homeworld but did on a few of their colonies, though they called them 'debtors,' not slaves. While they tended to lean toward the entertainment spheres, they were also law-abiding, and IGA regulations required that all people with a slave status on their homeworld be treated in accordance with their owner's native laws. For Gaians that meant tagging so that a boy's movements could be tracked by various computer systems or authorities at any time.

Joanna pushed Scott forward so the clerk could scan the number on his collar.

"Everything checks out. Here's your key card. Have a wonderful vacation, and if you need anything ask for A'Tarick; that's me."

"Thank you. I will," Joanna replied with a smile as she took the key card from his hand and turned to leave.

As they hurried to the elevator, Scott kept looking back at the receptionist, so Joanna slowed to his pace. While he knew that the officers were of different peoples and sexes and that they'd be playing roles, seeing a man with some authority, no matter how minor, must be a bit disconcerting, Joanna realized as she caught him looking. "Just try not to stare at people, chill? I don't want to have to be the baddie out here in public, but we are building a set of expectations, so ..." Scott merely nodded as they continued.

They continued in silence to the spacious suite. It had a mini-bar, a kitchenette, and a living room with a large screen TV in the center. Two archways leading to a bathroom and a bedroom. The bed was as big as her one back home, so Joanna placed her luggage on it, then looked around with a frown. Scott followed her out to the main area again. "Renee, darling, where are you?" The words were still difficult, even after deciding that she'd not use any endearments that she'd shared with Judy.

"Right here, babe," the older woman said, looking out of the bathroom. "You're a bit earlier than I thought you might be, given that you brought him along. I just got back from lunch a couple of minutes ago." Renee made a circular gesture with her finger and tapped her ear.

"Please don't start that again; you know Grandmother wants us to give him a try," Joanna replied as she took out her scanner and started going over the room slowly. She motioned for Scott to start unpacking while the two women continued their planned dialogue, just in case they were being watched. E'Lige had said he didn't do that in his resorts but, given that they had made this vacation semi-public in this sector, they wanted to be certain, since the doctor had been gone for a few hours.

"We each had a ride or two, or was it three for you?" Renee teased back, and Joanna felt her face go slightly warm as she watched the readout.

In a moment the doctor was out of the bathroom and had Scott by the chin; Joanna swallowed but forced herself to continue the scan. They had agreed to try and be in role as much as possible, which was less of a challenge for Joanna than she expected. Joanna hoped that the way her MOI partner was acting was a role and that the other didn't enjoy being the baddie. "How's your arm, boy?" she demanded of him.

"Better, Miss Renee; thank you for asking," he whispered as he looked in Joanna's direction.

"Don't look at her when I'm talking to you, boy!"

Joanna bit her lip as she walked into the bathroom. She'd been scanning the room for any device that might be watching or listening in, double checking what Renee would surely have done before. Joanna flinched when she heard the slap from the main room. "We're clean," she announced as she hurried out to find Scott on the floor in a penitent pose.

Renee released a breath and held out her hand to him, but he jerked back just slightly before taking it, so Joanna rushed to them and held out her own hand. "Take her hand, boy; she'd be the one you should be clinging to in this little drama," Renee reminded them all.

"We have a couple days to work with these covers before Maggie is scheduled to arrive," Joanna told him as he stood up, holding her hand. "Are you going to be chill with all this?"

"Yes, Miss Joanna. I'm still nervous that I might cock things up," he added, looking down at his feet.

"You should be. We all should be, because if Maggie is doing what IGA thinks, she's one of the most dangerous people in the galaxy right now," Renee pointed out.

Scott lay very still on his back, with Miss Joanna on his left side, holding him as she had every night outside of that freeze pod thingy, and with Miss Renee on his right, turned away from them both. This was a first; two women with him in one bed, just sleeping. He'd been hired a few times for parties and ended up the center of multiple women's attention, but they always sent him back to Dells when they were done with him or had him sleep on the floor.

He wished he was awake from being well-used, but no. They just continued to play their parts, even going out into the resort for meals and some casual shopping. As they did, they checked to make sure each IGA agent knew they were there. The entire game seemed to have caused both women stress, his client more than the medic. Miss Joanna had even taken some medication for a headache she had. There were no lights or sounds here to help soothe emotions as there were on Gaia.

For Scott, acting subservient to both women, even in this strange place, felt reassuring. He knew what to do and say, how to keep his wits about him to gauge what each wanted. If only it was what his client really wanted, he would be learning so much more about her. Instead, he kept reminding himself that these were roles they were all playing.

Miss Renee made a soft sound as she slept, not really a snore but just more audible breathing than Miss Joanna. She insisted he wear full pajamas again and had one of her hands fisted in his shirt as he slept. This was nice, and even if there was never any sex, he could live this way … if he lived. This Miss Richards was bad, worse than Jones bad, though he wasn't quite sure yet how. The IGA and the two women in bed conveniently sent him to check equipment when they discussed those specifics. It was probably for the best, helping him keep to his role, because the test husband for a power couple wouldn't know who Miss Richards was.

Scott looked up at the ceiling and took several deep breaths. He could do this. He glanced at his client, her auburn hair half tumbled over her face, her unseen hand along his side just touching him. He had to do this.

Chapter Seven

The casino was buzzing with activity when Joanna, Renee, and Scott entered the next afternoon. Using the leash on Scott allowed Renee to jerk on it, something that looked crueler than it was. Joanna didn't like those things back on Gaia, and she didn't like it here, but it allowed them to stay in character. It also allowed her to slip away to the rendezvous on her agenda after a few moments.

"Don't lose too much, babe," Renee told her with a kiss on the cheek.

"I don't plan to lose at all," Joanna said with a chuckle. "Behave," she directed Scott, who was at the leash's limit, and he smiled at her. "Don't be too harsh on him, please, darling; this is all very new to him, too."

Renee's answer was a snort and a jerk on the leash, pulling Scott forward two steps.

Joanna shook her head but made herself smile, and then went to the tables that Agent Noulayia, who was working as floor monitor right now, had assigned her to stake out. He briefly touched her arm and softly reminded her of the series of bets she was to make, even though she remembered. Her rental wasn't the only one who could memorize information; it just took more work for her.

She placed the bets, in the prearranged order, on the color or symbol that came up on the tube the croupier rolled down the table. Her winnings went up and up until a person from one of the minor worlds – male or female she couldn't say, given the dress and even the rather neutral sounding voice –

asked if she'd mind if she mimicked her bets. "Oh, I don't really know what I'm doing, so it's your risk," she teased with a giggle. She, too, started to win, though of course the winnings went down the more bets were placed on the same color or symbol.

After a bit of time that one person thanked her and scurried away to cash out. Another player, a Fortixe woman with graying tufts around her rather impressive horns, took the previous person's place and asked if she might borrow Joanna's luck. Another floor monitor had stepped in earlier, decreeing that only one player could copy either her color or symbol and needed her permission, so the others around the table started to protest until Noulayia stepped in and said they'd go around fairly.

Joanna glanced at him as he spoke into his headpiece. It was time to move to stage two of this undercover mission.

The casino owner approached without any entourage and just stepped in next to her after the older woman left. "Hello. I'm Evan E'Lige, owner of this casino," he introduced himself just loudly enough for the nearest guests in the small crowd that had gathered to hear.

Joanna blinked, then smiled as she offered her hand. "I'm Joanna McMillin. Is there something wrong, Mr. E'Lige? I, for one, am having a wonderful time." Several of the other gamblers made a noise or a motion in agreement.

"No, my dear. I just happened to be visiting the floor today and noticed your lovely red hair. It's the most beautiful shade I have ever seen."

"Thank you," she replied, blushing, and glancing back at the table. Several of the other players were going away, but none looked worried, just cautious. Perhaps the resort dealt harshly with trickery, though Joanna was doing none of this; it was all rigged for 79 rolls in her favor. She had four more rolls to go. "Green," she called, placing five chips on that color.

"May I buy you a drink? Perhaps dinner?" E'Lige offered smoothly.

The table roared as green came up. "Starburst," she announced, placing her five chips on the symbol. "It's kind of you to offer, but I don't eat with people I've just met."

"You don't bet more than five?" he asked, and Joanna shook her head right before the "starburst" symbol landed upright at the end of the table.

"I promised my wife that I wouldn't lose. Black now." She placed her chips.

"You are certainly not losing," he said, motioning to her stack of chips. Black came up, and she placed what they both knew would be her final winning bet on spiral. "We can just have a drink at the bar over there, in public, so you can get to know me in a public venue, if your wife won't mind." Spiral came up, and the crowd went wild.

E'Lige offered his arm to her with a small plea, "Please, I would be most honored."

"Just one, though," Joanna gave in with a small smile. He motioned for the floor monitor to bring a bag and help her put the chips in it while the remaining players protested.

"Now, now, let the lady leave. You should all rely upon your own luck," E'Lige insisted, and this got the players to back down quickly, making her very curious. She shook her head at his offered arm but accompanied him to the nearby bar, where they were seated at his private table, which overlooked the floor and was thus not particularly private.

"What would you like?" E'Lige asked, handing her the menu.

Joanna read over all the listings before answering, "I think I'll just have the tea. I don't drink alcohol very often."

"Ah, I wish I could say the same, but my business requires that I partake occasionally." He turned to the server and said, "Two hot spiced flowers."

"You sound as though you dislike this casino," Joanna asked her host.

"Oh, no. I like entertaining people – who doesn't? Sometimes the focus on gambling gets boring, and the growth factor is limited. People only have so much credit." He nodded as the server left their drinks. E'Lige looked over the redhead's shoulder as they sipped their tea.

"You look a million parsecs away, Mr. E'Lige."

"Not that far," the Karkan replied, smiling at his companion. "I am just thinking of a new venture of mine."

"A new way to entertain people at your resorts and casinos?"

"More like a way for people to entertain themselves."

"Now you've intrigued me." Joanna leaned forward slightly.

"Perhaps later I will tell you more. But I want to know more about you." He set down his glass as his smile faded. "So why would a Gaian woman agree to have a drink with a man? A married woman, at that."

"Ah." Joanna settled back into her chair. "You didn't just see me, did you?"

"I did, but then I made inquiries – just the basics. I must say I'm a bit surprised that you would come out here to this region for a honeymoon. We do get Gaians from time to time, but only a handful every year; almost all are stopping briefly, not staying for a vacation."

"My mother wanted to expand her business off-world, and my wife has several business contacts off-world in her job."

"Which is?"

"Xenomedics and xenogenetics – no offense at the terms."

"None taken. We are all 'xeno' to others, are we not?" They both laughed lightly, then sipped their drinks a few more times. "I must confess that I am more surprised that you accepted my offer. I have heard that your people do not trust males. You are from one of the leading families of your world, are you not? I thought you'd trust males the least."

Joanna set her glass down slowly and licked her lips. The reputation was well earned, so she didn't have to play a role to feel like she'd been kicked in the heart by the comment. "Yes, my family is … important back home, but we are also a bit more traveled than most Gaians. It makes us a bit more open-minded, you could say."

"So, you have no problem being out where men are running things?"

"I have no problems sharing a drink with a man I think is my intellectual equal." Joanna picked up her glass as he tilted his head back. She took a very slow sip, keeping her eyes on him. "I have no problems sharing anything with men I like, equal or not, once I get to know them."

The resort owner chuckled softly. "Then perhaps we may share dinner some night before you leave, so some of your luck at the games will rub off on me."

"Perhaps."

"I will call on you again." He rose after a brief glance at his watch. "If you will excuse me, I have a meeting I almost forgot."

"Yes, sorry to have distracted you, Mr. E'Lige." Joanna rose and offered her hand.

The casino owner paused, then kissed it lightly. "No meeting is worth more than such lovely red hair and the beautiful woman who possesses it. I'll ask one of our hosts to show you the entire resort if you would like."

"I would prefer a tour from the owner," Joanna hinted. She was going off-script, but he knew something, and if she was undercover on this story, she'd push as far as she felt was safe.

He only paused for a second, searching her face, then he nodded and bowed. "I'll meet you here after my meeting. It shouldn't be too long."

"I'll be here, Mr. E'Lige." Joanna sat back down as he left. She hoped that was enough of a show to explain their spending more time together. Time was slipping by, and they needed to make sure everything was in place before Maggie arrived. Whatever he was hiding, she needed to gain his confidence faster. "Another tea, please," she asked the server, who smiled but also brought her a fruit appetizer with a word that it was on the house. Joanna looked around the casino as she waited. Her eyes fell on Scott and Renee. More information would protect them all.

This was almost relaxing, because it was normal, exactly what he was expecting, Scott realized as he stood just behind Miss Renee with his head bowed but looking stealthily around him at the same time. She might not be ignoring him as much as she acted; she seemed a lot like his client, with some very strange ideas.

Miss Joanna was too far on the opposite side of the room for him to casually seek his client out to see how she was doing. The last time he'd seen her, she had been surrounded by people who were cheering as they shared her luck. He wondered if she'd get to keep the money she was winning; if she won enough, maybe it would be easier to convince her to take him on or at least become a regular. She was supposed to be meeting the casino owner, a male owner. Ah, there she was; he could just see her if he stretched up on his toes to get a better angle.

The specialist crossed her arms as she watched the escort standing next to her stare down at the redhead. She tugged gently on his leash.

"Miss Renee?" Scott looked over with a swallow, both for effect and to damp down the rising unrest in his stomach as he wondered which rough treatment he might be in for next. Truth was, he was really more interested in the woman below than any big story they were investigating, and he wasn't skilled at faking interest – his friend Todd, his trainer at Dells, and even a few clients had told him so.

She yanked on his leash, so he faced her. "You're supposed to be with me," she whispered harshly.

"Yes, Miss Renee. Sorry, Miss Renee," he said, slightly louder than he would have in the same situation back on Gaia.

Miss Renee's hand hit his cheek sharply enough to send him to the floor. "Get up!" she ordered and pulled roughly on the leash. She grabbed him roughly by his hair as he struggled to stand, bringing him close to her face. "You chill? We have to make it look real," she whispered quickly into his ear.

"Yes," he mouthed back as he cringed from her other hand.

"Don't ever speak to me in that tone again!" Miss Renee shook him by his hair before turning back to the woman she'd been talking to, who appeared to be of the same people as the chief of the IGA they were working with.

Working with. He was working with them, not just for them, or at least it had felt like that when they had tried to include him in the conversations. His dorm mates weren't going to believe this either.

"Let her look at you, boy," Miss Renee's voice commanded, and he lifted his head but averted his eyes as the woman touched one of his cheeks, then the other, and made an untranslated sound before she complimented him.

"He's a good looker, but he can be uppity."

Scott flinched at the comment, his hands tensing behind his back. This all felt so normal, but his heart was racing when Miss Renee grabbed his chin and sneered at him as she continued to speak. "He's behaving today, but, well, aren't your males rather juvenile, too?"

"Oh, yes, but they are capable of making some decisions and can be very helpful, if it doesn't require a lot of forethought or interfere with their necessary playtime," the other woman said as she tilted her head and continued to look at him.

Miss Renee squeezed his chin just a bit, so he gasped to make it seem like she was hurting him before she chuckled and released him. It wasn't difficult to imagine how that would have hurt, since it had been done to him enough in the past. She could have hurt him; they said it might be necessary, and he'd even agreed to it, for whatever that was worth, because he cradled how important this story was to his client. Yet she just turned back to the woman and continued her conversation, ignoring him once more.

"Are you having a good time?" A feminine voice and a touch on his arm made Scott jump and turn, causing Miss Renee and her new friend to stop their conversation. It was Agent A'Jaliou asking as the entertainment concierge for the resort, and she was smiling at him. She was pretty, with light straw-colored hair that fell in thick ringlets over her olive-green skin, framing her light gray eyes that seemed to really be interested in an answer, so he almost spoke before the other Gaian stepped in and jerked him away by his arm.

"He's fine. I could use a bit more respect for our traditions," she added, narrowing her eyes.

"Oh, you're Gaians – so sorry, I thought maybe he was Fortixe from the back. Are you having a good time?" she asked Miss Renee directly but with widened eyes.

Miss Renee's eyes softened in response, and she smiled as the Fortixe woman circled around to check out his other side. Scott could almost feel the woman's body, because she was so close to him, but she didn't touch him again. "Do you have chocolates, cocoas? I think my wife would like that."

Agent A'Jaliou thought for a moment, then nodded. "We do, and," she answered, taking a pad from a bag she had strapped across her torso and making a few notes on it, "if you give me your room number, I can give you a discount coupon for our import boutique."

"Room 289. Thanks," Miss Renee replied as she took the coupon and the agent walked to check in with another guest. "Do you like what you see?" she teased the returning Fortixe woman.

"He basically does look like our males, though a bit more," she made a grabbing motion with her hands, "full, you know. Ours have more discreet organs."

Miss Renee chuckled and pulled Scott in to stand right next to her, so he bowed lower to make himself a bit smaller, which was unnecessary, since she was bigger than his client and him. It was a reflex, a means to send the message that he was a good boy to curb the swings of her moods. She patted his arm while she spoke, "You want to check him out in private?"

"You sure your wife wouldn't mind?"

Miss Renee waved the little coupon around. "I got a pass right here for any miscommunication."

With that he was escorted to the other woman's room for another new experience his dorm mates weren't going to believe.

"How did it go with E'Lige?" Renee asked Joanna later that afternoon when she returned to their suite.

Joanna sat in the other chair, glancing down at Scott, who was kneeling at Renee's feet. "I think it went well. I doubt they will let us keep the winnings, though."

"One never knows – of course, if you just spend it all, as we should be doing," Renee reminded them all, "it won't matter."

"How did it go with you?" Joanna turned the subject back.

"I think it went fine, if fine means acting like a dick when the boy you have is so very well behaved."

Joanna saw Scott grimace and bow his head until Renee ran her fingers through his bangs and his loosened hair that he had almost rebraided that morning out of habit. "You're both chill with this?" Joanna asked after a moment of watching the intimacy.

Renee shrugged and muttered something about doing something nice for him later, which made Scott look up at her with a blush. "Something else, not that," she hissed, then chuckled as the boy's face reddened.

"I'm missing something. What exactly did you two do today?" Her tone surprised them all, making both Renee and Scott look sharply at her, causing her to cough a moment before rephrasing it less severely.

"Scott here got touched by a non-Gaian woman and got to see a bit more skin than he had been expecting," Renee explained as she kept caressing his hair.

"Excuse me?" That tone was back in her voice, but this time Joanna just glared. "I don't recall agreeing to you whoring him out to anyone other than Maggie."

Scott's mouth fell open as he returned his gaze to the floor, and Renee just sighed and withdrew her hand from him. "Boy, go take a bath, and make sure you close the door."

Neither woman spoke until they heard the bathroom door close.

"I accept the blame; don't be mad at the boy," Renee offered before Joanna could release her annoyance further.

Joanna blinked and let herself relax just a bit. "Why did you let someone else touch him?"

"If we want Maggie to accept that it's normal for me to lend out Scott, then I have to establish that now, don't I? Just like you need to be seen with E'Lige so it isn't too unusual when he takes you to his meetings, or at least around her."

Joanna growled, and Renee's eyebrow rose a bit. "Yes, I understand, but I don't like it," she forced out.

"Apparently not. You know, the feeling is mutual."

"Feeling?"

"That you are starting to care for him. He is clearly enamored of you."

Joanna sat back with a sharp wave of one hand. "Please, that's all attention to his client; it isn't personal."

"Right …" Renee replied slowly as she sat back. "He couldn't get it up for my Fortixe friend, or for me either, but he watches you every chance he gets."

"He's just hoping I'll become a regular."

"Hmmmm … yes, that would be a terrible thing," Renee sarcastically agreed with her waspish tone. "Oh, I brought you a gift," she quickly added before Joanna could get out a retort.

Joanna sighed and looked up at the ceiling. While Renee went to fetch this gift, she listened to the water and other sounds from the bathroom. Maybe she should make him sleep on the other side of Renee, but the thought of being that close to another woman felt like cheating. No, Renee might be an expert in other peoples, but she clearly wasn't reading the situation correctly with Joanna, and hopefully she wasn't reading Scott's expectations right either. Joanna had repeatedly been completely clear about her intentions.

Joanna continued to tell herself that even as he licked the chocolate off her fingers when she shared one of the four truffles with him after he got back from his shower. He had helped pick it out, she'd been told, so it was only right to share it with him. It wasn't because she had anything other than the feelings she'd have for anyone she was working with.

By the next evening, after they had each played their roles in all the public areas of the hotel and casino, Joanna was certain she disliked their cover. There were too many windows unblinded, too many ways to lose control of the situation. Richards was on schedule, so she and E'Lige had made plans to have a private meal that evening to create more buzz about their forbidden relationship. The restaurant he picked was central and drew people who simply watched those eating there. If Richards had spies, she'd learn about it. Her MOI colleague was happy about it.

"We could use the extra time," Renee said. "We'll go out and make a fuss to generate a more vicious rumor mill. I got approached today by a woman and man, Fortixe again, who said they'd heard we were giving out views for the curious. They didn't say anything that made it seem like I was roughing him up too much, and we have to fix that."

"I should think that bruise," Joanna said, pointing to the one now blooming over Scott's left cheek, "would convince anyone that you mistreat him!"

"That's only one bruise," Renee pointed out.

"Actually, it's two, Ma'am," Scott added quietly, touching the arm she had gripped tightly when they were in the elevator after leaving for breakfast that morning.

"Two?" Joanna frowned and crossed her arms over her chest.

Renee faced her with a tired shake of her head. "How many times have you worked with a man on a story?"

"Never, but ..."

"No buts. I've worked a lot under the slave-mistress guise. I know what I'm doing, and it's what has to be done."

Joanna took a deep breath. At least Renee wasn't saying something stupid like "ward" or "guardian"; she was being honest about their society. Scott seemed to know it, too, because he visibly relaxed at the words. It only heightened Joanna's worries. "Are you sure this is necessary?"

"Yes. Richards is rather an odd character. She likes her men roughed up, but she doesn't like to do it. We've been through this." Renee walked back to Scott. "That doesn't mean she won't hurt you, especially if you don't convince her that you are totally sincere in wanting to please her."

Joanna wiped her eyes as she returned to the front room and stood in front of her rental. "Are you going to be able to handle all this ... roughness?"

Scott nodded, his eyes respectfully on her feet. "I've had much worse, Miss Joanna. I can help, I want to help."

"I know, I appreciate it," Joanna said softly.

Renee nodded gratefully to the redhead, who only shook her head and walked to the bedroom. "We'll put on another public performance while you're out tonight," she called after her.

"I need to get ready for dinner now," Joanna just replied as she went into the bathroom to do so.

She sighed and looked in the mirror. The chance that Richards might say something in front of Scott, give them another piece of evidence – was it worth knowing he was being bruised up just to make an impression? If he were enjoying it ... but it was obvious that he wasn't. Betty's boys, her former dorm boy, they'd all enjoyed it. Joanna knew the difference after the talk with Jack. Scott was too focused on her, pleasing her, possibly keeping her as a client.

Joanna clenched her hands into fists as she looked at her reflection, debating whether to punch the mirror.

With a growl she pushed back from the counter and turned to the shower. She had her own role to play that evening. She used the time to get into the proper headspace.

E'Lige sent a vehicle for her, and two hours later she was at the dinner, but he hadn't come himself, which wasn't part of the plan. His driver, another Karkan male, accessed a voice message from E'Lige for her when she met him in her hotel lobby – something about an emergency. They would need to dine at another branch of the resort, some distance away.

Renee had expressed some doubts, as a slightly worried but open-minded wife might, but had then let her go with an uncomfortable kiss for those curious onlookers. Joanna had been gathering crowds with her lucky streak in the casino and her luncheon with the owner. The tour had fallen through, but she'd keep trying. Renee and Scott had their own groups of onlookers that were tittering about the bruise on his cheek as well as the wrist wrap. Goddess, she hoped none of this really drew gossip columnists to them, because there was a tiny chance that it might get back home. While she could ignore her mother, her grandmother was an entirely different obstacle.

Looking outside the window had been pleasant at a certain level, seeing the results of Karkan terraforming a millennium ago. According to the brochure her driver handed her once she was seated to "occupy her time," the planet was a failed colony attempt that the E'Lige family had purchased two generations ago. It was only under Evan's guidance – yesterday they had decided to go to a first name basis – that the resort was flourishing. About half the planet was water, and the brochure laid out some plans to refurbish some of the older abandoned platforms that had once housed fisheries that the resort didn't need.

It was very odd that a colony couldn't survive while a workforce of some 10,000, primarily from Karka, Fortixe, and many minor worlds, could do so well. This little promotional guide didn't go into many historical details, but part of her expected it was simple masculine aggression at the core. The galaxy had far more habitable worlds than one might guess from the IGA's membership, but she recalled from history classes that most civilizations destroyed themselves soon after they managed to explore space to the edge of their stellar systems, if not before.

She could speculate about it all; any normal woman would, but instead she found her mind going back over the growing number of bruises on Scott's body and the way he'd flinched tonight when Renee had shoved him to his knees to say good evening to her before she left. The display had made the crowd silent for a moment before the whispering started up again. Renee might be a medic, but she seemed far too comfortable with hurting him. Did MOI not even vet the moral code of its members anymore? They'd put Joanna through a background check and were still watching her, as Mi's comments about The Chain clarified.

Tuning out her thoughts by watching a documentary she'd discovered on the back seat viewer answered some of her questions about the planet Bragg but did little to ease her worry about what was happening back at her hotel or the club that her partners were planning to be seen in. Yup, there it was in the documentary. Competition for leadership and economic power had released a wave of violence on Bragg that the authorities had been unable to stop without calling in the homeworld.

She was grateful when they arrived at the most elegant restaurant in the Resort and the driver helped her out of the vehicle. A few steps and she was inside, facing a well-coifed minor-world man with a bifurcated mouth that was just a touch off-putting. She didn't recognize his species – he might not even have been male – but it didn't matter for the part she was playing.

"I'm Joanna McMillin. Mr. E'Lige, the owner, asked me to meet him here for dinner," she introduced herself to the host.

"Yes. Mr. E'Lige has asked that you be seated at his table. Follow me, please," the host instructed as they took a menu and started down the steps to the dining room proper.

Joanna followed the host to a large round table at the other end of the dining room. Several people from different planets were sitting there already.

The casino owner rose at the sight of his special guest. "Please sit here, Joanna," he asked, pulling out a chair next to him. With a nod, he dismissed the host, then reseated himself at the head of the table. After a smile at his newest guest, he addressed the rest of the table. "My friends, let me introduce Miss Joanna McMillin, from one of Gaia's leading families."

After a few polite nods and brief introductions of most of the guests from all the major peoples and a few upcoming minor ones, E'Lige placed a hand on the shoulder of the man sitting right across from her. "Joanna, let me introduce my business associates. This is Jinn O'Rray, my resort manager here on Bragg."

"Nice to meet you, Mr. O'Rray," she said, holding out her hand as was common on Gaia. The other Karkan took it, placing a kiss on the back of it after a prompt from his boss.

"Miss McMillin, is that the proper form of address?"

"It works," she told him with a smile and got one in return. O'Rray looked nervous, though, compared to his boss. While he had seemed willing to be part of this investigation at the final meeting several days ago, it was only willingness, not eagerness, that she'd noticed then, and she could confirm that right now. He was loyal to his employer but afraid of something. Perhaps later she might find out what, but for now she tried to participate in the conversations.

She found it difficult to contribute much to the various branches of discussion. Gaians isolated themselves to an extent, but not as much as the Sorzlex – although the single member of that people at the table, a male who headed security in the third casino, seemed far less the stereotypical military pawn than she'd expected. The Vancazie at the table, the gate chair for this system, came to dinner once a month to keep contact with their clients; as usual, he said little but watched everything. The Fortixe woman and the Karkan male, regular casino guests whose high roller and elite resort membership status had earned them recognition from the resort owner, were more stereotypical but charming.

The three minor peoples were from different worlds, and only one's gender was easily identifiable to her, a female from Geunol who was clearly attempting to find allies in their pursuit of Federation status; the other two peoples – Qoibin and Lysop – were vaguely known to her as heavily unequal worlds whose wealthy explored the galaxy at their whims while the masses fought their wars and struggled to survive. There had been periods, according to her history classes, when Gaia had been that way. Everything she knew might also be utterly incorrect, given how isolated Gaia was.

Luckily most of the guests seemed to know each other from previous weekly dinners with the resort owner, so they let her primarily observe or discuss her luck in the casino. Apparently, their cover was generating more interest than they'd hoped, and a few mentioned the "rare Gaian male" or her marriage. In those cases, she fed the image they were trying to portray by indicating how the marriage was one of family alliance and convenience, something all of the peoples at the table accepted as normal.

When most of his guests appeared to be finished eating, E'Lige rose. "I would like to thank all of you for dining with me tonight. Joanna," he said, holding out his hand to her, "would you care for a tour of this part of my resort?"

"I have been looking forward to it very much." With a smile to the rest of her eating companions, Joanna took the offered hand.

"What do you think of my resort?" E'Lige asked her some time later as they approached one of the balconies that surrounded the third casino floor and looked outside to the cool night with its orange sky turning black.

It was late when they walked out into the fresh air, so she took a deep breath, feeling slightly high from the higher oxygen content. "I think having these," she indicated the balcony, "is a great idea. It gets rather crowded and noisy in there."

"Ah, so it is true, then, that on Gaia there isn't much gambling, drinking, or drugs?"

"We have a … difficult history with those forms of … entertainment. We've moved on from them," Joanna replied, a bit colder, and moved several mills away.

"I apologize. We have mostly rumors in the rest of the galaxy about what happened. So, few of the rest of us visit your world … I should not have pressed," he finished by stopping and bowing slightly until she spoke up.

"I should not let such topics annoy me. As I said, I should know how to interact with my intellectual equals, regardless of people."

They stepped forward a bit more to rest against the railing, where Joanna gathered her wrap closer around her. The Karkan glanced back at the casino, then turned to his guest with a smile. "I know what you need," he said, pointing a finger at her.

Joanna stiffened, well versed in what such a phrase might mean from a male in Gaia's history meant. Most of the classes she'd had said that was male nature, Gain or otherwise. Her reaction was ridiculous. She knew that he was just playing a role and would keep to his agreement with MOI and IGA or risk losing their help in the future, so she smiled and countered, "What is that?"

"A cup of hot tea."

"That would be wonderful," she said as she took one step toward the casino.

"I will go get them." After a kiss on her hand, he hurried inside.

Joanna smiled as she watched him leave, glad that once again stereotypes were simply that. They needed to be focused on the goal, all of them. Then she turned back to the night sky. She sighed as she tried to locate Sol.

"You are doing all that you can to protect him?" The voice was sudden, and she turned to find O'Rray just a few steps from her.

"That's a question more appropriate for IGA," she pointed out as she moved closer.

He didn't look convinced as he frowned. "I understand why you're here; revenge is a powerful motive, but have you asked why my boss is really part of this?"

Joanna tilted her head to one side, then nodded. "The good citizen spiel seemed a bit too good, perhaps. But I try not to buy into stereotypes when I can avoid them," she added to convince them both of that ideal.

"About peoples or professions?"

O'Rray was getting more intriguing by the second, so Joanna arched an eyebrow but said nothing to discourage or encourage him. Perhaps she'd misjudged his loyalty after all, but he'd have to reveal that on his own if it were the case.

He held out a data crystal and motioned for her to take it. "Here's the financials. I think you'll find that this isn't his first partnership with your Maggie Richards."

She looked at the crystal, then at him, but didn't move to take it. "Are you saying he's part of her schemes?"

"Her schemes? Not part of them in any real sense of that word, and definitely not a partner." When she didn't move to take the information, he sighed. "IGA will find out about all of this when they take her down unless she torches her records. I just want you to understand that he's been very afraid of her for some time. He has thousands and thousands of employees whose families depend on their salaries. He thinks about that whenever he makes a decision, even if I suggest otherwise."

Joanna stood for a moment and considered the request. She understood carrying the weight of thousands of others on your shoulders, even though that responsibility fell primarily on her mother and grandmother. If IGA had enough evidence on Richards, they wouldn't need more, but if they were struggling to make a case ... "As long as Richards can be put away for the rest of her life, I'll protect this," she agreed, holding out her hand.

"Thank you, Miss Joanna," he said, placing the crystal into her palm.

They stood for a second, and then O'Rray lowered his voice and asked, "Why don't you protect the man you came with? You're protecting a stranger, and yet you just allow Scott to be hurt."

Joanna frowned and tilted her head to one side, and the Karkan copied the movement but kept his eyes on hers. "I don't understand; this is part of our cover."

"But you're his Protector; shouldn't you be protecting him?"

There seemed to be a translation problem, so Joanna tried again. "I'm his Guardian – well, not really; I've rented him, and we're acting as co-Guardians," she started to explain, but this only made the alien's frown deepen. "Maybe the chips aren't working quite right; the words are similar. I heard you say Protector, but I say Guardian."

"Different words?" O'Rray guessed. "I'm hearing the same word."

Damn, that was inconvenient, so Joanna thought as quickly as she could. "We don't protect our men from women. We protect ourselves and our world from men. We guard them so they can't harm the world." There, she'd said it; it felt like a half-truth at best, but it seemed to work, as the resort assistant just nodded.

"Ah, I see; a mistranslation, then," O'Rray simply replied. He looked back toward the building and then bowed before leaving her at the balcony railing.

Joanna barely had time to put the crystal away before her host returned. "That didn't take you too long," she greeted him.

"When you own the place, you get first-rate service," E'Lige said with a chuckle, handing her one of the steaming cups. "I noticed you looking at the stars before I left."

"They're not in the same places, but they're just as pretty as those seen from Gaia."

"We all see the sky differently. I know most of them here on Bragg, as well as my homeworld, though I haven't seen it in many, many years." He moved slightly closer to her. "Would you like me to point some of them out to you, Joanna?"

"I would like that very much, Evan." Joanna leaned against the rail, sipping her tea.

"When we look up, we see ourselves out there among the stars," he began. He pointed up and to the right and said, "That grouping is the great Arka Fruit, with its tendrils growing from its base. We say that our first mothers wanted this fruit so badly that our first fathers grew legs to fetch it for them." Her host made every myth about the plants in the night sky come alive by using different voices and gestures to represent the characters.

Joanna enjoyed the new information, but she really wanted to know what was on that crystal, because if he were a threat to this mission for any reason, IGA and MOI would need to know. She excused herself as quickly as she could. She held onto the crystal tightly during the ride back, not trusting the technology not to relay what she had right back to E'Lige. The ride back seemed much longer than the first.

Joanna entered her dark hotel room quickly. Without turning on the lights, she knocked on the bedroom door. "Renee! Scott! I need to talk to you!"

A few seconds passed before the sleepy brunette stumbled out and stood facing her with squinting, tired eyes. "What time is it?"

"It's three in the morning, Miss Renee," Scott answered with a yawn as he followed her.

"Three!" the xenospecialist repeated loudly.

"Please," Joanna whispered, "I'm tired, too." She handed Renee the tiny crystal. "I was given this earlier in the evening by O'Rray. I just couldn't get away before now."

Renee shook her head violently as she tried to force herself awake. "Let's look at it."

"Mistresses?" Scott alone seemed fully awake as he stood at attention, nearly naked with just part of a sheet held around his hips. "Would you care for something to drink?"

"No time for that," Joanna said, and looked at him for the first time that evening. Her smile fell when she saw he was only in pajama bottoms and bore several bruises on his chest and arms. Her face started to burn as she turned to look at the other woman.

"Go put the top on, Scott," Renee ordered. They were silent as he scurried into the bathroom, shutting the door behind him. He'd learned to just do that automatically now when sent so they could talk about him.

"He would rather be working directly with you," Renee reminded Joanna.

She snorted once and shook her head, clutching the crystal in one hand as she counted to ten. "It's better for you to play this role. As you said, you have more experience in this area than I do."

"True," Renee's one word agreement annoyed her, but Joanna let it go. "By the way, none of those bruises caused much pain. I gave him a pill this morning that increases the risk of marking from even minor pressure. Just the one dose – he should be back to normal in a day," Renee added at the horrified look that crossed Joanna's face.

Renee sat down on one of the nearby chairs. "He'll be ready by the time Richards sees him. I'm thinking on her second day, not before. Seems too much like a set-up to have it be sooner. You should try to meet her first – maybe mention your wife and this trial husband thing, how easily annoyed I am by him. She might even seek us out."

"Good idea," Joanna replied through tight lips from the closet where she had their equipment. "Scott," she said, noticing he had returned. "You need to listen to this, too."

As they read through the documents IGA had given them and listened to the various recorded conversations on the crystal, Joanna started to smile. At the end, she pressed the rewind button. "It's her. Her and E'Lige on the phone just a few days ago, confirming their meeting here." She turned with a grin to Scott, "Listen very closely to the woman's voice. It's Richards."

The two women watched the slave carefully as he sat on the floor, ear close to the player, listening intently as they replayed the entire thing.

"Could you recognize that voice in a crowd?" Renee asked after the tape ended.

Scott paused before answering. "Yes, Miss Renee."

Joanna leaned toward him, "You have to be sure. We can't risk any mistakes. Starting tomorrow when she arrives, we all have to be completely sure we're in character and remain that way.

Scott nodded as he stared at his clenched hands. He glanced at each woman. "If this one may be so bold," he offered with a glance at each.

"Be bold; this isn't a time for any doubt," Renee pointed out, and Joanna nodded.

"I don't feel like much of a potential husband for both of you."

Joanna put her head in her hands, and Renee began a chuckle that soon turned into a full-blown laugh. "That's a very polite way to word it," she gasped out with a few breaths as she tried to calm down.

"I said I wasn't renting him – MOI wasn't renting him for that," Joanna insisted.

"And you didn't, and apparently you haven't, which is very stupid of you, by the way." Renee's laughter died at the glare Joanna threw her. "He's good, not great," she added with a glance at the boy, who just bowed his head.

"Wow, talk him up more so I'm really eager," Joanna countered. She knew this had been coming, given the cover; it was the reason she'd argued against this idea. After Judy's death she'd had The Chain and Raven for company at least once a week, not to mention her own hands and tools. At first, she'd thought it was a sign that she hadn't really loved her fiancé that her sex drive hadn't dried up, just shallowed. This trip was really a dry spell for her, and it was getting tougher every day. But giving in, using him, seemed like losing the argument with Mi all over again.

"Use me only as you desire, Miss Joanna," his voice, low and needy, pushed her over the edge, and a low moan left her lips as she looked at him.

"I'm going to take a walk, since I'm not really tired," Renee said before she disappeared into the bathroom, leaving Joanna to deal with the opportunity in front of her.

It was an opportunity, she realized when she stepped toward him and tilted his head up to look at her. Seriously, if MOI thought they could get her to accept him on future stories, and she revealed that she hadn't given him a fair try, Mi would just dismiss her arguments again. With that thought she leaned in and kissed him.

He opened his mouth up slightly, but instead of being passive as she'd feared or hoped – it was more unclear to her with each passing second – he moved his hands to her hips and kissed back, tilting his head in harmony with hers, moving his body when she leaned and guided.

She started walking them back toward the bedroom. He gasped against her lips when his legs met the side of the bed. She gave him a little shove, and he fell onto the bed, his feet still on the floor, the smile growing on his face as he lay looking up at her. His pajama bottoms were tented, but it was his eyes she searched for desire and found it reflected back more than she thought she might.

Joanna smiled and felt her own arousal burning low as she stretched her neck with one circular turn before pointing at him with one hand. "You remember what I told you about me liking it rough?"

"Yes, Miss Joanna. Please be rough with me," he stated more than asked as he raised one hand to his pajama buttons.

"With this pill," she said as she almost paused, but he rolled his eyes and started to unbutton his shirt, "you don't care if you're going to bruise more?"

"Not really, not right now," Scott confirmed as he bared his chest and motioned to the tented fabric covering his groin.

"Well, then, I guess we'll see if you are merely good or better," she giggled as she slipped out of her shoes and started to undo her own clothing.

After a moment of watching his eyes follow her more openly than ever before, she paused in her undressing to stand in only her underwear. She placed her hands on her hips as she considered him back, and she saw him swallow, but not break their shared gaze. She let herself smile, then directed him simply, "Take them off, and show me how hard you are, boy."

He blushed but quickly tossed his pajama pants to the side. He ran his hands along both sides of his inner thighs to rest on either side of his swollen cock.

"Renee said you couldn't get it up for her curious new friends or for her, but tonight?"

"Tonight, yes, I managed, because Miss Renee was patient in spite of what you might think," he said, indicating a newer bruise on his chest. "This is for you to use as you wish, Miss Joanna," he intoned. He used his hand movement to draw attention to the little jump his cock made in response, but he didn't touch it. "All of me," he added, licking his lips.

Joanna frowned, not at his cock, which was what she wanted to see in this context, after all, but at the bruise. While their target might like such things, Joanna did not like to see marks from anyone else on her partner … was she really starting to think of him that way? She needed to do this for the mission, even if she wasn't getting wet, and that was something she could change. "Is Renee right? Do your clients often hurt you?"

He tilted his head with a swing of his gaze to the left before shaking his head. "Not often. I'm not listed as a roughboy, but," he quickly added, recalling her self-description, "we're all trained in how to react to rougher stuff. My dick reacts easily."

"But not to the people Renee introduced you to …"

"No, I'm sorry; I'm not sure why. Boys are generally good to go," he added with a grin.

"So they say," Joanna replied as she changed position so she was straddling his hips, his cock pushing up just above where she sat down on his thighs. He moaned and arched up, then licked his lips. "What about this do you like?"

He blinked, then lifted his head to view as much of her as he could see before meeting her eyes. "You, on top, so close but not touching me yet, not letting me touch you. So difficult to refrain," he said, clenching his hands before slipping them up toward his head.

"I didn't tell you that you couldn't touch me."

Their eyes kept focus on each other as he frowned just slightly and considered what she'd said. Joanna could almost imagine what he was thinking, because she'd heard it from the boys she rented through The Chain, but also her occasional female bottoms. "I'm not trying to trick you. I'll tell you when I don't want you to do something. Chill?"

Scott just lowered his hands and touched her knees, then caressed up her thighs, his eyes locked on hers. He ignored her center and stroked his fingertips up her hips and then over the sides of her torso, his touch gentle and slowly moving. His hands lightly outlined her bra, and he sat up as best he could with her on top of him, stretching one arm far back to provide leverage so he could skim over her chest to one shoulder. From there he trailed down her arms with both hands, his body trembling as he slowly lowered his torso down. He had a lot of control under his very lean frame, and his muscles tightened from his movements.

He was breathing hard by the time he was lowered again, and his hands simply stroked along the top of her thighs. "I could do more, Miss Joanna, but you have me a bit trapped," he pointed out, licking his lips.

It was an unexpected comment, and she lifted her hand, automatically freezing when she saw his look of terror at her hand as his gaze shifted away from her. He was trained to suffer it; he didn't naturally enjoy it ... Joanna's eyes widened when she realized this brought a sudden rush of moisture to her groin.

He must have felt it, because his gaze went back to hers, and he frowned slightly. "Miss Joanna? Did you want to hit me because I spoke out of line or because I said something right? You did tell me to ask questions," he quickly amended. This entire time his hands had continued to caress her thighs, not even pausing when he was afraid.

Joanna lowered her hand and stopped one of his with hers; its companion stopped as well, and his eyes bored into hers, hanging on the moment. "I like a bit of attitude, so it was a good thing."

He paused for a second, then spoke up in a stronger voice, "You should let your hand fly then, since this is your pleasure I'm trying to figure out."

Instead of slapping him, she used her free hand to reach down and grip his cock, tugging it up and into her fist. He groaned and started to narrow his eyes before opening them wide and maintaining focus on hers. "I do not like being told what to do, attitude or not," she told him with a lopsided smile.

"You've got my attention, Miss; I'm listening and learning how to please you," he replied. He used his free hand to stroke down to her inner thigh and up to the spot of moisture she knew had soaked through her underwear.

"Are you blocked?" she asked, using the slang term for the most common form of male birth control.

"Yes, breeding's an extra fee that no one's paid for yet, Miss," he replied, arching up into her fist, moving her hand so it teased the wet spot on her panties.

"No one, huh? I'll house that away for later," she said as she used her hand on his to raise it to her bra as she leaned down, forcing him to move his other hand and run it along her arm as she kissed him.

As they kissed, he used his hands to caress her breast and then ran his hands along the band to the back, where he quickly undid the clasp. The bra was an odd piece of clothing: once despised as a form of patriarchal torture, it had become a useful and lovely item for the more ample-chested. Thinking of that brought Judy to mind again, so Joanna tried to push that sad thought into a more useful one by remembering that while she wore bras more for utilitarian reasons, she'd learned to use them as a tool in her lovemaking kit. Of course, with men, a bra never failed to arouse interest, as it teased by refusing to share what was underneath.

She wagged her eyebrows at him as she pulled back just a bit, and he smiled as she sat back to take her bra off. Using the motion of tossing it to the side, she stood up before settling back down, her center trapping his dick underneath. He moaned and fisted his hands in the sheets but kept his eyes on her. She pulled his hands up and placed them on her waist. She ran her own hands over her breasts and nodded for him to follow course.

Joanna arched her back to thrust out her breasts as he ran his hands under them and cupped them before reaching up with one finger on each to rub each nipple. She rewarded him by grinding down on his cock. After a few minutes he tried pinching, but her pause in grinding made him back off, and she smiled with a "good boy" comment that made him gasp and arch underneath her.

As he learned about her, so, too, did she learn about him. He liked feedback, especially positive comments. He became less verbal the more aroused he got, yet never tried to push them faster, only gently adjusting his touches and sounds, his eyes always meeting hers when she looked down. He was trained to read his client; she'd noticed it before, but what she had thought might be boring in bed turned out to be a slow steady rise in enjoyment.

"Stop," she said as she felt herself start to tense up a bit too much. Immediately he stilled his body, dropping his hands to her hips to hold them lightly. Joanna stood up, and he moaned but didn't move. She surveyed his body and found new bruises along his thighs, hips, and even stomach, but his breathing was steady if a bit fast; his cock jerked a few times as his hands scratched against the bed cover. "Saddle or ride?" she casually asked, making herself wait for an answer.

Scott rolled his head to the side and down so he could look at her without moving much, though his fingers were now digging into the bed cover. "Both? Either? Neither? Miss, please," he offered every option without any arrogant tone. The pleading seemed genuine, not faked, not afraid.

Joanna glanced at the clock on the wall over the bed and tried to calculate how long they might have. What had Renee and he done exactly? She hadn't gotten to really ask, and she wondered what the gentler of two owners might do in such a situation. Gentle or not, she slapped one of his thighs and told him to move down a bit, so his feet were flat on the ground, but his butt was firmly on the bed.

"Giddy up," she chuckled as she climbed on top of him. He grinned up at her as she spread herself and took his cock in one hand to guide him. They both moaned as she settled him deep inside and then began to ride. He reached out to her but stopped, so she captured his hands in hers and settled them on her hips while she leaned down just enough to use his chest as a brace for one hand.

In a few seconds he arched up with his hips, and she hissed out, "Yes," so he continued. Soon they were matching strokes well, and he had moved one hand to one of her breasts while she forced the other to his head, guiding him to sit up. That created another slight tremor through his body as they adjusted their positions so that they were sitting up, her legs wrapped around him, before they resumed their thrusts.

He moved his hand from her breast to stroke her clit, and in a few minutes, he was gasping as she came hard around him, biting down on his shoulder hard enough to bruise without the medication. "Please," he moaned, and Joanna pulled back in surprise, her eyes trained on the red welt. "Please may I come, Mistress?" he continued, his eyes barely open now but still meeting hers when she looked at him.

She forced their hips down hard as the final waves of her own orgasm hit. "Yes," she screamed as she pulled him tight against her in a hug.

His own cry came immediately, and he stiffened for a few seconds under her before slumping as much as their position allowed. His breathing was shallow, interspersed with other sounds. Joanna pulled back and found him looking away until she forced him to face her. "What's wrong?" She was utterly confused by his reaction.

"Thank you, thank you, thank you," he was babbling with a smile as tears streamed from his blue eyes.

Joanna clutched him to her with a sudden horrible question about what his regular clients and Renee must be like to create such a reaction from a very average yet enjoyable sexual encounter. The idea that she could hurt him, or even harm him, had been a bigger turn-on than she'd hoped, but this certainly hadn't been an evening with Jack in terms of intensity, at least not for her. It had been … good; it had been relaxing, but it hadn't been great for her. If his continued babbling was any indication, he considered his orgasm to have been beyond anything he deserved, though Joanna loved to see all her partners come.

Joanna couldn't stop thinking about it all as they took a shower then redressed and lay down to try to get a few hours of sleep. As he lay there looking at her until his eyes closed of exhaustion, she found herself petting him and wondering just what she was starting to feel. Luckily Renee just smiled at them when she returned and didn't press things the next morning, when the investigation was swinging into full gear.

Chapter Eight

"There she is." E'Lige took Joanna's hand and led her to meet the shorter, black-haired woman. "Miss Richards! Welcome back to Bragg," he said, stretching out his hand and putting on what was clearly a strained smile.

Joanna tried not to stare at the unimpressive woman who shook hands with the Karkan. In her mind she had created a monster the size of a small vehicle, one with horrible features who was capable of taking away the one she loved. Instead, the woman looked very ordinary. The imperious air about her came from the way she moved, the look in her eyes, and the precision of her smile. Her photos and descriptions didn't do her justice, and Joanna bit her tongue to keep from punching her in the face right here and now. Looks could be deceiving and could be used as an advantage; even small girls learned that from their history lessons.

"This is my special guest, Miss Joanna McMillin," E'Lige introduced the two women.

Richards shook the redhead's hand with a slight frown. "McMillin? As in the McMillin Family." She emphasized the last word and bobbed her head once.

"Yes. Technically I'm the Scion, but I'm here on honeymoon, not Family business," Joanna answered with a forced smile.

"Interesting. I've had some … dealings with the Great Families," Richards replied bitterly, and Joanna heard the monster underneath her voice. No, this was the right target. Richards then turned to the Karkan. "Mr. E'Lige, we have business to discuss, but I would first like to go to my room. The shuttle ride was a bit bumpier than it should have been."

"Of course." The resort owner motioned for the bellhops to help with her bags.

"Don't ever speak unless I give you permission!" an angry, loud female voice broke through the crowd.

"What was that?" Richards demanded.

The Karkan looked and found the source. "It is them again. Miss McMillin ..."

"Oh, I'm so sorry. I'll deal with it," Joanna promised. She took off toward the direction of her "wife's" voice with both E'Lige and Richards behind her.

"Renee!" Joanna hissed as the other woman kicked their "husband" lying on the floor. "I can't leave them alone, not even for even a second?" Joanna muttered, turning to Richards.

The crime chief's grasp on the redhead's arm was tighter than expected as she whispered excitedly, "What do you mean?"

Joanna pulled out of their target's grip and kept her eyes on the scene as security joined them, Agent Markeni eying her for a moment before jerking Scott up by one arm. "Renee, do you have to cause a scene out here in public?" Joanna tossed out. "I brought him here because you said you wanted to check out this gift, but if you can't get yourself under control ..."

"Oh, yes, you think he's so sweet, so obedient; that's a game he plays with you, my dear," Renee replied as she frowned at Markeni and grabbed Scott's other arm.

"My grandmother would never give us an inferior gift," Joanna retorted as she crossed her arms over her chest.

"I think I may be able to help," Richards spoke up as she stepped between the angry Gaians and E'Lige. "We are all sisters here; we can solve this without other ... interference," she said, casting a disgusted look around them.

E'Lige interjected, "I am trying to be understanding of your culture, but I must ensure all my guests' pleasure in the resort. If you cannot control your behavior in public, I will have to insist that you leave. Which I would hate."

E'Lige directed a pleading look to Joanna that Richards followed with her dark eyes just as Joanna tracked her reactions.

"What did he do?" Richards asked as she returned her gaze to the man being held by one of his mistresses and a security guard.

Joanna caught Scott's eye and nodded very slightly to let him know this was his target. "You know what, Miss Richards, if you can talk some sense into my wife," she emphasized the term, "more power to you. I'm sure if I say much else, I'll regret it later."

"We'll just talk," Richards pointed out to Renee, spreading her hands out in a welcoming gesture. "I have an idea that could help both you and me."

Renee and Joanna exchanged looks until the larger woman sighed and nodded. "Fine, fine, I don't like us fighting, so ..."

"I'll leave it in your hands, for now," said E'Lige, whose tone implied he would have his people watching, then he asked, "Miss Richards. Would you still like an escort to your room?"

Renee spoke up. "I'll walk my sister to her room. He can carry the luggage. You are capable of that, right?" she added, dropping Scott's arm. Agent Markeni released his arm at nods from Joanna and the resort owner.

Scott nodded as he scrambled to accept the bags from the other woman. He glanced at Joanna briefly but then shrank back as Renee came over and adjusted his grip on the bags.

"Well ..." The Karkan looked at his new business partner.

"This will be fine," Richards answered, a smile clearly directed more toward Scott than any of them. It hadn't taken much at all to intrigue her. She turned to the resort owner and said, "I will call your office in an hour or so, Mr. E'Lige."

E'Lige waited until the group was dispersed and he was alone with Joanna. "I've never seen her react to anything in the resort like that. She had a fire in her eyes I don't think I've ever seen. It was a bit unnerving."

"I'm sure it will all work out," Joanna tried to reassure them both as she narrowed her eyes at the retreating trio. When Scott looked up as they entered the elevator, she gave him a simple nod, then allowed the resort owner to take her out for conversation and food in a public venue.

Miss Renee glanced at Scott as they both waited for their target to open her room door. "Come in, Dr. Brownlow," Richards invited them. The women had chatted during the elevator ride and the walk, while Scott had just carried the bags and stayed as much in the background as he could. "Put my luggage on the bed, boy," their target ordered him, so Scott did so as he kept his eyes and ears open to everything happening.

This morning there had been some minor reprogramming with his chip, activating the recording part of it that Dells sometimes used during training to track and grade their work . He didn't think it had been used in a few years, but then again, he couldn't access the recordings, so for all he knew it might have been recording this entire time, though Miss Joanna had insisted it be turned off before she'd used her access code that morning. The specialist had used some device to ensure that its live feed went only to IGA and the two of them, and that it wouldn't go to Dells, which couldn't get a feed this far from Gaia anyway. Scott prayed that was correct.

"It was very nice meeting you, Ms. Richards," said Renee, offering her hand to the other woman.

"Must you run off?" The shorter woman frowned sadly while also obviously checking out Scott. He thought that there was something about her that seemed a bit too eager, even though he knew this was what they wanted. "Please stay and talk a while. It's been years since I've spoken to a sister from Gaia. Even women on natural worlds seem a little strange, and don't get started on the oppressive ones."

Miss Renee looked from Scott to Miss Richards and smiled slightly. "I imagine there are many things you miss about Gaia."

Miss Richards chuckled softly as she approached Scott. He stood perfectly still as she looked him over slowly. "Isn't gold the symbol of private ownership?" she asked, touching his silver chain.

"Yes, but he's really owned by the McMillin Family. He's with us as a potential husband; we haven't decided to keep him yet." Scott swallowed and looked down at the comment. "My wife has many wonderful traits, not the least of which is her Family, but it's ridiculous how soft-hearted she is; she tends to be too lenient with him." With one step Miss Renee had him by the ear and snarled at him, "I'm getting tired of him already!"

"I would gladly pay you for a few hours with him."

"Hell, I'd give him to you for a while each day to keep him out of my hair. It might save my marriage to have some time away from him. She brings him all the way here, then decides she needs to connect with the owner – some business thing for her Family, I guess. Leaves me with him for the bulk of what's supposed to be our honeymoon; what kind of honeymoon is that?"

"Well, the Great Families … they play by different rules, don't they?" Miss Richards' cold tone made Scott glance up at Miss Renee, who gave him a tiny shake of her head, so he looked back down.

"That's the way things are," Miss Renee simply replied.

"For now," Miss Richards stated softly, and Scott couldn't help but suck in a breath which luckily both women seemed to have missed. "No, no. I insist on paying." Miss Richards took out her wallet with a smile. "Owing anyone a favor can be a problem, I've learned the hard way."

Miss Renee put a fist under her chin while she considered, and Scott's stomach tightened with every passing second. "I'll tell you what, Ms. Richards. I'll let you have him, starting tomorrow, for a credit an hour."

"Surely you're joking."

"No. You'd be doing me a big favor, giving me time to calm down and figure out what is truly fueling my anger. But –" and her sharp directed tone and grabbing of his chin made Scott tremble as he met her eyes – "you will be a very good boy while Ms. Richards watches you, understand?"

"Yes, Miss Renee, this boy understands."

"Wow." Miss Richards released the word with her breath, and Miss Renee lifted one eyebrow at Scott as she released him. "It's a deal." Miss Richards shook hands with the specialist. Taking one last look at the boy, she escorted them to the door. "That's the best deal I ever made," she laughed, pinching his butt as he walked out the door.

"I hope he behaves better for you." Grabbing Scott by the ear, Miss Renee led them down the hallway to their room.

Scott could feel Miss Renee watching him take their dinner from the room service personnel and set it out on the table. Unlike his client, she didn't expect him to sit with her but did allow him to take his plate and set it up on the other chair's seat while he sat near her on the floor. They'd stayed inside the rest of the afternoon and evening while she primarily ignored him to look over something on her computer until she'd ridden him hard just a short while before ordering their meal. They were both just in hotel robes, and he wondered if he'd be used again before his client got home.

For some reason it had been more difficult to get and keep his cock up this afternoon; he hoped he'd be able to manage with this Miss Richards. He'd probably have to think of the single session he'd enjoyed with his client. And he had enjoyed it, something that he found rarer in his profession with each passing year. That's what they made the pills for that Dells gave out. Too bad he hadn't been allowed to bring any because of travel restrictions.

"The meal is served, Miss Renee?"

Miss Renee nodded. "Did I hurt your ego back there?" she asked.

"Miss?"

"When I told Richards she could have you for a credit an hour. I thought that might have bruised your ego."

"No, Miss Renee," he replied quickly, though in fact he had been disappointed with the sum. "I understand that I have to get close to Miss Richards, and that I need to obey you." Scott set the last of his table setting on the chair, then knelt by her feet so they could eat.

They ate in silence with just the occasional petting from Miss Renee's hand on his head. It felt familiar and calming, yet he found himself frowning simply because it wasn't his client. Another woman, a dangerous woman, would soon be touching him, so he damped those feelings down and leaned into the touches.

"Go ahead and clean up," Miss Renee ordered as she stood, and he rose as well. "I'm going to take a shower, then you may as well." She caught his chin in her hand and gave him a smile. "You did great with everything today."

"Thank you, Miss Renee," he blushed, then stepped back and bowed so she could leave.

A few minutes later, the door opened, and Miss Joanna hurried in. "Scott!" she said, looking around. "Where's Renee?"

"In the shower, Miss Joanna."

"Oh." Miss Joanna came to a stop by the table and looked at all the plates and remaining food.

"Would you care for anything, Miss Joanna? We could order again if there isn't enough, or you'd prefer something else." Please stay and eat; please let me do this for you, he pleaded silently.

"No, I already ate with E'Lige after his meeting with Richards, who seemed in a better mood, though I think she's far more cold-blooded than her façade. How did it go?" she asked, surprising him just a touch, because he realized he was expecting those sorts of queries from her now. It didn't feel normal, but it was feeling more comfortable, so he tried to consider what information she would need.

"Miss Renee arranged for me to meet with Miss Richards tomorrow for a credit an hour," he replied.

"A credit an hour?"

"She insisted on paying something," Renee explained as she returned from her shower. "We'll split it fifty-fifty."

His client rolled her eyes at the comment. "Do you want me to leave?" Miss Joanna asked, noting the bathrobe the brunette wore.

"No. We've all seen naked women here."

Miss Joanna nodded, then focused on Scott, even though her next question wasn't directed at him. "Isn't one credit an insult to him?"

"Yes. I'm sure he normally earns far more back on Gaia, but I felt it would show my disdain more and play into her desires. She loves them abused. As far as I'm concerned, he's a worthless piece I'm just tolerating out of respect for my bride and her powerful family. She hates the Great Families, by the way, as we thought she might, given her history with them. She might tell him more if she thinks I won't believe him and that you don't care much to interact with us now that you're on family business."

"That's how you described me?"

"She seemed to buy it. Did you get into their meeting at all?"

Miss Joanna shook her head and moved closer to him, so he leaned into her just enough to touch his arm to hers. She ran a hand up and down his arm, but he kept his eyes on her as she had liked earlier that morning. "No, not into the meeting, but afterwards while I was spreading my luck around for him and a handful of special members," and she flipped her hair with a chuckle, "he did mention that she'd confirmed the timetable. Apparently, she has a shipment set to arrive in just a day."

He caught Miss Renee's eyes flitting from him to his client a few times; she didn't look annoyed or jealous, but instead oddly satisfied by what she saw. "I've promised he'll be at Richards' door first thing in the morning, so perhaps we should call it a night, given that it's getting late."

Scott stood outside Miss Richards' door. He looked nervously up and down the hall, then knocked on the door once more.

"What the hell are you doing here?" Miss Richards stood in her robe, glaring at him from her partly opened door.

"Please," Scott pleaded, kneeling in front of her, "my mistress told me to come."

"It's seven in the morning! Go away!"

It was time to play the abused boy at full tilt, so Scott threw himself through the doorway and across her feet. "Please, Ma'am. My mistress is very angry with me."

After a few moments, the woman opened the door all the way. "Come in, boy," she ordered with a chuckle.

"Thank you, Ma'am."

Miss Richards rubbed her eyes as she shut the door. Scott knelt and she turned to stare down at him. "What's your mistress' room number?"

"289, Ma'am."

Miss Richards walked around him as she reached for the phone. She watched him with an amused smile as she listened to the rings. "Dr. Brownlow? ... I have him here ... No, actually, I would like to keep him for a while ... Yes." She tapped the slave with her foot. "She wants to talk to you."

"Thank you, Ma'am." Scott moved forward a couple of steps on his knees before taking the phone. "Yes, Miss Renee ... Yes, Miss Renee." He hung up the phone and glanced at the crime chief, trying to make his gaze pathetic and hopeful at the same time. Those were feelings he'd had often, so it shouldn't be hard to fake them, and it seemed to work, as she smiled.

"You're staying here with me for a few hours," she informed him, that smile turning into something darker, something he'd seen on other clients' faces, on Jones' face. "Do whatever I tell you to, and we'll get along fine."

Scott fell back onto protocols. "Yes, Ma'am." He crawled to her feet and bent down to kiss them. He smiled slightly as she led him to the bed by his hair. He made sure to follow closely, since loose hair tended to hurt more than braided hair when gripped and Miss Renee had insisted that he keep it loose while they were at the resort. While his client and her target – no, their target – might like it rough, he never sought it out unless he knew it would please the woman who held his leash.

"Take off your clothes, boy." Miss Richards sat watching as the man undressed slowly and deliberately. She reached up and gently pushed him onto his knees. "Do you know how long it's been since I've had a man, a real boy from Gaia?"

Scott just smiled and turned his head, so his lips brushed her hand resting on his shoulder possessively.

Miss Richards took him by his hair but was gentle as she directed him up onto the bed next to her. Scott lay on his back, lifting his hands over his head but keeping them relaxed. Slowly she ran her fingers over his face, pausing for him to lick each one of her fingers.

"Please me," she ordered, throwing her robe onto the floor.

Scott moved to the floor and knelt in front of her. With a fake but practiced smile, he started at the bottom of her feet. He imagined he was pleasing Miss Joanna, so slowly his cock started to rise. By the time he was done with Miss Richards' feet he was hard enough that she chuckled.

Joanna stood silently as Renee talked on the phone. "Is she letting him stay?"

"Yes. The plan is working well."

"I hope he can handle her," Joanna stated as she sat down to listen and watch the action being monitored. MOI's technology was allowing them to tap into the monitors that Dells had sent, using Scott's chip to access his visual and auditory senses. The fact that both the escort agency and the organization she fought for could do that was terrifying. Only an idiot thought the chips only monitored health and controlled database access. Seeing it in action made Joanna feel a bit sick. She added that to a long list of things she didn't like about Gaia.

At least the readings were coming through, and they would help IGA get Richards locked up. A giant view of the crime boss was not doing anything for her appetite. The breakfast they'd had delivered earlier was only partly eaten.

"He's basically doing what he does for Dells," Renee's voice interrupted an intense exchange of passionate sounds from the feed.

"Don't remind me," Joanna practically growled, but that only made the other woman chuckle as she popped one of the native fruits into her mouth.

Scott moved his cuffed hands slightly so that he could get a better look up at Miss Richards, who was perched on his chest to return his gaze. They'd been at it for three of her orgasms, with none for him, which was very normal, and she had finally gotten a bit more creative around lunchtime. "What did you do to upset your mistress so much? It certainly can't be this," she stated, running her hand up his arm to his cuffed wrist.

"I'm no good, Ma'am."

"I think you're very good."

"Thank you, Ma'am." Scott glanced sadly away.

"Tell me what you did exactly," she ordered, nipping at his ear.

"Her tea was too hot this morning." He closed his eyes as her teeth closed on the earlobe. They'd come up with a list of errors he could say he made that reflected more poorly on Miss Renee than on his service.

"Then I won't tell you to make me tea." Miss Richards stood up and reached for her robe. She tied the belt, then unlocked his wrists. "Come help me with my bath."

A half hour later, Scott was helping Miss Richards dress. She slapped him on the ass as she slipped into her shoes, but when no other physical contact followed, Scott smiled and thanked her. "Get dressed and get out of here. I may see you again. Just shut the door behind you."

"Yes, Ma'am." Scott bowed as Miss Richards left. Quickly he dressed and walked out the door into the hall until he was around the corner and could break into a jog to use the stairways. Could he use the elevator by himself? Not back on Gaia, and since the resort was supposed to respect the traditions of the worlds their guests came from, he wasn't going to try. At least going down was much easier than going up a few floors. Soon he was back at room 289. He knocked on the door three quick beats.

Miss Renee opened the door to let him in. "How'd it go?"

"I planted the bug in her shirt, just as you ordered, Miss Renee. I don't think she knows."

"I should think not, given how many times we practiced that the past few days."

Miss Joanna hurried back into the living room from the bathroom. "They should be having their meeting soon," she told them both, pointedly not looking at Scott. Had he done something wrong with Miss Richards? Was he supposed to ask her questions?

"Yup, we're getting a second feed from IGA cameras in E'Lige's office," Miss Renee confirmed, pointing to one monitor and then to the other, "and the feed he placed on her shirt is there." She tapped the screen that showed the hallway on the way to the resort owner's office.

"Looks like you did a good job," Joanna told him as she sat down. He paused, then knelt on the floor between both women sitting on the couch. This gave him a view of both monitors but also let him lean into either one should they touch him, though he moved just slightly closer to his client to begin with.

"Ah, Miss Richards. You're right on time, as always."

"There are no hidden cameras in here, are there?" Richards' voice asked tautly.

"Of course not. I'm offended you should ask again after we already met yesterday. After all of our meetings," E'Lige emphasized.

"We can't be too careful," Richards replied, and they saw her take a disc-shaped device from her pocket and carry it around the room. As promised by MOI and IGA, it didn't detect their equipment. The entire team sighed in relief. "I would not like to think you were stupid enough to try to cross us."

"You have my complete cooperation, Miss Richards."

"You do not sound too happy about that."

"Your people have hardly given me a choice in the matter."

"Yes. I am sorry it had to be this way. In the end, you will be glad you agreed to this partnership."

"Umph. Just what do your people want my resort for? More drugs, correct? I do not want the IGA linking me to any of your business."

"Once everything is in motion, they will have no reason to even look at this place."

"When a new wave of drug dealing springs up around here, they'll come straight to me. They do not like my business as it is, Miss Richards, as I've pointed out to you in the past."

"That particular venture of ours will not be dealt with from here."

"I put my foot down on your slave dealings! That may fly on many planets, but it is not how I was raised, and while I must allow guests to bring their ... people with them, I won't be part of the trade."

"We won't be trading in slaves from here – hardly enough room in the underground for that. Just some research."

"So, drugs."

"No. Our scientists will not be dealing with known illegal substances."

There was a pause then, of a good five beats, before the resort owner could be heard sighing. "What exactly will they be dealing with then?"

"Something beyond your understanding. Not a slam on your maleness, I assure you. It is also beyond mine. You really don't want to know more; trust me on that. There might be some profit in it as well if you prove to be amiable. Fight us, and we cannot say how safe the rest of your resorts will be. People are unlikely to come to places they are likely to die at."

E'Lige shot her a fierce look but nodded his head slowly. He reached into a desk drawer and took out an envelope. "As requested, the codes have been opened for you to reset, so you can control your little research facilities."

"Excellent!" She stood up suddenly and left without another word.

In a few moments E'Lige took a breath and looked directly into one of the IGA cameras. "I hope you got that, because that woman is pushing my patience, and even we peace-loving Karkans have limits."

Joanna looked up as they saw Richards leave the resort owner's office. "This doesn't help us very much. We already knew they were developing a new drug."

"We'll see where she goes, but if our device works, we'll have her security codes, and maybe she'll venture into the labs," Renee pointed out. Joanna reached down and massaged one of Scott's shoulders for a second until the women's eyes met and the younger woman leaned back in her seat, leaving the boy to look down at his legs. Renee shook her head, then closed the connection to E'Lige's office, opening a second screen for the bug showing Richards, who was going down in a service elevator at the moment.

"If she doesn't go into the labs?"

"We have a man on the inside, literally," Renee chuckled as she patted Scott's shoulder, making Joanna frown again.

Unfortunately, all Richards did that afternoon was reset the code and meet with two women, both Gaian, it seemed. That night Joanna found herself pulling Scott a bit closer toward her when they lay down to sleep. Perhaps she could convince Renee to watch his ... arrangement with Richards the next day while she went back over records on the criminal activities in the galaxy. There had to be something there, something that could get IGA to allow her down into those labs. Before she'd been worried about being uncovered, but now she was so close to discovering what could make that monster pay that she was thinking of acting more like Judy.

"Come in, Dr. Brownlow," Miss Richards invited when she opened her resort room door for them the next morning. This time their target was dressed and smiling, looking quite pleased and almost relaxed.

"This works out quite well for me." Miss Renee walked away with the shorter woman so the boy couldn't hear. "I received a call from one of my research colleagues right before your call. There seems to be a small problem at one of the nearby colonies. Part of being a xenospecialist means doing such things from time to time. My wife is still enamored of her alien, so ..." and the brunette glanced back at Scott with a tight smile. He was kneeling, eyes on the ground, hands folded on his lap, a slight tremor running through his body, acting every bit the abused creature he was supposed to be, which wasn't difficult to do if he just kept thinking about the disciplinarian at Dells. "I could just leave him in our room, but that's like asking for problems."

"True, very true. Give them too much freedom, and they wreak havoc on the world," Miss Richards agreed as she walked over to him. He knelt up immediately under her direct gaze. She folded her arms across her chest and glanced back at the medic. "I do have to make an inspection today, but I imagine he won't understand what he's seeing in a lab."

Scott glanced at Miss Renee, who just gave him a tiny shake of her head while Miss Richards reached out and stroked his hair. "Boy, do you know what a lab is?"

He quickly played dumb by answering, "Isn't that a dog, Miss Renee? A type of dog?"

Both women chuckled, and Miss Richards patted his cheek, then looked back at the doctor. "I'll take good care of him."

"I appreciate it greatly. Joanna may want him back in the evenings, but frankly, who can tell, since she's indulging in her alien fetish. Great Families, huh?"

Miss Richards rolled her eyes and agreed but continued to focus her attention on him, so he sighed and leaned closer to her. He knew it was all a trick to get closer to her, and he knew that Miss Joanna was really just a client, but he badly wanted to correct them both. She didn't have any strange alien interests; their one time together had shown him that, as well as just how much he really needed to find a way to stay with her.

"Scott, walk me to the door," the specialist barked, so Miss Richards stepped back so he could stand up. At the open door, Miss Renee grabbed him firmly by the shoulder, whispering quickly. "Be calm and chill, we're always watching and listening. If things get out of hand, keep it together, and we'll get to you as fast as we can."

"Yes, Mistress," Scott said, loud enough for Miss Richards to hear. As he shut the door, he felt the target's hands slide up his back. He straightened as she laid her head against his back.

"You're going to be staying with me for a while, boy," she purred. Miss Richards turned him around and peered hungrily up at his face. She felt him shudder as she ran her fingers down his cheek to his chest. "I think we'll have a very interesting time, don't you?"

Scott looked steadily over her short black hair. "I hope to please you, Ma'am." He closed his eyes as she slowly unbuttoned his shirt and slid it off. He had yesterday to gauge from, so he knew that while he wouldn't get much pleasure himself, he wasn't going to be hurt either.

Miss Richards pulled him to her bed, where she sat and felt his long, strong legs through his thin pants. "Go get me a glass of white wine," she ordered with a nod toward the bar. Wine was plentiful at the casino, and though his "owners" didn't indulge, Miss Richards did. It might help loosen her tongue, so he decided to try to steer her toward more consumption during his visit. He hoped that would only be during the day and that Miss Joanna would call for him in the evening. He needed to try stay in the here and now while attempting to get information his client could use.

Scott bowed his head and started to rise so he could fetch the drink but found her fingernails dug into his arm. "Not so fast. I want to enjoy every moment," she whispered and released his arm.

Scott walked slowly, making each movement as fluid and as sensual as he could. Though his eyes focused on pouring a full glass, considerably more than what was considered one serving, he felt her watching his every move. He purposely licked his lips slowly as he lifted the glass up and headed back to her and was rewarded with an audible sigh. He returned and offered her the wine on bended knee.

Miss Richards took a long sip as her smile widened. "I just made arrangements that will make me rich enough to buy my way back to Gaia – hell, to control Gaia. Fuck up every not-so-great family."

Her laughter made Scott's stomach drop.

"I have lots to celebrate, and you're going to help me." She leaned back on one elbow. "Remove my shoes, then stand up and remove the rest of your clothes, slowly. Turn on some music while you're at it. Put on a show."

Scott bent over her shoes, his lips brushing each before gently sliding them off her feet. After a quick massage of each foot, he reached for the radio and turned it on. He rose with the beat and began to unbutton his shirt as he swayed in time. Control Gaia? He hoped Miss Joanna and Miss Renee and IGA and whoever had power were watching everything, because that sounded very bad to him.

Scott took a few deep breaths as Miss Richards got off his face to answer the phone; he knew better than to make any move to wipe her moisture from him, and given that she was being kind to him, he rather liked the reminder. His sides still ached a bit from the bruising Miss Joanna had left when she'd ridden him, even if it had been more from the medication the doctor had given him than her being rough . He watched Miss Richards' every move from where he lay, one arm under his head, his eyes half closed, as she spoke to the caller who had interrupted them. After a few minutes, he shrugged and glanced up at the clock opposite the bed near the in-room entertainment kiosk. An hour had passed since he'd arrived.

Miss Richards chuckled lightly as she hung up the receiver. She mussed her hair as she stood at the foot of the bed, looking him over. "I've had the best news," she announced as she crawled on top of the covers to straddle his hips.

Scott lay still except for his one free hand, which he used to caress her knee.

"I'm just dying to share this with someone." She leaned down over him, so her elbows rested on either side of his chest. "Why shouldn't I tell you? Who would you tell, boy? I'm sure neither of your owners care, and I believe Renee might even find it shameful if you attempted to tell her. She might be a bit … rough, but I sense she has honor, natural honor."

"Mistresses Renee and Joanna are both honorable," he whispered, but the woman didn't seem to hear him.

"If you did," she said, moving close enough for his tongue to reach and lick tiny tickling strokes along her arm, so he did so as he remained focused on her words, "I'd just have to make sure you never spoke again. And it would be a pity," she went on, running a finger over his lips as he hungrily licked the digits, "to see you lose such a talented part of yourself." Scott froze for a moment. She might not like to hurt boys herself, but her tone told him that she had no problem ordering others to do so. Richards rolled off him and lay on her side, one leg still thrown over him. "Ask me to tell you what's on my mind."

"Please, Ma'am." Scott focused his aqua eyes on hers as his free hand stroked her calf slowly. Dells had trained him for almost any response he might be asked to give a client, and it rarely failed to get the desired results in that moment, even if it didn't create repeat clients. "Share your thoughts, just a little, so I might help you celebrate better."

She moved his hand up to her mound so he could arouse her once more as she spoke. "That wonderful new business I mentioned earlier is going better than planned. Our first trial subjects have been installed. I'll never have to worry about finding new customers again, and soon every world will be eager for our products."

Both Joanna and Renee sat up straighter as they heard the threat against Scott. "We should …" but Renee was interrupted by the buzz from their IGA private communication device, which she answered by putting it on speaker.

"Did I just hear Richards say that they already have test subjects in their lab?" Chief Blim's voice asked as she frowned at them on the screen.

"That's what it sounded like to us," Renee agreed while Joanna moved over on the couch so they could both see.

"Can we go in yet?" Joanna asked as politely as she could.

"I'm getting a plan set in motion. Agent A'Tarick will contact you when we are ready; I'll send Agent Markeni to your room when we are good to go. Do not," Chief Blim emphasized, looking directly at Joanna, "go down there alone, no matter what happens. Understood?"

"Yes, yes," Joanna shook her head slightly but agreed verbally, which earned her a glare from her MOI partner.

"We'll be in touch," Chief Blim assured them before signing off.

"Nothing to do but watch the show, then," Renee offered with a chuckle.

"I wish he didn't have to do all … that," Joanna angrily said with a wave toward the monitors. She hadn't felt this protective of a boy in years, not since college and losing her twin. She didn't even feel that way about Jack. Paying for her regular time was simply protecting her spot, not protecting him; Betty did that. But that boy doing all of this for her – Joanna ran her hands through her hair in frustration.

"He's used to it; it's what men were made for," Renee pointed out, making Joanna roll her eyes at the medic, "and there's no other way to get so much information in such a short time. And I don't think you or I are Richards' type. Everything I've seen about her suggests SexCompt 5, or close to it," Renee added.

"So, she's a pervert as well as a criminal," Joanna tossed out. She liked men, liked them a lot, but to never have a female lover? It seemed so very unnatural. "I need a drink," she declared as the sounds and images transitioned to something more explicit than she really wanted to see.

Joanna drank her third cup of hot chocolate an hour later as she watched uncomfortably. Cocoa was expensive off Gaia, so she was now very glad she'd brought a stash of it with her as she squirmed in her seat when the moans reached a climax and the female voice cried out again. Joanna looked over at Renee with an exaggerated glare when the other returned with room service. "If they do it again, I'm going to be sick." She stood up to stretch her legs. "Fathersucker! I really have a headache now."

"This food will help, plus I've talked with Agents O'Heironul and A'Jaliou while I was out."

"The real reason you went out."

"Indeed," Renee confirmed as she brought the containers over to the table. "They are just as anxious to get down to that underground network as we are, but they won't disobey Blim unless things get really cocked up."

On the monitors another round of sex was interrupted by a buzz at the suite's door. Richards turned her head and growled as she hopped off Scott and grabbed a robe. It was weird seeing everything from his perspective; it did little to reassure Joanna that he was chill with it all, but he had code words to use if he felt in danger, and so far, he hadn't used them.

"I sent them food from the resort as a thank you for watching him," Renee explained. "Figured it would give us a break to eat as well."

"Thank you," Joanna heaved a sigh of relief as she opened her box and found a selection of some of the best food they'd had here on Bragg, along with another chocolate truffle. If she didn't know better, she might think her MOI partner was trying to flirt with her.

Scott turned to the wet woman with a towel as she emerged from the tub. She slapped his cheek firmly as he tried to kiss her wet shoulder. They had just taken a shower together, and her actions surprised him, given how often she'd allowed him to touch her over the past few hours. He backed up a few steps and stood with head bowed, uncertain of whether he needed to assume a punishment position or not. "Turn around," Miss Richards instructed him.

Scott's buttocks tightened reflexively as he turned away from her. After a few minutes, he found the towel lying over his shoulder.

"Dry off and get dressed. I have to go out, and you are not staying here."

"Yes, Ma'am," he said, adding a bow before backing out of the room. As he pulled on his clothes, he whispered, "Red flowers are my favorite," the code phrase for being on the move. His gut tightened as he slipped on his shoes and caught Miss Richards looking at him far more coldly than she had all day. He hoped his client and IGA would do something very, very soon, because every part of him was tensed up as she took his arm in a firm grip that surprised him and led him from the room.

"We've got to follow them," Joanna declared as she stood up and slipped into her shoes, grabbing the wrist monitor with her free hand.

"Blim told us not to go in there without them."

"Actually, she told me to not go down there alone; you'll be with me." They stood and stared at each other for a second before the other woman shrugged and pulled on her shoes as well as the other wrist monitor.

Renee chuckled as she followed the redhead to the door. "Tell me. Which upsets you more: the fact that he's pleasing Richards, or the fact that he isn't pleasing you?"

Joanna immediately turned angrily around. "Dr. Brownlow, we are here because of MOI business. I didn't ask for Scott or you on this story, but I have to deal with both of you."

"Hey, I didn't mean to upset you." Renee walked closer to her and spoke more gently. "I know why you were chosen for this mission. I heard about your fiancé's death, and I'm sorry. I've also heard about your search for your twin. I understand that you have very personal reasons for your involvement in the movement, but you are incredibly uptight when it comes to that boy, and it doesn't make sense."

"If you know why I'm here, about Judy and about Joseph, then you should understand why I dislike having him here. He represents what I hate about Gaia. Plus, he doesn't know what he's doing, and he could ruin any chance I have to bring Richards down," she added quickly.

"And you aren't a bit concerned about his safety, are you?" Renee asked sarcastically.

Joanna sighed as she stopped right in front of the door. "Of course I am. Richards is a very dangerous woman."

"Yes, she is, but your concern is beyond that." The older woman ran a hand through her hair, then placed it on the door to keep it closed when Joanna moved to open it. "I'm a bit older than you; I've had my children, a daughter who is studying to be a medic too – family business. A son I had to hand over to someone else because I couldn't come up with a legitimate reason to keep him. You talk the message, but you also believe the propaganda, as do I. As we all do because it's all we know from the moment we're born. I can say all that stuff about men because deep down I know that part of it's a lie, because I care about them, or I wouldn't be in MOI. How can any mother, any woman, help but care for her own flesh and blood?"

Joanna looked up at the other woman. "Wish my mother had cared about Joseph."

Renee sighed and changed the subject. "We need to stay calm and let him go down there with her, assuming that's where they're going. I'm ready to head there at a moment's notice, but for now, for his safety, for ours, for this case you are heavily invested in, we need to do more than adhere to Chief Blim's words."

Joanna looked up, took a deep breath, and then nodded after a few seconds. "You're right, of course. But I'm calling him back tonight."

"Obviously," Renee agreed as she steered Joanna back to the couch and the two monitors.

In just a few moments they saw Agent A'Jaliou on screen, stopping Richards to just do a friendly check-in on a guest as they headed across the casino floor at a fast pace. The agent took the time to look directly at Scott and say, "We're here if you need anything," before letting them go. His lingering look back at the agent made Joanna's stomach tighten, but she continued to watch.

They took a service elevator to the ground floor and then another one further down, using the code that Richards had reset. When they exited, the underground network was finally revealed, and it was much more complete than E'Lige had led them all to believe.

There were several women in formal lab coveralls marking them as scientists or techs walking around, and a few others in more combat-ready gear, but the thing that stuck out in Joanna's mind, and apparently in Scott's, as his gaze lingered on them the longest, were the rows of cages set along the hallways before they got to a big open lab area.

"Whoa, that is very cutting-edge genetics equipment," Renee whispered next to her.

"Those cages look too big for one person," Joanna countered. "There were beds in them, but no bathroom facilities, and they're so public."

Renee leaned forward as Scott turned and gave them another view of the cages before following Richards as she talked with one of the women in lab garb. The medic slowly turned to Joanna. "You can't experiment too long without replacing your subjects."

Joanna's mouth fell open at the other's thought. "Breeding? That would require both males and females, of multiple peoples."

"Very easy to get, through illegal slave trafficking. You may not be aware of this, but this crime syndicate deals with traffic from almost all planets in the known galaxy." The medic called up Blim and set the device between the monitors. "Are you seeing this, Chief?"

"I'm seeing something, and Doctor E'Leun's going nuts over here about breeding or something," Chief Blim replied.

"He's right," Renee said. "Think about it a minute. There are a dozen planets that have just male slavery; at least that many planets have just female slavery. A majority of planets, particularly the backwater ones, have slavery based on economics, religion, skin color, or military conquest. Most of the major worlds won't even use terms like 'slave' or 'owner' anymore, but none of us are stupid. Slavery still exists under nicer terminology. The market is there; the market has always been there. You have a trade that could reach into every sector of the galaxy."

"We already know that Richards has her hand in the slave trade," Chief Blim pointed out. "That's legal under the IGA constitution."

"We know," sighed Renee sharing a look with Joanna. "But what's the one problem that all of these slave systems have in common that Richards and her crew might want to exploit?"

"Controlling the slaves," Joanna tossed out and got a nod from the IGA agents on the screen. "Though most worlds have that figured out to some degree, it's never easy." Joanna was drawing from years of formal education and her own informal studies with contacts and MOI. "A captive population just doesn't reproduce easily. Whether people or animals, captivity seems to kill sex drive and curb biological fertility. That's why systems based on sex thrive more; they can be portrayed as natural. Fertility never becomes a problem, since only one half of it is forced."

"Oh, dear." Renee let out a long breath as she sat back and pointed to the monitors. "I can read their genetic charts now that he's looking at them casually; can we freeze clips? I think I just figured out why this would cross from legal to illegal."

Chief Blim barked out a few orders, and after a few moments a secondary screen popped up on one of the monitors. Behind her Doctor E'Leun gasped.

"What are they trying to do? Make a new breed of slaves?" Joanna asked as she saw her MOI partner grow pale.

Renee sat silently for a moment before meeting the redhead's gaze. "Of course. If you had a monopoly on water or the known universe's food supply, what would you be?"

"Incredibly rich and powerful," Joanna stated.

"Right. On many planets slaves are also a necessity, like on Gaia, where we might call it by a polite name, but we all know what men are." Renee stood and began pacing. "Controlling those necessities is next to impossible, right? Back home there are constant negotiations between families. We need men for their role in reproduction, because no matter the science, the reality of biology, the old-fashioned approach, turns out to be the most reliable and most productive."

Joanna nodded and stared at the monitors as Scott continued to give them as much of a view as he could.

"Now let's say you want to breed a slave class for maximum profit, marketability, and power," Renee offered, but E'Leun interrupted. "They're set up to create a hybrid people, a separate slave people."

"Wait," Chief Blim said, holding up one hand. "Are you saying that they're looking at cross-world breeding? Cross-dominant species breeding? The results of previous attempts have been utter failures; it can't be done."

"Then it wouldn't be illegal, if it couldn't be done," Joanna replied as she sat back. It was making a very sick sense to her, but she let the experts explain.

"They're using genetic and drug treatments to increase the success rate of the hybrids," Doctor E'Leun added. "The major and minor peoples have enough in common across worlds simply because of how and what the galaxy is made from that you could manipulate the differences as well as enhance the similarities."

"It's more than that," Renee added, pointing to another part of the charts that were frozen on the screen. "They've found a way to make a slave who is a slave by nature. Not just the rhetoric of it, not just using fear, but the reality. A slave who unquestioningly follows commands, one whose biological pleasure is driven by obedience."

"Considering how big the legal and illegal trade is, I bet it could take over entire economies," Joanna said as she sucked in a breath. "So much is spent on controlling enslaved populations, so many people are used to control them, you'd throw entire political systems into chaos, take over." Joanna doubled over as the possible enormity of the plot started to overwhelm her.

"But after a while, the slaves would be reproducing on their own," Chief Blim pointed out.

"Unless you controlled their reproduction." Renee thought for a moment. "If I'm understanding this chart correctly – Goddess, I wish we could see it better – they have the ability to limit the reproduction of these improved slaves. A drug trigger that they'll control, perhaps?" Renee suggested.

"Are you sure of this?" Blim demanded, looking between the man next to her and the screen.

"We'd need to study their hybrids, if they have them," Doctor E'Leun replied.

"This equipment strongly suggests that this is their production facility, not a research lab," Renee countered.

Joanna shook her head. "But Richards would be using other females."

"You assume that she agrees with Gaian society? There must be reasons why she left Gaia that go beyond a rejection from the Great Families. I'm guessing she's no true believer."

They all watched as Richards led Scott back out of the underground breeding facilities.

Scott sat on the hall floor waiting for Miss Richards to open the door, which she had shut in his face when they had returned. His head was hanging down between his knees, his hands resting across his neck. He could use the code words right now. Something was wrong; he felt it. He hadn't seen enough of the papers and the equipment, even though he feared he'd gotten too close and looked too long.

"Boy." Miss Richards' angry tone surprised him into looking directly up at her when she returned a few minutes later. He returned his gaze to the floor, then silently stood up and followed her into the room.

"Get me a glass of wine." Miss Richards sat down in one of the cushioned chairs as she watched him pour her a glass of the wine she'd brought back with her from the supply room down in the underground area. He hadn't understood most of what he saw, other than that it wasn't a lab like any he'd ever seen in a show or movie. She took the glass from him without a smile.

Scott stood in front of the woman, anxiously waiting for her to speak to him. After a few moments he took a deep, quiet breath and ventured to speak. "Ma'am?"

Miss Richards looked up at the boy slowly. "Oh, yeah. Come sit next to me," she ordered, patting the side of her chair.

Scott knelt next to the chair. Miss Richards ran her fingers absently through his hair as she silently sipped the wine. He glanced up at her as he spoke, "Ma'am? Is there anything you'd like?"

Miss Richards took a long, slow sip, then spoke quietly, staring straight forward. "Just sit there."

Scott really wanted to say the emergency code words, but he refrained as he felt her fingers tugging on his hair. She'd noticed him looking at everything down below; he just knew it, but he was too afraid to do more than just sit and wish that Goddess listened to the prayers of boys.

Chapter Nine

"Something is wrong," Joanna stated as she stood up from where they had been watching the monitors for over two hours of an uneasy nothing. She should have been pleased that Scott and Richards weren't having sex and hadn't taken another shower together. Richards was not her type, so the voyeuristic thrill wasn't a factor, even if she'd been able to forget Judy's lying unresponsive on the floor after their short-range slip. Richards wasn't touching Scott and wasn't having him do anything but just sit on the floor while she poked around on her computer, facing him, and glancing at him from time to time.

"Just be calm; it isn't like she's hurting him. She's trying to run a galactic crime syndicate; we shouldn't be surprised if she ignores him for periods," Renee answered with a sigh as she studied the stills that the IGA had sent and conversed with E'Leun on a private line.

Joanna huffed and went to pick at the leftovers from her lunch but kept one eye on the screens. Beneath each was a reading of his life signs, and it was clear that he was worried, as his heart rate had increased since he came into the room. Why the medic, specialist or not, couldn't see that was beyond Joanna's understanding. She pushed back one lock of red hair that had come loose over the course of these two hours. "I'm going to put in a call and have him brought back, say I need him."

"No, she's heard how much time you're spending with E'Lige; if you call now ..." Renee trailed off as there was movement on the monitors.

Richards had stood up with a deep frown, ordered Scott to stand, and was advancing on him with a glare that radiated rage, even on the monitor. His life signs were going crazy as he moved to kneel up, bowing his head and shoulders, seemingly bracing to be struck. Joanna reached out and grabbed the communicator for Chief Blim. "Are you seeing this? Something's wrong."

"We're watching. Please, just relax. Our agents can be in there and at your room shortly."

"What if that isn't fast enough?" Joanna said as she glared at Renee, but the medic was already on her feet and slapping the wrist monitor on. "We're heading over there …"

"Don't you dare! Miss McMillin, I understand that on your world you are an important woman, used to being obeyed. In the IGA I am an important woman, used to being obeyed. You are in my sphere right now."

Renee looked at her, and Joanna pressed her lips together but ground out, "We're ready to go, and we will if that woman harms my boy in any way." Joanna, too, strapped on her wrist monitor and added the gun holster the IGA had given her.

"Understood," Chief Blim replied, "I'll tell them to double-time it."

Joanna looked up to find Renee struggling to keep from laughing. "What is so funny?"

"You said 'my boy' – he's under you, and you're rocking it hard," the older woman laughed, even though she was preparing her gear to go at a moment's notice.

Joanna just rubbed a hand over her face until the monitor turned to static before their eyes. "Go! Go!" she ordered, grabbing a camera out of instinct, and bolting for the door.

Richards' room was only a few minutes away at full speed, given that IGA had given them access to the staff elevators too. They had easy access to the room as well, but it was empty when Joanna and Renee stepped in, and the light automatically came up. "Fuck, where are they!" Joanna swore as she kicked a wall.

"All is not lost," Renee countered as she stepped in and grabbed the computer Richards had left behind. "She was in a hurry if she left this behind.

I'm stowing this," the older woman added as she slipped it into the backpack that held the emergency medical and testing supplies that she always kept within arm's reach in the suite. She didn't have a gun, though, so Joanna hoped hers would do, because they weren't waiting on the all too slow IGA.

"She knows, then. That means he's in danger; if he's still alive," Joanna replied and put up one palm. "Regardless of my feelings, his being in danger or dead puts us in danger. We can't wait around for IGA to get hard enough to do something about this." She was being vulgar – Joanna knew that without the other woman's frown at her language – but as she'd feared, the situation was quickly deteriorating. She should have refused this covert garbage and just done the basic documentary that she and Mi had talked about. If she'd refused to take the boy at all, then he wouldn't be in any danger.

"His life signs aren't coming in." Renee held up her wrist, showing nothing but the same static they were getting on the monitor. "He might just be unconscious – without our CS from home, any readings are hit and miss." Joanna didn't wait for the medical technology lecture and headed toward the door.

At the door Agent Markeni appeared and glanced around, gun drawn, until she spied Joanna walking straight toward her, frowning back, without a bit of fear. Joanna was literally shaking from anger, and she pushed past her MOI partner and the IGA agent. "Scion McMillin!" Markeni called, and this made Joanna stop. "Where are you going?"

"To get him back and stop Richards. You coming to arrest that whore or not?"

All three women paused at the use of such an ancient vulgarity applied toward a woman, but the agent recovered quickest. "Where?" Joanna heard Markeni ask.

"Underground, obviously," Renee replied, right before catching up with her.

Behind them the Gaian-born IGA agent's footsteps were audible, as was her call to the other undercover agents. Markeni kept pace with them and got on the elevator with them. Her ID allowed her ever more access than they would have had, yet Joanna was too angry that any of this was happening to do more than give the other woman a sharp nod of her head.

They went down to the level where they'd have to use E'Lige's code to go down further, but then, given that Richards had reset access to the underground network, they might have to use force.

Joanna pressed her lips together and placed her hand on her gun lightly, ready to act. With relief she noted that Markeni's gun was still out at a ready position. The agent checked the door and the area around them, sending a few casino visitors hurrying away when they changed elevators. The other four IGA agents met them at the second elevator while the resort security staff was keeping guests away and the speakers blared out commands for everyone to return to their quarters while attempting to reassure them that everything was fine. Joanna could imagine E'Lige downing several strong teas right now, and she hoped he was smart enough to stay away from all of this.

Though guns were rarely necessary on Gaia anymore, it was still standard practice for all women to get basic training, and the Great Families trained in a wider range of weapons and more often. It was that training that Joanna had stepped up during her mourning period. Although she still wasn't comfortable with the idea of shooting another woman, with each passing second, she considered Richards less woman than monster as her mind conjured up images of that lab and the possible things that might be happening to the boy she had never wanted to bring with her in the first place. Damn him for getting under her.

E'Lige was on the last floor they could access, with his assistant O'Rray and two of his other security staff. Guess he hated Richards as much as she did and wanted to make sure that IGA did their job. He nodded seriously at Joanna as they stepped out. "I'm sorry about your husband," he offered, but stopped when she interrupted.

"Sorry is worthless; action is what we need. Do you have something to bring down the doors?"

"Oh, we don't need that," E'Lige said with a wide smile, his light green skin almost glowing. "I never gave her the full access codes; I kept a secret backup for just this contingency. She may have threatened my other resorts and my people, but I'm not an idiot. O'Rray!"

His assistant stepped forward and put a device on the final elevator, and after a few moments it hissed and opened.

Joanna turned from it with a grin and grabbed the Karkan by the neck, pulling him in for a deep kiss. She broke it and looked away, "Just a thank you for thinking ahead," she mumbled.

E'Lige touched his lips and then smiled. "Strange custom I shall have to remember," he stated as he led the first group into the car.

"He's transmitting again," Renee said as she held up her wrist monitor. "Life signs strong, so he isn't injured. Must have used a weak sedative on him – probably don't have the right kind for us," she added with a glance between Joanna and the Gaian-born IGA agent, who was stepping in front of the car doors.

"Scion McMillin, I need you to stay behind me, please," Markeni stated simply as she fell into a bodyguard stance. The other agents all flanked the two civilians.

Joanna sighed and positioned herself right behind the larger woman. "I can't promise, Agent, but I'll try."

"That will have to do, but try to stay alive, because I have something I want to discuss with you when all of this is done, Ma'am." Joanna barely heard the agent as she divided her focus between the live feed from Scott's chip and the immediate situation around her. She smiled when Chief Blim's voice came over the agents' radios saying, "He's transmitting audio but a blurry and rather odd image."

When Scott woke up, his head groggy and a touch confused, he channeled his amazing memory to try to clear some things up. Miss Richards had backed him into a corner and then whispered that she knew he was a spy sent by the Great Families to destroy her family completely. It wasn't correct, but his attempts to tell her otherwise only earned him a needle in the arm, something she must have fetched from the bathroom earlier. He didn't know much about the chip in his head, but he was worried it stopped working when he passed out. It didn't take much time to figure out that he was lying on his back on a strange table that had padded bars over his limbs and center and around his face. He couldn't see much, though, because he was afraid to open his eyes more than slits, but he kept quiet and observed as much as he could, hoping that his client and her IGA friends knew where he was and what was going on.

"Director Richards," said a voice, which Scott identified as the voice of the main scientist Richards had spoken with earlier. All her staff were Gaian women, he guessed, making it very easy for him to read their tone of voice, something he was sure the translation of the chip struggled with. The researcher's voice was strained much like that of an irate client, trainer, or even his mother, suggesting that she was on the verge of yelling. "I demand to know why you have burst in here with a guard and this ... boy! You are disturbing our work!"

"Just calm down, Doc." Miss Richards voice was low and cold, just as it had been back in the room.

"Why did you bring him here? I thought we were saving your people for the final stages of testing. We haven't even worked with the minors yet."

"I believe we're being spied on. Those damned Greats are determined to destroy me and everything I've built."

"Then why are you here?" the researcher fumed. "You're going to draw them right to us. You are endangering years of work with your paranoia."

"Oh, please, it will take them quite a while to break through the security, and I have more firepower down here than I let that fool upstairs believe. My paranoia, as you call it, is what is funding your little experiment, doctor. You remember the ones that got you exiled from Gaia for unwomanly thoughts and traitorous behavior."

The scientist slammed her hands down on the table right next to his arm, hitting him in the process, but Scott just pressed his lips together as tightly as he could, hoping their argument would prevent either woman from noticing that he was awake, though women were frighteningly aware of so much, even when you thought they were focused on one or two things. "Fools didn't see I was offering a better way to control male reproduction in a more thorough way."

"But I saw that. I came to you just days after you left the system, your scholarship in my hands, offering you the chance to continue. I'm not endangering your work; they are, just as they've tried to dominate our world for almost a millennium." Miss Richards' voice had a sweet edge to it, but under it, Scott could still hear her anger.

After a few seconds the researcher took a deep breath and removed her hands from the table and his arm. "What do you want me to do?"

"I want access to his chip. I want it overridden so I can have full control over him." Scott held his breath. Could that be done? Full control? It was one of those rumors that circulated when you went to boys' training and one of you just didn't come back one day. Women were developing a chip that would make training, discipline, and punishment unnecessary, because they were working on turning boys into dolls, tools.

"I'm not specialized in that technology," the scientist confessed, offering Scott slim hope for a moment, until Miss Richards spoke up with a snort.

"Oh, please, use your chip and figure it out. He's just a boy; it can't be too complicated, given his simple mind."

Scott opened his eyes just a bit more, just as the table was rotated and he was left facing the floor. He felt hands brushing back his hair over the chip, and he flinched.

"Awake already?" Miss Richards hissed, and someone, probably her, slapped his ass hard. "Well, then, this is going to hurt."

The scientist's voice interrupted, "We need the code, or it will do him severe harm, leaving him in a catatonic state, useless to us then."

Scott felt his hair gripped hard and his head shaken as much as the restraints on the table allowed. "What's your code?" Richards demanded.

"I don't know, Ma'am, really, I don't. Please. This boy doesn't understand." He fell back into rote phrases as a drop of sweat fell down his face and landed on the floor. "Forgive me, Ma'am? Please? Beat me, bruise me, take me, use me."

"Shut up!" she ordered with a thrust downward on his head that left it throbbing. "Can we turn it off, then, Doc? Disable it? Remove it?"

"That's very risky; he'll be useless or dead or worse, revert to a purely male state, if I make even one mistake. I simply don't have the necessary equipment to know what I'm doing, so I'd literally be stabbing in the dark."

There was a pause. "Wouldn't you be able to harvest his sperm, though, even if he died, so we could start preliminary tests on our own men sooner than planned that way?"

Scott started to struggle. The scientist yelled for someone to give him something, and soon he felt another jab in his arm. "Yes, that would still be possible. We have those storage facilities all set up."

Before things went dark, he heard Miss Richards say, "Our first subjects arrive tomorrow. Several females among them, whom I'm sure will be grateful test subjects when we explain that this way they don't have to worry about rape. We'll save that special treatment for the difficult ones."

Joanna had been trying very hard to stay behind Agent Markeni, but each word she heard from Richards enraged her. One by one the IGA agents and E'Lige's security team had taken out the forces below, quietly, quickly. It was like watching a movie about an assault on some patriarchal military lab, back in the war, heroes sacrificing themselves for their sisters left and right in their just cause – but here and now it wasn't just women. IGA and resort security must have coordinated at some point to be working so well together, and the fact that males and females were working side by side might have made Joanna smile more, and want to get it on vid, if she hadn't been so focused on getting to Scott before it was too late.

They were only steps from Richards, a few of her scientists, and a handful of guards; all of them looked to be Gaian, or at least from one of the colonies. What would possess women to so betray their morals that they would talk about raping other women as though it were a reasonable practice? The scientist closest to Scott was taking some device out of a surgical pack and heading straight for his head. It was going to be too late if she didn't act now.

"Gonna go," Joanna hissed as she stepped around Agent Markeni and walked straight into the lab with the Gaian agent hard on her heels, the rest behind them.

"I wouldn't do that, Richards!" Joanna called out as soon as the mercenaries fell to the floor thanks to the accurate aim of the IGA forces backing her up.

The crime leader turned around with a smile. "It's about time you came out, McMillin – I refuse to call you Scion!"

Joanna took a few more steps as Markeni stepped around and positioned herself partly in front of her. "Let the boy go. It's me you want. I'm a Great; I'm the one who's been targeting you," she said, playing into what the other woman had described as paranoia.

Richards chuckled. "Yes, I do want you. It took me a while to figure out who you were besides a spoiled brat, but then that stupid little adventure on one of my ships came to mind. Your family must be so disappointed with your gallivanting all over the galaxy instead of attending to their business. It's a pity my people didn't get rid of both of you back then. Would have saved me so much trouble today."

"You know you've lost. We've just shot your guards right in front of you, and clearly, we're here," Joanna went on, motioning backward with her arm as the rest of their group stepped forward, "so your other guards went pretty fast." The three scientists stepped away from Scott, but Richards moved closer and picked up a scalpel. "Just let him go. What good would it do you to kill him, a simple boy?"

"It will make me feel wonderful, especially since you seem to want him to live so badly," Richards hissed as she stepped toward Scott's head.

"I really don't care one way or another." Joanna took two steps forward and held her breath for a moment as Richards held the blade over the access point in the back of Scott's head. "If he dies, I'll make sure there are two murder charges against you. You know I have the pull to make sure he counts as a full person, even back home, and my friends in the IGA, well, they really don't see the difference when it's illegal."

"Home?" This got Richards to turn from Scott as Joanna and Markeni circled to his other side and two of the other IGA agents corralled the scientists and took them away. "I don't have a home because of you Great bitches running over every family on Gaia!" she screamed as she lunged across the table with the scalpel.

Joanna was attempting to undo the table's restraints, her eyes focused on Richards, when Agent Markeni shoved her aside, took the blade in her upper left arm, and shot out her right to grab Richards' shoulder and shove her away from them all.

"Fathersucker!" Richards screamed as she slumped forward from several shots to her lower back from E'Lige's security team. Over Scott's strapped body, Joanna thought she saw the resort owner nod and his assistant smile. They'd kept Richards from testifying about any of their business problems that O'Rray had slipped to her earlier. IGA might not like that, but right now Joanna just felt a cold satisfaction curling in her stomach.

She turned to see Agent Markeni flexing her left arm as she kicked Richards' body further away. "You're hurt," Joanna stupidly pointed out as the agent looked at her.

"Are you, Scion?" Markeni countered.

"I'm fine, thanks to you," Joanna told her as she looked around for something to stem the flow of blood.

"I'll take care of it – been awhile, but I think I can manage," Renee stated as she stepped forward. "You get the boy out; he may be unconscious again, since the feed isn't up, but I think we made it before they cocked up his chip."

Joanna fiddled with the table, and in a moment, she was able to flip it over, so Scott was lying face up, his eyes struggling to open. "There you are, Scott. I guess whatever they were using doesn't work very well on our people, thank Goddess," she said as she placed a hand on one of his cheeks.

She smiled at him when he managed to open his eyes just a bit, squinting against the bright lights. She lost that smile at his words, "Forgive me, Miss? Please?"

"I'm the one who agreed to this operation; we should have stayed on the ship and just documented their side of things," she muttered as she released the restraints to free him.

"She figured it out; I didn't tell her, I promise," he continued to babble.

"Don't let him sit up until I've looked at the readout," Renee tossed out as she continued to clean up and close the knife wound in Markeni's arm.

"Just stay still," Joanna told Scott, placing a hand on his chest. Soon she was petting him as he continued to plead his refusal to cooperate with Richards. Joanna glared down at the woman who had taken away her mate and almost harmed the boy she'd been entrusted with. She let him continue to ramble on until Renee gave him a shot that should keep him out for some time.

Once she was sure he wasn't going anywhere, she got out the camera and started moving around with Renee, asking questions, and zooming in on equipment as the team worked. She paid particular attention to E'Lige and was able to corner him by one of the cages being disassembled.

"Mr. E'Lige, did you have any idea of the scope of Richards' activities down here?"

He turned to her and shook his head. They weren't pretending to be interested in each other now, so he was all formality, as was she. "I figured it must be something big, given the amount of space down here, but …" he trailed off, shrugging with both arms spread, so she zoomed out a bit, then back down to the immediate area. "While we have used slaves on some of our colonies, we prefer not to do so when it can be avoided. It is not a status native to my people, only to the planets I've acquired land on, you see." He turned around, then turned back to her and the camera she was holding. "I hope IGA will tell me and you, all of us, what was actually going on."

"Your staff killed Richards. Had you been planning to do that?"

That question made him narrow his eyes and put his hands behind his back as he stood up straighter. She had told him that by his side she'd be an amusing tourist, but that didn't mean she'd throw him easy questions once she was reporting again. She pushed a bit harder, "Her death might be seen as a victory for you in many ways. I'm sure people would not be surprised if you planned it."

"I'm sure they wouldn't be pleased – do believe me when I say that we were merely helping to protect you and the others, especially myself. Her death is … unfortunate, as any death would be," he offered diplomatically, so she gave him a nod before moving to the next question.

"Any plans for this space, then?"

O'Rray had moved next to his boss, so Joanna zoomed out to include both men. "We'd only explored some of it, since as you may know we have reused existing buildings. I think now we may invest time in that. No solid plans yet," E'Lige replied.

"I just saw a history video on Bragg speculating about a previous civilization; I assume you've heard of this?" she continued, moving on to the next and final topic she wanted to address for right now.

"Oh, yes, and we have found some evidence," E'Lige said as his assistant shot him a displeased look, and the resort owner waved a dismissive hand at him. "It is a point of debate among my people how much we should share, but I think, given how much IGA has helped me, that I may open this area up to scholars as well. A museum to a lost people could be a good tourist attraction."

"Indeed. Thank you for your time, Mr. E'Lige," Joanna concluded, ending that interview with a smile before moving on to continue to document without an imagist to back her up. Really, what had been the point of renting him if she was doing this all by herself, she forced herself to ask, so she didn't go after him as the medics arrived to take him back to the ship.

Chapter Ten

Scott slowly opened his eyes and tried to focus on the face looking down at him. As his vision cleared, he smiled and spoke softly. "Miss Renee?"

The specialist smiled back. "You're awake, finally," she said. "I didn't think you'd be out much longer."

Scott shook his head and sat up on his elbows. He had a few IV lines running into his arms, but he didn't dare disturb those. Such aftercare was sadly common for him if Jones got angry. His client was nowhere to be seen at the moment, so he focused on the other woman. "Where are we?"

"Aboard the IGA ship. I gave you a proper sedative, so you've been out a while."

"Miss, um, Scion Joanna?" he amended quickly as he took a glass of something that she held out to him.

"She should be back soon from Bragg. She's doing interviews, documenting, you know – the reason she really came here."

Scott frowned and bunched up the blanket on his lap in his free hand. "I should be down there; she rented an imagist, not a patient," he declared softly.

"I did," said Miss Joanna's voice, which got him to look up as she walked into the room, "but you'll just have to make up for it by covering everything from here on out."

"Miss Joanna," said Scott, setting the glass on the table near him and moving up into a kneeling position, taking Miss Renee's arm when offered to steady himself. "I'm sorry, Miss. I really messed up."

"Oh, not this again," she teased him as she stopped by his bed and folded her arms across her chest. "You sure his chip isn't damaged? He's talking nonsense." His client was looking at him but clearly speaking to the medic.

"E'Leun could tell you more, since he is the actual medic in charge of this case, but I think he's fine physically."

Scott wasn't stupid; he knew they meant he was supposed to stop apologizing for things that had been out of his control. It was nice to find women who understood that, so he moved to a different topic, "Did they get Richards?"

"She's dead." Miss Joanna sighed. "I would have liked to have taken her alive, but that's not your fault. She insisted on fighting, attacked me with a knife; I'm fine," she added as soon as he started to open his mouth to apologize again, but he spoke up anyway.

"I almost got you killed," he whispered, looking away.

Miss Joanna nodded. "Several people almost got killed, including yourself." She sat down at the edge of his bed and took a deep breath before continuing to speak in a surprisingly emotionless voice. "I said something like this might happen, but they insisted that I take you along. Maybe they'll listen to me next time."

"You told me that I'd screw up, and you were right, Miss," Scott pointed out. He turned his cheek toward his client. "I deserve the back of your hand." There; it wasn't an apology, more an offering of compensation, an attempt to defuse a woman's anger. He couldn't lose her, not now, after everything he'd been through; he had to make her want to keep renting him. She didn't move to slap him but continued talking.

"You didn't screw up," she admitted. "Richards' people got some illegal import software that hacked into your chip – saw that it was transmitting. IGA should've known that could happen, should've prevented it from happening." Sitting in the chair next to the bed, Miss Renee sighed and nodded as well. Miss Joanna reached out and turned his head by the chin, so he had to look at her. "Hitting you won't change what's happened. To be perfectly honest, after all the excitement and interviews, I'd like to just eat a whole lot and then sleep for a while." She grinned, so he smiled weakly back in return.

"Aren't you mad at me, Miss?" he asked.

"Oh, I'm sure I'll be very mad about this whole thing in a day or so. Who knows why she got suspicious of you? She's dead, so we can't ask her," she replied with a resigned sigh. Her tone was lighter as she stood up, saying, "Right now I order you to get well." She picked up the glass he'd used moments before and handed it back to him. "Doctor E'Leun says you should drink lots of this, and since he's a medic, you should probably do it."

Scott took the glass but didn't let his fingers brush against hers; now was not the time for that move. "Yes, Miss." As he sipped it both women left him alone, so he slid back down to sit. If she rented him again, if she bought him, would his life always be like this? Was it really better than the other futures he'd heard about for old boys? She'd said this was an unusual story for her … it would take some further thinking, but he was pretty sure this was still his best hope.

They spent the next several days documenting the procedures involved in closing the case, from agent debriefing and evidence evaluation to two press conferences that Joanna merely watched from another room while Scott handled the cameras. He was good, able to move around people and out of the camera's view most of the time, making adjustments, either physically or over the connection. He wasn't good enough to rent again, though, she told herself whenever her mind went stupidly down that hallway.

In their room on the ship or at the station once they'd returned there, he was chatty and hadn't apologized again after the medic had released him. He was attentive, though not overtly sexual in any way. They still slept together in the lone bed, and she found his presence next to her comforting. Not comforting enough to rent him again, though, she told herself whenever her thoughts turned that corner.

Around the other people on the ship and then at the station where the bulk of the wrap-up happened, he was more relaxed, though always deferential to the females. He stayed back and let Joanna do all the talking when they were documenting, but when it was just mealtime or a down moment, he could be charming. Not charming enough to rent him again, though, she told herself whenever she caught her pulse speeding up while looking at him.

Renting him hadn't been a good idea, but before her thoughts started to drift down that hallway again, Joanna used the fact that she was watching the IGA team go over the files on Richards' computer to refocus her mind on the issues at hand. Now she could ask the question that had been on the edge of her mind. "Is there anything on there about E'Lige's other businesses? It seemed a bit convenient that his guards killed her, didn't it?"

A'Tarick looked up from the computer; he was sitting directly in front of it because he was this team's cracker, gifted in breaking into all manner of security systems. It had taken him a few days to break Richards' security until he had finally asked the Gaians for some information about the woman that only they might understand. Back home they would have had it open in a few hours, but cultural differences mattered a good deal when personal security was so stupidly personal as using a line from a children's show she'd grown up with. Was Richards a little boy, using something like that? Thank Goddess the McMillin family attorneys insisted on complex security systems that used three-factor. The IGA agent considered Joanna with the camera pointed at them for a moment before answering. "Only what we knew of their dealings. Still nothing that suggests he was directly benefiting from her illegal activities."

"It did seem like they used too much force," added Noulayia, the male Fortixe agent who was sitting at the next desk diving into the financials showing who was backing the project. So far questions on that front were going nowhere for Joanna.

"When we use force, we use it," A'Jaliou told them about her people with a grim face. "Homeworld is generally quite peaceful, but we've had to learn to be more aggressive out here, so sometimes we get carried away. I'm sure E'Lige and O'Rray were just overreacting."

"Yeah, don't take her to a shooting range unless you want to be humiliated," the other Karkan agent, O'Heironul chuckled, making A'Jaliou's skin darken all over in what passed for blushing among their people.

Agent Markeni wasn't with them today, saying that she found computers boring, and went instead to the lab with Chief Blim, with Scott in tow to document everything. The Gaian agent had made an appointment to have dinner with them that night to discuss something that Joanna had a gut feeling she would have difficulty saying no to, but she promised herself to act like she was surprised when she agreed.

"So, it was just normal Karkan overreacting – is that what you're saying?" Joanna pushed. A'Jaliou and A'Tarick exchanged a glance. Did the beginnings of their names mean something on their homeworld? Joanna pushed that question aside for a possible later investigation, or one she could share at GNA for another reporter.

"Probably," A'Tarick replied, "unless you have other information. You did spend more time with him than the rest of us."

All four agents were looking at her now, so Joanna just shrugged. If the evidence of her blackmail was only condemning to Richards, why add to their pile with the crystal, which she didn't even have at the moment? Besides, she had promised O'Rray that she would protect his boss, and McMillins kept their promises. "No, we played it pretty close to script, because we were never really alone."

They went back to documenting the money maps and discovering a lot more ties back to Gaia than Joanna had suspected. True, all of Richards' security forces and researchers were Gaian women, but as she and the IGA worked the evidence, Joanna found that all of Richards' minions had something else in common: exile, either self-imposed or by Council directive, Great or worldgov or both. Once she was back home, Joanna suspected she would find even more commonalities, but out here she simply didn't have the resources or the time.

One image caught her eye, and she made a note of it, even picking up the camera and zooming in. A lavender labrys symbol appeared on certain documents related to the military forces that Richards used, some of whom also wore the symbol as a patch on their uniforms. It seemed familiar, but Joanna couldn't remember why.

Scott moved as quietly as he could around the office, documenting the final interview between Chief Blim and E'Lige, the resort owner. It still amazed him that the strange man ran an entire planet, plus several other businesses on other worlds, and apparently quite successfully. He really wasn't paying much attention to the details of their conversation beyond when it seemed like a change in angle, or a close-up might be a good option to give his client. That his client trusted him to do more than just monitor the equipment from a separate room to capture such an important meeting meant he was doing well.

Or maybe this wasn't as important as it seemed. Either way, she trusted him to make the best images for the final piece. She hadn't mentioned his helping her edit yet, but he was hopeful, since he had the entire trip back to Gaia to finish impressing her. Of course, they might just do the editing aboard the ship to the moon after getting out of the Slip. Oh, those tubes and the cold did not bring up good memories, and those eyes ... Scott pushed those creepy thoughts aside to move out of the way as the two men stood and shook Chief Blim's hand. Wow, men and women shaking hands like equals; the Dells boys would never believe this unless he got permission to show them the story when it came out.

Scott hopped in front of the two Karkan men and filmed them walking out of the office and back toward the port where their ship was docked. A drone camera would help so much with all of this – maybe if this turned out well, he would take the risk and mention that to Miss Joanna. Don't get ahead of yourself, boy.

After a few feet they stopped, and E'Lige looked directly at him and addressed him, "Don't you have any questions for us? Scion McMillin always asked questions."

"Eh? Oh, no, see, I'm just her imagist, not a reporter, sorry," Scott was mumbling, unsure how to talk to a man who wasn't his equal. Did she expect him to ask questions? She hadn't said that at all. She could always edit his voice out, though, he thought as the two people just looked at him expectantly and didn't move. He recalled all the questions he'd heard her ask and repeated one, "Now that you have your resort back, what are your plans?"

The two men smiled slightly and resumed walking as they answered. "Besides just running the business?" O'Rray paraphrased.

"Run it very well, investigate the underground, which it turns out is indeed of interest to several historical groups," E'Lige enumerated, counting on his fingers as they walked. Scott zoomed in on this for a few seconds then went back to their faces until they were at the docking port doors.

Follow-up question. Miss Joanna would have a follow-up question. "Would having a historical group be good for business?"

The two men smiled at each other, then at him. The assistant took a step back, indicating the other should speak. "It will be a different type of business," said E'Lige. "Keeping your business varied can be good, can help you weather economic downturns, political storms, harvest new customer bases. Someone interested in history still must eat, may want to watch a show, or even gamble. I believe your McMillins are quite good at diversification back on your homeward. See what sprouts." The two men laughed so Scott did as well, though he didn't really understand why they were chuckling.

"And what will you do?" O'Rray asked, looking directly at Scott.

"Me?" Scott felt his face heat up at the question. Did these strange males even know what sort of query that was, given Gaian customs? Very few people had paid much attention to him during the investigation, but since his time in the clinic here he'd been getting a few nods and words of acknowledgment, all of which felt very odd. He shrugged and turned the camera off; she didn't need to know about what he was going to say next. "Whatever Miss Joanna wants, hopefully for a long time to come."

"Ah, so your people's men are capable of thinking ahead," E'Lige said with a smile toward his assistant. "I thought you might be. It's easy to let what we see out in public, what we're allowed to see, influence what we think the truth is."

Scott swallowed. That didn't seem like a safe thing to say at all. He looked down at the machine he was holding, glad that it really was turned off.

The two men seemed to feel that he was uncomfortable and ended things by taking a couple of steps toward him. "Well then, I wish you luck, and thank you for your help in this matter."

Scott stared for a moment at the outstretched hand and tried to copy the handshake he'd just witnessed back in the office. It was making him nervous, so he stepped back and held up the camera again. "Could I take a closing shot of you two going through the doors? I believe Miss Joanna had an earlier scene like that, and it could be a good framing technique."

At their consent he brought up the camera and filmed them waiting for the doors to open, going through them, and then walking down the small corridor that led to their ship. Scott turned the camera off and studied his hand, the one he'd just had shaken as if he'd been a valuable member of the team. If these strangers thought that he was, then maybe so did she … a beep went off, then there was a visual reminder from his chip of their dinner appointment. Although Miss Joanna had had the recording features turned off, she was now using his access code a bit more. That had to be a good sign.

Markeni stood up when Joanna approached the table in the mess hall, Scott close behind carrying both of their trays, while she carried the two glasses, a compromise she'd discovered back on the ship from the moon to the Transway Gate that didn't make either of them too uncomfortable or draw too much attention. That Richards had seen through them was worrisome, so Joanna had been a bit more careful with Scott when it wasn't clear she needed him to be more independent as her imagist.

As a member of one of the Great Families, she had an idea what this discussion was going to be about, and bringing the boy was a way to test the waters without directly asking the suspicious questions. "Thank you for agreeing to meet with me, Scion," Markeni politely greeted her and then gave Scott a nod and smile; one point in the woman's favor.

"No problem – you may have saved my life back at the lab," Joanna pointed out as she and then Scott took the seats next to her. She'd given very clear orders that he was to sit at the table and eat with them, but she could sense his discomfort from his stiff posture and bowed head. Markeni didn't even glance at him or frown; she simply ignored the unusual practice of having him join them at the table – a second point in the woman's favor.

"Just doing my job," the agent countered.

They all ate their food, and then when they were nearly finished, Markeni raised the matter with one simple question. "Do you have a bodyguard, Scion?" A direct yet not pushy question – point three in the woman's favor.

"Not currently, unless you count Scott, which I don't," Joanna added when she felt Scott turn to look at her. "I had a feeling you might ask me something like this, so I asked your Chief for information about you." The other woman didn't flinch or stiffen at the news; point four in her favor. "Do you want to tell me what I found out?"

The agent sighed then and sat back in an exaggeratedly relaxed pose before she spoke. "I was fired from my last position on Gaia because I refused to shoot a boy that my client was tired of."

Next to her Scott gasped, then muttered an apology, until Joanna put a hand on his knee. The information that Markeni was about to give her wasn't so important, but how the woman spun it was.

"I wasn't a disciplinarian, but I'm also not a murderer, and to be blunt, Scion, I don't believe death is ever an appropriate punishment for any boy unless he's killed someone, raped someone, or been found guilty of treason. It's almost the eleventh century; shouldn't we be beyond that?" All the words were good, but the lack of emotion was a bit difficult; no points earned or lost.

"You worked for the Vedova family," Joanna stated.

Markeni nodded and clarified, "Candelora Alba Vedova, not the entire family. My understanding is that each member hires her own staff, though connections often form over generations. My family had been one of several who had worked for the Vedovas. I was the first to be dismissed. My mother wasn't pleased." That admission clearly made the agent uncomfortable, and given that said mother was still alive, it was a point against the agent.

"I don't normally need much protection, but if you're able to handle basic home security and only being on call most of the time, I might be able to find a position for you. I live in one of our family's semi-public housing complexes, the one in Cape Elizabeth, and I'd need to see if the residents would be chill with it." Markeni was smiling now, looking relieved, so Joanna twisted things with a different question. "However, Chief Blim speaks very highly of you; I'm not sure she'd be happy to let you go. As she pointed out to me, you are one of only a handful of Gaians in the entire service."

Markeni tensed for a second, but why was unclear until she spoke. "Don't get me wrong, Scion; I've found working with IGA rewarding. Turns out I'm good with other peoples, but it isn't home, you know?" Nothing about the gender roles or discomfort, just simple homesickness was evident in her tone and body language; no points gained or lost.

"That I can understand. Well, then, Agent Markeni," Joanna said, standing up, causing Scott to rise and back up a couple of steps behind her, "let me and my people look into things, and I'll send you a message if I have a position for you. Is that acceptable?"

"Erin, please just call me Erin," the agent replied with a nod and a handshake. "Regardless of what you decide, I'd like you to call me Erin. No one ever does out here, and I kind of miss it." Was she flirting? If so, that was a point against her, but it didn't outweigh the pros of having another person she could rely on if Markeni passed the background checks that both MOI and Liz Kourns, Joanna's attorney, would run.

"Erin, then." Joanna accepted the handshake but held on to the agent's hand a bit longer. "But only if you leave the 'Scion' crap for public use only. I find it annoying."

"Of course ... Ma'am." Good, she stayed formal but not too formal, sending the message that any job would not involve intimacies. She had enough to worry about in that regard with the boy, who trailed after her as they left the mess hall.

Keeping things more formal in public areas was starting to wear on her, and with each passing day the boy seemed to be a touch chattier and more attentive, especially when she brought up the trip home. Soon they could go their separate ways, which would be the best thing for both of them, she reminded herself as she glanced at him walking next to her, as she preferred.

Scott was packing up his luggage when the sound of someone clearing her throat made him look up. The specialist was watching him, so he stopped and stood still. "Miss Renee?"

"Aren't you happy to be going back to Dells?" she asked, making him blink.

He paused, then went back to packing. He'd already done as much with his client's luggage as she'd allowed. They'd be going through the Transway in a few hours; he wasn't looking forward to that, but until now he'd been trying to ignore his return to Neuvo and Dells. "Of course, Doctor Brownlow," he replied, falling back into a formal title.

"You don't sound too thrilled to be returning to Gaia," she pointed out. When he didn't reply, the specialist sat on the edge of the bed his client reluctantly shared with him. "Hey, you know I was just playing a role on Bragg; I'm actually a pretty caring person. I can cradle that you're unhappy about returning. Why don't you tell me about it?"

"I belong to Dells. It's my home." He frowned as the words came forth with venom he seemed unable to contain. He felt the woman's eyes upon him, awaiting the truth. Kneeling at her feet he begged, "Doctor, I don't want to go back. I know I'm being an ungrateful dick, but for all the danger, I really feel like I could do this for Miss Joanna. I could be her imagist."

There was silence, so he just bowed his head and waited for the lecture about how men came from women and should be grateful for every breath, every moment of life. The thought of that life back at Dells … he clenched his hands into fists on top of his thighs to steady himself.

"I've heard about Dells, particularly the one in Neuvo." Doctor Brownlow leaned toward him. "Is Emma Jones still the disciplinarian there?"

Scott shuddered at the name. "Yes, Ma'am," he whispered hoarsely.

"I wouldn't want to go back to her either," she told him.

He looked up slowly, surprised by the declaration. "You know her, Ma'am?"

"I know of her. Before I was a xenospecialist I was a regular medic working for the Great Council. I was part of a team that once investigated Dells Escort Service worldwide. There were several complaints from clients about bruising and misleading advertising. But as these things often go, nothing came of it, even though it was shown how poorly some Dells employees treated their … wards." Doctor Brownlow looked over his head as she gave a low chuckle.

"That's when I decided to leave my old job. I've kept an ear out for more complaints, and while I didn't use Dells myself, I did have a son I signed over to a rival company, because he and my wife asked me to," she added, though Scott was unsure why she sounded like she was apologizing. Most male contracts were held by companies or even government entities. Most women didn't have the time or desire to oversee one. A private contract was the dream, but it wasn't reality.

The specialist continued, "He tells me he's fine when I check in a few times a year. He's just turned 20, and I think one of his clients is a bit too regular to stay just a client."

That wasn't fair, Scott thought briefly, then frowned. He didn't have a right to be so jealous of her son. He was clearly a better man if she stayed in touch with him and he was already in line for a private contract. Scott shoved that feeling down and just gave the medic a smile. "You made wonderful choices, Ma'am."

The specialist sighed then blew out a breath. "Tell me about you going to Dells in Neuvo," she demanded. "Was it always as bad as it is now?"

Scott shook his head slowly. "It was better to begin with. I had just been taken in, so I was mostly in basic training. But I recall a lot of the staff mentioning something about outsiders nosing around. Older boys claimed that the food improved, the lessons weren't as intense, but I didn't know if that was just talk. She left me alone."

"Who left you alone?"

"Jones likes me – xe always has, even when I wasn't supposed to be used that way ..." He glanced up at the woman, unable to control his fearful trembling completely. "Xe takes me at least once a week now."

"Xe just takes you?"

Scott looked down again but was forced to look up as the doctor pulled his face up by his hair. "No, Doctor Brownlow," he used her full title hoping it would make his next statement seem as serious as he felt them to be. "Xe does whatever xe wants to me. If anyone asks why, I get written up for punishment, but I'm not a bad boy, I'm really not."

"I saw that with my own eyes." She released him with a sad smile then commanded gently before she left the room, "Finish packing."

"We need to talk now!"

Joanna looked up at the sudden outburst from her MOI partner as she and the Chief IGA Agent were finishing their final interview. "Thank you, Chief Blim; please do let me know if there are any further developments, and thank you for including me in this case. I'm sure our viewers have found it very interesting."

Now she turned to the xenospecialist as she turned off her camera. "Thanks for interrupting and adding more editing." With that she walked out of the office and down the hall, back toward the room where the boy was packing.

"I'm sure that Scott is more than capable of handling such a small interruption," Renee tossed out, with an edge to her voice that was screaming anger.

"What's the problem?" Joanna demanded as she set the camera on the nearest table and faced the other woman.

"What are you planning to do with him when you return to Gaia?"

"Do with him?" She didn't want to be having this conversation. Joanna took a second to run through the procedures she assumed she'd follow once they were back in Neuvo. "I'll return him to Dells, thank them for the use of their imaging equipment, and let them know he did a good job."

"And then?"

"I'll tell him that he did a good job, too; maybe I'll buy him a gift," she offered with a forced shrug.

"A gift?" Renee mimicked, but Joanna just rushed on.

"Then I'll try to forget about having to rent him at all and look around for a qualified imagist." There, that sounded as convincing as she could make it. She even rested her hands on her hips for emphasis.

"Oh, you won't forget. I read your personality file." Renee leaned forward as she lowered her voice. "You don't forget people you work with easily, and I think that you're too dedicated to our fight to just forget this experience, especially him. You know he's terrified of going back to Dells and growing more so by the day as he gets closer to his 25th birthday."

Joanna did, but she'd been trying to ignore it. "How is that my problem?"

Renee tilted her head with a huff and folded her arms over her chest, moving her legs in a defensive stance that Joanna forced herself not to mimic. "We are fighting for better treatment of men ..."

"Equality ..."

"Get realistic! You know that's not happening in your, and probably not your children's lifetimes. There's too much history for that to happen. Hell, the millennium approaching is going to make it more difficult." Renee lowered her voice but not the intensity of her words. "We fight for better lives for our boys one revelation at a time, one case at a time, one story at a time, one legal change at a time, one boy at a time."

"What are you suggesting I do? Send him off to one of the free planets between here and Gaia? Maybe see if E'Lige could use him at the resort?"

"No," Renee said firmly. "That would make people suspicious of you, not to mention getting worldgov authorities on your trail as well. No Great name could protect you then."

"Most people are already suspicious of me," Joanna added with a tired sigh.

"Which is why you need a better cover in your daily life."

Joanna narrowed her eyes angrily as she spoke. "What are you suggesting, Dr. Brownlow?"

The older woman reflected the question. "How much do you know about Dells Escort Agency?"

"Enough to know that it gave me more creeps than a run-down house," Joanna replied, letting her arms sag as she shuddered.

"I think you should look into it further. I think you'd be interested in knowing how that boy has been raised and treated. I can send you some information that I had from my earlier years with MOI. If you dig more, have your attorney dig, maybe have that archivist friend of yours ask their colleagues for recent history, heck, talk to your friends and family, I think you'll know what you should do."

Joanna's stomach clenched. How much of a background check had the xenospecialist done on her before they met? MOI had given her nothing about Renee beyond a few facts. She'd been foolish enough not to do more research, too busy saying goodbye to Raven and Jack and worrying about Scott.

"Unless you're afraid of the truth, and of doing something about it instead of just reporting on the sins of others." With that the doctor said goodbye and went to her own room, leaving Joanna just standing in the hall for a few seconds as she thought about a similar suggestion she'd received years before while she was still in college.

"What exactly do you know about a man's life on Gaia, Joanna?" The professor looked up from Joanna's paper and into her student's eyes across the desk in her office.

Joanna looked blankly at her history professor. Just weeks ago, she'd discovered that her twin had been sold. She returned to campus early from the year-end holidays. Finding the boy who came with her dorm room was the last thing she needed, so she'd fled to this professor's house, where she'd lived with her for a week. During that time, she'd discovered the professor's association with the secret organization MOI, an acronym that seemed familiar from her own family's history, though at the time she didn't grasp why or how.

A month into the new semester, she wanted to impress this woman, but she was struggling with an answer to her question. "That it's not as free as my own. That my mother treated my twin like cum."

The professor frowned. "That's not enough to join our particular organization." She held the student paper up, then threw it down on the desk. "You need to investigate what's going on around you before writing such revolutionary remarks!"

Joanna took her paper from the desk as her face turned red. "I thought I could trust you," she whispered.

"You can. But I'd hoped you would have learned that ignorance isn't bliss." The professor sat down in her chair with a shrug. "Frankly, I'm surprised that a woman from your background could even think about anyone besides herself."

Joanna started to protest but was yelled down.

"We need people who are really motivated! Your rich ideal of freedom isn't going to get you through one bit of brotherfucking hardship!"

Joanna stared at the floor in silence, then looked up at her professor with tears filling her eyes. "I may not know firsthand what it means to be male, but I know treating men as slaves wasn't the original goal of the Great Mothers! Not for my family, it wasn't. If it's become that now, then we've betrayed everything they fought for."

Joanna moved around to stand at the side of the professor's desk. "I never back down from a job or a challenge! If your group gives me a chance, I can prove myself."

"You have to feel anger before you can use it to help us fight."

"I am angry!"

The professor sat down on the edge of her desk; arms folded across her chest. "You're angry about your twin; you're personally offended. That isn't the type of anger we need for our mission. If you really want to learn about boys' lives, then go back and reclaim your dormboy before it's too late. Save him, observe him, learn from him. Unless you're a coward."

Joanna's face flushed a red so deep it started to approach her hair's color as she picked up the rest of her books and stomped out of the room. She would never own a man again, never, she swore with each step until she was back in her eerily quiet suite.

Joanna frowned as she looked down at the floor for a few seconds, the camera gripped tightly in her hands. When had she picked it back up? Her stubbornness had stopped her from getting that dormboy back – Zack had been his name – and she'd refused any suggestion of taking on a new one. She'd treated Zack horribly when she'd found him following her outside around campus over the course of two months, ignoring his pleas, trying to ignore his clearly worsening physical condition. Then one day he wasn't around, and she'd told herself then that he'd just been reassigned to another student.

Coward. Afraid. She'd just stared down a crazy woman a few weeks before, but she was afraid to investigate one boy's life?

Joanna walked into her room and found Scott packing the last of their luggage. She silently watched him as she remembered her conversations with Renee about the boy's usefulness and MOI's agenda. This led once more to memories about her old history and journalism professors, who had introduced her to MOI. To the discovery of forbidden documents in her family's personal archives that mentioned something quite similar. Even Scott's words and behaviors since this entire assignment began were running through her mind. All these thoughts harassed her with the choice she knew she had to make: to be either an agent for change or part of the continued problem. If she clung to her ideals and just observed and reported, was that really helping MOI's agenda? It hadn't even gotten her brother back.

"Miss Joanna." His soft voice made her stop the recollections and take a deep breath. Only now did she realize that he had already taken the camera from her hands. "Everything is packed, Miss."

He wasn't looking directly at her anymore, and his body language was exhausted, his manner meeker again. He was shutting down, and Renee might be right about why. She wanted to pat him on the back, but instead she just ordered, "Take it all to the shuttle, and I'll join you soon."

As soon as he was gone, she contacted Renee one more time before they went their separate ways. "Send my private account all the information you have on Dells. I'm giving you an access code."

Joanna looked at Scott when she joined him on the bench that would take them to the ship. "The trip back will be much the same. Remember – conversation, and don't just let me win Mixed," she said as lightly as she could.

He stared at her for a moment, his lips trembling, then he smiled. "I would never let you just win, Miss Joanna," he said softly.

She nudged him with her arm and tried to act as normally as she could without getting his hopes up. She tried to be friendly without letting her guard down during the journey back to Gaia.

Chapter Eleven

"Ms. Jenson is very busy, Scion McMillin," the secretary stated as Joanna walked toward the executive office doors. Yet the woman made no effort to stop her, so she kept going, pausing only long enough to throw the doors open to let her walk in.

"Just how busy are you?" Joanna asked as she seated herself across the other woman.

The normally jolly blonde was frowning, looking over her glasses at her unexpected guest. "When did you get back?"

"Just a half an hour ago. I dropped some things off, then came right here. My luggage is still in the car." Joanna paused for breath as she crossed her legs at the ankles and folded her hands in her lap. "Are you very busy?"

Kathey pushed her glasses back up with an amused smile, "Well, actually I am ..."

"Great!" Joanna cut the other woman off. "I need to ask you a few questions."

Kathey sighed as she laid the report on her desk and placed her feet back on the floor. "Judy once told me to just go along with you if you seemed excited about something, which you do, so my quarterlies can wait. I can assign them to others; that's what I have employees for."

She held up one hand, spoke into her intercom for a few moments, and tapped a few buttons. Joanna held back a sigh. This behavior was one reason she always liked the Jensens; they didn't fawn over the Great Families, at least in informal settings or in their home spaces. After only a few minutes, Kathey had sat back and was giving Joanna her full attention. "What has you so excited? I'm assuming you helped avenge Judy's death? Which you cannot confirm or deny, so just move your head one way or another to appease me please."

Joanna nodded and took out the crystal she'd made of information for Judy's family. It had the basic facts that the IGA had said Joanna was allowed to release to the family. IGA and worldgov were keeping Joanna informed of when the case would be officially closed so that she could arrange to release the documentary that same day on the various news outlets her family controlled or worked with. "This will tell you everything that I can for now," she said, placing it on the desk without releasing it, "but I need you to promise to keep it quiet until after my documentary comes out, which won't be until I get the go-ahead from IGA and worldgov both. They're not authorities you want to challenge by speaking about it publicly."

"Understood, but could I show it to my grandmother; tell my mother about it ...?"

"Yes, but just keep it between close family members, please."

"I can do that." Kathey took the crystal and gazed at it for a moment before placing it in a pocket. She tented her fingers under her chin and considered Joanna for another moment. "This isn't what you want to ask me about, though."

Joanna leaned forward, placing her hands on the desk. "Tell me everything you know about Dells Escort Agency. About all your experiences there."

Kathey lowered her hands and placed them on top of Joanna's with a wide grin. "I'll tell you what. I have a lot of work to do, but I'll be done by four. Meet me at Cafe Le Mare at four thirty, and I'll tell you over dinner."

Joanna felt her face flush as she realized what a spectacle she'd made by storming in here. "Right; you're working. I'm sorry I interrupted you."

"He made an impression on you," Kathey remarked, standing when Joanna did. "I knew it would happen," she added with a chuckle.

"Yes," Joanna admitted. "He's piqued my interest."

Scott set the bag down on the floor next to his bed, then sat down. He held his head in his hands, releasing a tightly held breath. Madame Sandy had informed him that Jones was out of town, so he had some time to just bask in the aftermath of a successful rental instead of paying for his time away. Jones liked to make him pay after any rental.

"The man is back!" Scott looked up to see the wide smile of his best friend. "Stand up and let me see what almost eight weeks away from here have done for you," Todd exclaimed, clapping his hand on Scott's back.

Scott rose and gave a mock bow. The two friends stood looking at each other a moment before hugging tightly and for just a few seconds longer than they should, though not as long as they wanted.

"I'm glad to see you, but I'm not so glad to see you back in this place," Todd stated as he sat down on the same cot.

A worried look clouded Scott's face as he sat next to his best friend. "What's been going on?"

"She's been in a rage ever since you were rented," Todd replied. "She took Johnny after a week."

Scott rubbed his hands down his face as he tried to speak. Each branch of Dells had only one boy per name, so sometimes a boy was moved if a better Paul or Simon came into their holding, but the practice made it easy for everyone to know who you were talking about with just one name. "He's just a kid; he just came here."

Todd nodded. "He freaked out. They took him to the clinic," he said, spitting the word out, "but they messed him up more."

The medics at the clinic had always helped him; the idea that they had harmed another boy made Scott feel dizzy with worry. He stood up. "I've got to go see him. This is my fault for being gone so long."

Todd grabbed the blond by the arm. "No one can see him. He's in solitary, all doped up."

"Why?" Scott collapsed on the cot at the news.

"He just keeps screaming and crying. The drugs were the only way they could shut him up. They even let some of us try and talk to him." Todd looked at the floor. "It didn't do any good. He just sits staring into space now."

Scott's face grew red as he sat silently. His fear was being replaced by anger, which he knew was dangerous to acknowledge. Slowly he glanced at the open entrance. "Where is she?"

"You'll never believe it." Todd's voice got excited as he nearly bounced on the bed. "She's been sent to LA to talk to the owner about this."

"Good." Scott stood up and started to unpack the bag he'd been sent.

Todd watched for a moment, then shook his head slowly. "What are you doing?"

"Putting the clothes away," he tossed back as he let them slide down the chutes to the laundry, where they'd be cleaned and stored until the next boy needed them. He looked at the T-shirt his client had gotten him and tucked it in the back corner along with the one an old client had given him, praying that this one, too, would be overlooked by any staff member who might find it.

"Did you hear what I said about Johnny?" Todd demanded as he walked up beside Scott.

"Yes, but you also just reminded me that I can't help!" Scott's hands tightened on the handle of the laundry chute as he let the dangerous feeling drain from him. He turned around with a half-smile. "I was going to tell you, all the guys in this room, some things about the trip that might interest you, but I think I'd only hurt you by mentioning them now."

Scott took a few steps forward, looking into the air. "You know, I actually thought that maybe things didn't have to be this way," he said, waving his hand to indicate the room. "But coming back has reaffirmed my belief that things will always be the same for us, Todd." Scott returned to unpacking after a few seconds, sending down the shoes through another chute and then laying the equipment on a conveyor belt so it wouldn't fall and be damaged.

The other man stood silently, shaking his head. "You gotta think positively, Scott. Why, just two weeks ago one of the older bucks was bought privately."

"Privately?" Scott stopped unpacking. "From this Dells?"

"Yeah. Well, no, not this one, but one in the Midwest." Todd pointed a finger at his friend. "It's like I keep telling you. If you treat each client like they're someone special, one day you'll have a new life in the private world."

Scott scowled as he set the bags themselves on the conveyor.

"One of your regular clients got lonely, so I was assigned to her." Todd looked away as he spoke.

"What?" Scott stopped unbuttoning the shirt he was wearing. His voice was edged with worry and stress as he huffed, "It went well, I suppose."

"I showed her a good time."

"And I suppose she said you were better than me?" Scott resumed taking off his shirt and dropped it down the chute so he could put back on the regular clothing they wore within Dells.

"No, not better, just more ... 'pleasant' was the word she used," Todd answered defensively.

"Pleasant?" Scott's anger disappeared quickly when he looked up to see the concern on his friend's face. "What does that mean?"

"It means she doesn't like your negative attitude, boy."

Scott looked down at his feet with a sigh. "Did you say this was a former client of mine?"

Todd nodded and stood up. "She asked me if I had time to spend with her on a regular basis. I lied and said I didn't have the time in my schedule. I couldn't do that to you, Scott. I heard she canceled your contract anyway."

Scott dumped the rest of his clothes down the shoot. Naked, he walked silently back to his cot and lay down on his back.

The two men refused to look at each other for several tense moments until Todd broke the silence. "Well, maybe you'll have a new regular now. One who'll take you places," Todd suggested with a grin.

"Ha!" Scott hmphed once, then closed his eyes. "Things were really strange on this trip, Todd. I thought I had a shot. She wanted so much from me, and I thought I met her goals 'cause she was nice to me, nicer even, on the way back. But then she just dropped me off, didn't even come in, did all the forms remotely. Didn't say anything about using me later."

Todd sighed and sat down on his own cot next to his friend, pointedly looking away. "I'll tell you what. I'll give you some of my secret tips on how to please women and have a more positive attitude if you promise to try them."

"Sure. They can't hurt me more than I've already been hurt."

Both men let their gaze drift toward each other, then Todd smiled and slipped off the bed to sit on the floor. "I do want to hear about the trip. The boys and I in here have been gossiping about it, making up stuff that I'm sure pales in comparison. You can tell us when they get back, yeah?"

Scott looked up and nodded. "Sure, though you probably won't believe half of what I tell you. I'm only going to tell you the truth," he added with a pointed look.

"Yeah, you suck as a liar; we all know it, so don't worry about it. How can we judge? The furthest I've been in the past few years is a thirty-eight-minute ride to a beach house for a weekend every quarter with Miss Margie."

"You're unpacked, yes?" Madame Sandy asked as she strolled in, causing each man to stand up and at attention.

"Yes, Madame Sandy," Scott replied as Todd stepped a few paces away to stand nearer to the door.

"Good," she said with a genuine smile and a glance at Todd. "Your being gone under the care of one of the Greats has apparently made you more attractive. That listing on your profile on our site helped with that," she added, but Scott was struggling not to grin as Todd made a double-fisted gesture of pride behind the host's back. "You have a client coming here in a few hours to see you."

Scott felt his mouth start to fall open but quickly shut it. "Yes, Madame Sandy; how should I prepare?" Great, he didn't even get a day off, but then again, that meant no thinking about Johnny in solitary or Jones being gone or Miss, no, Scion McMillin not wanting him.

"Just rest, then shower and do standard viewing dress, no nudity, and I'll be back to get you in an hour and 53 minutes," she told him, consulting her computer pad, and making a few taps on it. "You," she went on, turning to Todd, who snapped to attention, "make yourself scarce; try the common room, since you don't have a client until tomorrow evening. I can also assign you chores if you feel the need to be a nuisance."

"Understood, Madame Sandy," Todd replied with a bow and a glance at Scott before he left.

Scott bowed as well but waited to lie down on his cot until after the host left. He rolled over and tried to get to sleep. Maybe this was a regular? No, Madame Sandy would have mentioned that. Given what Todd had said, he had no regulars left. Probably someone wanting to see what a Great might see in him, an average boy with a weird specialty that hardly anyone wanted. He was so limited in what he could say, given all the promises he'd had to make to IGA, MOI, and Scion McMillin. He'd just fall back on client privacy and pleas for understanding about the Greats. With that resigned thought he just started counting his breaths until sleep came.

Scott placed his hands in front of himself and felt cold metal walls. He stumbled in the darkness as someone prodded him in the back. He continued walking, his bare feet now touching the cold metal floor.

"Stairs. Up!" the female voice commanded.

Scott found the step with his toes and went up five steps. He felt hands grab him and strip his pants from him. Suddenly the hands removed his blindfold, and a bright light dazzled him. He lowered his arms as his eyes adjusted. Several women stood below the platform he was on.

A woman he didn't recognize was standing on the same platform as him, giving him an appraising but not impressed look before reading the information on

her computer. "Remove the collar," she instructed another woman, whom he recognized as Madame Sandy.

Scott tensed as his silver collar was removed and tossed into a basket. He didn't even know what to say as he struggled to figure out where he was.

"Not too bad for 25," the woman with the clipboard commented as she examined him closely. "I think we'll start the bidding at 500."

"Please," Scott began speaking, but stopped when the woman struck his chest with her riding crop.

"Silence!" she ordered. "Show these ladies your stuff, boy."

The auctioneer turned to the crowd. "Ladies! Here we have a fine boy. Age 25, height five nine, weight 163, and it's mostly muscle! Trained at Dells Escort

Agency in Neuvo, he was one of their modest line, for clients looking for variety at a reasonable fee!"

Scott almost moved out of attention stance when the women started chortling at that information. He looked around with his eyes as the bidding began. None of his clients had wanted him, so now he was here in open auction for anyone to claim guardianship over. Open auction for unwanted men never ended well, the rumors said.

"650. Who-will-give-me-seven? Seven. Seven! Who-will-give-me-750? A bid for eight! Eight. Who-will-give-me-nine?"

Scott watched each woman bid but noticed that one hand in the back kept rising.

"1500, going once. 1500, going twice. Sold," the auctioneer announced, pounding her gavel, "to Emma Jones for 1500 credits!"

Scott backed up on the platform as his tormentor pushed xyr way through the crowd. Two guards grabbed his arms, forcing him to kneel as his private owner walked up the platform steps. "NO!" he screamed as xe placed the gold collar around his neck.

"No!" Scott sat up in his cot, sweat running down his face. He looked around his empty room to reassure himself. Slowly he got up and went to the mirror. He was still 24; he had nine, no less than nine, months before he turned 25. He glanced at the clock on the wall and noticed he just had time for a quick shower before this new potential client came. This time he had to get it right; he couldn't screw up the viewing as he had the last time.

Scott waited in the viewing room for his appointment; the walls were red, and the music was mostly rhythmic to generate more interest in prospective clients and proper arousal in the boys. He was ignoring the system's attempt to manipulate his feelings as he thought about why he might be here in the first place. Normally he'd get a few days off after such a long rental, or so it seemed when it happened to other boys. Best to keep busy, though, when the months were ticking by. He knelt on the floor facing the door. He looked over his clothes as he waited: khaki pants, white gauze shirt, brown sandals. Hearing footsteps approach, he stood up, smoothing his pants down.

"Bet you didn't expect to see me again!" Miss Joanna announced as she opened the door.

Scott blinked for a few seconds as his previous client approached. Today she was dressed in shorts, T-shirt, and sandals. He paused, correcting the words that wanted to come out of his mouth, trying to control his heart's pounding. "Miss Joanna," he stated as he stepped forward, then knelt on one knee to kiss her hand.

"Let's get this thing on you," she said, and he lifted his head. Miss Joanna sighed as she attached the leash she must have been given at the reception desk to his collar.

"How may I please you?" he replied to the click, though his head was spinning with questions.

"Is the ritual over now?" Miss Joanna asked.

Scott glanced up and let himself smile, remembering how little she liked the formalities. "Yes, Miss Joanna."

"Good, then let's go."

Miss Joanna hurried them out of the building. They strode down the sidewalks, nearly side by side, until she paused and dropped his leash to lift her hands into the air. "The fresh Gaian air! Normal gravity! The prettiest colors filtered through our atmosphere! Don't you love it?"

"It's wonderful, Miss Joanna," he replied as he picked up the leash and handed it to her as casually as he could.

Miss Joanna sighed but nodded as she took it. "I know; it's the law. The law sucks," she whispered, and he felt his mouth fall open a bit.

"You know, you can talk any time you want," Miss Joanna told him brightly as she held the leash short, forcing him to walk closer to her toward a nearby park.

He knew that, so why was he hesitating? They passed two women pushing a baby stroller, so he merely smiled at his client and offered a formal response, "My duty is to please."

"Can't you talk except in those rote phrases? I know you can; my memory isn't as great as yours, and I remember that." Miss Joanna looked around.

"Is there something I can help you find, Miss Joanna?" Scott offered.

"Ice cream vendor," Miss Joanna said. "There's got to be one around here. It's Nuwath, the season for ice cream and other cool delights to try and beat the summer heat. Every park should have a frozen treats vendor, shouldn't they?"

"There's one by the bridge," Scott replied, indicating the direction by pointing. He'd spent time in this park with clients on several occasions over the years.

Miss Joanna smiled and led him to the ornamental river with a bridge over it. A frozen treats vendor stood near the bridge, on their side. "What kind do you want?"

"Miss?" Scott looked at the vendor, an older slave, his silver collar attached to the cart by a chain. That was one place an unwanted man could end up, property of the company that ran those little shops, working long hours. Did he get to eat the treats he sold? The paunch on his tummy suggested he might. That wouldn't be a horrible life.

"What kind of ice cream do you want?" Miss Joanna repeated when he didn't reply. "I was rude this morning when I dropped you off, but I had a good reason. Still rude, though. I've always found that ice cream or whatever you prefer is a good counter to rudeness."

Scott felt himself blush. "You're a busy woman. I didn't think it was rude, Miss Joanna," he said. Terrifying, certainly, but not rude.

"So, what kind do you want?" his client got right in his face as she asked again.

Scott shrugged. "I don't know. I've never had ice cream, Miss."

Miss Joanna stepped back. "Crazy, 'cause even Joseph got ice cream when I did, usually because I demanded he did," she added softly.

She turned to the vendor and looked through the glass on top of his cart. "What flavors of premium ice cream do you have?"

"Ma'am, this service offers a wide variety of flavors of ice cream today. Chocolate, vanilla, chocolate chip, mint, butterscotch, fudge swirl, cookie, chocolate cookie, rocky road ..."

"Bio bowls for two. I'll have a double rocky road," Miss Joanna interrupted. "And a single," she continued, glancing at Scott, "chocolate. Let's not overwhelm him with too much of it for his first time, huh?"

"You are very kind," the vendor whispered. He quickly scooped up the orders, then handed her the bowls of ice cream.

"Thank you," Miss Joanna replied, pressing her finger to the scanner and adding in a tip. "Keep the change."

"Thank you, Miss, thank you," the old slave called after her as she led Scott away.

Miss Joanna found an empty snack table and motioned for Scott to take the other seat. He looked around, then bit his lower lip before doing as ordered. If the militia came, they couldn't claim he was disobedient to a client. He doubted she'd just let them beat him or haul him away. Once he was sitting, she took up a spoon of her ice cream. "Try yours, but take a small spoonful at first."

Scott did as she instructed but bit into the cold brown mound and found his teeth aching.

"Don't bite into it." Miss Joanna handed him a napkin as his face filled with pain. "Just place it on your tongue and enjoy the taste before swallowing."

Scott waited until the pain left before trying another spoonful. A moan escaped his lips, making her chuckle.

"It's good, huh?"

"Yes, Miss Joanna. Thank you so much." Scott took another spoonful with a grin. He finished his treat as she did, pacing himself so he finished just before her.

"Admit it," Miss Joanna said, wiping her mouth. "You didn't expect to see me so soon after our adventure on Bragg."

"I didn't expect to see you ever again, Miss Joanna," he replied, then clapped one hand over his mouth. Even she had limits to his speaking openly, he'd learned over the course of the trip.

"I promised you ice cream," she pointed out with a bit of a pout.

Scott nodded slowly, tossing the empty bowl and spoon into the blue recycling bin within arm's length, but he kept his mouth shut as he took hers and tossed it likewise into the bins.

"You probably hear lots of promises that aren't kept, huh?" Miss Joanna rested her head on one hand, propped up on the table by her elbow. She was watching him closely; her tone was a bit wary.

"I just didn't think I made a very good impression, Miss Joanna. I certainly didn't expect you to treat me to something this wonderful when I couldn't perform to your expectations." He placed both hands flat on the table where she could see them as he said each word slowly and carefully. The movement and purposeful tone were the only things keeping him where he was sitting when he wanted to fall at her feet and beg.

"Oh, you didn't do that badly," Miss Joanna replied, but her voice sounded shaky. She leaned toward him across the table, her chin on both hands. "I'm glad they said I could see you so soon. I was told that you normally get a few days' break, but my name does have benefits. I probably ruined your day, though," Miss Joanna stated with a half frown. "They said you were free all day."

"I'd much rather be with a client, especially you, Miss Joanna," he assured her more softly. He tried to make his eyes meet hers, but it felt too exposed out here. He was picking up bits and pieces of disgusted conversation about his sitting there from passersby and folks sitting a few tables away.

Miss Joanna nodded as she adjusted her position and moved closer to him, lowering her own voice. "I understand. If I don't have a story for a week or two, I start making up stuff to investigate."

"Do you have another story? Need an imagist?" he asked, hopeful that maybe she might need an imagist again. She'd given him a lot of set-ups on his own and a few solo filming assignments on the IGA ship; she'd even asked his opinion, as he'd been allowed to sit next to her during the editing of the days and days' worth of images and sound while they traveled, between the station, the Transway Gate, and the various ships back to Gaia. He thought he'd made several good suggestions, and even those she rejected never made her angry.

"Yes and no. I'm looking at a company now, trying to figure what's going on with them. Seeing if they're worth my attention." Miss Joanna went silent, then stood up suddenly. "Well, let's walk around. I need to have you back by four so I can make a dinner appointment."

Scott followed his client around the park, looking at the art and natural environs that populated the expanse. At a quarter to four they headed back across the park to Dells, and he knew he had to speak up now or never. "Miss Joanna?"

"Yes?" Miss Joanna brushed her hair from her eyes where the breeze had tugged it loose from the band she was trying to control her curls with. She was giving him her full attention.

His leash hung around one of her wrists, allowing him to walk next to her. Everything he wanted to say died in his throat, and instead he foolishly asked, "Did you want to do anything else? There are some shaded and private spots here."

"No," Miss Joanna said with a disappointed sigh. "I just wanted to get you some ice cream, spend some non-business time together." She stopped at the steps of the escort agency. "That was a nice time. Reminds me of hanging out with Joseph."

"I'm glad I pleased you, Miss Joanna," Scott said. Since she was smiling, he hadn't completely cocked things up. This Joseph boy – from the way she said his name, he had been important to her, was important. It was best not to push that right now; he might be able to find out more if he could get use of the database again. He bowed and kissed the hand that now held his leash.

Miss Joanna slapped him playfully on the back and led him up the steps to return him.

Kathey and Joanna followed their server to a small table in the back of the tiny café that Judy had brought her to a few times in the past. Joanna's coming back to this place symbolized that she had survived it all. Richards was dead, and her criminal empire would likely soon fall to pieces, leaving Joanna with both revenge and a great documentary that might win an award, one she'd dedicate to her fiancé if that time came. She'd make sure it came, invest the time to create the best documentary there could be. Whatever she decided to do about that boy, Scott was the logical choice to help with the editing, as long as he could keep his mind off his dick.

Kathey had picked the café and seemed very familiar with it, since she placed her order without looking at the menu.

The server turned to Joanna. "Would you like to order now?"

"Actually, I think I'll need a minute with the menu," Joanna said, taking one from the server. "I haven't been here in a while, and you're always adding new things."

"I'll return in a few minutes, then," the server said with a nod of her head and left.

"Whatever you get, make room for dessert," Kathey suggested. After a few minutes of allowing Joanna to silently go over the menu, she interrupted, "So you've been here before?"

"Yeah." Joanna marked her place with a finger and looked up. "Judy brought me here a few times when we had business in the city."

"Judy loved to try out different restaurants," Kathey said, sipping her water. "But I dare say she liked my spareribs best of all."

"Oh, is that an invitation to dinner at your place?" Joanna teased as lightly as she could as she placed the menu on the table. Except for the funeral, and her contact with Kathey over a month ago and earlier today, she had been avoiding the Jenson family.

"Yes, and I hope that we can do this more often." Kathey paused as the server approached.

"Yes, I'm ready to order," Joanna said, picking up the menu and pointing out the dishes she wanted.

Kathey waited until the server had left before speaking. "I don't have a lot of close friends, Joanna. I concentrate on business and family. Without Judy, it feels a bit lonely."

"I haven't been very supportive," Joanna confessed as she looked down at the tablecloth, picking at it with her fingers.

"We all grieve in different ways. I spent more time at Dells, at work. Ann could cradle it, but she has her limits; she wants me to have other friends like she does. Plus, I should be a better role model for Nell." Kathey moved in her seat. "Listen, I was hoping that maybe we could get to know each other better.

Judy talked about you a lot, but with seven years between us, I just never really got to know you while you two were dating."

Joanna sipped her water for a second. "How is your mother doing?"

"It's difficult losing your youngest, especially when you have unusual health concerns," Kathey answered, leaning on the table. "I've had to step up into her family position a bit earlier than I'd hoped as well as staying on top of the day-to-day operations."

"Your grandmother?"

"She's taken on a huge role in Mother's care," Kathey stated and looked away as their drinks and starter courses were brought out by a rare male server. She let her eyes follow him as he walked away.

"Owen and Ann have their hands full with you, don't they?" Joanna chuckled as she picked up her fork.

"I'm just looking," Kathey retorted as she took a sip of her cool tea. After a few seconds she sighed and spoke softly, leaning forward to make the comment more private, even though she had gotten a table off in a corner for a reason. "Grandmother does blame you a bit."

Joanna stopped and set her fork down, swallowing that bite as she nodded slowly. "She should ..."

"No, she shouldn't, but," Kathey began, then paused and sighed, "it's normal that she does, even if it isn't rational."

"Judy was only out there for a story that I found us, that I used my name to get us ..."

"Judy loved that about you. That you weren't willing to use your family for easy things, for material things, only for matters you were really passionate about."

"I did it hoping to get contacts to find my twin, not to find a multi-system conspiracy."

"Exactly. Things you're passionate about," Kathey repeated. "It's something we don't have a lot of in our family, maybe because of the defect," she said, referring to the odd genetic anomaly that seemed to pop up in their family every now and again no matter what the medics did. "If you know that every third generation is going to start losing their minds around the age of 40, you just don't bother getting too attached to anyone. But you do, and that thrilled her."

Third generation, huh? So Kathey's grandchildren would have this. That might be why Judy never wanted to be the birth mother, but for now that wasn't the topic, so Joanna pushed the idea away. "Should I do something about your grandmother? Make an appointment to talk with her? Send her something?"

Kathey just shook her head. "Let me deal with her. I think what you've given me is going to help with that." She took out the crystal and held it up before placing it back in her vest pocket.

"Good, good, and I'm going to mention Judy in this documentary, since she was my partner when this started. If anything positive comes out of this, it all began with her."

"Don't make a big deal of it, please. That will just rub Grandmother the wrong way," Kathey warned softly. "Be tasteful."

"Of course," Joanna said, frowning as she pushed aside several ideas that she'd had about a memorial inside the docu. After a few seconds they went back to eating until the next course was brought and her companion took the opportunity to check out the boy's ass again as he walked away.

Kathey turned back to her with a grin, then started to cut her main course. "So, why did you want to eat with me? I'm sure it's not for the delightful small talk or the occasional view we've been sharing."

Joanna took a deep breath, then said it again. "I want you to tell me everything you know about Dells Escort Agency, especially the one in Neuvo."

"You did get interested in him; I was right," Kathey stated with a waggle of her eyebrows.

Joanna rolled her eyes but nodded. "Yes, yes, you were right, but I'm interested in him because of how helpful he was on this story. He helped me edit huge sections of the footage on the trip back, was competent during the investigation, even risked his life ... that isn't something I planned," she hastened to add at her companion's narrowed eyes.

"Just promise me that you'll stay on-world for a while, and I'll try to tell you everything I know."

"I promise to stay on-world for the foreseeable future. We have the millennium celebrations coming up, and I think GNA wants a lot of personal stories. Not ideal, but I think I can spin it," Joanna pointed out. She often twisted what the Gaian News Agency wanted so that she had edgier stories that could fit into MOI's goals. At this point, GNA knew better than to assign her a topic if it didn't want some corruption revealed.

"Where should I begin?" Kathey asked.

"Well, I've learned about the boring stuff – when it was created, profits, legal matters, including some abuse investigations." That didn't get as much of a reaction as she'd hoped, but Joanna pressed on. "I really want a customer report from you. Start with your first visit, and proceed from there," Joanna directed.

"Chill." Kathey smiled as she remembered. "Well, I was in my first year of college. After finals I wanted a little excitement. You know, the boys in the dorms are nice, but I wanted a change. I'd just met Ann as well, so we actually went together, though she's not that fond of men."

Joanna settled down to let her talk at her own pace, since she had a good idea of what she wanted to do, even if she was making herself go slowly this time.

Scott sat down next to Todd at his dorm table in the mess hall. Two of their other roommates, Polo, and Elias, were present for the evening meal. "Slow night?" Scott asked when the bell signaled that they could start eating.

"I have one at eight," Polo said, pushing his dark hair back from his face as he ate.

"I just got back," Elias explained, showing off a bruise on his lower right arm before pulling his sleeve back down.

"I'm on break, as you should have been," Todd pointed out using his spoon.

"It wasn't a new client; it was the one I just served," Scott replied out.

"Hey," Todd said, nudging him with an elbow. "I told you."

"Maybe," Scott conceded, eating some of the nameless food on his tray.

"How was your big trip?" Elias asked in a hushed tone. They could talk while they ate; in many ways it was less frowned upon than their gossip sessions back in the room, but some things weren't dinner conversation.

"Very interesting," Scott replied with a twinkle in his eyes.

"Was the food good?" Elias asked as he frowned at his own bowl.

"You're always asking about food," Polo chuckled, hitting his benchmate on the arm. "I'm surprised you get hired with all the food you must eat."

"I don't eat that much," Elias insisted.

"Boys," Todd interrupted. "Let's just listen to Scott so we can eat before the bell sounds."

Scott waited for each man to apologize before speaking. "The food was great about half the time. I didn't have to prepare anything."

"Where did you go?"

"A resort. Off-world," Scott added for the looks of admiration that followed.

"How was usage?" Elias asked what all three of his roommates really wanted to know.

The one time they had sex? There was no way he could tell them that. Not the boys he shared a room with, certainly not any of the staff here. "It was fun, really," he admitted, letting himself blush at the memory.

"So much better when it's fun," Elias sighed wistfully.

"Thought you always had fun," Todd teased back with a huge grin. The roughboy just shrugged, and they all let it drop. Everyone had their limits, even those who weren't supposed to have them.

"You were gone for six weeks. You've never been gone that long," Polo pointed out, getting a glare from Todd sitting across from him. "That's true," the younger man squeaked.

"It took time to get where we needed to go and then do what needed to be done," Scott replied vaguely. He couldn't give them details. Not only wouldn't they understand, but he knew it was against the wishes of IGA, worldgov, and Miss Joanna.

"Where was that?" Elias insisted. They all paused as another boy joined them, releasing a breath when they saw it was Cal, who gave them all one of his always too sunny smiles. Polo whispered to him for a few moments, then the gardener nodded at Scott with wide eyes, urging him to go on.

He used the time to figure out what he could say. "You have to just believe me and not draw attention to the table by overreacting, chill?"

"Chill," each man agreed.

"Off-world," Scott said. Each boy opened and closed his mouth while Scott paused to give them time to process. Then he added, "First to the Lunar Base, then to the Transway – you may know it as the gate – then out of the solar system to a resort planet. Think an entire planet that's one big resort."

Polo started to stand up, but Elias and Cal quickly pulled him down between them. Scott's gaze went to the nearest guard who was watching the room, but she was turned away from them for a few moments. Once everyone at the table calmed down, Todd was the first to speak. "My boy does not lie, but I am struggling to accept it."

"I have a tee-shirt I'll show you," Scott simply said as casually as he could.

After several more silent minutes of eating, Cal asked a question Scott had been dreading. "How were her punishments? If you had any?" That got a snort from Elias. He might not have meant it as a comment on Scott's behavior, but it felt that way.

"She was very kind, very fair." Scott looked at his plate in silence. "Let's just finish eating. If she comes back like she says, I'll have more to tell you later."

Todd looked at him with a grin. "Told you it was just a matter of time," his best friend boasted.

Scott returned the grin but glanced over at the guards before he took another bite. Timing might be everything, and he didn't know how long he'd have before Jones was back. The disciplinarian was going to beat him bloody if xe got into trouble at headquarters but was allowed to come back anyway. He'd seen how Miss Joanna had reacted to Miss Renee's hurting him for their cover … it could be a good or bad thing if she had to see what Jones did to him. He thought his chances to survive Jones were worse than his odds had been to live through his encounter with Richards.

It was dark when Joanna looked up at Kathey's unexpected words. Everything that she'd been told was either good – the boys were obedient but not boring, and well-trained in something useful – or sadly expected, based on the investigations, including the latest one involving the lead disciplinarian right here in the Neuvo office. The sudden change in topic took her by surprise, so she said, "What did you say?"

Kathey sighed and took a sip from her second glass of hot tea. As long as they kept ordering something, they could stay at their table as long as they wanted, especially once a few local reporters snuck in and took a few images of them, stirring up interest in the café tonight. "I said you'll need to tell him about your others."

Joanna frowned and looked at the table for a second. "He'll be my partner." The other woman arched an eyebrow at that, but Joanna kept talking. "My imagist. I don't really think that has much to do with others in my life."

"Will you hold his contract or will your family? Perhaps one of the affiliate news stations? MOI?"

"No; if I do this, I'm doing it; he'll be under my guardianship."

"Then living with you ..." Her companion let the obvious implications trail off until Joanna nodded.

"I doubt Dells is going to want a rider like you have with Owen's family. They're a business; I'll just acquire him flat out."

Kathey sat silently for a second and then sighed before making the next statement. "It isn't easy to get the right to hold guardianship without any riders. It's a long process, with background checks, meetings with various parties, written exams, oral exams, and, of course, the virtual immersion to see if you've been lying." Joanna frowned and squirmed in her seat, but her companion continued, "Then the visitations for the first two years, just to make very certain you're adhering to the law. Judy told me about your dorm boy. This time you wouldn't be able to just send him away. He'll have to live with you. Can you do all of that?"

Joanna tried to smile back confidently, but she stuttered her words a bit. "I can be a good ... guardian. I do what's necessary. I do that all the time at

Great meetings, with my family, at GNA, worldgov, everywhere." She let her words die off as she realized what she was saying.

Kathey frowned at what she said but didn't push. She took the final sip of her drink, and Joanna did the same. "You said you went and saw him today, expressed some interest, so I assume, given your philosophies" – Kathey said that word with a slight mocking tone that had Joanna stiffening in defense – "that you want him to be consenting for this change in his status."

The elder Jenson might not agree with her sister's ideals, but she knew enough about what they'd done to use it to make her point. "You're right," Joanna said, getting the other to smile brightly and flag for their check, "I'll tell him. I'll figure out a way."

"Of course you will," Kathey agreed as she shooed away Joanna's offered finger to split the check and simply scanned her own ID for it. "I want to see it when you do. In fact, I insist we have a party when it's all finalized."

"Why?"

"Because my dear, according to my sister, when you put your mind to home, you put your passion into it. Your passion is what makes you so damned stubborn that you take whatever you've set your mind to and see it through to the end. That sort of thing is the reason why your family is a Great Family, whether you want to admit it or not."

Chapter Twelve

Joanna paused in front of the entrance to Dells' downtown club in Neuvo a few nights later. She gave a sharp laugh as she read the club's name. "Ha! 'Dells Heavenly Haven,' huh?" She pulled her foldable black leather hat down over her eyes and the matching jacket collar up around her face; she'd decided to go rough tonight, just in case he hadn't believed her. Her attorney had said the process would simply speed along once it was started, given her family name, so this was her final opportunity to figure out what Scott's life was like and give him a taste of what she could offer. Ideally, they could have stayed at Dells, but she'd been told he was out at one of their clubs tonight because of a shortage, dancing. He had told her that he could dance and that he did so at these clubs; she just hadn't remembered unprompted.

After a slow glance around to make sure that no one was trailing her, a problem she'd had since returning on-world, she entered the club.

Once inside, Joanna loosened her collar. She blinked as her eyes adjusted to the dimly lit room. "May I help you?" A woman suddenly appeared in front of Joanna as she tried to walk further into the club.

"Yeah," Joanna handed the woman a card the receptionist from Dells had given her. "They said I could use him tonight," she replied with a weak smile.

"Let me just check our reservation book." The woman led Joanna back to the entrance, where her reception desk was. "I assume this is your first time here, Scion McMillin?"

Joanna's stomach tightened at the uncomfortable title, but her face showed no signs. "Yeah, it is. How'd you know?"

"You keep looking around," the receptionist replied as she sat down at her desk.

"I expected more light than this in a club," Joanna stated, folding her arms.

"The stage and bar are fully lit, as is each of our displays when approached." The woman consulted the card, then the book. "Yes, here we are. McMillin – the Safari Room," she said, raising her eyebrows as she took in her cap and jacket. Joanna had wanted their "dungeon," but it had already been booked when the receptionist at Dells had tried to reserve it. "That's a fun room. Equipped with both sauna and play area. Swimsuit optional." The host handed her a card, which she explained would allow her access to the room and other facilities in the club.

"Sounds great." Joanna looked around with narrowed eyes now that she could see better. Membership-only dungeons such as The Chain were well lit, though she'd only played on-site a few times there. She guessed the average woman wanted the naughtiness cranked up by dimming the lights. "I have two guests coming as well," she added, tilting her head and trying to see the computer screen, but she couldn't see it from that angle.

"Yes," the host replied as she continued to read, "Raven Eliane Windsome and Jack." The host looked directly at Joanna with a frown. "We don't normally allow outside boys, but I see that an exception has been made since you've reserved time with Scott. Good thing you did – he tends to draw interest when he dances."

Joanna smiled, pleased that he was more popular than his comments during their trip had led her to believe, and glad that she'd made the reservation. "Where's this Safari Room?"

"Follow me, please." The receptionist led the way to the entrance but only pointed out the directions. "Go past the bar and down the hall marked 'Heaven.' It's the third door on your left." The woman handed Joanna a green card. "Your time doesn't start for twenty minutes. Have a drink on the house," she said, tapping the card she'd given Joanna, causing it to light up, "and relax for a moment; you can even see Scott dance, since he's scheduled for the next song. We'll send him to your room when your time starts, so he has a chance to refresh himself – unless you like him raw?"

Joanna shook her head. "Nah, he should clean up a bit, thanks."

"May he take your coat?" the woman asked quickly as a man stepped out of the shadows next to her.

"No, it has things I need for tonight." Joanna smiled tightly as the woman gave her a grin and the man slipped back into the darkness.

The smile disappeared as soon as the woman returned to her desk. Joanna took off her jacket, placed the hat inside a pocket, and draped it over her arm. "You have to go in, Joanna," she whispered to herself as she stepped through the doorway and into the unnecessarily dark club. If the gossip parlors ran her face on their pages tomorrow, so be it. Given what her dorm boy had been like, it wouldn't be a shock to her mother or grandmother.

"Miss?" A soft masculine voice stopped her after just a few steps.

Joanna took one step toward the sound and was surprised when a large silver cage was illuminated before her. It hung about three feet off the ground and contained a boy dressed only in a white loincloth. The boy knelt close to the bars and reached out tentatively towards her. "Let me be your angel tonight, Mistress?"

Joanna swallowed as she stepped closer. The boy's pale skin contrasted sharply with his black hair and eyes. He flinched as she touched his hand. She noticed a dark mark under one eye that wasn't completely hidden by the powder, which made him even paler. "How old are you?"

"Sixteen, Miss." The boy moved closer to the bars.

"Nope!" Joanna pulled back from the pleading boy as her own face turned pale.

"Miss, please!" the boy called out to her as she hurried away.

Joanna stumbled across the dark distance, ignoring the sudden bursts of light and cries of boys for her attention as she moved. As she entered the lit area, she hurried to the bar, fully aware of how ridiculous it was that this was freaking her out, yet unable to stop. This could have been Joseph. These were someone's brothers or sons, and those kids in the cages ... she'd fooled around some with boys when she'd been that age, but the clients here were clearly adults.

"Would you care for a drink?" the bartender asked suddenly, making Joanna nearly jump in the air. The older woman gave her an amused smile, simply stating, "You need a drink. What will it be?"

Joanna placed the green card on the counter. "Wine, whatever's your house best," she ordered after a moment's hesitation. Once she had it in hand, she leaned back against the bar, sipping, and trying to calm down. Soon the music from the stage drew her from the bar to stand closer. The dancer was good, working his audience with well-timed moves and graceful execution; he had the crowd of women clapping and screaming. Zack, her former dorm boy, had danced for her a few times, but he hadn't been nearly this skilled, plus he'd lacked the entire stage and accompaniment. She was about to sit down at one of the many tables to enjoy it when she recognized the dancer as Scott.

Joanna shuddered and sat down, feeling her mouth fall open. A moment later her eyes met his as the last bit of cloth fell from his body. Her face turned red as he stood frozen for a few beats, staring back at her.

Quickly Joanna stood up and pushed back through the crowd as it hissed its disapproval. If she couldn't control herself, she needed to leave him be, or he'd get into trouble, and her research had shown that was the last thing she wanted.

Joanna turned her wrist pad and messaged Raven. Her lover had just left to pick up Jack. "Problem, Ma'am?" the other woman asked.

Joanna moved into the hallways, away from the dance stage, the cages, and the bar, and took a breath. "I'm just eager to introduce you all," she sent a voice message back.

There was a pause for an extra couple of seconds, then Raven's voice message replied, "I hope we will all get along, Ma'am."

Joanna smiled and closed her pad. She looked at the room card, found the corresponding label on a door at the edge of the hall, and went straight into the Safari Room.

Scott remained frozen for a moment before catching the beat again and finishing his routine. After the weak applause, he hurried off stage.

The show manager roughly grabbed Scott by the arm. "What the hell happened out there?" she demanded, giving his arm a jerk.

"My client for later is here, Ma'am. She surprised me," he muttered.

"Why did they send you guys over here if they're just going to schedule you out before the customers have a chance? Not that you would have gotten one with that performance," she added, looking at her computer. The stage manager released him and pointed toward the locker room door with her thumb. "Well, hurry your ass up, boy! She wants you cleaned before you report to her."

"Yes, Ma'am." Scott hurried past the manager, oblivious to the rough pinch on the butt she gave him. That had not been the best way to impress his client, but he hadn't known she was going to be here; he hadn't heard anything about her in several days. At least he didn't have any damage, since Jones was still at headquarters, and the one client he'd had since the ice cream outing had only been interested in a quickie saddle at the agency.

He found Miss Joanna crouching in the center of the room, by an artificial pond surrounded by artificial flowers. She was peering down at her reflection with a sigh. Like everything else in Haven, it was all for show.

"Miss Joanna?"

She looked up at him but returned her gaze to the water as she spoke. "You said you had a bit of dancing talent. You have quite a bit, actually."

Scott walked around the pool to kneel beside her. "I didn't know you were coming, or I could have tried to get you a better room," he said and nodded at the leather jacket next to her.

"This will do – not ideal, but it will serve its purpose."

Scott nodded and just waited, keeping his gaze on hers, as she seemed to prefer. "Thank you, Miss," he whispered after a moment of silence.

"For what?" Miss Joanna glanced up.

"For complimenting my dance routine," he reminded her.

"I tell it like it is. You are better than you claimed. Like you were with imaging," she said with an odd tone he couldn't quite understand. She was sipping wine. How many had she had? She'd only had alcohol a few times at Bragg, and then just for show. Women didn't usually get drunk without a reason. It was never good when they did. He just watched until she spoke again. "What are you doing here dancing, though? I figured you'd still be on a break – hoped you'd be on a break." He almost didn't hear that last sentence, so he ignored it.

"Some of the dancers got sick, so some of us came over to entertain the matrons." He glanced at the water as he added, "I worked here for about a year."

"Really? When?" Her voice had a surprised tone to it, so he looked back at her.

"Before I legally became an escort, Miss Joanna," he stated.

"How old were you?" she asked, recalling the boys in the silver cages.

"Sixteen. Your serious training starts at 15, do the club circuit at 16, then become an escort when you're 17." Scott noted his client's eyes widening and amended his comment. "I mean, a boy becomes an escort when he's 17."

Miss Joanna just nodded with a frown. Perhaps reminding her of all the years of clients he had pleased was a bad move, but it did no good to lie when she could easily check his profile.

"I have you until closing," she told him as she picked up her jacket.

Scott pressed his hands together tightly as she frowned. "You can leave at any time, though. You'll get your money back, Miss."

"If I left early, would you be," and she paused, "rented out to someone else?"

"Perhaps; there is a lot of work here."

"I bet a lot of those women out there would love to be back here with you."

Scott sighed sadly, "I don't think so."

"What do you mean? I saw all those women clapping and screaming. Even I was entranced for a moment," she admitted.

"They were also booing me," he added.

"Because you saw me and got distracted?"

Scott shrugged. "When I saw you, it threw me for a few beats. It's entirely my fault; a professional shouldn't let that happen."

"Well, I was a little thrown myself when you turned around, even though the receptionist told me that you'd be dancing." Miss Joanna crouched down and reached out to run her hand through the warm water.

"It's a whirlpool, Miss."

"Not really what I'm in the mood for," she said. She sat down, pulling her leather jacket onto her lap. Her voice had a deeper edge to it now, darker than the one she'd had the single time she'd truly used him on the trip, but he knew that tone of voice and what it meant.

"There are many toys and devices here for your amusement, Miss Joanna. Some rougher toys as well," he added.

"In a moment," Miss Joanna muttered as she took her scanner out of her jacket pocket and got back to her feet. She walked around the room, giving it a once-over. He knew what she was doing, and part of him was offended; Dells would never spy on their own clients. He just stayed by the pool and watched until she returned and sat down on one of the artificial rocks.

"I came here to spend a bit more time with you, Scott. Have some fun – my type of fun."

Scott straightened up as he moved within easy reach and lifted his gaze to meet hers. "Yes, Miss Joanna, I look forward to your use."

Joanna paused, then asked, "Do you like me?"

"Yes, Miss Joanna. You are the nicest client I've ever had." He gasped when her hand struck out and slapped him hard enough to almost tip him over. She let him get his breath and move into a kneeling position by the rock, right in front of her. This time he blinked when he met her eyes. "I'm not lying; I think that you are the best client I've had."

She slapped him again, this time on the other cheek, before stating, "That must be why I'm hitting you, 'cause I'm so nice."

"I almost ruined your story," he offered. "I deserve to be yelled at, beaten without mercy, Miss Joanna. You were being, you are being, very lenient with me, if I may say so?"

She didn't say or do anything for a couple of moments, so he let his gaze move up again. She had brought one leg up to rest on top of the other knee and propped her elbow on it; now she was resting her chin on her hand, studying him.

"I always want you to tell me what you think," she reminded him gently. He nodded, forcing his stance to relax, his gaze to stay on her. "Things weren't ideal on Bragg, but I think you'd do fine under the normal stressful conditions I operate under. What did you think about working with me?"

"I felt really out of place at times, most times, but," and he paused. Miss Joanna leaned forward with an encouraging nod, so he continued. "I helped you when I was behind the lens, at the editing desk, and I think I didn't do so bad as a companion either." Scott stopped speaking but smiled.

"I doubt I could have gotten all that information on Richards without your help. In fact," she went on, taking a folded letter out of her shirt pocket, "I just received word this afternoon that our assistance is going to be up for an IGA award for civilians helping the authorities. And we have the go-ahead to finish the docu, get it ready to release."

"I'm very glad for you, Miss Joanna." His smile widened, and his heart was pounding at the news.

"For us. It will be us winning if we do." She placed both feet on the floor as she said, "I need someone to help me a lot now, because as much as we got done, there's so much more to do on this docu, on the next." Miss Joanna paused and took a deep breath, then said more softly, "My partner was killed; I believe I mentioned this to you."

He nodded; his heart was racing.

"I think you might be able to learn the skills to be a first-class investigative imagist. You already have a lot of those skills." Miss Joanna moved the couple of steps between them, and he made himself hold still as she took him by the shoulders and looked directly at him. "I'm thinking of buying you."

Scott's eyes widened, and his mouth fell mutely open.

Miss Joanna's smile widened as she viewed his reaction with amusement. When he just continued to stand there, she loosened her grasp and stepped back. "Is there something wrong, Scott?"

Scott shook his head violently, then lowered his eyes respectfully. "I'm afraid I wasn't listening very well. I don't think I heard you correctly, Miss," he whispered.

"What do you think I said?" Miss Joanna asked in a neutral tone as she returned to sit on the rock as she had before.

Scott swallowed before answering, "I thought I heard you say that you were thinking of buying me, Miss Joanna."

"That's exactly what I said. Do you not want that?"

"I do!" he immediately replied but whined in his throat at the same time.

"It's a lot to cradle, I guess." She let her leg fall so she was straddling the rock. "Is there anything you want to ask me?" He simply stared at her as he nodded, happy to have permission to release all the thoughts running through his head. "Go ahead and ask me anything, Scott."

"Would, would you privately own me, Miss Joanna?" he asked haltingly.

"Yes." She said yes; she wanted his contract for just herself, not her family, not her career; he was about to reply when she stood up and took a few steps away. "The people I really work with offered to buy you for me, but I'd prefer to do it myself. You don't need lots of people telling you what to do, especially in some of the situations we might find ourselves in. I also don't want them to have the power to interfere in my life more than they already do."

Scott closed his eyes as he ventured another question when she turned back to him with a wave of her hand to signal that he should continue. "How many others do you own, Miss?"

"None." Scott sighed happily. "You'd be the first – well, actually, my second, but he's not with me anymore."

That stopped the other questions. She did have rules, then, and limits to what she'd accept, even if she didn't know it or was unwilling to directly tell him. He could ask, but it wasn't a done deal yet. Better to wait until the contract was signed before asking about those details.

Miss Joanna sat down on a rock and looked intensely at him. "Would you like me to buy you, Scott?"

The sudden touch of her hand on his shoulder made Scott glance up, tears in his eyes. "Yes, Miss Joanna," he managed to softly say.

Miss Joanna pulled a handkerchief from her jeans pocket and handed it to him. "Here. Use this. I didn't mean to make you cry. I won't buy you if you don't want me to."

Scott sat up on his knees so he could be closer to her. "Oh, Miss, I do want to be bought by you. To be owned by you and only you," he added dreamily. It was so freeing to be able to use the words that were real instead of the lying terms. "I'm sorry I'm so emotional."

"That's how men are," Miss Joanna stated with a little chuckle.

He didn't bother to disagree when he knew it was true; he had the annual recounting of the Sins of Men to show the danger of the weaker sex's emotions. Dells drilled them to have more control, to focus on their clients, but here he was, thinking only of what he had been wanting for so long. "Here," he said and turned a dried cheek toward her, "please continue, Miss Joanna. My pain is for your pleasure."

"Whoa, that's like so passive. How can you stand it?" said a masculine voice. Scott turned to find a man and a woman walking across the floor toward them. He hadn't even heard the door open.

Scott must have been trembling, but Miss Joanna reached out and put a hand on his shoulder to steady him. "Just my guests," she whispered.

Boys were highly competitive, but Scott bit his cheek, and the pain helped him focus as they both stood up. She went forward and motioned to the two new people. "Scott, I had some of my lovers come here to meet you tonight. I thought we might get to know each other, since if I become your … guardian, you'll be seeing them." She was using the euphemism again.

Scott tried to keep his hostile reaction quiet, but the other smirked back. "This is Jack; he's a roughboy whose company I enjoy a couple of times each month," Miss Joanna said. Scott merely smiled tightly, as did the other boy, who came right up to his client. The roughboy spread his legs in a wide stance, arms crossed over his chest, and gave Miss Joanna a cocky grin. She hit him so hard that Scott could almost feel it in his own bones, but the other boy only went to his knees and started rubbing his head against her leg.

She looked back at him, her eyes daring him to keep their gaze, so he did. "I don't intend to give up Jack. Do you understand?"

"Yes, Miss Joanna," Scott made himself reply. Thank Goddess, he allowed himself to say silently over and over.

"Jungle, huh?" The other woman said as she looked around. "Not quite what I was expecting, Ma'am."

"You know I do like to keep you off balance, pet," Miss Joanna teased back, which made both new arrivals chuckle. At this exchange Scott blinked and looked down. Who was this other woman? "Did Jack behave for you on the trip?"

"He was obedient and stuff, really uncomfortable," the other woman confessed as she stepped toward Miss Joanna and went to her knees. "I brought him from The Chain like you said," she added with a bow of her head that mimicked positions he been taught at Dells.

"This is Raven, my … girlfriend," Miss Joanna introduced the other woman finally.

The other woman blushed and rose to her feet. She looked disappointed, and that only confused Scott more.

"Raven is an officer with the Nuevo militia, but she only works with Great Families, which is how we met," Miss Joanna went on to explain.

Scott put a hand on the fake grass to help steady himself. The room felt too warm, too humid. Was it spinning?

"Miss, I think he might be sick?" he heard the other man's voice say in a tone that wasn't cocky anymore, it almost sounded concerned.

Stronger hands, slighter larger hands, helped him stand up and set him down on the rock where his client had been sitting. Another pair of hands pressed a cool glass into his. "Sip this," Miss Joanna ordered, so he did.

In a few minutes, he could focus again. The two newcomers were there. The woman named Raven was standing looking at him, xyr hair, dark brown and nearly black, in a loose braid over one shoulder. The other man, also a blond but with darker tones to his hair and skin, his eyes brown, not blue, was kneeling but in a relaxed stance. The woman was in a long skirt with a tank top, while the man had torn jeans, tank top, and some leather accessories like Elias might use. Definitely not prepared for this room, Scott thought, and that made him start to giggle.

"Now he's gone nuts," the other boy said, getting a tap on the head from the woman. "If you're gonna do it, do it harder," he tossed up.

"In your dreams," xe snorted.

"This was not my best idea," Miss Joanna said. She was sitting by him on the rock, one arm around him.

He looked at her and stopped giggling. "Why do you need me if you have them?" The words were out of his mouth before he could stop them.

Miss Joanna glanced at the other two, then at him. "I'm complicated. I love more than the average woman usually does." He glanced and found the other two were nodding. "My partner, who I was going to marry, who was my imagist, she knew both Raven and Jack. We were a family. I want that family again. If all of you can accept that?"

"I know that you have needs that I can't fulfill, that no woman could; I don't have a problem with you adding another boy, Ma'am," Miss Raven immediately said. "If this one," xe directed xyr gaze at him, and Scott looked down, "I mean if you have the skills to be an imagist, I think it can work out. If you can accept us."

"So weird," the other man began, then quickly changed his tone as he stood up, "This guy flinched like you'd hit him with a truck just from that love smack you gave me. He isn't a threat to what I do for you, Miss Joanna. You asking us, though – I'm with his reaction; that's not how most women are."

"Scion McMillin isn't most women," Miss Raven pointed out.

That settled every scurry of worry that he was feeling. Scott lifted his head, looked at each of the newcomers, then turned to his client. "I want you as my guardian," he used the term she had for their sake, hoping his tone and eyes showed he understood what she would truly be. "I will be the best imagist a boy can be, and then I'll be more."

Miss Joanna considered his statement for a moment, then nodded as she pulled him in for a brief hug. "Fair enough," she agreed.

There was a pause, and then the other woman stepped forward and knelt at Miss Joanna's feet. Her feet, not theirs; his were merely in the vicinity. "But you brought us here for more than that, Ma'am. You want to see if we can all play together well. Right?"

The other man frowned for a moment, then he grinned. "Oh, with the new boy. See if he can handle the truth." He looked at Scott with that smirk back on his face again.

"Only if everyone is chill with group play here tonight. Only if each of you knows you can say "no" and just go to the other side of the room if you get too uncomfortable," Miss Joanna insisted. One by one each person nodded seriously. When Miss Joanna looked at Scott, he did the same.

"Let's start simple, then. Just hugging; everyone come and hug me, and then we'll exchange hugs," she began, directing them.

Thirty minutes later, though, Scott kept looking up from where he knelt just a foot or so away. Part of him felt like moving, but he hadn't been given permission, and he was determined to be very good for Miss Joanna, tonight and every day she had him. He was struggling with what he was seeing before him. Miss Raven and Jack were both Miss Joanna's roughboys … no, there had to be another word for it.

Scott could almost feel what he was seeing turning him on. Goddess had made males a certain way; it was normal to get a bit hard from seeing any sexual act, any physical act. Jones had shown him that much. The thought of the still-absent disciplinarian made him shudder, so he closed his eyes for a second.

When he reopened them Miss Raven's skirt was up over Jack's head, and Miss Joanna was playing with the other woman's bared breasts. That was his cue to move, to take advantage of the blanket permission to go to the other side of the room if things got too intense. He was used to seeing other boys tormented for fun, but it bordered on unnatural to see a woman in that type of pain. That had to be pain, right?

No one noticed when he stood up and headed toward the hidden snack bar in the room. He gathered up glasses of water plus a pitcher, filled it with ice and more water, several protein-rich snacks, and some sugary ones as well, and put them all in a bamboo basket designed to fit into the theme of the room. He was about to turn around when a different feminine voice started crying out. Scott bit his tongue to keep himself quiet; Miss Joanna hadn't been nearly that loud when she'd used him.

Straightening his shoulders and back, he waited until the noises died down and then turned with a smile on his face to carry the basket back to them just as Miss Joanna called out his name.

She looked down and pulled up her jeans, pushing Jack back and prodding Miss Raven with a foot as Scott came back and knelt with the basket at her feet. "We didn't mean to ignore you, Scott …"

"I did," Jack replied, so Scott gave him a glare, then smiled again as Miss Raven pinched the boy, making him gasp in unwanted pain. Good; it served the little dick right for taking time away from Scott tonight.

"Jack!" Miss Joanna's verbal punishment seemed to have the greatest effect as the boy almost folded in half on the floor. "Scott, oh, how sweet," Miss Joanna said, taking the water from him.

Miss Raven was holding xyr top close to xyr chest with one hand and just nodded at him when he handed xem a glass. Even Jack looked ashamed, maybe even shocked, to be offered a glass.

"I brought snacks, too; they help after play," Scott heard himself say, though he felt like he was watching from a long way back. Would this be what life was like with Miss Joanna? Knowing that he'd have to help take care of her lovers because he wasn't enough? He could find a way to learn to be more like Jack, just like he could learn more about taking care of a house and keep up to date on the latest imaging tech. There had to be a way. There was nothing wrong with being the boy who took care of others. She didn't live with them; it wouldn't be all the time.

He flinched when he felt himself pulled into a hug by his client. "See, this can work," she said rather loudly. "Why don't you set that basket over there, Scott?" she instructed him. Then she leaned toward the other two and whispered something as he did as he was told.

Soon he felt two other pairs of arms and hands around him. This was not the sort of night he had envisioned when he'd seen her from the stage. As six hands caressed his arms, back, and shoulders, and even ventured down to his ass and legs, he felt himself relax into it until he was on the floor on his back with Miss Joanna looking down at him.

She sat back, and Miss Raven popped up over him with a piece of fruit in xyr fingers, which xe gently pushed into his mouth with a chuckle. When his client's female lover moved out of view, her roughboy entered his line of sight with a piece of cheese in his fingers. "Sorry for being a dick," Jack said as he brought the light-yellow cube to his mouth and let him take it without taunting him.

"Now we'll pay attention to you," Miss Joanna said as she took the boy's place, then leaned down to give him a kiss.

It was the weirdest thing he'd done – some of Dells' movies could get pretty intense, but it was up there, because women were never the givers in those vids. It was also much nicer than he'd been hoping for just a few minutes before.

Miss Joanna saddled him, meeting his eyes the entire time while Jack took him deep into his mouth. "You're doing great," Miss Joanna kept telling him. After a while, they changed positions, so that he was fisting Jack's cock, while Miss Joanna took him in hand. Miss Raven just lay alongside them and stroked Scott's arm.

Miss Joanna lay down along his other side, her and Miss Raven's hands tracing patterns on his chest and stomach as Jack returned to suck his dick. When Scott was close, he looked up at his client, licked his lips, and pleaded, "Miss Joanna, this one begs you to allow him to come."

Jack stopped all movement with his cock all the way in his mouth, taunting Scott, who had to grind his teeth to keep from moving his hips.

The two women looked at each other, then Miss Joanna nodded once.

Scott shuddered and cried out, "Thank you," over and over while the other man drank him down.

Scott just watched, jealousy and worry distant feelings, as Miss Joanna leaned over and kissed Jack on the lips. He felt only warmth as he watched her kiss the other woman. Then they all held him as his balance returned.

After Miss Raven left, taking the roughboy with xem and leaving Miss Joanna lying half on top of him, Scott's smile faded just a bit. "You chill?" she asked him with a concerned frown.

"Please buy me," he whispered as he stroked her arm, which was resting across his chest. She just smiled again and gave him another kiss.

Chapter Thirteen

Scott breezed into his dorm room with a grin and nodded at Cal, Todd, and Elias, who were in various stages of getting ready for bed. When he just lay down on top of his cot without bothering to undress or get under the covers, the other three looked at each other until Todd made the approach.

Todd raised an eyebrow at his best friend's behavior as he stood over his cot looking down at him. "You've never acted this way before after working at the club. While I am exhausted after teaching the newbies tonight, your attitude is making me curious."

Scott propped himself up on his elbows and looked at his friend. "When did you get back?"

"About fifteen minutes ago." Todd moved into a sitting position, his face frowning at the movement.

Scott glanced around to see the other two roommates moving closer as Todd continued to just stare at him. "Wow, I must be one sorry whore, then, for you all to be looking at me like I'm some kind of reprogrammed doll boy when I get back from a rental."

Todd looked at the other two roommates before meeting Scott's gaze. "Jones is back," he said solemnly.

Scott chuckled as he flopped back down, rubbing a hand over his eyes. "Of course, xe is. But I don't care; I just want to relax a minute."

Elias's gasp was audible and drew Scott's eyes as the other man lowered his hand from his mouth. "You don't care? I like it rough, and I care about xem being back," the other man said with a wary glance at their open doorway.

"Nope."

"We are talking about Emma Jones, the agency disciplinarian, right?" Cal pointed out as he sat down on the bed opposite Todd.

Scott shrugged.

Todd frowned and put a hand on Scott's arm as he motioned for Elias to watch the doorway. "The woman you fear most in the world? The one you have nightmares about?"

"You always say that I'm too negative," Scott reminded him. "Xe'll do what xe wants to me anyway, but right now I just don't care," he sighed as he smiled up at the ceiling, remembering.

"Something obviously happened tonight to change your attitude. You gonna tell me about it or not?" Todd pressed as he motioned for Cal to move away.

"You gonna tickle me if I don't?" Scott asked with a chuckle.

"What? Did you get concussed?"

"Just a joke, Todd." Scott sat up cross-legged on his cot then softly recounted the events of the evening. The other boys stayed away, eyes warily on the door. "Miss Joanna came to the club. She rented me for the entire evening. Brought her female lover and a roughboy she rents often with her to see how I'd fit into her world. See if we could all get along."

"The Scion who rented you? What did she do to you, Scott?"

"It was a very interesting evening, Todd." Scott unbuttoned his shirt to show off the light marks that the trio had left him with after feeding him. He hadn't even realized they'd hurt him because none of it had hurt at the time.

Todd's dark eyes narrowed as he examined the marks. "I thought you said she was the nicest woman I could possibly imagine?"

"That's just it. I didn't feel these while they were happening. It just felt good. It was weird at first, but I wasn't really involved in the weird stuff," Scott vaguely explained, earning a shake from Todd's head. "I'm not supposed to tell anyone more," he added with a glance at the other men, who were trying to act like they couldn't hear, which was impossible in their room. They had moved slightly closer to the beds again.

"Guys, why don't you go use the toilet again before bed," Todd instructed, still in that mindset from teaching introductory massage that evening.

"Just as it was getting good," Elias mumbled as he left his guard post and followed Cal out of the room into the attached bathroom.

Todd waited until they heard several of the sinks turned on and a toilet flushing before insisting, "Aren't I your best friend? Your lover?"

"Yes, and I'll die if I don't tell someone," Scott admitted.

"Then tell me!"

Scott took a deep breath, crossing two fingers to make sure he didn't jinx things. "Miss Joanna said she wants to buy my contract. She wants to privately own me because she needs my imaging skills and knowledge. She was impressed with my work, all of it."

Todd pulled him into a hug, then released him before hugging him again. "This is it! I told you that you just had to be patient and things would work out. When does she pick you up?"

Scott shook his head. "Apparently there's an interview process, her and me both, some government and business meetings, I don't know what all. I guess guardianship doesn't just happen, like we thought. She explained some of it to me after the other two left. I'll be here a while longer."

Todd sat back and looked at the bed, then back up at him. "Jones is here to work again, but Madame Sandy told Cal that xe was going to be monitored more closely, and also that xe was getting Johnny as some sort of benefit."

"Benefit?" Scott felt anger build up, and he quickly damped it back down. He was not going to let this ruin his mood after the eventful and hopeful evening.

"Can we come back yet?" Elias's voice made both men on the cot chuckle.

The next morning, Joanna waited impatiently in the director's office at the Korawinian Archives Center. She twisted her gold pinkie ring as she tried to think of the best way to approach the subject with her friend, whom she had not seen in the months since Judy died. Dr. Vivian Deborah Blakley was the only woman near her own age who Joanna knew was the solo private owner of a boy, and she had some questions she needed answered before the process to acquire him got too far along. Kathey and Ann owned Owen together; that was a different procedure. Talking with her grandmother or mother would bring up subjects she didn't want to discuss yet. Her attorney suggested Vivian, who had helped Joanna find some archived documents about Dells. This would be more personal.

"Vivian," Joanna said as she heard footsteps and rose. "Vivian? Wow!" Her eyes widened at her obviously pregnant friend.

The strawberry blonde director smiled as she patted her stomach and sat down across from the younger woman. "You noticed before I could tell you."

"Yes. I'm surprised," she said, sitting back down. "When did this happen?"

"Five months ago," Vivian stated.

"Five months?"

"I was going to tell you, but you were so withdrawn after Judy... I didn't reach out like I should have..." Vivian smiled as she rested her hands on her desk and took a deep breath. "How have you been, Joanna?"

"I'm getting better. I'm very happy for you, though a bit surprised," Joanna confessed. Vivian was only three years older, right at the start of what were considered prime mothering years by most women. "I'm sorry I didn't visit sooner. Is there anything you need? The HCS is supposed to have the technical matters in hand, but also, I know your mother lives on the West Coast."

"Island City isn't that far by plane. She flies out about once every two weeks or so. I think she wants me to come out there so I can learn the business." Vivian rolled her eyes.

"I thought you had an older sister who was going to take that on," Joanna said sympathetically.

"Yeah, but I think my mother would prefer my being a sea farmer to my dabbling in the dark world of history." Vivian laughed at Joanna's growing frown. "No, I'm just fine. Chad is taking good care of me."

Just then, the mentioned man walked into the room carrying a tall glass of special mother's formula, which he set in front of his mistress.

"Would you like something to drink, Joanna? I have to drink one glass of this stuff every three hours," Vivian explained, sticking out her tongue, "but we have a lot of options for everyone else to enjoy."

Joanna shook her head but spoke up as the man started to leave. "Chad, could you stay while I talk to Vivian?"

The man glanced back at his mistress, then nodded and stood behind her.

"What did you want to talk to me about? I thought you were getting what you needed from my contemporary archivist colleague?" Vivian asked as she patted her baby's sire's hand, which rested gently on her shoulder.

"I really wanted to talk to both of you, if that's chill?" she added, looking directly at her friend.

Vivian nodded and directed the boy to pull a chair up close to hers and sit. "Of course, it's chill, Joanna. I share everything with Chad."

Joanna smiled warmly as she tried to figure out how to begin her questions. "Vivian, why did you decide to buy Chad?"

The historian blinked a few times as she took in the question. "That's a rather odd question for you to ask, Joanna. I thought you disapproved of joining the masses," the archivist said.

Joanna blushed at the reminder. The two had met through Professor Houten, their mutual mentor at university. The "masses" weren't just anyone who wasn't part of the scholarly world but specifically those who weren't part of the secret organization that both currently served. "I was younger, more naïve. It just made me wonder about your position in MOI at first; later I just accepted it as part of your mundane cover, like Houten herself."

"A reasonable concern," Vivian admitted, pausing for a moment before continuing. "I met Chad at the house of one of my old college professors – Radform specializes in archival recovery; not one of us. He's her cousin's child, and she was trying to find someone to take guardianship of him. They didn't want to turn him over to a company, not even as dorm boy." Vivian glanced at her husband and said, "Feel free to jump in at any time."

"My mother had wanted to keep me, because she had no daughters, but given that she wasn't head of the family and the government's concerns on why she chose not to use selection for another child …" Chad trailed off while looking straight at his mistress' guest.

"So, you bought him because you felt sorry for him?" Joanna asked hopefully.

"No, not exactly." Vivian smiled as she remembered her decision. "I had been visiting Radform's home for several weeks, because she was helping me work out my thesis problems. Chad was still there, so I spoke to him one day. He'd been carrying a tray of drinks into the office where I was headed, but when I spoke, he dropped it. It startled him because he'd been raised very strictly. "

"My aunt became very angry at me," Chad added with a sad grin.

"And you swore something very vulgar as you were cleaning up, at which I just laughed." Vivian chuckled again as she saw her slave's face redden. "Anyway, I just told my professor right then and there that I would buy him. She reminded me that I was going to pursue my doctorate and didn't need the distraction. But I think she was pleased, because she agreed with me when I pointed out that a laugh every now and then would do me some good. Plus, even though the Radform family is strict, she still wanted a good life for her nephew." Vivian patted her boy's hand lovingly. "He's been with me ever since."

"You two get along every well," Joanna observed.

"Of course; I wouldn't have chosen him to sire my baby if we didn't. He's an excellent husband; I think he'll be a wonderful father, plus he's a big help here at the archives as well."

"I love my mistress," Chad declared, kissing her hand.

"Why are you asking about this, Joanna?" Vivian turned seriously to her.

"Well," Joanna began and stood up so she could pace as she spoke. "I don't know if Kathey has told you anything."

"I haven't seen her since the funeral," Vivian stated with a frown. "Not that I like her much anyway."

"Good," Joanna said bluntly, bringing a look of shock to the archivist's eyes. Joanna gripped the back of her chair as she leaned over it toward them both before releasing the chair and pacing. "I rented someone from Dells Escort Agency a little while back and took him with me on an investigative feature. He has excellent imaging skills and a good editorial eye," she added at the other two's surprised looks.

"MOI suggestion?" Vivian asked.

"Yes. I didn't want to, but you know they generally get their way." Joanna resumed her pacing. "He turned out to be more helpful than I'd hoped."

"Will you please stop pacing?" Vivian sighed. "It tires me out just to watch." Joanna stopped immediately; one should always do what was best for an expectant mother, and only that woman could know what was best for her unless her medic said differently. "Go on talking, though."

"He's very good with camera equipment. With some training he might be as good as Judy someday." Joanna paused and took a deep breath. "I'm thinking of buying him."

Vivian shook her head. "What did you say?"

"I'm thinking of buying him," Joanna restated. "In fact, I talked to him last night, and he seems to think it's a good idea."

"You'd think it was a good idea too, if you worked for Dells," Chad replied softly, earning glances from both women.

"You know about Dells?" Joanna directly at him. "What can you tell me about it?"

Chad glanced at his mistress, who nodded for him to continue. "Every man knows that they don't want to be owned by an escort agency; the only thing worse is a private dungeon or a mining company."

Joanna didn't let the dungeon comment threaten her. MOI might know, but she kept some matters from even her dearest friends, though given how much she'd been ignoring everyone recently, she might not have many of those left.

"While we don't keep the modern records here, we do keep up on the news. Boys do, too, even if we all want to pretend that they don't," Vivian pointed out as Chad helped her stand up. Then she shooed him from the office with a promise to finish her drink.

Once they were alone, Vivian took Joanna's hands. "Don't buy him because you feel sorry for him, Joanna. That's the best advice I can give you. You might also want to talk to a few other private guardians, get different perspectives on how your life is going to change. It is going to change. It will change you."

Scott smiled at Polo as he entered the domestic training area. Madame Sandy had listened to his request to get further training in a few areas and assigned his own roommates to the task of teaching what they were specialized in. Polo's contract was promised to one of his regular clients when he turned 25, but he was still sent out on rentals from time to time. Most of his time was spent helping to teach the new boys some basic domestic skills as well as a few advanced classes. Scott was so happy this was working out so very well that he gave the darker haired man a big hug.

Polo stepped back and looked him up and down, then nodded his head, apparently satisfied with his outfit of basic pants and shirt with soft athletic shoes and his braid pinned to the back of his head. "Well, you're dressed the part, but how much do you remember about your initial classes in husbandly arts?"

"I remember it all, but I lack practice," Scott explained, and the other man just nodded; they all knew that his memory was one of his special skills, even if it hadn't seemed to help him keep clients until now.

"We don't have to do it all today. Madame Sandy told me that as long as you and I have free time and this facility is open, then we can practice until you feel you have it down. It's really quite womanly to be thinking of ways to make yourself more attractive," Polo complimented him. They were being watched, so neither mentioned Miss Joanna's promise, only exchanging knowing looks.

"I'm not getting any younger," Scott stated firmly. "If I want to find a private guardian, I have to try and figure out what she might want. I can at least be more useful when I'm not behind the cameras."

"See, thinking ahead like that might come off as too serious for the clients who just want a good time, but trust me, no woman wants a husband or a father around who can't plan out a week or so in advance. So, we'll start with cleaning. Most people, regardless of legal gender, find cleaning to be both boring and tedious. If you can learn to do it well without going crazy, think of how pleased she'll be!"

"Sounds great," Scott offered with what he hoped was an agreeable shrug. "Tell me what to clean and give me pointers while I do it."

Polo narrowed his hazel eyes slightly but nodded. "Then we'll start with the bathroom – the least favorite but the most necessary." With that they went into the first of two model bathrooms.

"It's a very difficult decision to make, Joanna," the Reverend Pamela Ilona Asher admitted to her when she came by for an appointment the next day. "It was a difficult decision for me to take on Louie as well, and I was older than you. You say that you have talked to this boy about acquiring his contract?"

"Yes." Joanna sat properly and straight up, across from her minister. The Temple of Family was a fairly liberal organization, and her spiritual leader, while not a member of MOI, had always been open to her questions. Still, she was using the current euphemisms for the legal status of males and females to be on the safe side. She wasn't sure whether MOI had religious leaders among their numbers. The subgroups tended to avoid contact with one another, for their collective safety, with directors and agents acting as go-betweens. "He seemed thrilled at the idea."

"I've heard that escort agencies are not a good place, so I'm not surprised." Reverend Asher got up to sit on the edge of her desk. "I also understand that you would like the boy to be your imagist, a business partner like Judy was. Have you actually thought about how unusual that is?"

Joanna gave her a crooked smile, "I am unusual, after all."

"Or forward-thinking," the older woman replied with a gentle smile. "There is a balance between genders in the world, a balance necessary for the creation and maintaince of family, just as Gaia herself is a balance of all life.

That balance was horribly skewed for so long that even now our world is still struggling with the consequences."

"Controlling men is the proper balance?" The question was a touch dangerous to ask anywhere else, but her minister was used to odd questions and actively encouraged them. Her services were often half praise and half community discussion. They never countered the prevailing mores, but they often pushed the congregation to think rather than merely accept.

"For now, it helps to correct the balance, but these things take time." The reverend motioned toward the sanctuary of the temple, where everyone met for weekly services. "Consider that most of the men and mas who are brought here are sent to the back to sit, while little boys, fem, and girls take separate classes during our services. Why is that?"

Joanna shrugged back her snotty response and settled on a simple, "It's always been that way." It didn't pay to push too far when she really wanted to gauge whether she was truly welcome to bring Scott or anyone here with her. The temple was one of the few places she felt both connected to the world and yet comfortable with it. She'd give it up if MOI ever discovered some dark secrets about it, but until then she didn't want to push her ideals onto the good woman who headed the faith.

"As far as you and I and our mothers for over thirty generations are concerned, this has been the norm, men separated from single women, guarded by those in charge of them. But before the dawn of the reclaimed world, men and women either sat together, or women and men were completely separated, even forced to worship in different buildings or at different times. All of these separations, ours now and those from the past, are because of fear. Yet we know that a family that has fear at its core is unhealthy; it cannot thrive for long."

Joanna blinked. Her minister's words went just a touch beyond the standard beliefs of the temple; that was a hopeful sign. "Why are you telling me all of this?"

"With your name, people look up to you, so I was thinking that if you brought this boy to service, maybe he could sit with you in the main room ..."

Well, well, maybe Reverend Asher was even more progressive than Joanna had believed, but she decided to play it cautious. "Well, of course, I don't intend to change how I worship merely for some boy."

Scott refused to look at Jones as two junior disciplinarians tied him down to the wooden table. Jones was supposed to be monitored; how was this even happening? Xe'd pulled him from the gym just moments before, with Johnny looking on wide-eyed with terror behind her and her juniors falling close behind him. A glance around had shown him that the gym's trainer was busy with another boy off in a corner.

Scott had come in early to exercise during an off period before meeting up with Todd. He'd deviated from his schedule, thinking that it was a good idea. He should have known something like this would happen – Jones always seemed to know when he was most vulnerable. He felt foolish. He'd taken the initiative, and now he was paying the price.

He closed his eyes and concentrated on his client's order not to tell anyone that she was thinking of buying him. So far Jones hadn't said much; xe'd merely ordered xyr aides to grab him and walk him to xyr room. He never even considered resisting; there was no point when he thought xe'd be stopped at any time. Where were the monitors?

"You've requested some training in the rougher arts, yet I was told I wasn't allowed to do it," Jones said in a low whisper.

Scott opened his eyes and stared straight into xyrs, but he remained silent. Great. He hadn't asked for anyone in particular to train him, but he'd been hoping that Elias might just be allowed to give him some pointers, or maybe he could see a few rougher clients.

Jones rose up slowly in anger. Xe grabbed the whip from the nearest trainee. "I won't disobey; I'll merely oversee. Ladies, this will be good practice for you both. But I'll tell you a secret first," xe added in a very loud whisper that Scott knew xe meant for him to overhear. "This boy, like all of them, enjoys it, because his body is nothing but one cleverly disguised cock support system. As long as you touch that tool between his legs, he'll get hard. So don't hold back, ladies, just keep coming back to that nasty piece of meat."

The first assistant stepped forward, taking the whip in hand. She began in earnest, with no build-up; even Scott knew this wasn't how the rougher sex was supposed to go. After she'd beaten his front soundly, leaving him feeling hot and slick with sweat, someone flipped the table upright, and he jerked against the straps. The one striking him stopped, and she and the other junior pulled apart the table until there was only an I-shaped frame behind his spine, spreading his wrists above him and his ankles below him about two feet. He was basically hanging now, and he knew from experience the pain would be much worse.

That's why he wanted the training, so he'd know why some things hurt and others didn't, or why it might hurt with one client but not another. He knew that when he was fucked, he needed to relax, but would that help when he was beaten? Xe did say this was training, so maybe he could ask and that would be acceptable right now. But before he could get a word out, the other assistant picked up another whip and started in, her strokes coming harder and faster.

It continued for several minutes until he felt the sweat replaced by a hotter, thicker liquid. There was only one thing Scott could do, so he opened up his mouth and started to scream as loud as he could. He hoped that Todd would show up at the gym as promised and try to get someone to find him, because he could already feel blood covering him.

He could make it stop or make it worse by telling xyr that he was being sold and that Dells wouldn't appreciate the risk to such a deal if her assistants kept up this pace of torture. As the lash wrapped around his hip to contact with his cock, he considered it. No, he wouldn't betray Scion McMillin, so he bit into his own cheek instead and tried to close off his screams.

"Excuse me," Joanna said, holding up one hand as Reverend Ackley walked her to the entrance of the temple. They'd had a good chat, a hopeful chat, but the ring was from Dells, and that might represent a problem with her plans, so she needed to check it. "Yes?"

"Scion Joanna McMillin?" the unfamiliar male voice on the other end of the line asked quietly.

"Speaking," Joanna switched on the viewer and was surprised to see an unfamiliar boy staring back at her. "Who are you?"

"Scion, you don't know me. I'm a friend of Scott's at Dells Escort Agency," the caller explained, his eyes downcast.

Joanna frowned as she let her minister look over her shoulder. No reason to hide information that likely pertained to their conversation. "Why are you calling me?"

"Scion, I'm really sorry. I wouldn't call unless it was important." The boy took a deep breath then looked up. "Scott has been hurt really bad. He said you were a new regular client, so I thought ... I was hoping you could ..."

"What do you mean, Scott has been hurt?" Joanna put her hand on top of the minister's, which was now on her shoulder; the older woman was reciting a prayer.

"The disciplinarian, he wasn't in official trouble, and she shouldn't have ..." The boy's eyes begged as he asked, "Would you please come down and help him, Scion?"

Joanna was silent for a moment as she recalled the last conversation she'd had with the disciplinarian. All those documents of complaints against Jones and against the agency flashed through her mind. Her eyes narrowed in anger as she pictured her twin being placed in the same room with that barren.

"Scion, please. I can't hear him screaming anymore, but the lashes keep coming. Madame Sandy gave me the phone so I could talk to you while she tries to stop it. Please come help him," the boy begged over the phone.

The sobs snapped Joanna out of her thoughts. "I'll be right there." She turned to her minister, who nodded and continued her prayers.

As she hurried to her car, she called up her attorney, Liz, and arranged to meet her at Dells. Surely if abuse were happening, they could use this to get guardianship faster.

Elizabeth Mena Kourns, or "Liz," as she allowed Joanna to call her, was waiting outside of Dells when the reporter arrived. The militia vehicles had been there when she had arrived just a few minutes before, but none of the officers were outside with them.

"What's going on here?" Liz demanded as Joanna hopped out of her Vega and hurried to her open window.

"I don't know. I just got a call from one of the boys here, telling me that Scott was in danger," Joanna explained as both women headed up the steps to the building's entrance. The Kourns family had been legal consultants for the McMillin Family for seventeen generations, though as the newest member of their board, Liz was assigned to Joanna almost exclusively. She could trust Liz, if not with all the details of her life, then at least with the legal ones. The police cars couldn't be a good sign, but neither woman said a thing as they hurried.

The boy who had called about Scott, who turned out to be fairly tall, dark, and lovely, approached them as soon as they entered. "Scion McMillin?" he asked as he stepped forward, then stopped and looked at the floor.

"You're the one who called me," Joanna stated. "Are the militia here because of Scott?"

"Yes, Scion. Madame Sandy had a receptionist call them. I don't know why, but I was told to wait here for you, then take you to his room to wait."

"This is my attorney, she's coming with us," Joanna said, getting a shocked look from each before she motioned for the boy to lead the way. "Did he tell you what I talked to him about a couple of nights ago?" she asked as they hurried down several hallways deeper into the building, several boys going down on one knee and staff members turning to look at them as they went.

The boy glanced at her with a worried frown. "Yes, Scion, but neither he nor I have told anyone else."

They entered a room with six cots, three on either side. "This is his room?" Joanna looked around at the small space.

"Yes, Scion. Six of us live here." The boy motioned at one cot. "Would you like a chair, Scion, Ma'am?" he added with a bow toward the other woman. "We don't have chairs, but I can find some."

"We're fine, boy." Liz stepped forward as Joanna looked around.

He'd mentioned sharing his room at Dells, but she'd had no idea it was such a small space with so many men. Given that they were naturally competitive with one another, how did they all manage to function in such a setting? She had no time to speculate, as several militia officers carried a bloody mess into the room and gently laid him down on the cot that had been pointed out to her.

"Oh, Goddess!" She knelt beside the bloodied body of the boy she'd just seen a few nights before as tears streamed down her cheeks. She took one of his limp hands while the other boy took the other, their eyes meeting briefly.

"How very touching," came a deep woman's voice, breaking the silence. Joanna looked over her shoulder to catch Emma Jones' dark stare as the police escorted xem past the doorway. Xyr contemptuous laughter echoed down the hallway.

Joanna turned back to the beaten man and touched his cheek, one of the few parts of him not covered in his own blood.

Scott flickered open his eyes. His eyes focused after a second as he smiled weakly. "I didn't tell her, Miss Joanna," he promised softly. "I didn't tell her anything."

"Shhh ...." Joanna leaned closer to his face. "Be quiet, Scott. I'm here now, and I'm not leaving you."

She looked up at her attorney, who was staring wide-eyed at the scene. After a few blinks, the older woman turned on one heel and called for the militia member still in the room. "My client has filed intention for guardianship forms for this boy," Liz said.

Joanna looked at Scott's hand, which lay across his chest, then at his other hand, held by the man who had called her. "What's your name?" she asked in a voice rougher than she wanted it to be. The darker boy flinched but only held tighter to the limp hand in his. "Keep holding onto him. I can tell you care about him. I just want to know your name."

"Todd, Scion," the man dipped his head and shoulders once, then met her gaze.

Joanna nodded as she repeated his name a couple of times. "Thank you for calling me, Todd. I won't forget this."

Chapter Fourteen

"Scion McMillin, I need you to come with me for a few minutes, answer a few questions."

Joanna heard the unfamiliar voice behind her as she stood staring at Scott lying on his stomach on the cot that served as his bed.

"My client and I got here a few minutes ago. Dells CS will confirm that," Liz's voice stated.

"Be that as it may, Ma'am," the unfamiliar voice said, "someone called us, and the number traced to Scion McMillin's private pad."

Joanna turned around shaking with anger. Both her attorney and the militia member whose insignia marked her or xem as a squad leader stepped back. It gave Joanna even more fuel for the emotions churning inside her. "You traced the number even after I clearly stated that I was the one calling? Do people commonly call claiming to be members of Great Families these days? That's an issue that needs to be brought up before the Council or worldgov then. Liz, make a note of that please. Is my name the only reason you came into Dells to investigate?"

"Well, we've never had a complaint about this agency," the squad leader began, but Joanna waved back toward the bleeding man and widened her eyes at the officer. "I personally checked the database on the way over, Scion. Not a single complaint about abuse here."

A woman in a red uniform marking her as a medic entered the room carrying a small case. She paused when she saw the scene, then hurried around to the cot. Joanna turned her head and watched the medic. She was only half listening to the militia leader explain how unusual it was for any sort of complaint to be called into their office about any escort agency, privately or publicly run. "Public agencies?" Joanna mumbled with a frown that deepened as the medic pushed Todd away from the bed.

"Just what the balls do you think you're doing?" Joanna yelled as she whirled and took two steps to get into the medic's face as the woman stood up, eyes blinking rapidly. "Leave your pathetic first aid kit and send someone who actually cares to help!" Joanna ordered.

The medic fled from the room.

"Let me answer your questions for now … Sergeant, is it?" Liz's voice cut through the pounding in Joanna's head.

"Help me," Joanna simply said as she held out a hand toward Todd, who had stepped back rather than fall from being shoved.

"Yes, Scion, happy to be of assistance," he agreed. His eyes flitted to the room's entrance then to her, and the two of them went to opposite sides of the cot.

A few minutes later, another Dells medic came into the room and announced herself, though Joanna didn't pay as much attention to her name as she did to the fact that Todd's smile seemed genuinely happy when he saw her. Both stepped back as the other medic worked.

"Why did they let Jones come back here?" the medic asked in a whisper that Joanna noted but didn't press her on.

"Can we help?" she asked instead.

The older woman considered them, then nodded to her larger medical case. "Wipes are in there. Gently help me remove the blood; that will help me see what I need to close. I'll give him a mild sedative while you begin. It won't put him to sleep, because I don't think that's wise right now, but it will dampen the pain."

Joanna took up a position across from her with Todd at her side. They worked as best they could; both flinched whenever he made a noise. A few minutes after the injection, he barely moaned or moved.

Joanna cringed each time she and Todd wiped some of the blood from Scott's bare and striped back. She knew what this was from. She could use the same torture instruments, because every woman trained with them as a teen, but she didn't use the toned-down versions for fun. Some things just didn't turn her on. None of her lovers had asked her to use them.

The medic made soft clicking sounds as she used a handheld tool to close up each serious cut. Joanna couldn't keep from counting. 31. 31 times he'd been hit hard enough to slice through layers of skin and muscle. 31 possible scars, were it not for the care of the medic. Each time, Todd sucked in a breath as though he felt the pain himself. The two were clearly close; the fact that the man had risked the same treatment just by making that call strongly suggested that, and his aid and reactions were confirmation.

Joanna damped down her desire to help him too. She couldn't save everyone. One man at a time. That's what Renee had told her back on Bragg.

"We need to flip him over; can I get your help? I'd ask my second, but you terrified her, Scion," the medic tossed out with a forced chuckle.

It took some effort and elicited a couple of screams from Scott, but in several minutes, he was on his back. While Joanna and Todd tenuously held him, the medic laid a cooling blanket on the cot, and they had to jostle him again, earning groans, to lay him out on it.

"Damn," the medic exclaimed when her wrist pad binged. "I doubt the injuries will be as bad on his front. The boy," she went on, nodding at the man who was helping Joanna, "knows how to call for assistance if you see anything like what I had to heal before. I'll be back as soon as I can. Thank you for your help, Scion."

Joanna met the other woman's eyes and nodded.

The injuries on Scott's front did not appear to be as severe as those on his back. None were actively bleeding and there were no open wounds or visible cuts. Whatever was on the wipes seemed to help the skin heal minor damage as well as clean. Joanna and Todd had been working silently for several minutes. It was starting to wear on her nerves, so she spoke as calmly as she could. "I hope they didn't hurt him when they moved him in here."

Todd flinched then nodded. He wiped away a tear as he replied in a whisper, "You're so kind, Scion," then he straightened up and tossed the hygienic wipe into the first aid case. He was looking at her with a fear in his eyes similar to what she'd seen in Scott's.

Joanna tossed out the wipe she was using and growled low in her throat. "I can't abide the silence. Conversation, please. Sorry," she added when he flinched again.

"I don't think he can feel much now that he's asleep, Scion," the man replied softly.

Joanna squeezed her wipe out again but left it in the cool treated water. She gave the other man a smile and nodded before looking back at the imagist she had been trying to help. She touched the blond's cheek and whispered, "Can you hear me, Scott? Say something, please."

"Don't you think it's best that he sleep, Scion?" Todd pointed out in a whisper as he wiped the last of the blood off his friend's front.

Joanna nodded mutely as she picked up her own wipe and laid it across Scott's forehead for lack of any other idea what to do. She got up, as did the darker man, and walked over to the door impatiently. Not knowing what to do was annoying, but Liz had told her to stay there while she talked with the militia and Dells staff.

There was no sign of anyone outside the door now. Her reaction to the medic must have scared them all away. Good. They deserved to be scared; they should be terrified of her, given what they'd allowed to happen.

Joanna leaned back against the wall; her arms folded across her chest. "Are you guys best friends?" She smiled as Todd looked down in embarrassment. "I think men are capable of having friends, being friends, with each other, possibly with other genders, too. That surprises you, doesn't it?"

"A little, Scion. But Scott said you were ... different." Todd took a step back as he spoke.

Joanna frowned sadly at his behavior. "You can say whatever you want around me. I am different, and proud of it. No point having a fancy title and a grand heritage if you're only going to go along all the time," she added with a forced chuckle. Joanna walked back to Scott's side and gently touched his hair.

"I'm going to buy him," she whispered, looking up at Todd. "I'm sorry that I can't buy both of you. Can't buy all of you, get you all out of this place."

Todd blinked in surprise. "I don't even know what to say to that, Scion." He ventured a step closer so that he stood directly across from her. "His life is much harder than mine."

Then he took a confident stance, one she was unfamiliar seeing men take, relaxed yet standing straight, meeting her gaze. "Scott's a hard worker, has a great memory, and he's a good imagist. He'll do his best to please you, Scion."

"I know he will."

The other man smiled but kept talking, and his forwardness made her smile in surprise. "He can be a bit moody; I won't hide that from you, 'cause you probably already saw that. That's just him worried about pleasing you. He has opinions, too, and if you give him permission to share them, he will, but he won't mean any disrespect by them."

"I need him to have opinions, about imaging and other things." Joanna was about to speak further when a small group of people arrived.

The staff member, Sandy, who had met her a couple of times, approached Joanna first. "Scion McMillin, on behalf of Dells I want to say how sorry I am that you had to see this. We're having a problem with an employee – former, I hope – and for some reason xe took out xyr masculine tendencies on Scott. I assure you that he did nothing to bring this upon himself; he's a very good boy."

Did they really think she'd reconsider her desire to take him because some crazy barren almost killed him? Of course, they did; it was always the man's fault.

"I don't blame him, though why you let it happen ..." Joanna began but trailed off as Liz looked over Sandy's head and gave her a firm shake of her head. Fine, let the legal stuff be worked out separately. Joanna turned to the chief medic here, who had dropped off the supplies before. "Will he be all right?" Joanna asked with a kinder tone than she used before.

"They are very sturdy creatures," the medic stated. "With a bit of rest – actual rest," she emphasized, directing her gaze toward Sandy, who nodded, "he'll be as good as new in a few days. It shouldn't interfere with any of the contract transfer steps as long as he's truthful and there are no unforeseen issues during the background checks."

"Which is what we truly care about," Liz spoke up as she raised one hand. "Scion McMillian, if I could get a few moments of your time to go over the proposed contract transferal?" she asked, using all the formalities as a show of strength.

"Of course," Joanna said, but she glanced back at Todd, who looked up from his lowered eyes just enough to give her a wink.

Once the formalities and legalities were done, and she was back outside and in Liz's car, Joanna growled and ran both hands through her now unruly hair. "I told you I needed this rushed."

"And this abuse, as horrible as it is," Liz quickly added, "is the best thing that could have happened to speed the transfer along."

"Goddess," Joanna fumed but nodded her head. "You're right – if they're allowing abuse to happen, as opposed to training or discipline, then surely a judge will agree that I'm a better guardian."

The attorney took a small booklet out of her briefcase. "Read this and memorize it. If you can pass the test this booklet is based on – I have no doubt the boy will pass his tests fine – then it should be just a matter of the time it takes to do the exams and schedule a hearing."

Joanna frowned at the familiar title, *How Males Should be Treated*. "I had to read this in high school. I thought it was stupid then, and I still do," she stated as she tried to hand it back.

"You need to study this," Liz replied, then hastened to explain. "Most women think they know it, but few pass the test the first time around. You didn't have to do this for your dorm boy; your mother got him for you. I bet you haven't read this since you were what, 15 or 16? Every delay … I know you don't want that."

Joanna looked at the booklet again. "If I have to memorize it word by word, recite it line by line, in order to buy him, then I'll learn it like no one ever has."

"Good, because that book is just the first of the materials you'll need to review or use. The rest is at my office. Should we go?"

Joanna rolled her eyes but nodded. "What about him?"

"Scion," Joanna stiffened at the formality of her attorney's words, "you have to trust now that Dells wants this sale as much if not more than you. If they value their business, they can't risk not only damage to him but pissing off one of Gaia's most connected reporters, the heir to one of the world's most important families, right?" Joanna nodded again. "Get into your car and follow me to my office. Let's get this done."

Almost an hour later, Joanna sat, nodding in exhaustion as Liz finished giving her all the materials. "All this stuff?" she asked. She stood up, picking up the bundle of paper and crystals. She had grown up with men – privately, corporate, and publicly owned – but she'd had no idea how complicated the process was. There was no way her mother had just decided to send Joseph away, then, as she'd always told herself. It had been planned, as surely as her going to university had been prepared for.

"Yep," Liz replied, standing up also. She groaned as she arched her back and removed her glasses tiredly. "What a day! My back and feet are screaming. Sasha is gonna lecture me about taking care of myself," she said, making Joanna wince at the mention of her wife.

"This was the last thing I was expecting to happen," Joanna promised.

Liz smiled sadly as she put her glasses back on. "I wasn't too surprised, given the investigations into Dells you passed on. I did a bit of my own digging; I want to make sure the McMillin Family won't be taken advantage of, after all."

"To quote my grandmother," Joanna said as she offered her attorney a hand to shake, "Trust the Kourns family with everything."

"We aim to live up to your trust, Scion," Liz agreed with a formal handshake before leading her to the door.

Joanna turned at the door and took a deep breath; she thought she saw the other woman tense a bit at that. "There is one more thing I need from you, Liz." The other woman just folded her arms over her chest and focused on her, so Joanna continued. "I want to hire a personal bodyguard – not someone from the Lindherse family, someone completely independent."

"You clearly have someone in mind."

"She's currently an IGA agent, but she's Gaian; she used to work for another Great Family but was fired for some reasons that make her appealing to me."

"That's what she told you," Liz guessed as she grabbed her work computer pad off her desk.

"Which is one of the things I want you to look into. Her name is Erin Zoe Markeni and she reports to Chief Traffaz Blim of the IGA," Joanna spoke slowly so that her lawyer could note it all down. Joanna transferred all the details via her wrist pad as well.

"I'll look into it personally, Joanna," Liz agreed, using her first name to show she understood the private nature of such a request. Joanna left knowing that she was in safe hands.

"When can I work again, Ma'am?" Scott asked the chief medic at Dells as she finished reading all his vitals on the third morning after the militia and Madame Sandy had rescued him.

"That's what I'd like to know," a friendly voice announced from the doorway.

Scott sat up with a grin, his wince from the pain lessened by his most important client's presence. "Miss Joanna!"

The chief medic turned to the client with a smile. "No escort service for another week, but he can get out of bed for a little while each day." She turned back to her patient. "Short walks, conversation. You hear me, boy?"

"Yes, Ma'am." Scott glanced at his future mistress – unless this entire episode had ruined that. He'd been plagued by doubt ever since he'd regained consciousness to find himself in the dorm room with only Todd by his side. His roommates had tried to reassure him. He'd pieced together what had happened. Right now, Miss Joanna was smiling, and her voice seemed light, cheery even.

"That's great," Miss Joanna said. Her hands were still behind her back, where they'd been since she'd come into the room. "Can he have visitors right now?" she asked the medic but didn't take her eyes off him, making him blush slightly.

"Yes, I'm finished." The medic packed away her equipment. "I'll be back this evening to check up on you again," she told Scott, who lowered his gaze.

"Yes, Ma'am," Scott replied. He remained still until the doctor left, then started to stand up as his client continued to stay, smiling, her hands behind her back.

He stood slowly, dipping his head instead of kneeling, hoping she'd understand. She simply nodded. "Would you care to sit down, Miss Joanna?" He glanced around and motioned to the sole chair in this part of the room near his cot. No one had remembered to order it removed, and his roommates had been sitting there checking in when they got back from practice or clients.

"Will you sit down?" she pleaded, laying her bag on the floor by the chair.

"If you want me to, Miss," he answered, stepping back, and motioning for her to sit first.

"I do," Miss Joanna sighed as she plopped herself down in the chair. "Back on the bed," she insisted, with a nod toward his cot.

"I brought you something," she teased once he was seated with his back against the extra pillows the medic had acquired for him.

Scott held his breath as she took the brightly wrapped package from the bag. "I don't deserve any sort of gift, Miss Joanna," he whimpered as his face reddened. He looked away from the gift and from her.

"People don't give gifts only when someone deserves it," Joanna informed him. "Gifts mean that you are cared about, and I do care about you, Scott."

Scott slowly looked back at her; his eyes rimmed with tears. "You do, Miss?"

"I wouldn't usually buy gifts for someone I didn't care about. Unless it's my birthday," Miss Joanna admitted as she shook her head with a frown and glanced at the floor. She shrugged and looked back at him. "Anyway, you do deserve it for not telling anyone but your best friend that I'm trying to buy you. Though everyone knows now," she added with a roll of her eyes.

"I shouldn't have told Todd, Miss," Scott observed as he let his eyes focus on the floor in shame.

"Forget it. I was talking with some of my friends before I had even made a final decision. It's a big decision; I wanted to make sure it was the correct one," Miss Joanna confessed. She placed the gift in his lap. "Open it."

Scott examined the blue paper with little silver stars on it. "It's very pretty, Miss Joanna. Thank you."

"I can't take credit for how it looks. The sales rep wrapped it up. If I'd wrapped it, it would be a mess," Miss Joanna chuckled.

Scott touched the big blue bow, letting a big grin appear as he felt a bit less apprehension.

"Just because it's pretty doesn't mean you shouldn't tear it open," Miss Joanna pointed out, making him blush.

"I usually only receive gifts from clients I've known for a long time, and then rarely. Never wrapped like this," he commented, knowing she liked conversation, as he untied the bow. "I don't know what to say, Miss Joanna," he whispered as his hands started to shake just slightly. He was acting foolish, but his stomach was tightening, and his head was starting to pound.

"You've already said 'Thank you.' Just open it!"

He couldn't even reply; he just reacted to the order and quickly but carefully unwrapped the gift. Inside was a plain brown box with writing and a picture of a turtle on it. With a blank look of awe, Scott glanced up at his client. "Thank you."

"Open the box, silly," Joanna teased him again.

Scott did as he was told. "Oh, my," he said, looking at the dozen pieces of candy lying in his lap once he had opened it and dumped the contents out.

"They're turtles," Miss Joanna explained.

Scott looked at the candy, then at his client, blankly.

"It's candy with chocolate, caramel, and nuts, tree nuts. I know someone who really liked them. I may be one of the only people I know who really likes them, so I hope you do, too," she confessed as she glanced away, her memories drifting into her mind.

"Hey!" Joanna shrieked as her twin grabbed another turtle from her box of Family Day candy.

The little boy pouted, hands on his narrow hips, as she grabbed the candy back and placed it in her box. "You said I could have a piece," Joseph whined.

"You already had one piece," she sniffed as shook her head furiously, sending her curls bobbing up and down. "I wasn't supposed to give you even one," she reminded him sternly.

"I want another one," he howled loudly as he reached for the box.

"Be quiet!" Joanna hissed as she held the box tight to her chest. "If you get us in trouble with Mommy, Joseph, I'll never give you another piece of candy ever again!"

"But those are my favorite kind," he pleaded as he knelt in front of her.

Joanna raised her eyebrows in melodramatic surprise. "How many kinds of candy have you eaten? How would you know it's your favorite kind?"

"I've eaten all the kinds you have ..."

"Nuh uh," Joanna retorted quickly.

Joseph crossed his arms with a frown. "Yes, I have," he whined shrilly. "You promised me that you would bring me a piece of candy whenever you had some."

"One time I didn't," Joanna confessed as she placed the box behind her out of his reach.

The little boy's mouth fell open in shock. They both stood there in silence for a moment. "You didn't bring me a piece of candy?" He tried to hold back the tears that were building up in his hazel eyes. "But you promised, Joanna."

"I forgot," she screeched as she saw the tears fall from his eyes. "I was at that horrible Nancy's birthday party, and I was going to bring you a piece, but it tasted yucky 'cause their father burned it when he made it." Joanna felt tears rising in her own eyes.

"You promised," Joseph gasped between sobs.

Joanna rubbed her small hands together in worry as she watched her twin cry. After a moment she scooted up beside him and put her arm around him. "Don't cry, Joseph. Mommy will hear you and come and yell at you and then take you downstairs," she warned him. Downstairs to the punishment room, where the fathers and brother went, where Joanna was forced to go and watch them be punished when she acted unladylike. She hated that place.

When that didn't silence him, she took a turtle from the box. "Here, you can have another one."

Joseph looked at his sister, then at the candy. He wiped his eyes with the back of one hand and stuffed the turtle into his mouth with the other.

"Will you stop crying now?" Joanna begged, wide-eyed with concern and a glance back at her bedroom door.

Joseph smiled and kissed her on the cheek. "You're the best sister in the world … universe." No, that wasn't what he'd said, was it?

Scott leaned closer to his client after a few moments of silence, her eyes looking into the distance, not really at the wall across the room. "Miss Joanna?" he whispered as he gently touched her arm. "Miss?"

"What?" Miss Joanna blurted out as she looked up at him with surprise in her eyes. She took a deep breath and shook her head before addressing him, "Sorry, Scott. Were you saying something to me?"

"Yes, Miss Joanna." He smiled at her as he repeated his praise, "You're the best client in the universe."

Joanna's face paled as she stared at him.

"Did I say something wrong, Miss?" Scott set the box of candy on his bed and rose to his knees on the cot.

"No." Miss Joanna stated as she took his hand. "Someone used to say something very similar to me. It was a long time ago."

"I apologize for bringing up bad memories …"

"You didn't, and please stop apologizing so much," she grumbled, making him bow his head. After a sigh she continued, her voice lightening, almost jovial, "I think we should eat the entire box right now. I think that chocolate and nuts have ingredients that are important to the healing process."

Was that true? Before he could ask, she stuffed a turtle into his mouth. It was different from anything he'd ever had before. He'd had all the ingredients she'd mentioned at one time or another, but the three foods together were amazing. As they ate the candy, her mood improved, so he took the opportunity to ask her a few important questions.

"Miss Joanna, I was thinking of getting a bit more training before you bought me," he half-lied; he had already been doing some extra training, but questions from those tasked with training him about what she wanted from him had made an impression on him. She nodded her head. Miss Joanna had used the word buy before, so she knew what was really happening. Still, it was taking a risk to use that term here, even if both Madame Sandy and the chief medic had used it in private with him.

"I'm wondering if there are any areas you'd like me to learn more about? We all get the same basic training, but I could improve some domestic, personal, professional, or even other skills?" he offered before putting another turtle into his mouth to help himself stop blathering on.

"Well, now, the medic said you should take it easy, Scott. I don't know how long all this bureaucracy will take, but you may not have time to learn much. I'd have to know what you already knew, too," she pointed out, but she didn't take another candy.

"Madame Sandy could get you my records, Miss Joanna."

"I have them; I'd just have to read them again. I have a lot of material to look at for this transfer." She paused for a moment and then nodded again before stating, "You know, I can cook – sometimes I love cooking – but I'm not a big fan of cleaning. If you could take on some of that, it would be very helpful. Plus knowing how to act around a bunch of folks who think they're better than anyone else, high-level etiquette in other words, would be vital. Eventually we'll have to spend time with my family and the other Greats." At that comment she took another candy, so he had another as well.

He didn't know anything about interacting with the Great Families, not formally. Did they have classes about that at Dells? He made a note in his memory to ask about that, then stayed tuned in as she continued.

"Do you know anything about communal chores? You know, solar panels, wind power, water treatment, gardening, that sort of thing? I live in an apartment complex, and I do put in my hours. I think you'd need to put in hours, too. We each have to do our job to keep everything in balance," she repeated a phrase he was familiar with, then looked expectantly at him.

"Yes, Miss Joanna. Dells has all of that, too. Each of us boys puts in our hours when we don't have clients."

"That will be a big help, then. Not a lot of men at the complex. I'm trying to think. Who is there? Maybe one father in my building? A few buildings. I'm sure once you're there I'll suddenly meet neighbors I didn't realize I had." She picked up a turtle and put it into his mouth but didn't take one for herself.

"You'll need to make sure you're up to date on all the contractual and ownership stuff for our tests and interviews – of course, the interviews are really just another type of test," she reminded him. Suddenly, the candies didn't taste as good.

Chapter Fifteen

A week and a half later, Joanna sank down into the chair across from her attorney's desk for the fifth time in fewer days. "How many more of these meetings?" she asked with a yawn.

Liz checked over her list. "Not many more." She laughed when Joanna grumbled and tried to find a more comfortable position in her seat. "You did pass that oral exam yesterday with flying colors."

"You said it was going to be written," Joanna snapped as she glared across the desk at her attorney.

"It usually is. I'm not sure why they wanted to interview you – probably a way to get face time with someone of your heritage. You did a good job," Liz chuckled as Joanna made a face. "I was watching on the monitors, as I promised I would be, getting a recording for our records, just in case things didn't go as we wanted. Although I'd never have thought the examiners would accept such sarcastic answers!"

Joanna allowed herself to relax into a grin as she recalled the few moments of pleasure she'd gotten from that meeting. "You said I just had to know the booklet, not that I had to believe it."

"True." Liz laughed a moment longer as she continued, "But if I didn't know you, I'd have thought I was listening to an extremist from one of the colonies that was tossed off Gaia a couple of centuries back. For instance, when you got tired of all those questions about what words a boy should use and what tone of voice is appropriate, I almost fell out of my chair laughing at your answer!"

Joanna frowned as she sat up straighter, as she had during the exam, and paraphrased what she'd said. "Liz, don't you agree that vocal cords only get males into trouble? They just don't know when to shut up."

"I agree completely," Liz mimicked the examiner's voice. After a second, both women continued their laughter.

"Liz?" Joanna directed their attention back to more important matters than merely making fun of the bureaucracy. "What did the judge say after meeting with Scott?"

Liz pulled up something on a big screen on one wall so they both could look at it. "Here are the transcripts from yesterday," she added, sharing those to both of their pads. "She agreed that undue violence had been done to him and that it would be best for him to be removed from Dells as soon as possible."

"What did she say about me?" Joanna asked seriously.

"She indicated that she would grant you the right to buy Scott if your test results next week are within reasonable parameters." Liz smiled as she read further, "She also said that Scott seemed to sincerely want to be under your guardianship, not just to get away from Dells." They glanced through the transcript, which her attorney had obviously read before, given the speed she scrolled with. "The judge said that it was logical that you wished to acquire him, given his particular skill set, and that he seemed a bit excited by the idea of using those skills for you."

"Did the judge get the affidavits from my grandmother and mother? I took your advice and had a conversation with both of them separately, though I can't say it was a pleasant visit with my mother." Her attorney arched her eyebrows, so Joanna continued, "I met Mother at headquarters, so we kept things professional."

"Wise," Liz agreed. "And your grandmother?"

"Had to do a phone conference, since she's in Perimbia, checking on our cocoa connections in the south."

"Is there anything the McMillins don't have a room for?" Liz replied in a low impressed tone.

Joanna shrugged, then said, "From the start we've been focused on versatility. In this case it meant that they were both chill with Scott as long as I remember my duty when it comes to sire, husband, or father selection. In other words, I promised to consult with them and allow them to start accepting inquiries"

"Are you even thinking of the boy in those ways?"

Joanna waved a hand and snorted, "No. Scott has skills I need, and we can work together. I'm only 27, too young to think of kids or settling down yet."

Her attorney just pressed her lips together as the two women looked at each other silently. "Scion," Liz interrupted the silence, and Joanna braced for the comment about Judy, "there is one more test the judge wants."

Talking about Judy would have been preferable to the information that followed about the test she was most dreading. The one she couldn't bluff her way through: submergence.

She told her current lovers everything she could over a group call.

"If you get my contract, do you have to do that again? Will I?" Jack asked first.

"Not me, I'm sure about you," Joanna told him. "Did you have to do it for Betty's guardianship?"

He rolled his eyes to the left and pressed his lips together. "Yeah, but it was like a mockup of her layout. I don't know if the ladies testing everything were government or not. Sorry, Miss Joanna," he offered with a shrug.

"We could roleplay it out, Ma'am," Raven suddenly said. Jack's face lit up. Raven wasn't really attracted to men, males or mas; actually, xe wasn't attracted that much to fem or other fifth-genders either. Xe had been chill with the situation in Haven, but it wasn't something that xe'd ask to do again, Joanna knew.

"I'm good at roleplaying," Jack tossed back, with excitement in his voice that quickly faded with Raven's cool-toned reply.

"We'd play out the scenarios that you think were part of previous submergence tests for first-time guardianship. I could narrate, be any additional women who might appear, and Jack obviously would be the boy in question. You'd have to play the eager-to-please and scared new privately owned type of man," Raven pointed out.

Jack's demeanor entirely changed, then he said, "This boy is honored that you are offering him this opportunity, Mistress. This boy will do his best to serve your household."

Joanna squirmed a bit in the seat at her desk where she was having this call. It turned her on to hear him say those words, in that tone, with that look. It probably shouldn't.

"See, I got it!" Jack exclaimed as he clapped his hands once.

Neither lover said that they could tell how it affected them, but Joanna felt her face heat up anyway, so she changed the tone. "You go back to work, Jack. Can you stay on, Raven, so we can set up a time with Betty to pick up Jack?"

Liz had acquired old recordings of submergence tests, possibly only borderline legal, so no one knew how much would be the same. Joanna, Raven, and Jack spent an entire afternoon going through as many scenarios as they could before Jack had to go back for another client and Raven had to return to Neuvo. Joanna could do it; the roleplaying showed her that she could.

In the high likelihood that it wasn't the same, Joanna told herself that she could apply similar principles, as she had with the written tests and oral interviews. She could think about the pleasure the three of them had enjoyed afterwards to direct her body's reactions. If that didn't work, she could always remind herself that she was better than Jones. Scott wouldn't be with xem if she could just pass this final test. She wasn't male; her body didn't run her; she could control her reactions. She had to.

Two days later, Joanna circled the mostly bare final examination room. It contained only the virtual meld chair, a comfortable recliner with computer equipment attached to it. Liz was outside observing.

The submergence test was a way to gauge how a woman would deal with a man living with her. It cut through the conversations to get right into your head by placing you in a virtual world where you were the first-time guardian of a boy. By taking the applicant through the expected process of delivery, setup, and one week of interactions, the governing body that oversaw all transfers of men assured that males were properly guarded, and that the world continued to function in balance.

According to the document that Liz was allowed to read to her before she entered the room, twenty percent of all applicants were denied at this point for "lack of control," whatever that meant. Rather than worry herself, Raven, or Jack further, Joanna just spent the past two days overseeing the setup of her home according to legal standards but also her own expectations.

"Scion, the bathroom is up to code, and the products are acceptable," the other woman said when she exited that attached space. "The boy will like the ample lighting, I'm sure."

Joanna wanted to roll her eyes but resisted. The recommended vanity reflected cultural expectations that men decorated their bodies. Frankly, she found it annoying.

For the second time, the inspector went over the bedroom itself, lifting and opening everything, while Joanna watched, a knot forming in her stomach. "This is all acceptable, if a bit luxurious, but you have high standards, I'm sure," the woman said with a tight smile.

She knew she shouldn't say anything, and yet the words came out. "What is particularly luxurious?"

The inspector arched her eyebrows and then turned to look directly at the desk and chair. "I have never seen that in any other boy's room."

"Ah, yes, this boy is to be my imagist, so he'll be working with me outside my home, too. If there is some work I want him to do while confined to this room, I want him to be able to continue it. Governance is a duty of mine; I won't let it interfere with his work for me." There, that tone sounded like she was all high and mighty, using a boy for all he could be used for, right?

"Is that the same reason for the larger than normal media screen, too?" the inspector asked, indicating the currently lowered unit that could be seen from either the bed or the chair by the desk.

Thinking quickly, Joanna revealed a bit of her future plans. "I'm going to acquire other boys; this will allow them all to see the screen without conflict. I don't want unhealthy masculine competition." Unlike the supposedly healthy type that made them peacock their appearance or attempt to please women with proper attitudes and behavior.

"In that case, I do have one criticism, though it will not prevent you from getting a pass today," the inspector said as she typed something on her pad. "Hold yours out please, and I'll send your copy now." Once that was done, the woman continued. "If you have a larger room, consider using it for a boy's dorm. While it is the fashion to stack them, it can cause ill feelings, and that increases the likelihood of infighting. Surely you have a larger space in an apartment this size."

Joanna didn't nod but instead motioned toward the door, saying, "Thank you for the advice. I will certainly not be using bunk beds. Thank you for your time today."

If the inspection pass was from being a Great, then she might be in trouble today. If it was because the house was arranged within their standards, then she should be fine. She just based how she set up the apartment on how life had been growing up. It was a bit unnerving how well she remembered the rooms and access that her family had given the various fathers who had lived in the house. Hilda had a hard time adjusting all the wall colors to counter the stress and worry Joanna had been feeling. Wasn't becoming a Guardian supposed to be a joyous decision? Not if you knew what you were really becoming. Joanna closed her eyes, picturing Raven and Jack kneeling at her feet, wanting to be there, lowering her heart rate.

"Please sit down," a voice commanded firmly. It didn't breach the calm that imagining her lovers had created, so Joanna turned slowly with a smile to find a medic in the room with her.

Joanna let the woman access her chip and set up the equipment as she sat in the chair. This wasn't a film or a walk-through holoprojection, but a virtual world created in her mind based on scenarios the examiner supplied and could monitor. This wasn't the same virtual-reality equipment that the average woman had in her home, or that even the most prestigious school used, or the most cutting-edge jobs required. This was the most important matter on Gaia. No one else was allowed to use this technology. MOI would have sacrificed dozens of agents to get access to it.

Suddenly Joanna was standing on the bottom steps of her apartment complex. It looked and felt exactly as her home did. She could smell the same fragrances in the air from the gardens, the river, the cookies someone was making. A delivery agent was holding out a computer pad for her, so she took it and signed her name. Looking down, she saw Scott kneeling at her feet. He was dressed in very simple clothing with a shiny new golden collar around his neck, his hair a bit longer than she liked, and he was staring at her feet. His face was blank, but she attributed that to the presence of the other woman.

Joanna took the leash and thanked the delivery agent. She waited until the woman left, then turned her attention to the simulation that her mind was interpreting as Scott. Was it helping her to keep reminding herself it wasn't real? "I want you to look up at me. You need to be able to see what I want, so you need to look at me. Understand?"

"Yes, Mistress," he replied as he looked up. His eyes were that lovely aqua color, but she didn't see the intelligence there that she knew the real Scott possessed. Their program wasn't perfect after all.

"Come on, let's get you settled into your new home, Scott," she told him.

Once in her virtual apartment, a series of first-week scenarios flowed by with only a brief break for a narrator to explain the passage of time or the background for each. It was far more intense than the immersion games she was used to playing, but Joanna never let her guard down as she worked her way through them.

Every time she thought about going easy on the boy, she only had to look into those eyes to be reminded that it wasn't Scott at all. That made it easier to do what they wanted when he dropped a glass or jacked off without permission or just made a noise without permission.

She only paused once at the door to the punishment room. She pulled her hand back from the knob, turned to him, motioned him forward, and told him to go in ahead of her. She took the opportunity to then put her hands on his shoulders and whisper in his ear, "You are going to pick out the instrument of your correction since you chose to repeatedly misbehave." It was something her mother had always done.

Liz was waiting for her with a cup of lightly flavored water when Joanna left the testing room three hours later. She took it, blinking in surprise at the tremors in her hands, and downed it quickly. "Can we get out of here?" she croaked, glancing around as she tried to brush off the memories of the scenarios she'd been presented with.

"Not yet," Liz informed her quietly as she motioned down the hallway to a door. "They told me that once you were done we were to report to a waiting room. The analysis was ongoing, so we should know how you did soon. You want some food? They said they could bring some to the room for us."

Joanna paused and looked at her attorney with distaste. "A hit right now would be great," she hissed.

"They did mention alcohol, too," Liz replied seriously as they walked through the door into another hall, where one of the staff showed them to a nicely decorated room.

Joanna started to pace while her attorney spoke to the staff member. She didn't even pause as Liz took a seat and just watched her. In a few minutes the staff member returned with a cart holding food and a bottle of something amber.

Joanna waited until the other woman left, then faced Liz. "No food, I said."

"What you said and what's good for you are two different things," her lawyer pointed out. "Your hands are shaking, you're pacing, and you've been in a high-stress virtual environment for over three hours. No alcohol until you have food in your stomach."

Joanna just went and poured a drink, downing it almost as fast as she had the water, but she didn't pour a second one. Liz frowned as she joined her and poured her own drink, downing it almost as fast. They both took the platters of food to the table and sat adjacent to each other.

"I've read that it can make you dizzy or dissociate, confuse your senses," Liz said softly.

Joanna huffed. "It was intense. Almost too real." She didn't mention the eyes or falling back on her mother's habits. She reached out to the food. Soon both were nibbling while they waited. "I don't think I can tell you more," Joanna stated after a few minutes of silence.

"No, you can't." Liz got up and snagged the alcohol, juice, and seltzer from the cart along with some larger glasses. "I can make us much better drinks – healthier, but still with a hit – and tell you some other news."

"Spotless news?" Joanna guessed as she watched the other pour far too much juice and water into the glasses compared to the alcohol.

"The boy passed his submergence, along with all his interviews and tests. Plus," she continued, pushing the filled glass toward Joanna before sitting down and finishing her sentence, "he is almost fully recovered physically, our independent medic confirms."

Joanna held up her glass, and they clinked before each drinking a quarter. "This is good."

"Don't sound so shocked. Who do you think has been spying on the bartender at your family parties and her own for decades now?" Liz chuckled.

They went back to nibbling on the food, sipping the drinks, and looking at the vids and stills Joanna had on her pad for the layout of the apartment. A delivery of reports from IGA via Mi provided a welcome distraction. They were about the Richards case; Joanna hadn't kept up on it while she was prepping for all of this. She'd have to get to work on that docu once she got the go-ahead and Scott was moved in. That had to happen.

In less than an hour the door opened, and a woman entered; she'd been the first one they'd met when Joanna had reported for testing that morning. "Good news," she told them, holding out her computer pad to transfer the data to Liz's. "You've passed with flying colors, just as we'd expect from a Great Family. We've sent our analysis to your judge, Scion, and I hope you enjoy your future with the man you'll be guarding."

Joanna looked at the offered hand for a second, then shook it. Flying colors sounded eerie to her, but she said nothing until they were outside in the parking lot.

"Get in first, then I'll read the results to you, since I know you don't want to wait," Liz instructed as Joanna paused by her Vega IV.

Joanna got into the driver's seat and waited impatiently for her attorney, who was looking over the results.

Liz snorted at a few points and finally turned the screen so that Joanna could see it. There was a graph with the scores for each of the twenty-one scenarios she'd worked through. "Not only did you pass, you placed within the perfect range set up by the Great Mothers."

"I couldn't have placed there," Joanna exclaimed as she looked over the scores closely. "Oh, damn! Oh fucking fathersucker!" she screamed, hitting the dashboard with both of her palms.

"Joanna!" Liz blushed, shocked at the language. "Those are very good scores. Nothing to get so upset about."

"Oh, no?" Joanna exclaimed as she wiped her eyes angrily so she could glare at her lawyer. "You know me, Liz. You know what I do and why. You are one of a handful I haven't kept certain aspects of my career from. How would you like to find out that one of the people that you hate on this planet is yourself?"

"The score doesn't mean that," Liz said, and tapped on the graph. "Look, you're on the gentle side of perfect. The buying range extends farther on the crueler side than on the gentle side. What the Great Mothers thought was perfect is hardly strict by today's standards, it seems. Most women who are allowed to buy privately score in the cruel range."

Joanna's glare softened as she considered the new facts. "What exactly does it say about me?"

Liz scanned the next paragraph briefly. "It says that you're stubborn – don't I know it – empathic, yes, logical, and very punctual. You have a desire to integrate a boy into the household in a way that require less direct oversight. You see men as useful tools who can also be entertaining companions." Liz rested her curly dark brown hair against the driver's seat as she looked over her client silently. "It sounds like an accurate description of you. And one which the Great Mothers thought would be best in our society."

Joanna nodded mutely, facing forward with a frown. This wasn't the balance they'd meant, was it – a hierarchy of genders? Her attorney seemed quite pleased and was using her pad to tell her mother and wife the good news, ignoring the fact that they were just sitting there. Perhaps she was giving Joanna time to process what it all meant. That was more likely the case. In a few minutes she was calm enough to drive them back to Liz's office.

"You've now met all the requirements for private guardianship," Liz announced proudly as she sat in the car, one hand on the door. "I thought you might, so I've already arranged for us to meet with representatives from the government and the agency at the start of next week to finalize the transfer."

Joanna didn't reply, but simply looked down at the results that had been transferred to her own computer pad. She was a perfect woman, according to the system, the type she said she opposed. It still didn't sit well in her center.

"You haven't decided against buying him?" she vaguely heard her lawyer ask. "Joanna?"

Joanna shook her head and met Liz's gaze. "No, he's mine now. He's out of that nightmare. Let's finish this as soon as we can," she decided with a firm nod of her head.

Scott stood up from his kneeling position and stared at his image in the mirror for a second. He had been practicing the appropriate greetings and positions for a good hour now but still was not satisfied. "Mistress," he said, bowing a bit lower than before, his hands spread to the sides, palms facing the woman he was imagining. He shook his head. "Mistress," he repeated the word and gestured again and again until a laugh interrupted him.

"What are you doing?" Todd chuckled at him as he walked into the room.

Scott ignored the other man and moved on to another position.

Todd watched with a sad smile as the blond knelt on both knees and bowed his head to the ground, repeating the title over and over. "What are you doing?" Todd asked again, with a little nudge at his friend's shoe.

Scott stood up and smiled. "I'm practicing," he explained, turning back toward the mirror, and straightening his shirt collar.

Todd shook his head as he sat on the edge of his cot. "What for?"

"For my mistress," Scott replied.

"Why?"

Scott threw his best friend an exasperated look. "So, I'll please her," he said slowly as though he was explaining to a small child.

"Isn't she buying you as we speak?"

"Yes."

"Then she's already pleased with you," Todd pointed out.

"Just because she's buying me, that doesn't mean she'll keep me," Scott told his friend and his own reflection.

"She may not even be buying you." The voice of Madame Sandy made both men jump. The host hurried to Scott and fastened a leash to his collar. "I'm supposed to take you to an emergency meeting," she explained.

Todd spoke for his confused and worried friend as he followed the host down the hallway. "What's the problem, Ma'am?"

"It seems that Scion McMillin may have changed her mind about the transfer," she explained in short form, then added, looking directly at him, "Your job is to make sure she goes through with this, no matter what you have to do. This is an important deal for Dells, and whatever you cocked up, boy, you will fix, or there will be a punishment you can't imagine waiting for you here."

Scott had little time to exchange horrified looks with his best friend as Madame Sandy yanked him out of the room and down the hallway.

Joanna placed her hands on her private bathroom sink, facing away from her attorney.

"What's wrong with you?" Liz hissed quietly. "We've been working for almost a month on this, and now you change your mind?"

"I didn't expect that audience out there. A party?" She was grasping at something to say, to do to put this off. "Did Kathey arrange this, 'cause I know you didn't, Liz."

"Other than you, me, the gov agent, and the Dells rep, everyone else just started showing up with these invitations on their accounts. They just showed up and flashed their pads, and your HCS admitted them. I think it grumbled about it."

"Hilda shouldn't have let them in," Joanna hissed.

"Shall I call the local militia, Scion?" the HCS's voice made both women look up. They knew it was always on, always the nanny everywhere, but it rarely did more on its own than change lighting or add music.

Joanna looked at Liz hopefully, but her attorney just gave her a sour look back. "No, no, Liz, you didn't do anything wrong. I just don't like surprises."

"Neither do I," Liz pointed out. Joanna hung her head again and closed her eyes.

"This is because of that submergence test, right?" Liz guessed after Joanna remained silent and still for several seconds. "That profile must have been wrong. You are definitely stubborn, but not too understanding. The test says that you will be a wonderful guardian. Whoever set up this party agrees and wants to show their support for what will be a big change to your life. Matriarch McMillin is out there with my grandmother. You are not going to embarrass both of us."

Joanna looked at her reflection in the mirror in front of the sink. She looked exhausted; even if women used makeup, it wouldn't have hidden that. She couldn't admit that she hadn't slept one hour since that day. She needed to think of something to say, any excuse. She tossed out, "One hundred-fifty thousand is a lot."

Liz scowled and waved off that attempt. "We both know that hardly scratches your personal bank account. I've known you since you were born, Joanna Lily McMillin. What are you afraid of?"

Joanna turned to glare at her attorney. Tears stained her cheeks. "What if the tests are wrong? What if I'm like the average woman, on the cruel side, and what if I lose control and really hurt him?"

"We all get angry at times." Liz's voice drained of negativity as she tried to reassure Joanna. "It's only normal for us to let go and just hit them sometimes. He's used to it. He'll understand why you're hitting him. He'd probably freak out if you didn't from time to time."

"Wonderful," Joanna moaned, wiping away a tear. She screwed her eyes shut for another moment and then tried another tactic. "If I'm so perfect, then why two years of visits from both Dells and the government?"

"I don't like that part either, but they won't move on that; it's standard for every private guardianship for the gov to check in, and Dells wants to make sure you're satisfied. It's only for the first two years. I bet you'll be off on some new investigation most of the time and they'll hardly be able to find you, just like the rest of us," Liz pointed out.

Joanna started to speak but was interrupted by the doorbell.

"You get back out into that front room and answer that door," Liz ordered, pulling her client by the arm toward the swinging kitchen doors. "I'm going to try to smooth things over so the gossip parlors don't steam up about this in a few hours, 'cause you know that Dells will talk if this doesn't go through."

When the door opened, Scott stood frozen for a moment as his hoped-for mistress stared at him from within a beautifully furnished apartment, the walls slowly melding from golds to greens, creating a sense of prosperity and calm. Just beyond her were several other women, including the Dells heir, their attorney, and a court official whom Scott had met with a few times. Scott only hesitated for a moment, then he gracefully fell on his knees at Miss Joanna's feet. He had to do anything to get her to change her mind, so he hugged her legs and pressed his cheek against her stomach. "Mistress," he pleaded, just loud enough for everyone to hear.

Miss Joanna's body started to shake, so at first, he thought he'd made a horrible mistake, until she started to stroke his head. She pulled out of his grip but kept one hand on his head and stepped toward the court official. "Give me the pad. I'll sign."

Scott remained on his knees, listening, as the deal was completed. "Congratulations," he heard the women exclaim. Soon the door to the apartment closed, and Scott rose to his feet, nerves eating his heart.

He was pulled into the room by the woman who had come to the agency the first time he'd met his guardian, Miss Kathey. She steered him around the room, introducing him to people, while Miss Joanna was being congratulated by others. This wasn't going at all like it had in the submergence.

The attorney who had questioned him soon after the severe beating – her name was Miss Liz – was speaking to a group of frowning women whom he had not been formally introduced to yet. One looked a bit like his guardian, but much older. He felt like he should know her, or know of her, but her face wasn't pulling up any names in his supposedly wonderful memory. They were glancing at him, so he bowed his head for a few seconds. When he glanced back up, they were looking elsewhere, talking to another woman.

Scott looked around as casually as he could without moving. Joanna was nowhere to be seen, and Miss Kathey had released his arm. What was he supposed to be doing? He didn't know the layout of the apartment, or he could go to the kitchen and check on the food and beverages. He didn't know all the guests, or he could circulate, see if anyone needed anything. Why was no one serving any food or drinks? Even he knew you were supposed to do that at a party this large. There were two dozen or more people.

He nearly jumped out of his skin when Miss Liz approached him. "She's just so overcome with joy," she said loudly, then grasped him by the arm and whispered in his ear, "Go after her. Go out the way you came in but turn left toward the river. Keep going till you see the piers. Find her. We'll cover for you."

Scott glanced up to find Miss Kathey standing with them. Now both she and Miss Liz were blocking the guests from seeing him. The HCS let him out of the apartment and the complex.

He found Miss Joanna out at the end of one of the apartment complex's piers. She was leaning over the railing, her head cradled in her hands. As he approached, she looked up at the river, slamming her palms down on the railing. Scott stopped a short distance away and called out, "I'm sorry, Mistress."

"For what?" Miss Joanna shook her hair back from her face. "For being male?"

"Yes," Scott said softly after a moment's pause.

Miss Joanna turned around to face him. She looked devasted. "That's stupid. This is my fault, you know," she tossed out as she turned back to watch the waves rolling in. "I don't know why I'm so upset. I knew there would be restrictions on owning you for the first couple of years or so. I knew I could never do exactly what I wanted. Who can?"

A cool breeze off the water made her entire body shiver. Scott took off his jacket and placed it on her shoulders. He could do that now, touch her now in these careful, helpful ways that he couldn't before. He still needed to be careful. But she had told him repeatedly that she needed more from him.

He leaned his back against the railing and looked directly at her. "You can do pretty much whatever you want to me, with me. I can do pretty much whatever you say I can, too. You do own me now, Mistress."

"Legally," Miss Joanna muttered.

"Exactly, Mistress," he smiled as confidently as he could manage.

Miss Joanna laughed harshly once as she shook her head. "There's a big difference between what's legal and what's right, Scott." She paused for a second.

She was looking intently at him, her eyes darting around his face. She took a couple of steps toward him and lowered her voice. "Should I tell you how I first realized that?"

"Yes, Mistress," he replied automatically. He shuddered just slightly as though something was crawling along his skin, warning him about what was coming.

"Are you cold?" she asked him and moved closer, lifting his arm up and guiding it under his coat and around her waist. They both caught their breath but soon relaxed against each other.

Miss Joanna turned around, leaning back against him, so she could look up at the apartment complex as she spoke. "You remember what I told you about my late partner, Judy?"

"Yes, Mistress." Scott hung his head, rubbing it soothingly against her shoulder, adding, "I'm sorry for your loss, Mistress."

Joanna sadly smiled as she continued. "I have a twin, a twin brother, Joseph, but he was just the start. I'll tell you more about him later." Scott's breath caught in his chest for a moment at the name as the mystery started to unravel.

"I met Judy at university, our second term there. Right from the start we did everything as a team. All our study groups, all our projects, and when I decided that I wanted to go into reporting instead of history, Judy was behind the camera. She always supported me even if she didn't feel as strongly as I did."

"Then what happened, Mistress?" Scott urged her to continue when she paused.

"We met at this really great class on the history of slavery on Gaia during our second year, both patriarchal and matriarchal societies; it was a controversial course. We got so interested in the topic that the history professor and my advisor, Professor Houten, suggested that we visit one of the mining companies up in Alaska for our junior projects. Of course, we jumped at the chance. We thought it would be a great project, tracing the historical nature of industrial slavery but bringing it into the modern context. Besides my twin and men owned by our mothers or their friends, we didn't really know how men are treated. We were so naïve."

Scott turned his gaze to the waves as she paused. He had a feeling that what she was about to tell him, he already knew.

"For two days, we watched men half dead from work and hunger being pushed from daybreak until midnight. If one of the slaves – because that is what they were, slaves, not just men – fell or refused to work, the overseers would beat him horribly." Miss Joanna shuddered. She turned to face him, with the sincere expression of someone who is sharing a great discovery that they believe no one else knows about. "They beat a man to death right in front of our eyes. They just threw his body into one of the smelting furnaces. We complained to the chief executives, but they didn't care. They just gave us a lecture about how men are animals, how they waste resources." She paused, waiting for some response from him.

"You did everything you could, I'm sure, Mistress," he offered quietly. "You are the kindest woman I've ever known. I can't imagine anyone else even caring enough to say anything at all."

"Do you know that short of killing you, I can do anything I want to you? Doesn't that scare you?" Miss Joanna pulled away from him as he shook his head. "It should, Scott; it really should."

"Mistress." Scott stepped closer to pull up the sleeve of the jacket that had slid down her shoulder. "I'm yours now. I'll try not to misbehave. If I do, I understand that you must punish me."

"That's not what I want!" Miss Joanna grabbed him by the arms. "I don't need a slave. I need a partner!"

He stood staring at her for several moments until he realized she was crying. He was making her cry, and she hadn't even held his contract for more than a few hours. "I'll try," he whispered, his voice about to crack with emotion.

He looked up when she stopped crying. They just stared at each other, so he repeated, "I'll try."

She pulled him to her and hugged him, saying, "So will I."

They stood there, side by side, watching the river for a few more minutes. With a sigh Miss Joanna turned around, looked back at the apartment complex, and said, "I didn't know about the party until everyone was there. I thought it was going to be me, my attorney, the Dells rep, and an official from the government."

Scott felt himself smile. He turned toward he as he nodded. "I'm glad I wasn't the only one surprised, then."

Her expression saddened, and she tilted her head up with a sigh before looking back at him. "I left you alone with all those people you didn't know."

"Miss Kathey was showing me around." He didn't add how short a time that had lasted.

"Goddess, that's worse!" She was touching his arms now; his coat was threatening to fall off her shoulders. He felt himself tremble as she ran her hands up his arms. "Oh, you need this coat. At least I've got sleeves," she said before removing it.

"Thank you, Mistress," he replied, taking her handing it back as an order to put it on. Since it was summer, the shirt he had underneath it was vest style, and her shirt had a solid tank and sheer sleeves that reached down to her wrists.

Was she blushing? She reached over and adjusted his coat collar, touching the metal links around his neck which she had just fastened on a short time ago. He hadn't even had a chance to admire it yet. The look Miss Joanna gave him told him that gold must be a better color than silver on him.

"Let's go back, together," she said firmly. She took him by one wrist and turned toward the buildings. He finally had time to look at where he'd be living. It was nice, like a small town, with multiple structures. He saw the energy and water systems, the small farm, a playground, and what looked like the edge of a pool area.

He followed her back, staying close as she led him by the wrist. It wasn't how she would have walked with her fiancé, her partner, but he was her new imagist, her boy. He'd try to be what she needed.

"Ready?" she asked when they reached the building.

"Ready," he simply agreed, and her radiant smile confirmed he'd made the right choice.

Author's Note

There are five legally and socially recognized genders on Gaia, and these are the pronouns used for them.

	Female	Male	Fem	Mas	Fifth-Gender
Nominative	she	he	ze ("zee")	ey ("A")	xe ("zee")
Objective	her	him	hir ("hear")	em	xem ("zem")
Possessive	her	his	hir ("hear")	eir ("air")	xyr ("zer")
Poss. Adj.	hers	his	hirs ("hears")	eirs ("airs")	xyrs ("zers")
Reflexive	herself	himself	hirself ("hear self")	emself	xemself ("zem self")

Almost Partners is a series that I developed over decades. I want to thank my fifth-grade teacher, Mrs. Koch, who secretly sent my short story off to a professional writer's workshop which in turn told me that there was a bigger story hidden inside. Thank you to my beta readers and editors who have given me their opinions and advice: Elizabeth, Emilie, Jennifer, Peter, Ryan, and Tom. To the groups at conventions over the years who showed up for readings I gave from this book and have been asking me for years when the series is coming out: This is it, everyone! I hope it has been worth the wait. To Terrie, who suggested Liminal Press to me. Finally, thank you to Between the Lines for taking a chance on the worlds I create.

Since 1995, TammyJo Eckhart's fiction and non-fiction work has been challenging readers to look at themselves and their world through a different lens. Her fiction routinely crosses genres and doesn't pull its punches when it comes to subject matter. Almost Partners is the first book in her long-awaited science fiction series expanding upon the "future is female" motto in critical and entertaining ways. Her previous Liminal Press books show her range. Day Unto Night is an experiment in storytelling which crosses genres from alternative history to science fiction and horror. True You 101, published under the name TJ Eckhart, is an LGBTQIA positive YA novel that refuses to accept that the way humans view the world is the only way to view it. You can find her online by visiting https://www.tammyjoeckhart.com/. Those interested in her more mature work can learn about her life and see her new creations on Patreon (https://www.patreon.com/tammyjoeckhart).